GRAVE CONSEQUENCES

GRAVE CONSEQUENCES

DEATH OF THE PARTY
BOOK 2

Kleggt

Podium

Cover design by Kart Studio

ISBN: 978-1-0394-6608-1

Published in 2024 by Podium Publishing
www.podiumentertainment.com

Podium

GRAVE CONSEQUENCES

CHAPTER ONE

Early Mourning

The dim morning light barely pierced through the rolling mists, hampered by the encroaching clouds and natural gloom of the start of the Swamps. Deep within the dense tree cover, the wail of a single zombie echoed out. A flock of birds flew from the canopy, startled by the sudden noise.

"Ugh," Sally said as she deflated. "Why did we have to leave so early in the morning? I'm still tired."

"You're the guild leader." Theo shrugged. "You have to set an example for the others."

She glared up at him. He looked way too happy to be up and about during the early hours. His suit may be various shades of boring gray, but his eyes beamed with excitement behind his crimson glasses. He had been itching to go up to the Wastelands—the second area of this game world—ever since he had hit Level Ten.

With a sigh she looked back at the Death Knight, but his skeletal face offered no encouragement in her favor either. He had been staring off into the mists at the edge of the woodlands for most of the journey. Behind his thick plate of dark crimson armor, Theo's coffin was strapped for transport. At his side, a satchel bag held the sleeping ball of ginger fur called Archie.

The cat was still no clearer on whether he was the Architect or not. It seemed a far reach, but with everything that had happened to them in the last couple of weeks, she couldn't discount the idea. As for the lack of information about the murderer of the actual Architect, both of the Observer-fueled Party members were keeping their lips sealed if they knew anything.

She brushed her hands off on her red skirt. Despite the novelty of being able to change into different clothing now, there was something about it that felt comfortable. She had swapped out the white, linen blouse for a black shirt and red jacket, however. In her line of work, wearing white was just asking for trouble. "Work" being eating people.

Ever since they had defeated three of the villages and claimed them for the Unique Monsters—and then gained validation from the System by way of the Capital accepting their presence—there had been a nervous ball rolling around in her stomach. Nothing *worrying*, but there was bound to be trouble looming in their near future. There always was.

Being a Party member short was concerning too. All the Unique Monsters had decided to either become Leaders for the new villages or were just not built for the dangerous adventuring life they led. Jackie had filled the much-needed gap of ranged damage dealer, but after seeing the mobster and the dark elf happily running the tavern, it had melted her dead heart, and she couldn't fault them for wanting to live a less blood-soaked existence.

And that was what it had all been about in the end. She glanced over at Theo, who looked to be counting the trees as they passed. Maybe a certain type of tree. Their adventure had started as revenge against an unfair System that had wronged her. Somewhere between making odd friends and eating brains, it had melted into just trying to make a good life for the Unique Monsters, who only had one life, to be as equal to the human Players as possible.

That is where the nerves came from. Heading through the Swamps into the Wastelands and starting the process all over again. Humphrey had warned them that the second area would have a much higher density of Players due to how late they started compared to everyone else. It sounded like more of a feast for her and Theo—but a lot more anguish. Starting back at the bottom of the totem pole might make them easy pickings when they looked so much like bad guys themselves.

They rounded the top of a hill, and her dead legs ached. She hadn't eaten a human brain in days, and she was starting to feel run-down. Monster brains just weren't the same. As they crested a peak of cut-down trees, she found herself wishing that a meal would just drop into her—

"Oh." She stopped as the Party moved up alongside her. They met the gaze of at least two dozen people standing in wait in the trees across a small clearing. *Players.* A dirt road began at this point and eked out a weak path between the trees beyond these gatekeepers blocking progress forward.

Her eyes narrowed as she walked closer with the Party and was not surprised to see the slicked-back greasy hair and scarred face of Walter, the Fighter they had met before. In dirty white armor he stood as the leader of the Player-killing Party *Zero*.

Walter gave them a friendly wave and a less-than-friendly shit-eating grin. "Seems you got here before the rest of your little friends." He scratched his chin as he leaned against a tree. "Be a shame if they arrived to see you all dead already."

Sally wrinkled her nose up. "Looks like they have sixteen—"

"Twenty," Theo corrected.

"Twenty Players in a guild too. I don't really want to drag the others into this."

Humphrey shuffled around and brought Archie out, waking him up by placing him on the soft grass. "This is certainly not ideal, *ha-ha*. But perhaps a good chance to bond or impress our guild members once they arrive?"

The zombie sighed and rubbed the bridge of her nose. She was too tired for this. Her voice raised to speak to the man opposite from them. "Alright. Any chance we can hang about and wait for them?" It had been a long walk—if she could sit down for a little bit before any bloodshed, that'd be really nice.

The Fighter looked around at the gathered Players among the tree line. "We can wait a few minutes, gang? Don't want the rest of their troupe to turn tail before they get here once they see their leader has been crushed, huh?" A gaggle of nods and agreements answered his question.

Theo put his hand over his brow to shield his eyes from the light and squinted into the woods. "Hands up if you're a Fighter or Paladin?"

A few hands went up into the air before the glares of the leader quieted them.

"Rogues are good, too, right?" he murmured to Sally. "That's a decent number of potential stats for you."

Her tired eyes just narrowed at him. If the vampire had gotten that stat gain skill, he would eat every Player he saw to min-max all his numbers. All three of them had attributes that were already skewed thanks to their strange classes and layers of Party auras. Theo would become a god and consume everything in this odd world. Part of her thought that would be pretty neat.

The leader of *Zero* raised two fingers and gestured a familiar figure forward. "How about a little entertainment while we wait, then?"

Their teleportation Rogue, in her trench coat, stormed forward to the front—daggers in her eyes aimed at the vampire. Her face, scarred from the burns he had inflicted in the Mines had nothing but seething rage bubbling up through it.

"Duel me again," she hissed at him, drawing her rapier aggressively.

"I'm sorry about the face." Theo rubbed the back of his neck. "I had hoped you would have just died." He turned to Sally with a slight shrug, to see what her thoughts on this charade would be.

"Go on then." She rolled her eyes and went to sit on a convenient rock. "If you die again, then I'll be *really* mad at you."

Theo held up a finger to the antsy Rogue, slowly removing his jacket and handing it to the Death Knight, who begrudgingly took it. As he walked over into the open space, the vampire unbuttoned his shirt sleeves and rolled them to his elbows. Eventually, he stopped, somewhat amused at the anger built up in his opponent. He clasped his hands behind his back and raised an eyebrow in anticipation.

Unable to wait a moment longer, she dove toward him. "Die, you time waster!"

[Heartseeker Strike]

The woman lunged forward, dark energy swirling around the tip of her rapier as it aimed straight for the chest of the vampire.

[Dread Parry]

The tip of the blade pressed against his chest, his gray shirt indenting slightly before the sword started to bend and flex. Theo raised up his right hand, red electricity crackling as he tensed his fingers as if to claw the woman. The Rogue stumbled backward and onto the floor away from him—but after a couple of seconds the energy dissipated from his raised hand.

"Ooh," he cooed and turned his gaze back to the Party. "I *can* cancel the guaranteed critical strike after the counter."

Humphrey shrugged; his arms folded. Sally gave him a tired thumbs-up. Archie was watching a bug move through the grass. All in all, Theo was pretty pleased with that response. Not that canceling the damage would be useful in many situations, but another mechanic of the System was his to know.

"Just because you've got a nice suit and some new tricks doesn't mean anything, Novice." The Rogue spat and climbed back to her feet, withdrawing a dagger into her other hand.

"Stat bonuses must be cumulative rather than additive," the vampire murmured as he rubbed his chin in thought. "Otherwise, Sally would get way too powerful from these bonuses."

The woman growled, either upset that he was ignoring her or embarrassed at making a bad show of her revenge in front of the rest of her guild. "Fight me, asshole. Where's your toy sword? Should we kill your little girlfriend first, as motivation?"

Theo looked back at the zombie again. Sally gave him a shrug and a twirled hand to get him to hurry up. As he turned his attention back to the Rogue, she began using skills to buff herself. Her trench coat now shimmered in the light as if vibrating. Her rapier glowed orange, and the dagger pulsed a foul green. Around her feet, an etched circle of blue runes turned slowly.

"Oh, you were actually serious?" Theo grinned widely, exposing his fangs.

The Rogue opened her mouth in shock as a wave of concerned murmurs began spreading around the grouped *Zeroes*.

The vampire snapped his fingers.

[Perfect Dark]

Immediately, the drab, overcast sky became pitch-black, plunging the area into dim darkness. Looming behind Theo rose a large moon of glowing crimson, silhouetting his figure and bathing the battleground in hellish light.

He pushed his glasses up his nose to cover his gleaming red eyes.

"Let's see what you are made of, then."

CHAPTER TWO

From Zero

An eerie silence washed over the clearing, as all eyes of the *Zeroes* turned up to question the sudden night and blood moon that painted the area in a dull, reddish light.

Sally yawned as she sat on the rock and kicked her feet back and forth. "Can you believe he used this skill a few days ago to try to *woo* me?"

"Yes." The Death Knight narrowed his empty sockets at the vampire. "Did it work?"

"We kissed, and it was super gross, like frenching a cold fish."

Theo physically cringed. "I can hear you, you know."

"Focus on your life and death fight!" Sally stuck her tongue out at the back of the vampire before turning back to Humphrey. "We *are* both corpses. It was a nice evening otherwise, though. We went and found those rampaging boars instead. Killed them all."

"I gathered." The Death Knight kept his gaze narrowed on Theo. "You told me he was taking you to hunt for cards."

"We found two Boar Cards, so technically correct." She had even equipped them despite the effects being useless. Mostly because farming for cards was way too boring for her, and she had only been lucky enough to find the Cyclops Card previously. Theo, of course, had a new full set already. It was still a mystery how he found enough time to level, hunt for items, and remain present for most of the Party's activities.

Sally cupped her hands around her mouth. "Tell her about your cool new card set, Theo!"

Theo's right eye twitched, and his mouth opened and closed before he exhaled. "You probably don't want to know—and it'd take too long to explain it when we should be fighting." He bit his tongue and congratulated himself for not unloading all the information, half hoping she would ask him to tell her anyway.

The Rogue held a grimace across her scarred face as she circled around the vampire. Part of his casual attitude toward the fight was putting her off-kilter. "D-do you not have a weapon? You expect me to fight you while you are unarmed?"

Theo stood still, hands again clasped behind his back. "Don't pretend you have any honor now, *Jess*. You are a Player-killer, after all."

"So are you," she spat in return, wincing at her name being spoken. Once fully behind him she lunged forward with weapons raised. Theo spun away, lashing out with a fist that she dodged easily. The Rogue stepped away to circle him again.

"My error last time . . ." Theo began, clasping his hands behind him once more, ". . . was trying to beat you in speed. Your meme build was just faster than mine at the time."

The Rogue whipped around both blades again. Theo dodged one, but the smaller dagger caught him on the forearm with a hiss of acid.

"Now, of course, I know what you sacrificed to get your Evasion and Movement Speed. I don't have to beat you in speed to win—I just have to strike you harder when I do."

Jess growled and activated *[Triple Cut]*—dashing straight at the vampire and crisscrossing crimson lines on his torso. Shreds of his shirt fell to the floor as she passed him.

"Woo! Take it all off!" Sally cheered from the rock before catching the glare of the Death Knight. "What? He is still *objectively* a stud, even if we can't do anything more than hold hands."

"You've been holding hands?" Humphrey somehow wrinkled up his skeletal face as the red flame from the back of his helmet increased in intensity.

Theo sighed and looked down at his ruined shirt. *Why did it always have to come to this?* He opened up his STAR and switched from cosmetic to equipped armor. Now, instead of his smart suit, he became wrapped in black leather armor, reinforced in places by tarnished iron.

"Grimband set?" the Rogue hissed from behind him. "I won't mind taking that from your corpse."

"You'd have to kill me first." He turned with a smile. "Or, technically, I think I am already dead? So be my guest."

She struck out at him again in a flurry of swipes. Some of them he avoided, but his raised arms bore the brunt of several gashes to protect his head from being cut. As he gained footing and retaliated, the Rogue had no issue avoiding all his thrown punches.

Sally hummed to herself. She was not looking forward to going through the Swamps. Mostly because she would no doubt end up falling into a bog and get her clothes all dirty. Although, if they were to be covered in blood in a few minutes anyway, it probably wouldn't be so bad. It's a good thing the System didn't charge for dry cleaning. She felt terrible for the rest of the guild, currently unaware and about to stumble upon the *Zeroes,* who had been awaiting their attempted travel to the second area.

She had considered contacting the Swordmaster, Dent, as he said he would repay them when they arrived in the Wastelands. By now, he must be higher than Level Fifteen, surely? Watching Theo dodge around and regenerate hits, they might not need the assistance after all. Depending on how terrible the Wastelands actually were.

Neither Archie nor Humphrey could tell her much about them. Other than they were a mix of desolate plains and sand dunes. If her previous life could tell her anything, then she would probably be facing giant scorpions and reptiles. Neither seemed like a particularly good food source for her brain-hungry stomach. If there wasn't a steady supply of Players, she was liable to get grumpy.

Theo was slowing now, his forearms streaked with his own blood. Briefly, she considered intervening—but she was still somewhat sleepy, so continuing to sit won out.

[Heartseeker Strike]

The darkened rapier again shot toward Theo, this time piercing straight through his chest. The false night vanished, returning the area to the overcast day as the vampire slumped against the Rogue.

"*Shit,*" she growled at him. "Why are you so heavy? Could you just . . ." She stumbled for a few feet as he failed to drop to the floor and continued to weigh on her.

"Hey . . . *Jess,*" Theo whispered weakly in her ear. "Have you seen *[Perfect Dark]* before?"

"N-no, what are you—" She struggled to pry his limp weight off her rapier.

"I can only cast it at full health. Increases some of my stats and looks pretty cool. Usually lasts ten minutes but goes away if I go beneath 90 percent health."

She growled. "Why are you telling me—"

Theo lifted his head, his eyes burning with crimson fire. "Do you want to know how much health I regenerate per second?"

The night sky returned, sending a dark shadow across their duel and leaving only his eyes and wide, fanged smile visible as her eyes adjusted.

"Oops," he hissed into her ear, "spoiler alert!"

"What . . . what *are* you?" Jess finally gathered some strength and pushed him away, the end of her weapon retracting from the wound with a wet *pop*.

Theo raised his hands, and two punch-blades of dark metal popped into existence from gloves he hadn't been previously wearing. "I'm a fuckin' *nerd*." He beamed.

"Language, Theo!" Sally yelled out from the sidelines before she turned to the Death Knight. "Honestly, did you really have to teach him how to hot-swap weapons?"

"Yes, *ha-ha*. Does it not look cool?"

"It does, but I'm trying not to let his ego get bigger than mine. I'm the main character." She wrinkled up her nose. If that were true, why was she sitting over here and not having a fight so soon in the adventure?

Her foot tapped on the floor before Archie rubbed against her leg. She looked down into his emerald eyes. "Arch, would it be bad form if I got involved?"

"Most likely. Do you not think Theo can win?"

"I just think *I* should win." Sally ran her fingertips over her dagger sheath. Surely his win was a win for her too? For all of them. Perhaps it was the nerves talking. Theo deserved a bit of time in the sun—or crimson moon as it were—and there were still nineteen other Players she could have her own time fighting with soon enough.

Theo dodged to the side and flicked his blade outward. Other than a gash through her trench coat, the Rogue had avoided most of his attacks—but he had a few splits between his armor where he was bleeding. The glow from his eyes had faded, but the crimson moon and pitch-black sky still loomed over their battle. He wasn't looking tired, though, just . . . bored.

"Did you realize you always attack in the same pattern?" He winced as he received a light slash across his arm. "I've been counting your steps, Jess. Every breath you've taken. It's a complicated pattern, but after time it becomes rote."

"Quit talkin', you bullshitter!" The woman was seething. Sweat ran down her face as the melee had progressed no further despite the damage she had dealt.

"Okay." Theo moved forward and blocked her next attack, sidestepped the follow-up, blocked the next, and moved forward to block her retreating slash. He put one hand behind his back and advanced, slowly and methodically, as if practicing dance steps. As the woman was on her back foot, he blocked each quick attack with calm precision, inching closer to her.

[Vampire Bite]

Since Theo had chosen the improved version of this base skill, the Rogue became incapacitated almost immediately as his fangs sunk into her neck. Like the paralyzing bite of a snake, she became stunned as he drank her blood. Her arms dropped to the side, and now inert weapons thudded against the soft earth, released from her grip.

The vampire released his snack, punching a blade into her stomach and then throwing her limp body over to his Party like a rag doll. The Rogue rolled across the dirt as crimson ran from her neck.

[Eat Brains]

+5% Melee Critical Chance

A sickening *crunch* echoed through the area, and Sally rose, her face caked in the gore of what remained of the insides of the Rogue's head.

Shocked panic and anger radiated through the disgusted *Zeroes*.

"*Fucking kill them!*" Walter shouted, sending forth a signal to charge, as he frothed from the mouth in rage.

Sally and Theo beamed at each other, their faces marred with red, as the Death Knight sighed and unclasped the coffin from his back.

Arrows, thrown weapons, and a variety of spells careened over the gap toward the Party as groups of Players charged forth against them.

CHAPTER THREE

To Nothing

The plated boots of Humphrey dug through the dirt as he slid in front of the two undead and raised his hands into the air.

[Impenetrable Defense]

"You have ten seconds," he growled, the flames of his helmet rising as the spells and arrows coursing toward them bent and changed their trajectory in the air to aim toward the Death Knight.

"Well, then," Theo said as he raised his empty hands, "looks like it's time for *fun*." His black punch-blades popped back into existence as he grinned wildly. "Although there's only one minute and twenty-three seconds left of *[Perfect Dark]*."

"If Jackie gave up smoking for Fran, you should be able to stop doing *that* for me." Sally scowled at him as she withdrew her *[Dagger of Luck]* into her right hand.

"Six seconds." Spells fizzled out, and arrows were deflected by a flickering barrier of pale blue around the Death Knight.

"Aw, but it makes me look like that cool superhero . . . the *uh* . . . " The vampire scratched his head in thought, almost impaling himself with the wielded blades.

"The animal one?" Sally wrinkled up her nose as her own brain scoured the depths for memories long hidden away from their previous life.

"I think? He fought *Goreblaster* one time."

"Three seconds." Colors flared around them as the various spells and special attacks glowed in the dark night sky.

Sally shook her head and exhaled. "I still don't get that reference." She held out her left hand and pointed out toward the group of combatants only seconds away.

[Endless Dead]

She couldn't help but beam wildly as she cast her Level Nine skill. After all her zombies had been buried in the fight against the Champion in Sanctuary, this was an easy pick.

Scores of hands burst from the ground among the enemies. Twenty-five pairs if Theo's count was correct, which it usually was. The slow shamblers had finally started scaling, although they were only Level Five. Much better than the default, however. Having all her zombies stowed away for ready access allowed her to grow into the necromancer role without all the logistical problems of dragging a large horde around. She saw it as the System rewarding her for the good show at Sanctuary.

"I'm done." Humphrey lowered his arms to draw the large greatsword from his back. He pulsed with energy as he activated *[Adrenaline]*, *[Dead King's Court]*, and his improved *[Grave Strike]*. Most ranged attacks had been avoided and now the melee combatants were almost at them before the second volley started.

Sally tried to peer out from behind the large plated figure to find the leader of the *Zeroes*. There were too many figures, but there seemed to be flashes of his dirty white armor near the back.

"We've lost three . . . four zombies already." Theo licked his lips as his crimson eyes darted around the battlefield. "Let's go."

She gave him a nod as he darted forward and looked back to see what Archie was doing. The cat had been preening himself, seemingly content to just appear as the Party mascot. But now, with her expectant leer, he sat up straight and opened his maw.

His eyes and mouth were briefly illuminated by a radiant light, as if his head were a jack-o'-lantern. Blinding the area, a beam of white light shot from his tiny maw across to the tree line beyond the fight. Three Players were rendered from various limbs, with a fourth being totally cored by the blast.

Humphrey barreled into a group of *Zeroes* that were dispatching some of the slower zombies. *[Will of the Dark Lord]* stunned two, with the rest saving their willpower rolls. A wide slash of his sword knocked one of the stunned Players into the waiting grasps of a couple of zombies. A wide grin spread across his skeletal face as his large sword illuminated the fight.

Sally slid up beside the Death Knight and stabbed the other stunned Player repeatedly. As soon as the conditionals were met, she used *[Eat Brains]* before immediately being struck by a lightning attack. She rolled backward behind Humphrey and wiped the bloody mess from around her mouth.

+10% Melee Damage

The flickering blue text of the stacking upgrade reminded her that Monks were especially tasty to consume. Clangs of arrows bounced off the plated armor as the defensive juggernaut of Humphrey continued to swath a path into the melee. She took a quick glance to the side to see how Theo was faring. The unmistakable pink blur of his *[Sanguine Weapon]* combined with *[Novice Strike]* darted from enemy to enemy.

He stopped briefly to drink the blood of one of the Players and then *[Blood Shift]* away when someone came in to assist. Sally noticed that he hadn't killed anyone . . . *he was saving them for her!* Her dead heart did nothing, but she salivated at the precooked meals he was dishing up.

"Archie," she called back, "support Humps."

She darted off, weaving through the throng of zombies and assailed Players. A Paladin stood woozy from blood loss—*[Hex: Slow]* rendered the woman unable to turn in time before Sally rammed her dagger into her side between armor plates. *[Eat Brains]*.

The added boost of the temporary stat theft from the upgraded skill made her feel elated, and she didn't even bother to read the notifications telling her what permanent boost she had received. She twirled and moved to the next weakened enemy. *[Necroblast]* struck a disorientated Fighter in the leg, making them drop to a knee. *[Eat Brains]*. *Now this is why I chose the improved version!*

"Good job, big brother. Keep it up!" Archie called out from the back.

Humphrey sighed loudly as he blocked the thrust of an out-of-position Cleric. The flare of radiant energy ricocheted off his shoulder armor.

[Lord of the Damned]

The surrounding earth turned and radiated with foul energy as five Skeleton Warriors burst out around the Death Knight. Holding shortswords and shields, they mimicked the skeletal grin of their commander.

Despite the bravado of the enemy guild and the loss of half of the zombies, things were easily falling in the favor of the *Outsiders*. Sally dodged underneath the blazing amber of a Knight's skill and kept going, her eyes already set on another Fighter. Theo appeared in a cloud of mist behind the man and held his arms back as she ran up and used *[Eat Brains]*.

The vampire grinned as he dropped the spent corpse, anticipating it turning into a walking body shortly. "Hey, does this remind you of that time? You know, when we killed people?"

"Can't talk—need eating," she panted back, her eyes wide and blazing bright red. "Where's Walter?"

Theo wrinkled his nose up and darted his eyes over the battlefield. "There." He pointed a bloodied finger to near the back of the fight, the dirty white armor just visible. The leader looked sweaty and tense as he batted away some of the remaining undead from around him.

"Hey, Walter!" Sally shouted out.

The man turned with a furrowed brow to see where her voice had come from, and then his arms hung limp as his glare fell on them.

"Boy, you got some range on that *[Stunning Gaze]*, huh?" She ran off in the direction of the paralyzed man, stabbing into Players and dodging around undead as she went.

"I just didn't want Humphrey to get to use *[Compelled Duel]* first," the vampire murmured to himself as he maintained eye contact. He winced as an arrow struck him in the leg. A second one then embedded into his shoulder. The sound of a flaming special attack came from the side. "I'm busy right now," he growled, keeping his eyes focused on holding Walter in place.

As Sally stalked through the melee, flashes of blue light lit up in the darkness as remnants of the various groups made the decision to cut their losses. Walter twitched and then regained his composure as *[Perfect Dark]* ended and light washed back over the top of the incline. His hands immediately went for something on his belt—a teleport, she guessed.

She withdrew her crossbow and fired it immediately with practiced precision. Walter reacted just as fast and raised his sledgehammer as a golden light surrounded him—deflecting the bolt out of the air.

[Necroblast: Barrage]

As he lowered it, his eyes widened to see five of the eldritch energy orbs floating around the zombie's head in an arc. With a flick of her finger, Sally sent them out toward him. He flinched and tensed to move away, but the sudden *[Hex: Slow]* made him completely misjudge the time he had to spend. Each blast of dark energy slammed into him. His white armor absorbed the first two, with the third breaking it. Numbers four and five rode up into his flesh, a burst of blood painting the dry grass as he stumbled to the ground.

Approaching him, Sally kicked away his weapon and grabbed at his greased hair. Panic and anger reflected from his sweat-slick face as he tried to worm away.

"But how? There's only three of you," he spat.

"No," she said as she rolled her eyes. "There were like thirty or something. You are worse at counting than me."

His dark eyes darted around the battlefield to see most of his guild either teleported away or being cut down.

Theo came and stood beside her; his movements slow. He had six arrows in his left side, and half of his body was scorched. He narrowed his eyes at the captive leader. "Ask him if they have any Skill Books?"

"True, we did win the duel this time, right?" Sally nodded as she pulled back on the hair of Walter, exposing his neck a little more.

"N-no, we used them all already." The man winced as he slowly came to terms with his fate.

The Death Knight stood up beside them and sheathed his sword on his back. The sound of battle had quieted to a low murmur of the shambling dead. "Shame. I could really use one of those."

"It was for *me*. I won the duel." Theo folded his arms, almost cutting himself as he had forgotten to stow his blades away.

Sally pouted up at them both. "But I'm the boss—I should get it."

"Rock, paper, scissors?" the vampire ventured.

Humphrey shrugged. "I don't know what that means. I pick rock."

"Paper!" Sally beamed.

"S-scissors?" Theo rubbed his head.

Walter just looked up at them in despair. "How have you made it this far . . . while being this incompetent?"

"Easy." Sally beamed and held her hand out. *[Endless Sleep]*. The ability, paired with the mass zombie-raising skill, caused all the undead under her control to sink back into the ground to be summoned later. "I have a lot of friends to support me."

The last thing the Player-killing Fighter saw was the looming sharp teeth of the Queen of the Dead.

CHAPTER FOUR

Swampy Thing

Among the newly gathered guild members, the Druid, dressed in muted colors, ran his hand through his messy hair as he stood among the undead.

"I probably shouldn't ask, huh?" Chuck tried to cover his eyes from the bloodied destruction marring the landscape.

"Well, you could see this as our final test before going into the Wastelands." Sally now felt remarkably upbeat and wavered back and forth on her feet.

"But . . ." The Druid peeked through his fingers at the equally blood-soaked zombie. "The *four of you* killed them *all*, already."

Theo sighed as he lay atop his closed coffin. "Not all. Some escaped." Gradually, his UI was repairing his cosmetic outfit.

"Not that I'm ungrateful for you sparing us the bloodshed. I'm just shocked at your . . . *efficiency*." Chuck sat on the rock the zombie had previously claimed. Originally, Sally had thought he might have stayed behind in the forest area, to pursue a life less violent—going to the Wastes didn't seem the optimal route for his more pacifist style, but life was full of surprises.

Humphrey stepped heavily over to them, slightly jostling the vampire from his resting. "Both Theo and Sally have exceedingly high Strength and Constitution for their level. We also have more auras than a normal Party."

"Auras are really effective, though." Theo frowned up at the Death Knight. "They don't get chosen that often?"

"Normal classes get fewer chances to take one. The three of us have Monster classes, which are often more geared toward supporting our fellow . . . *villains*."

Chuck looked more concerned after the explanation, rather than contented. "What about Archie?"

Humphrey turned his head to the clearing, where the ginger cat was prancing around and investigating the corpses strewn about. "He doesn't seem to have any specific class, and some of his skills are too high level for me to know what they are."

Sally wrinkled her nose up. Archie would be a force to reckon with if he could concentrate on fighting properly for more than ten seconds. It was nice to have an ace up their sleeve, but something more consistently reliable would be less stressful. Then again, he was a talking cat—there was only so much she could ask.

She went over and kicked the wooden coffin. "Any good loot?"

"Nothing much for me." He put his hand over his eyes to block more of the sunlight. "There was a gem, though. Where is your rare sword?"

"I didn't lose it."

The vampire didn't respond.

Sally crossed her arms and scowled over at the rest of the Party looking at her. "*Okay*, so I lost it. But maybe some newbie will find it, and it'll really make their day. I was paying it forward, in a way."

After a brief moment of silence, Theo moved his hands away from his face. "I'll keep the gem for now, then."

With a huff, the zombie sat down on his legs and pouted. "They really had no Skill Books?"

"No, if they had, I would have . . . well, I would have used it immediately." He grinned up at her with a flash of his fangs.

"*Ass*. So would I."

The rest of the guild milled around, searching the bodies if they had stronger stomachs or just waiting in the wings if they'd prefer only to see Monster guts. It was a small point of shame that Sally didn't remember most of their names—but they were Players, after all. It was enough that she didn't eat them.

She put her chin in her palms. "I'm surprised the *Zeroes* got enough people to create a guild."

Humphrey exhaled and turned to look out over the dense tree valley behind them. "Player numbers in this first area are very few now. It became a thing of being *with them* or *against them*. Most Players do not want to die, even at the moral expense of killing others."

"Yeah, who would want to kill Players?" Sally rolled her eyes and brushed off some dried blood from her skirt. Seemed like a waste to be a Player-killer if you weren't going to eat them after—shame on the *Zeroes*.

"You shouldn't want to kill anything." Chuck wagged his finger before deflating. "Ugh. When did I become such a square?"

"When were you born again?" She stuck her tongue out. "Anyway, we are burning daylight here. What's the plan, Humps?"

The Death Knight shrugged and grinned. "The Swamps are a few hours of walking. There may be Monsters in there that will attack us, but as an almost full guild, we shouldn't have issues. You'll know when we are in the Wastelands by the way that it is."

"And we should get our Keystone Quests," Theo added.

"Alright." Sally stood up on the coffin, almost tripping as she stumbled around the vampire's legs. She took a deep breath in. "*Guild!* Ten minutes to wrap things up, and then we are heading out."

She frowned and looked back down at Theo. "There was really no other gear on alllll those dead Level Tens?"

He blinked through his crimson glasses and was now wearing his once-again immaculate casual clothes. "Thirteen shortswords, seven maces, five shields, six bows, eighteen daggers, ten iron helmets—"

"Just all the rare stuff, you reprobate." She gently kicked his leg and courted toppling off again.

"Stop jumping around on my bed, and I'll tell you."

Chuck rubbed his temples with both hands. "Are they always like this?"

"*Yes.*" Humphrey narrowed his eye sockets at the pair. "Although they have become more cordial since Theo became a vampire."

"Makes sense. Removes all tension then, I suppose. With the brain-eating thing, I mean."

The Death Knight tilted his head. "I am glad to see them happy. As if I didn't have enough cats to herd."

Chuck raised an eyebrow. "Going for the big stoic daddy thing, huh?"

"I can kill you in less than three hits, plant-boy."

With a smile, the Druid looked up to the sky. "Cool. A simple *yes* would have sufficed."

"I changed my mind," Sally growled. "Let's just go back and be rulers of the tree place."

They all stopped to watch as the zombie struggled to clamber out of a knee-deep pit of wet mud and stagnant water.

"If you quit jumping around, you wouldn't—" Theo began, before catching her glare.

Humphrey lent a hand and pulled her from the thick mud with a loud slurp, putting her on the more stable path.

Perhaps she should have repaired her normal clothes too. Between the dried gore and the wet swamp, it was decent camouflage. She tried to convince herself of that fact to give her some manner of joy. So far, the Swamps had been a miserable affair. It was cold and clammy in some parts and humid in others. The only thing that had attacked them was some kind of Mud Bear that died before she had a chance to withdraw her dagger.

Traveling with almost twenty other Players made combat short when everyone wanted to throw out an ability from the outset. It would be no surprise if any Monster ran in the opposite direction once getting a whiff of them. It made her feel like less of the main character. Where was all the struggling against the odds?

"You need any help?" Theo stood and waited for her to catch up.

"Not from you, item hoarder."

The vampire rubbed the back of his neck. "I was going to share."

She waved him off. Despite her grumpy disposition, she wasn't really annoyed at him. He had made sure they had almost the best gear possible in the short time between Sanctuary and now. There were few pieces of gear that would have been much of an actual upgrade for them among the dead Players.

There was just an urge to be a bit more alone. Not away from Theo or Humps—but the guild felt weird to be around. Chuck was okay, but most of the rest of them still looked like walking meals. Sure, they were allied with her—but for some of them it was no different from the Players joining *Zero* to stay alive. It was *become a Player-killer* or avoid her widening maw with the thin wall of the System holding them on the same side.

Her view of Players had somewhat dimmed. Now that they had beaten back the forces of the System to lay claim to villages for Monsters to live in unassailed . . . it had taken a bit of wind out of her sails. Sure, she claimed it as a Win with a capital *W*—but then was the question of *now what?* Head to the Wastelands and try to do the same there? And then to the third area?

She was the dog that had finally caught the back end of the car and now was a bit shocked at how metallic and unyielding it was. There was always the draw of getting more powerful . . . and that seemed to be the easiest part. They were already overpowered. But what was the point of gaining all that power? To be the new Architect—or to break free of the System entirely? That seemed like an issue for a time that she wasn't knee-deep in sludge.

Twisted trees of muted grays and browns hung low across the Swamps. The dense and moist canopy blocked most of the daylight, adding to the malaise of the group. There were no sounds of frogs or crickets or whatever animals were supposed to live in a swamp. Sally couldn't quite remember. Silence had started as a nice way for her to organize some thoughts away into the lidless boxes of her brain, but now it had become oppressive.

"I hope the Wastes aren't this dire," she eventually said with a sigh, and rolled her head to the side to give Theo an exaggerated pout.

"Well, I hope they're not as muddy, at least." He shrugged and gave her a glum smile.

Mud was indeed terrible. She was glad they could agree on that. Even Humphrey had been quietly simmering over how he kept sinking into the softer stuff—not only was he a large chunk of plate metal, but with both his sword and

Theo's coffin on his back, he was a bull in a china shop as he clattered through outstretched boughs of almost slimy trees.

Chuck and Archie seemed to be doing all right. The cat had curled up atop the Druid's backpack and fallen asleep—and the young man himself seemed professionally interested in the change of scenery. Every so often he would murmur something about a tree or the particular shade of a mushroom—but she tried to tune it out.

Once they had arrived in the Wastelands, Sally hoped they'd all split up to do their Keystone Quests, and the guild would be more of a loose collection than a social club of people she couldn't eat. It would be super awkward if the System sent them on to do the same thing, and they had to bunch together for longer.

It would be nice just to be the *Outsiders* again and find a fifth member too. Some one-on-one time with Theo would be neat—some with Humphrey too. Some *classic* adventuring time. That was only if they ever got out of this depressing mulch.

Sally huffed and looked out into the wet swamp.

The wet swamp opened a large, yellow eye and looked back.

CHAPTER FIVE

Humble Mud Pie

A gigantic Monster burst out from the fetid swamp, casting streams of slick mud and foul water around the area. The guild stood in shocked awe as the creature rose impossibly tall, almost striking the treetops, gray-brown rubbery skin, and a wide maw that sat beneath two bulbous eyes glowing yellow.

"That's a big frog," Sally said with a nod, frowning up at the beast.

Theo popped out his blades. "*Toad.*"

The Death Knight withdrew his sword and cast a glare at the ginger cat, now awake, who returned a nod. "Unique Monster, be wary."

"Already sent him a Party invite." Sally's eyes burned bright crimson, and she ignored the grimaces of frustration from the rest of the *Outsiders*. The empty space in their group wasn't going to fill itself, after all.

Arrows, ice bolts, and beams of fire shot out from the collected guild members. Most attacks were either absorbed or deflected by the gigantic beast. His baleful eyes cast around the gathered ants along the path with impassive disdain.

"His level must be . . . pretty high." Theo scratched his head, almost cutting a chunk of hair off with his blades. "To take *no damage* from all those attacks . . ."

"*Yes.*" Humphrey nodded, his face a stoic grimace. "We are in danger."

Sally wrinkled up her nose and looked between them both. *Danger* was fast becoming their middle name. Like a collective family name—oh, did they even still have surnames? Briefly, she tried to consider what it might be. *Outsider? Sally Danger Outsider?* That idea went straight into the trash can. At least, for now.

The Toad opened his mouth, and from within, an enormous tongue shot out, striking further down the group into one of the other Parties. It retracted, and several Players were stuck to it, a gross mucus covering the dull pink appendage. Straight back into the mouth of the creature, the Toad swallowed the Players whole.

Guild member Harriet has died
Guild member Jones has died
Guild member Stephen has died

"Fight, or run?" Theo's right eye twitched as his crimson glasses slid down his nose.

Sally clenched her jaw at seeing the vampire perturbed. As angry as she was, she was the leader here and had to keep her cool. She had to keep the little snacks alive. She took a deep breath and yelled, "Do not engage! *Everyone run!*"

The *White Foxes* were ahead of them and turned to sprint farther along the trail with no hesitation. Chuck cast a spell to allow them to pull ahead unhindered. The *Warriors* were behind them and pulsed with their respective defensive skills. Both Parties in the rear became the unlucky recipients of the Toad's ire, and a second tongue-lash struck out and caught one Cleric unprepared.

Guild member Edgar has died

A hideous sucking sound reverberated throughout the area, and Sally's eyes widened as she turned back to see the creature leap into the air. Droplets of water and chunks of thick mud rained down from the airborne Toad. The dark shape rose above the treetop and briefly obscured whatever dim light the day could offer. After the short and sickening silence, the Toad collided onto the path, the sounds of snapping branches and bones echoing against the large *thud* that vibrated through the ground.

Guild member Katie has died
Guild member Ryan has died
Party *Strength of Many* has left the guild

[Necroblast: Barrage]
Several bolts of eldritch energy flew out and struck the looming creature but seemed to have little effect. Whatever he was made of, it had incredible damage reduction.

"Any thoughts?" she yelled out to her Party.

"Try not to antagonize it our way, please!" Chuck was pale and doing his best to be as far ahead of the rest of them as he could be.

The yellow eyes of the Monster turned to look toward the zombie. As his mouth opened, the tongue shot forth.

[Dread Counter]

Theo turned and slid out to protect them. Immediately, he was struck by the four-foot-wide tip of the long tongue. With the crackle of red lightning, he punched back at the gross appendage. Blood spurted from barely a three-inch-long gash. "Oh," he said and grimaced.

Humphrey joined up beside him a split second later and tried to pin the fleshly blob into the ground with his greatsword, but it just slid off, and the tongue retracted. They both turned and ran back to the Party.

"I can't believe you picked *that* over being able to fly." Sally scowled at the vampire as he caught back up.

"Sure, I mean it has a long cooldown and everything—but, with my Strength, an empowered critical hit is very devastating to anything that may—"

"*Later, Theo!*" Sally turned back and raised her hand out.

[Endless Dead]

From the dirt and muck, the remaining zombies from the morning fight emerged among the last Party of Players. Some of them were the Level Ten opponents she had eaten—although she had only assumed that they were all that level. With no way to see that detail anymore, they could have just rolled a weaker force. Although judging by the stats that she had received—

The Toad stomped with a webbed foot, crushing a pair of zombies. As much as she hated to see them go to waste, it was better that they died serving as a distraction. At least, rather than she and her friends die. There were always more zombies to raise but a lot fewer *Outsiders*.

Between reverberating thumps through the muddy trail, the groaning echoes of zombies being pasted into the mulch of the swamp slowly faded away as the surviving groups sprinted along the trail.

It was several minutes later before they all slowed to a stop, each one of them panting for air and dripping with sweat. Sally closed her eyes and rested her hands on muddied knees. One of her guild Parties had become erased from this world, and the *Mighty Swords* had lost a member. They were currently in a state of mourning, and barely contained tears could be heard from their haggard breathing. All so quickly too.

That was the other problem with traveling with so many Players. Other than being a tasty morsel of temptation, they still had a tenuous acceptance of their own mortality. For whatever violence the System threw at you that you had been able to overcome—when your friend died or you yourself were in mortal peril—there was something very human about that fear, even in this world.

She had seen the cracks starting to show in both Theo and Chuck before their classes and worldviews changed. The former slowly eroded away from the trauma she had been dragging him through, and the latter quickly broke from the change-in-reality whiplash and found solace in trying to be a pacifist. She pitied the Players. At least, the nice ones that didn't want to kill her.

"You think we lost it?" Theo's cheeks were a slight pink from the exertion, rather than his usual pale white.

"*Ass*." Sally punched him on the arm. "Don't tempt fate when you're standing so close to me."

They waited and looked back down the path, eyes straining against the gloomy darkness. The fog was working against them, hinting at a dramatic reveal when they least expected it. Tension filled the group. Archie dropped down from the Druid and put his ear to the ground.

After a couple of seconds of concentration, he looked up at the zombie. "I don't think we are being followed."

Sally grimaced at this further luring of the Toad to find them. Maybe she had rubbed off on them, and they shared her reckless death wish. Killing the large Monster might have been nice. They had just used up all their fancy abilities to show how powerful they were in fighting the *Zeroes*, so perhaps this was the humbling they deserved. Although, she looked back at the morose humans, it wasn't her Party that paid for the hubris.

"Take two minutes, everyone." She raised her voice so that all could hear. "We want to move as soon as possible."

Murmured acknowledgments came from the remaining groups. Not like they had much choice. They must be at least halfway through the Swamps now. In a rare display of maturity, Sally opened up her map. It flickered as though weak. The Architect may have ensured most of the System was not tied to them before dying, but it still had issues.

"What do you think, Humps? Forty-five minutes to an hour?"

The Death Knight stood behind her and gazed at her open windows. "*Yes*. Also, you have unopened Daily Rewards from almost two weeks ago."

"Do I get them all at once if I open them now?" Her index finger wiggled in front of the button to claim.

"Possibly. Sometimes it's hard to remember."

Sally closed the STAR menu and gave Humphrey a concerned scowl. "Are you feeling okay? You're not suffering memory loss or have a short life span, right?"

"Hmm." He folded his arms across his chest and looked out among the recovering Players. "I have been gaining new thoughts, feelings, and memories from our travels together. Sometimes it feels like that overrides or pushes out prior information."

"Ohhh." She punched his plated arm with a metallic *clang*. "You're becoming *normal*. Come on, let's get out of this place."

Forty-seven minutes and twenty-eight seconds later, as Theo was keen to point out, the swamp began to dry out. The peat bogs and stagnant pools became damp mud and tough patches of grass. Trees became taller and a slightly richer shade of brown. This also eventually faded into cracked and reddish earth beneath their feet. Sparse trees of dry, amber leaves and fewer branches.

As the canopy receded and the glow of midafternoon light illuminated the guild, they emerged onto a plateau.

Beneath them, an enormous expanse of dried stone and barren earth rolled out ahead until the amber sands of a desert met the horizon. In the distance, there were gray shapes of buildings and structures. The area seemed impossibly large. Down below, at the foot of the cliff, a small town of dark wood and little movement sat.

As a breeze of warm air washed over them, Humphrey turned to the *Outsiders* with a wide grin across his skeletal face.

"Welcome to the Wastelands."

CHAPTER SIX

Escort Quest

Sally crossed her arms as the vampire narrowed his eyes back up the cliff they had just descended. "No, all I'm saying is maybe you could have *flown* us down."

"Is this . . ." He frowned back at her. "Is this going to be a *thing*?"

"Probably not—the Wastes look pretty flat. But *flying*, Theo."

"It was more of a gliding ability," he murmured to himself as the zombie walked off.

It had taken a short time to move down the rocky cliff onto the plains themselves, and not only did the heat hit them—but no sooner had they stepped away from the Swamps, then all their STARs lit up with notifications.

Sally stopped to bring it up. "Mine says . . . kill quest in the Underwarren."

"Underwarren," Humphrey confirmed with a wide smile across his skeletal face.

Theo wrinkled up his nose. "Mine says . . . *take a nap?*"

"Snap!" Archie beamed up at the vampire. "The System must know we deserve a break!"

"Sucks to suck." The zombie stuck her tongue out at him before turning to the rest of the guild. "Hands up if you have Underwarren for your Keystone Quest?"

One hand raised from the throng—Chuck's.

"Huh," Sally said with a shrug. "What are the chances? And if one of you says fifty-fifty, you'll be my next meal."

Theo opened his mouth but thought better of it.

"Alright, guild, go do your respective things and meet back at that little town down there called . . ." She quickly brought up the map as her finger pointed down at the dirty brown buildings farther along the road. "Bordertown? Really?"

Humphrey unhooked the coffin to pass it over to Theo. "Here, *ha-ha*. Good luck."

With a healthy amount of waving and scowls, the various groups of the guild split up to embark on their respective quests. The Players split into two groups to help each other complete each other's in turn, while the *Outsiders* plus Chuck did their own things.

"No bad blood from the *Foxes* that you're with us?" Sally frowned as she kicked her feet through dry grass and dusty stone.

Chuck shook his head. "All their quests are in the opposite direction. It's nice to have a little break from them, though."

"Girls, am I right?" She punched him in the arm and almost knocked him over. "They treat you alright?"

"It's like having four sisters, so pretty terrible. But it's at least marginally less traumatic than whatever you guys have been up to." He furrowed his brow at the zombie. "I'm hoping we are just killing Monsters here, right?"

The warm air seemed stagnant as they moved over the near-featureless plains. Sally decided she much preferred trees—even the swamp was starting to have some charm to it in comparison. She drew up the STAR.

"I need to kill . . . Two-Fang."

Humphrey tilted his head to the side. "Mine says I need to kill Three-Fang."

Chuck groaned on reading his quest. "*Save* One-Fang."

If there was one thing the System was great at, it was barely anything. Sally smiled to herself. This was a little bit of fun, even if it was a little wonky. "Been a while since it was just the three of us, huh?"

"I don't think it ever was just us three." Chuck wrinkled up his face in trying to recall.

The Death Knight slowly shook his head as she raised an eyebrow at him. *Oh.* Chuck was a zombie back then. Until he managed to de-level, and his soul took over. A process she had tried not to think about, as the ramifications would surely leave her panicked at the state of her current existence.

"You're right—uh, well, I hope this isn't our last, then?" She grinned a little too widely in an attempt to cover over the memories he didn't have.

The Druid nodded slowly and adjusted his thick robes. Not likely if they continued on their path of violence, but he was one of the decent humans and only the third person they knew who could actually remember their previous world.

It wouldn't be too much longer before they reached their destination, but nothing obvious was springing out of the scenery. Even narrowing her eyes, the distant hills or mountains were dozens of miles away, if not more. From the map, she knew this area was larger, but she hadn't expected it to be even sparser in points of interest.

"Where are the mounts, Humps?" She considered leaping atop him—if he could carry the coffin around, then her slight frame would be no issue.

"Level Fifteen. If you're good, I'll get you a pony."

Sally pouted. She didn't want a pony. She would much rather have a fire wolf—or even a dragon. That would be more befitting a queen such as herself. Maybe an *undead* dragon to fit the theme. It was unlikely she'd find one of those anytime soon, though.

"Didn't you have a horse, Humphrey?" Chuck rubbed his fingers idly on one of the various dark leather pouches along his belt.

"No."

Sally waited for him to elaborate with a wide grin on her face. She knew that he knew that if he didn't, then she would—and her version of the story was much less flattering.

With a sigh, he relented. "Petal was an Observer who merged with a horse. I did not like them. I did not want to ride them—"

"Because it was sooo *cliché*!" Sally hopped across the sand.

"*Yes*. A flaming undead horse—I am a Death Knight. They were very persistent and annoying, so I gave it one try. *One*."

Silence washed over the three as Sally held her mouth in anticipation. Chuck grimaced and took the plunge.

"What happened—"

"Petal almost died because I am . . . considerable in power."

The Druid looked over the massive form of the fully plated Death Knight. He certainly was considerable. It would take quite the warhorse to support the amount of weight—even if Petal had fit the theme.

"Has Theo ever ridden in the coffin while you carry it?" A slight smile curled up at the edge of Chuck's mouth.

"I am not a mount for the vampire." Humphrey narrowed his empty eye sockets down at the Druid.

Sally waved her hands at them both. "Enough. With only three of us here, there is supposed to be *less* talking, not more."

Chuck prodded her arm. "But we haven't even talked about how cool Theo looks now and if you guys are dating."

Humphrey stared daggers at the Druid, flame flickering around the back of his helmet.

"Not in front of Dad, Chucky—he gets overprotective. We aren't *dating*, but we aren't *not dating*, you know?" She rubbed at the back of her hair. It was hard to quantify a relationship when you were a living corpse. The human side of her cared for him, but the zombie side was mostly indifferent. As if being a partial murder hobo wasn't enough of a mood killer.

"Not really." Chuck looked up at the hazy sky. "Must be nice to find someone you can just be yourself with, though."

Sally watched him for a few moments before turning to the still-glaring Death Knight. "Can't you adopt him too?" she whispered way too loudly.

"We are here," Humphrey stated, drawing his greatsword to change the conversation.

She pouted and withdrew her dagger. Before them was a hole. Barely noticeable from over twenty feet away, the wide tunnel dropped into the earth.

"I've got a bad feeling about this." Chuck grimaced at the darkness. "Here." [Nature's Defense].

Small roots of hardened bark wrapped around Sally's torso to create a chestplate of thick wood. It wasn't exactly comfortable or fashionable, but neither was having your bloodied lungs dangling out of your torso.

"Neat! Do you want to join our Party for now? Our auras are out of this world. Figuratively."

He nodded his head back and forth before sending a message to the *White Foxes*. As reluctant as he was, he also knew he would be at least a little safer under their wings.

Chuck has joined the Party

"Hey, gang, gang." Sally punched him in the arm again, almost knocking him into the hole. "Either I'm really strong, or you're incredibly weak."

"*Yes.* Probably both. Allow me to take point." Humphrey moved in front of them and peered down into the abyss below. Sally withdrew a torch from her Inventory and passed it to him to hold in his off hand.

"As your queen, I allow it." She gave his tired glare a curtsy. He was slowly regretting giving her the crown, and she was loving it.

They stepped into the darkness, now briefly lit by the amber glow of the held light source. It was a wider cavern than expected. After a steep drop down, the angle softened until it was almost flat. In some ways, it reminded her of the Kobold Mines—but here there were no supporting struts or the usual signs of a more civilized foe.

The dark sandstone looked hewn by inaccurate tools—or perhaps not tools at all. Indeed, as she squinted around the almost circular passageway, it looked more like an animal burrow. On the floor, the dusty stone fell into the grooves of long claw marks. Perhaps the name of the place had been a clue.

And then it hit her—the smell. It was something familiar, but somehow worse. Wet fur, ammonia, and . . . death? She nudged the Druid beside her. "Got anything so I can see better?" Her voice came out whispered but carried louder through the empty tunnel.

Chuck slowly shook his head, his face pale and slightly panicked. He had spent most of his time getting to Level Ten as a pacifist, much to the chagrin of Theo. The vampire had tried to boost them to the keystone as quickly as possible, and not wanting to grind Monsters was pretty inefficient. It still didn't seem possible to her to actually get this far without killing anything. Certainly not as fun, anyway.

"Don't worry," she whispered again, causing him to wince as her voice carried.

Not being able to see Monster levels might be a problem. Thinking back to the Toad in the Swamps . . . but surely the Keystone Quest would just have them against Level Ten Monsters? In which case, between herself and the Death Knight, there wasn't much that could cause them issues. Hopefully.

She took a deep breath in before the plated finger of Humphrey pressed against her lips. He shook his head.

Sally rolled her eyes. Perhaps she shouldn't get too big for her boots. At least until she found bigger boots—that was how they worked, right?

As Humphrey turned back toward the ongoing warren, a shadow flashed against the dim wall farther in. They all paused and stood ready. Nothing.

Chuck took one step forward, and then a large shadow blocked up the entrance behind them. The stench of rodent flooded through the air as two fist-sized red eyes glimmered in the glow of their torch.

Sounds of long claws scratching against rock came from behind them as two further sets of evil eyes clambered around the darkened tunnel.

CHAPTER SEVEN

Warren You Like to Know

Rats!" Sally shouted, her voice echoing down the tunnel as she cast *[Hex: Slow]* on the giant rodent clambering through the entrance behind them.

"I think they're field mice, actually." Chuck grimaced as he tried to lower himself down and be less of a target.

Humphrey pulsed with energy as he cast *[Adrenaline]* and *[Dead King's Court]*, stepping into the middle of the rough corridor to face the two from within. His greatsword burned a deep crimson, illuminating the space around them after the torch was discarded to the side.

"Are any of these the one we *aren't* supposed to kill for your quest?" Sally held up her hand in preparation.

"Don't think so—" the Druid began.

[Necroblast: Barrage]. A sequence of five eldritch pulses of necromantic energy flew from above the zombie and into the large mouse that was scurrying toward her. At first, it looked like they did nothing but burn the fur from the impact areas, but as the creature moved toward her with anger in its eyes, she could see the darker shades of blood soaking through the dark gray coat.

Humphrey thundered forward to meet the two mice coming from around the corner. The tunnel was only wide enough for one to fight properly, but so eager to find out what this new meal was, they squished and pushed between each other to be the first to bite down on the glowing morsel.

[Grave Strike] caused his blade to flare with unholy energy, and the Death Knight leveled a large upswing, catching one of the mice in the jaw. Dark blood flicked up across the ceiling as a dark gash flickered across the front of the

assailing rodent's face. The companion giant bit downward but was on shaky footing and only managed a mouthful of rocky dust as Humphrey skirted away.

Sally rolled to the side to avoid being flattened and lashed out at the offending leg, giving it a superficial cut. A dagger was no way to fight something so large. Even if she could get close enough, the blade didn't puncture deep enough to do a lot of damage. She watched as a thick tail lashed around toward the Druid. *[Thorn Wall]*

Up from the ground, small structures made of thick wood and vine sprung up almost instantly. There was a dull thud that blew dry dust up into a cloud as the wooden shield deflected the tail. The wall cracked and immediately shattered from the blow, but it saved Chuck from taking the hit himself.

The looming maw of the giant Monster breathed warmly down on Sally; giant, yellowed teeth bared in a grimace as the creature hissed out in anger. She ran toward it and sent off a single *[Necroblast]*—straight into the mouth before it had a chance to react. As the giant gulped in pain, she slid beneath it and stabbed upward into the furred stomach repeatedly.

Chuck winced at the violence and watched as the mouse tried to back away and stomp upon the woman. With a sigh, he held out a hand. *[Earth Clutch]*. Vines wrapped around one of the flailing legs of the Monster and pinned it to the tunnel floor so that it couldn't stomp on the zombie.

Humphrey blocked the clawed attack with the flat of his blade and slid backward from the impact. One of the injured mice had retreated to lick their wounds, and the eagerness of the second to take the place in the melee was now waning as it had lost one of its eyes. Froth surged from its mouth as it gnawed at the air where the Death Knight kept retreating from, drawing it back farther to the support of the zombie. Then Humphrey stepped forward instead and thrust the blade out straight.

The giant rodent tried to dodge to the side to avoid taking the blade into the mouth and instead had its shoulder joint split by the greatsword. It collapsed on the weakened limb, and before it could scramble back up, the Death Knight had leaped atop it and crashed down with his entire weight—impaling the creature straight through the skull.

"I don't think I'll ever get used to this." Chuck grimaced to himself, watching the carnage play out.

The mouse near the entrance collapsed on top of the stabbing zombie, and the Druid briefly considered casting something before—

[Eat Brains]. Sally burst from the top of the rodent's head in a spray of fur, gore, and bone matter. "Wow, that was super gross!" She beamed, spitting out some remnants of the quick meal.

"How did you even . . . from that angle?" Chuck's stomach rolled at the thought of the journey the woman just made to reach her target.

Humphrey started to stroll up, having also dispatched both his opponents.

He was similarly lashed with crimson blood, and he reflected in a macabre hue in the low light of the torch.

"Broke your . . ." The zombie slipped from the head of the felled mouse and rolled along the tunnel back to her feet. "*Ah!* Broke your pacifism run there, didn't you, Chuck?"

"I don't think I hurt it." The Druid bit his tongue. "Plus, I've killed orcs with you guys previously. It's not that I haven't killed . . . I just don't want that to be my bread and butter."

"Well,"—Humphrey slapped him on the back, knocking him forward—"it's nice to have some proper support for a change."

Chuck looked past the Death Knight down the tunnel. It didn't look like they needed much support. He hadn't even needed to cast any healing spells— and probably could have gotten away with just the one to protect himself.

"There will probably be a lot more squeakers in the hole." Sally tried to squeeze some of the matted gore from her hair. "How'd my hair get so long and thick, anyway?"

The other two shrugged. With a sigh and nothing left to accomplish at the start of the tunnel, the group started off toward the interior of the warren.

Chuck became the designated torch holder. Not that he wasn't being useful, but if only for the fact that when they were assailed by a mouse or two, he didn't actually need to do much otherwise. The glow of the Death Knight was almost brighter than the held light when he was powered up.

"Sorry if you feel useless, Chucky." Sally wiped her mouth from the fourth brain she had eaten on the trip. "Odd that our quests led us to the same place."

He shrugged in return but narrowed his eyes off into the gloom. "I'm more worried that we'll accidentally kill the wrong one, and then I'll fail my quest."

"Unlikely." Humphrey grinned as he strode out in front of them. "The System knows what it is doing."

Sally and Chuck exchanged rolled eyes and caught up.

A notification came through on the zombie's STAR.

Theo: sit rep?
Sally: that like an exercise?
Sally: we are fighting giant mice.
Theo: I can't sleep.
Sally: . . .
Sally: seriously? You have the easiest quest ever.
Theo: it's the middle of the day!
Theo: also something weird is going on with the town here . . .
Theo: tele stone to me when you're all done?
Sally: yeah, yeah, speak soon.

"Theo is useless sometimes." She sighed and shook her head. How could he not have a nap? He had the coffin and everything—she was super sure she could nap right now if given the chance.

Humphrey said nothing but grinned wider.

"Trouble in paradise?" Chuck nudged her, but she remained unmoved.

"Don't start with that, *Mister Vines*. Let's focus on fighting and quests for now, gossip later." She wagged a bloodstained finger in the air.

Chuck grinned and rolled his eyes. "A surprisingly measured response from you."

She shot him a glare, but any further back talking halted as another pair of giant field mice leaped from a side chamber. Sally pushed the Druid to the floor as the large, furred rodent slammed her into the tunnel wall and knocked the stale air from her undead lungs.

"The worst thing is . . ." she growled as she grabbed at the teeth of the mouse to hold its jaws open, "I can't even raise these as zombies."

"That would be pretty neat though, *ha-ha!*" Humphrey rippled with power as he slashed back and forth between the pair of enemies.

Chuck raised a hand—*[Blinding Light]*.

The mouse trying to take a bite out of the zombie flinched away as a bright, radiant light briefly lit the tunnel. Sally took the opportunity to roll away and beneath the jaw of her assailant.

[Necroblast: Barrage]

The repeated blasts struck the creature point blank, just below its mouth. Landing in the same place bore a hole into the furred neck, and as it struggled to breathe through pulses of blood—*[Eat Brains]* put it out of any misery.

Humphrey cleaved a leg clean off and managed to pierce the heart of the second with a swift jab.

With a smile, he turned back to the pair. "I hope you've been looting these."

"What!" Sally wrinkled up her face. "I don't give a [Rat's Ass] about what they could drop—oh? Do they drop that?"

"No, these are *mice*." Humphrey lowered his blade and deflated a little.

Chuck shuffled nervously as he tried to dust some errant rodent blood from his druidic outfit. "I've been looting them. Nothing exciting, but it'll be good to start building gold up again."

Sally shrugged and wondered where she could find rats that dropped their little butts. On second thought, that might not be the best idea—that path was a route to ruin.

"So, uh . . ." Chuck tilted his head to the side. "When are we going to address *that?*"

The two undead turned from where they were standing toward where the field mice had sprung from.

Ahead of them, barely lit by their scant light, was an enormous set of wooden doors. Emblazoned about twenty feet up in tarnished gold was the symbol of a crown.

"A rat king!" Sally gasped.

Humphrey ground his teeth together. "*They're mice.*"

CHAPTER EIGHT

No-Fang

Sally scratched her head and looked over at Chuck. "Do mice even have tails this long?"

"Yeah. Maybe you're thinking of hamsters."

"No, not since *the incident*." She looked over at the door and pouted.

"Uh . . . what—"

"Just trying out a new catchphrase. Theo doesn't think it'll catch on." Sally avoided the tired glare of the Death Knight as he tried to gesture toward the door.

Chuck frowned and couldn't resist stepping further down this path. "You had a catchphrase before?"

"Not since *the incident*." She beamed back at him with wide eyes.

The Druid leaned to the side to see past her. "How do you put up with this?"

"Barely." The Death Knight shrugged. Resting his greatsword across his shoulders, he walked up to the large doors. Even with his large metallic form, he was minuscule in comparison, like an action figure. One tired of little zombie woman shenanigans.

Sally read the room and, with a sigh, relented and ditched the quirky mania. Theo was much more receptive to it than these sticks-in-the-mud, although maybe he was just more polite about it. The vampire was just as weird himself these days . . . how far they'd come since meeting in the forest near Hillan.

"What do you think, then, Papa Humps? Knock or forced entry?"

"Don't call me that," he said with a sigh. "Let's just enter and kill everything except for whatever Chuck needs to save."

She stood beside him and looked up at the handle that was a good dozen feet above her head. Whatever lived in here, she wouldn't have thought it would have needed a handle. The giant mice they had already slain weren't exactly high on the intelligence scale. Something more interesting was afoot—probably something tasty.

"Here, allow me—this shouldn't kill anything." Chuck paused with his hand outstretched. "Unless the door falls over on us or something inside. Hmm." Resigning to whatever fate had planned for his actions, he cast out a vine that shot forth and wrapped around the wooden handle above them.

After a couple of seconds of him struggling, Sally rolled her eyes and came to help pull.

The door groaned loudly as it gradually opened, a musky air pooling out as the gap widened. Humphrey stood at the ready and waited for it to be open enough for all of them before stepping forward.

A large chamber loomed before them; a roughly carved rectangle of gray stone illuminated by large torches equally spaced apart on the walls. The smell of damp fur was even stronger, and Chuck held his hand to his nose. Across the room opposite to them were three creatures.

Two large and armored mice flanked one that sat upon a throne. This supposed king sat with a ramshackle crown atop his orange-furred head, random metals glinting in the light as it slid down toward his eyes. In one hand, he held a scepter with a flowing yellow orb at the top. He also seemed to be wearing what looked like a purple smoking jacket.

"Adventurers!" the king rumbled. "Tremble and yield to the strength of my two wives, Two-Fang and Three-Fang!"

"Oh." Chuck rolled his eyes. "*King One-Fang.*"

"Did you try face down?" Archie stretched out and clawed at the wood atop the coffin.

"Yeah, there's no way I can sleep with a mouthful of pillow." Theo sat on the edge of his vampiric bed and pouted with chin in hand.

"Shame. I've already completed my quest." The cat beamed up at him with emerald eyes.

"Perhaps I'm just worried—you saw the 'Wanted' posters, right?"

The cat nodded. "They weren't very flattering, yes."

Theo scrunched up his face. Unflattering would be putting it lightly. Humphrey's was just a rectangle with a skull drawn atop it, and small flames sketched just above him. Sally's and his were a little more professionally painted, but that was a stretch of most of those words.

Whether it would become a problem was a matter of intent to enforce the bounties. Level Twelve or lower guards? Not an issue. Bored Level Twenty Players? Big issue.

"Hey, Theo?"

The vampire looked down at the ginger cat, still looking up at him eagerly. "Yeah?"

"You can keep a secret, right? From the others?" A flicker of light rolled around his large emerald eyes.

"One each then?" Sally winced as the mouse opposite the Death Knight charged forward almost instantly, knocking him into the rocky wall with a loud *clang*. That one had three prominent fangs.

Narrowing her eyes, the one ahead of her had two fangs. Although most of the mice had prominent—she stopped that train of thought as the Monster opened its maw wide, and a beam attack started charging up.

"This is more like it!" Sally growled out loud as she put *[Hex: Slow]* on the attacking creature.

Chuck sighed and raised his staff. "This is my Level Nine. Try not to let me die." *[Ancient Grove]*Vines and plant growth surrounded the king, enshrouding him in a wide orb of druidic power. The verdant greens and sprouting flowers of pink and amber were a stark contrast to the dim and muted colors of the supposed throne room.

With a quick nod to him, Sally sprinted off toward Two-Fang. What she wouldn't give for *[Dread Counter]* right now—although she wouldn't ever admit that to the vampire. *He could have been able to fly!* Or at least occasionally glide.

Blue energy flashed and blinded her as she dove to the side. The attack of the beast finally released, scouring across the room as a continuous attack. Pain flared up her legs as she rolled into the trusty crossbow-withdrawal, with a bolt piercing into the side of the rodent's face. This one had a dirty gray color to its fur, with streaks of pale brown near its eyes. The Monster turned, and the beam curved through the air, drawing a dark mark across the doors and entrance wall.

Chuck unraveled from his recoiled position, thankful that the beam had struck a good few feet taller than he was. He was still unsure of how he was supposed to save One-Fang, but protecting him from the carnage about to be wrought seemed like a good starting point. Given how effective the two undead were, once they had finished their bloodshed, they could sort the rest out after.

[Lord of the Damned]

Skeletal Warriors burst out from around the Death Knight as he parried and deflected a quick slash of large claws. Three-Fang was extremely fast for its size. A blaze of crimson circled in the air as he stepped forward with a flourish to distract the oversized mouse. It returned the action by running around the wall, an impressive feat, circling the corner of the chamber to drop back down behind him. Black energy enveloped the Monster's paws.

[Necroblast: Barrage]

The pulsing blasts of energy radiated as they struck the Monster, charring fur and splitting skin. Two-Fang screeched out in rage, and Sally leaped atop the side of the beast, dagger in her mouth so that she could grab handfuls of the fur. Against the writhing and warm creature, she began to clamber up, unable to be shaken as the mouse tried to snap back at her.

"*I huv a mnnt!*" she growled out with the blade between her teeth. From atop Two-Fang's back, she giggled in mad joy at her impromptu bronco ride.

Chuck deflated at the sight and looked over at the Death Knight to see if he was taking things a little more seriously. Immediately, he regretted the decision.

Humphrey was standing inside the maw of Three-Fang, the Monster's mouth pried open with the greatsword like a toothpick in a cartoon, and the plated Party member was trying to pull the tongue of the beast out.

They were goofy and irritating, each in their own different ways. But when it came to violence, they were always a step above whatever was asked of them. He had seen the aftermath of the fight at Sanctuary and stayed well clear of the other two villages they had taken. It was one thing to be allied with the *Outsiders*, but pure carnage just wasn't who he wanted to be, even if the cause was good.

A Druid was the best thing he could have become, really. Despite the class choice not having a tangible change to his personality, it had served as a guiding track so that he didn't go off the rails. He had also seen the dead Cleric, Marius. The things that hate and denial could lead you to. Sally and her Party bloodied their hands with the best of them, but they hadn't flown off the handle in that regard.

Even as his stomach turned as the Death Knight was successful in tearing his coveted prize from the panicked Monster, there wasn't the grim trauma that real people doing these things would face. They enjoyed it and accepted it. Just as easily as they'd banter or annoy each other, they would eat and kill anyone who opposed them. It was as scary as it was impressive. Even now, the zombie sighed as her mouth withdrew from the broken skull and exposed brains of her fallen enemy. He was stunned.

Sally dropped to the floor with a smile. "Whoop! That's my quest completed. Are you ready to hear all the amazing keystone skills I get to choose from?"

"I am done also." Humphrey wiped his gore-soaked plated gloves on his red cloak. The low gurgles of the mouse behind him did little to bother him.

"Oh." Chuck downturned his mouth and released the spell protecting the king. "I guess you are saved, One-Fang?"

"Thank you, little ones!" the king boomed down toward them. "I was hoping for an amicable divorce from both my wives, but I guess this way works out. For me, anyway."

"Huh." Sally briefly frowned up at him as she prodded at her STAR. "You must be a Unique Monster? Want to come join—"

"*Sally, no!*" Humphrey shook his head.

She rolled her eyes just before they were illuminated by the long-awaited skill choice.

Keystone Quest Completed
Pick One
[**Crypt Warden**] Undead allies receive a boost to STR/CON/DEF
[**Soul Witch**] Your kills temporally empower your Necroblast skills
[**Resourceful**] Luck and Item Find increases

CHAPTER NINE

Blood x Money

Sally hissed at the choices. This was like the affinity choice all over again. If only there were a way to select all three at once. Her hand hovered over the selections—*no*. She lowered it again. Trying that would be a recipe for just unlocking the one she least wanted.

[Crypt Warden]

No actions were without consequences, but this at least seemed like the best option for the Party. It was the boring melee affinity once more—but the longer her zombies could stay alive, the better. Plus, it stacked with Humphrey and Theo. The closer they got to invincible, the less likely the System would be able to sweep them under the carpet and allow itself to sink into ruin.

"*No*, I'm just happy where I am, thank you. I am a *king*."

She turned to see the Death Knight and Mouse King in a heated discussion. As much as she had wanted him to join as a Party member or neat mount, the giant rodent seemed unable to solve his own marital problems. How could he assist with their world-conquering goals? The Party were paragons of self-assured normalcy and competency.

"Hey, Humps, what did you choose?" she shouted across the chamber, her voice echoing down the tunnels.

The Death Knight turned away from his conversation with One-Fang, and his expression softened. "Can I not keep it a secret until it becomes a key pivotal moment in future turmoil?"

She shook her head. "It's my turn with the Chekhov's gun." She patted one of her side pockets. "What about you, Chuck?"

The Druid scratched at his head, his eyes drifting away from his STAR screens. He looked tired. "Just some healing spell."

"Really?" Sally crossed her arms. "I bet it's cool, though, like with a neat name. Are you going to hold out on me too?"

Chuck furrowed his brow. Before he could answer, he tilted his head and turned back to look at the entrance to the throne room. "Footsteps," he murmured.

"Oh!" The Mouse King grinned, his ramshackle crown sliding back atop his head. "More ungrateful interlopers to kill off my—"

"Hush already," Sally said with a scowl. "You're just scene-dressing now. Let the adults talk."

One-Fang opened his mouth but closed it promptly. Under the glaring presence of the zombie, he slouched on the throne and resigned to being browbeaten once again.

She could hear the footsteps now too—a *clip-clop* of feet against the rough stone floor. Possibly only one person running. Perhaps someone who had a quest to do down here and was horrified to find that all the Monsters had already been defeated. Maybe even someone with a quest to kill One-Fang.

"You guys ready to head back to *Count-von-Count-a-lot?*" She shrugged. They weren't getting stuck down here listening to someone whine or getting murdered by an eager Level Twenty. Even though she thought she could take one on . . . well, maybe with Theo here. Their quests were complete, and they had a world to explore.

Humphrey and Chuck nodded their acknowledgment and walked nearer to her so they could all teleport at once. Just as she raised the stone that would take them to the vampire, the sprinting figure slid into the doorway and raised his hands.

"Aha! I thought I smelled a new Party!"

Sally paused. She thought in all likelihood that this new character was probably a Unique Monster—on account of him being almost seven feet tall and a dull shade of blue. Dark horns rose from a tangled mop of white hair, and his luminous baby-blue eyes matched the striped suit he wore.

"Hey," she began, "do you want to join our—"

"*Sally!*" Humphrey huffed at her, narrowing his eyes at the newcomer.

She rolled her eyes. They would never fill the empty space if they kept stopping her from inviting every Unique Monster they came across. You had to shotgun blast those invites out in the hopes that some foolish sucker would bite. Although this figure didn't look much like a fighter, you couldn't let appearances deceive you. They could be a potent ally in the making if she just gave them a chance.

"My name"—the slim demonic-looking fellow announced with a bow—"is Edward the Inevitable. I am an appointed tax collector for—"

"Not interested." Sally gave a thumbs-down.

"It's not voluntary—you are required to provide a gold stipend of—"

"Theo has all our gold," she said with a shrug. "He likes to count it, even though the System already does that." Turning to the Death Knight, the zombie frowned. "We should probably talk to him about that. It's not healthy."

"Do not ignore me! You will incur the wrath of—"

"Yeah . . . bye!" Sally activated the teleport and with a brief flash of blue, they vanished, leaving the odd demon and Mouse King alone to awkwardly glare at each other.

A brief wave of vertigo flooded over them before it abated, and they found themselves in a darkened room of deep red wood, curtains drawn to obscure any sunlight. From a casket on the floor, a shadowed figure loomed up—crimson flickering in the back of his eyes.

"You could at least knock, guys." Theo sighed. "I almost had it."

"Skill issue." Sally hopped atop the actual bed in the room, which creaked at the surprise assault. "Humphrey and I got our keystones—so did Chuck."

"Hey, Theo. Sorry for intruding." Chuck awkwardly shuffled his feet. "I should perhaps go find the *Foxes*."

"No need to be shy." Humphrey grinned as his helmet flames illuminated the room in a further red hue.

"It's more that . . . you're all pretty dead and covered in viscera—it's quite emotionally oppressive."

Sally didn't prod him further. As fun as it was to wind Chuck up, she understood the difference between them. "Thanks for your help today, Chucky. We'll arrange that gossip sesh for a less gore-covered occasion?"

"Sure." He gave a smile despite his discomfort. "I felt like I was being carried, but I'm glad I was on your side of the pointy stuff."

"What was it you killed?" Theo piped up. "Any good loot?"

"Mice and assorted mice parts." Sally kicked the side of his coffin. "We settled a domestic dispute too. *I think.*"

Chuck nodded and gave them all a brief bow. "More mania for me to unpack at a later date. Keep in touch."

They waved him off as he turned and opened the door—before the Druid gasped, stepping backward as a figure loomed on the other side.

"Did I not mention I was *Inevitable?*" Edward grinned as he stepped into the room—with Chuck yielding to his advancement.

"Who's this asshole?" Theo stood from his coffin with clenched fists.

Sally looked between the two. It was unlike the vampire to lose his temper or evoke naughty words—especially in her presence. The inability to sleep must be eroding away at his human side again, even though it was still the day.

"Ah, you must be the Party coin purse?" Edward stopped to observe them all. "You're actually *all* rather strange."

"I suggest you leave." The vampire stepped out of his bed and started walking toward the man.

"Let me assure you, I do not care for idle threats. I am here to do my job and—"

Theo flashed forward, his fist-knives popping into existence as he slashed out at the intruder in an arc of crimson energy. Blood sprayed through the air, and then his arm hung limp.

Edward dropped to the floor; his neck cut wide open.

Theo turned with a sheepish smile to the Druid, who took the brunt of the arterial spray. "Sorry guys, uh—especially you, Chuck. Not sure what came over me."

"Could have just given him some gold." Sally swung her legs back and forth on the bed. "That was a *little* out of character."

"First"—Theo put away his blades and stood tall—"—you never give scammers anything." He stopped as he started the process of cleaning his outfit through the STAR.

"Second?" Humphrey sighed.

"Huh? Oh, and yeah—there's something odd going on, right?"

The three watched him expectantly.

"Sorry." Theo shook his head. "I'm feeling a little off. I shouldn't be this tired . . ."

Sally sighed and lay back on the bed. "Perhaps you're just sore that we are going to level faster than you."

"No, no. Not going to happen." The vampire shook his head, but his eyes told a different story. "Just need to sleep. But there's something—uh, there were 'Wanted' posters of us three."

"Yet we are not assailed?" Humphrey looked down at the corpse of the demon.

"That's the thing—there's nobody in the town. It's a ghost town in all but the literal sense." He raised a finger as the zombie sat up. "And yes, I've checked."

Humphrey scratched at the side of his skull, the metallic sound causing the Druid to wince. "There are abandoned settlements in the Wastelands, but this is not meant to be one of them."

Sally pouted. They had made it half a day into the second area and already the glitches of the System were rearing their ugly heads. Not to mention she met two Unique Monsters, and Theo had just murdered one in blind rage. That was against their new moral code—probably.

"Theo, why'd you kill the nice man? He may have been able to give us answers."

The vampire tilted his head to the side as if he were trying to listen to a whisper in the breeze. Eventually, his eyes focused on hers.

"I just have to kill all demons."

"Uh—I'm not accepting that kind of cliché. Fess up, fangs."

Theo stood for a moment, the cogs rotating in his head.

"No," he replied, as he turned and left the room.

CHAPTER TEN

Dry Waterfalls

The remaining Party members sat in the room in stunned silence as the vampire sucked the mood with him as he left. His footsteps descended a handful of stairs before there was silence.

"*Awwwkwaaard.*" Chuck grimaced.

"He's not usually that curt or abrasive." Sally frowned. If he expected her to chase him outside for answers, that wasn't happening. The bed was rather comfortable after having spent all morning in the mouse tunnels.

"He is going feral. We need to put him down." Humphrey glared out at the open door.

Sally rolled her eyes. "Humps! Just let him cool off. Let's find Archie and investigate the town for ourselves. You in, Chuck?" The last thing she needed was to push Theo further away if something was the matter. They needed to stick together.

The Druid looked anything but in. Although he had seen his fair share of violence, the damp covering of the demon's blood all up his face was unpleasant. "Rain check." He grimaced and went toward the door too.

"Still haven't seen you cast that." Sally piped up as Chuck's footsteps slowly clunked down the nearby staircase.

[Chuck has left the Party]

Sally: Archie where you cat?
Sally: at*
Sally: cat

She exhaled through her nose. "He's not responding."

The Death Knight shrugged. "Classic Humphrey and Sally adventure?"

"Yeah, let's go punch some doors in, or whatever." All her muscles decided that this would be a good time to melt. Maybe just stop existing until everyone came back to pep her up.

Humphrey extended a hand to help her up from the bed. "Well now, no need to seem so enthused."

With reluctance, she took it and stood up, briefly brushing the dirt from her skirt. On second thought, she changed back to her black jeans—the System equivalent of dumping the dirty laundry in a pile at the end of the bed.

"We were just all so united before," Sally huffed as they stepped over the corpse. "Now we are languishing again."

"New area blues. Remember when we spent hours walking through the same forest just to fight some goblins?" The Death Knight struggled to fit through the normal-sized doorway, having to turn sideways slightly as he scraped against the red wood.

Maybe they just needed to roll with the punches and eventually they'd fail upward into something more than just sand and terrible moods. "That was the spark we needed for our overarching plans, huh?" She stopped at the top of the staircase to look out of the window.

All the buildings were of similar design. Dusty, ruddy wood in basic shapes. Everything had a layer of abandonment to it, just as Hillan had. Except this was supposed to be the staging area for Players new to the area to populate. Could *Zero* have held off new Parties enough to starve the location of resources? It seemed unlikely.

"Indeed," Humphrey continued, following her gaze. "Shake up enough trouble, and we will find a path to cling to."

"*Trouble*," Sally repeated before following the staircase down. A familiar word that almost stuck as their surname, if danger wasn't more apt.

It looked as though they were in some manner of a small inn. A darkened room of few furnishings took up the majority of the downstairs. Behind a long counter was a shoe and coat rack. On the wall was a dust-covered board that held keys for five rooms—four of which were present.

"No System-created at all, huh?" She ran her finger across the counter. Definitely hadn't seen any cleaning for weeks at least.

"Even in the Player-run towns, there would be System-created. The Wastelands are only a sandbox figuratively." Humphrey glared around the room as if any secrets would seep out of the walls if they couldn't meet his intensity.

"Where would we go for answers? I don't want to spend all day opening doors to empty rooms. That's not an engaging adventure, Humps. This one's on you." She crossed her arms and tapped her foot.

The Death Knight looked briefly taken aback that he was in charge but quickly gathered a thoughtful look—accompanied by a stroke of his metal chin. "If we had 'Wanted' posters out, perhaps a sheriff's office or jail?"

She shrugged in response. Sounded like as good a plan as any. Didn't bring Theo back, locate the cat, or fill in the gap in their Party—but all roads led to rivers or something. With another sigh, she gestured for the large-plated ex-Observer to carry on forward.

With the sun now high in the sky, the town was warmer than she'd like. Even the earth was dry and cracked beneath their feet. The main road seemed to head straight through from one end to the other like they were on a movie set, like a pop-up fake town. Her eyes narrowed at the darkened windows, pits of shadow that could be hiding any number of opponents in wait. This could be a trap. Or just super disappointing.

Eventually, Humphrey stopped and pointed at one of the abandoned buildings. Three sheets of weather-worn paper rustled in the meager breeze. The words "Wanted" inscribed across the tops of each.

Sally hopped over to take a closer look. "Ha! Look at yours, Humps." With a wide grin, she jabbed a dead finger at the square with a little skull atop it.

"It's mostly accurate," he grumbled and turned to gaze off into the distance.

"Meh." She scowled at the other two. "They made me look like a wretch, and Theo looks like a generic vampire cliché."

"I know, right?"

Sally kicked him in the shin. "Forget that—there's not even a bounty reward? It just says, 'wanted dead or alive,' and we're already kinda both."

Humphrey hummed to himself and walked around her farther down the wall. She watched as he plucked another page from the dried wood of the building.

"Another poster? For Archie or Jackie?"

The Death Knight shook his head and read it aloud. "Final warning. Should the levy not be paid by the end of the week, this town and the surrounding area shall be rendered barren and inert. May your charity save you."

"Hmm. That's enough context clues for what happened here, then, yeah? Handy to have them all on a piece of paper. Is it signed?"

"*Yes.*" There was a pause as the Death Knight did not elaborate.

" . . .I swear, Humps."

He grinned. "Signed by Edward the Inevitable, on behalf of . . . the rest is torn off."

Sally narrowed her eyes. The System might like to swirl around something macabre in her cornflakes, but this bit of narrative peek-a-boo wasn't settling well on her grumbly mood. The mouse brains had tasted gross, and she didn't want to play detective today.

The Death Knight tucked the notice into his belt. "Shame Theo struck down the chap who may have had some answers."

"Psh." Now she just felt tired. Why couldn't her quest have been to nap—and Theo could have gone and slain the oversized rodents?

A *bloip* from her STAR indicated a notification.

"Oh, a private message from Theo. *Private!*" She turned and moved away from the Death Knight since he was able to see her UI.

Theo: Sorry, Sally.
Theo: a lot on my mind recently.
Theo: I'm just going to go blow off some steam.
Theo: talk later?
Sally: of course
Sally: find me some good items, punk

She closed the messages, still not really any less concerned about the vampire. "False alarm, nothing *salacious*, Humphrey." She waved her hands in the air. "Oh, that's an idea—do you think we could do, like, a pinup calendar for merch?"

"*Merch?*"

"When we're a famous Party, of course. Assuming we don't die before Level Fifty—we'll be well-known by then, I'd think."

The Death Knight tilted his skull in thought. "I'm not sure how marketable I—"

"You're hot shit, Humps. Naturally, Theo would be centerfold, though—no offense." Sally rubbed her chin.

Humphrey would have blinked slowly in response, had he any eyelids. "That is understandable."

"Like, you've seen his abs, right? How does that even work when he is dead? Like the muscle growth—I can understand the low body fat percentage when all he drinks is blood. But I don't really have abs, and I'm just as slim—if not more!"

"Sally."

"Everything I eat just seems to go to my hair. Which I'm not complaining about—I'd much rather have long, thick hair than end up with the thin and sparse stuff like an undead would usually have. I should just count my blessings, huh?"

"Sally."

"Plus, I'm remarkably strong and healthy for a corpse. That's obviously something that the System decides—but other than eating brains, it makes everything kind of arbitrary, right? Like just a veneer of undead gloss over basically a living demigod at this point."

"Sally."

"You're right. Perhaps that is a bit too egotistical—we are small fish in the grand scheme of things, even if we are stacked tighter than . . . sorry, I seem to be talking an awful lot. I think it's just anxiety over the Party falling apart—I have no idea what I'm doing, and I didn't think we'd ever get this far, with everything we've been able to change."

She paused for breath; eyes wide as the windup key slowly ran out of steam.

"*Sally.*"

"Yeah?"

The Death Knight raised a plated hand and pointed his index finger over her shoulder.

She turned to see a bloodied figure silhouetted against the shadow of a dusty awning. Having politely waited for her waterfall of words to finish, the man stepped out and into the light.

Crimson had now soaked through his purple suit, but a sharp-toothed smile radiated across the demon's face.

"I told you that I was *inevitable.*" Edward beamed with eyes a bright, light blue.

CHAPTER ELEVEN

Unavoidable

Sally snapped her fingers at the macabre figure approaching them, her mood dulling even further. "Ah, we were just talking about you."

"No." Edward shook his head, causing new streams of crimson to run from his neck. "You were having some sort of brain-to-mouth issue and couldn't turn the faucet off."

"I'm pretty sure I'm always like that." She shrugged and raised an eyebrow to Humphrey.

"Well, my condolences, then." The demon tipped his head toward the Death Knight.

He narrowed his empty sockets in response, and the flame at the back of his helmet pulsed a little higher.

"Forget the smarm. We want some answers." The zombie raised a fist.

"And I want your valuables—I suppose we will both be found lacking." A wide grin of sharp fangs spread across Edward's face as he stopped a dozen feet from the pair.

Sally exhaled through her nose. Normally Unique Monsters had a little more camaraderie to them. Very few had to be put to the sword or to her stomach. They had just as boring a flavor as the System-created, but with the added guilt that she should probably feel toward consuming Players. Edward was being particularly unpalatable.

"So you'll just keep coming after us if we kill you until you get the money?" Her hand drummed idly on the dagger sheath.

"Essentially. All I ask is a generous donation of—"

"What about if I ate your brains?"

The demon smirked and slowly drew a sword of purple-toned metal. "I've had a lot worse, believe me."

Sally glanced up at the Death Knight. He had remained rather impassive but was still on alert. Something was definitely odd here, but he was letting her take the lead on any actions. She ran her tongue across sharp teeth. "How much to get rid of you then, Eddy?"

"*Do not call me that.* And the price, including extra for killing me and wasting my time, would be—"

"Eddy." Sally grinned.

"I will just increase the cost if you—"

"Eddy," Humphrey added.

The blazing light blue eyes wavered as he narrowed them at the pair. The trickles of blood had all but dried up in the constant heat of the sun overhead, but his seething hatred continued to drip from his expression.

"I knew I heard someone talking shit over here again."

The three turned to the side to see Theo stomping his way from an alley. He looked . . . unwell—a pained expression darkening his pale face.

"Ah." Edward rolled his eyes, a pale glow flowing along his sword. "If it isn't bat-boy, again."

The vampire strode right up to the demon, eyes burning crimson as Edward raised his sword.

[Inevitable Ruin]

[Dread Counter]

Theo grabbed the offending sword arm, hand crackling with red electricity, and twisted, pushing Edward to his knees. The snap of a bone caused the purple blade to drop to the floor with a dull *clang*. Dark punch-blades popped into his hands as he pulled a fist back for a strike.

"Wait, Theo! We need information from him first."

"First?" Edward winced, trying to get his head and broken arm into a comfortable resting position. "You'll still let him kill me, knowing I will return?"

The vampire kneeled, his face beside the demon's. "Speak."

Sally grinned. Theo was still the best at the interrogation thing. Although they *should* probably ask some questions first before calling this a win. "Oh, uh, Eddy. Who are you collecting gold for?"

"Our great Lord of the Dunes, the great titan of the Wastes, he who grants us with—*aah!*"

Theo twisted the broken arm further. "Are these different people or just one?"

"Just one—Ruben C'tenphorus the Unyielding."

"Compensating much?" Sally sighed and rubbed the bridge of her nose. "What are they, and what do they want with all the gold?"

Edward grinned despite his pain. "They are a dragon, and they are a dragon."

"Uh-huh." She brought up the map and prodded a finger into the air. "What do you think, Humps? They probably reside just before the third area; they are a Level Twenty Champion, annnnnd they've been sucking the resources from the Wastes and making it hard for Players to progress?"

"A reasonable guess." Humphrey grinned.

"Do we still need this guy?" Theo's eyes had dulled, and he just stared blankly at the restrained demon. He looked cold and drained of his usual good nature.

"How much to make you go away? I mean Edward, not you, Theo." Sally looked at the vampire with concern.

"It will be a cost of . . . twenty gold each!"

"Oh." She deflated. "We can pay that, huh? I was expecting to be extorted a little more than that."

"No, no, no," Theo hissed, "that's how they get you. *No gold.*"

The demon recoiled against the renewed fervor of the vampire. "That seems a little unreasonable; surely you could spare—"

Theo rammed his blade into the demon's eye socket. The slim-suited body dropped to the floor as he withdrew it with a wet sucking noise.

"*Dammit*, what has gotten into you?" Sally stomped over to confront the vampire. "Normally, wanton violence is our bread and butter—but you're especially out of sorts—" She stopped as she came face to face with him.

He looked like he hadn't slept in days—despite definitely getting good rest the night before. The longer he went without sleep, the more unhinged he usually became. But this was different. *Troubled* would be the best word to describe it. Not loopy, or even bloodthirsty—but as though the weight of all their travels had hit him at once.

"I'm just so tired . . ." he relented, looking away from her and to the empty street beyond. "It's like sliding down a tunnel where the sweet release of sleep is at the end—but it doesn't end . . . I just keep sliding and sliding . . ."

"We can take a rain check on taking over the world. Let's go back to your coffin." She put her hand on his arm, and his shirt felt . . . oddly warm.

"No, I don't think I will."

Humphrey stepped up beside them. "That wasn't a suggestion, Theo."

The vampire slowly moved his eyes between them, and then sighed as his shoulders deflated. "I guess you are right."

"See"—Sally beamed, looking down at the corpse of Edward—"things will be fine as long as we stick—"

Theo vanished in a brief blue illumination.

"—together. *Ass!* Where do you think he has gone?"

The Death Knight shrugged and frowned off down the road. "Something is not right here."

Sally brought up the STAR chat window.

Sally: you doing okay, Chuck?
Chuck: yeah, found the Foxes
Chuck: steering clear of the town, though.
Chuck: the girls said they were getting bad vibes.
Sally: no shit, Theo has gone off the deep end

Theo has left the Party

The ball of nerves in her stomach knotted tighter and weighed heavier.

Sally: now he has left the party :(
Chuck: anything I can do?
Chuck: that doesn't involve my neck getting torn out
Sally: rain check
Chuck: you're a druid too??

Sally sighed and closed the window. The figurative steam train had run out of coal, or whatever furnishings could be coaxed into the fire-laden maw. Taking over the world seemed more possible when your friends were around you.

"Let us focus on what we can control rather than what we cannot." Humphrey put a plated hand atop her shoulder.

"I am hungry and tired and sad, but I can't control any of those things. Thank you, though, Humps." She needed a quest to nap now, and hopefully the reward would be everything being better again.

"Theo is strong and capable. If he dies, then perhaps he doesn't deserve you. Us, *the Party*, I mean."

Sally smiled and gave the Death Knight a light punch. "You're right. Let's go find some zombies and continue our classic duo adventure. Ah—how long before this guy wakes up?" She gave the demon a little kick with her shoe.

"Not long enough, I'm sure. It will be inev—"

"Don't you start saying it too." She rolled her eyes and took his plated arm. "Cross that bridge when it's burning time."

"An acceptable mixed metaphor, *ha-ha*." Humphrey grinned as they turned and started back down the street.

Sally tried to allow some manner of positivity back inside her head. There wasn't a lot of room in there currently. Not just because of Theo, but Archie hadn't turned up either. Had something similar happened to the cat? A Party of two made it clearer who was the main character, but she was coming to understand the importance of having a dependable supporting cast. Plus, the vampire had all their money.

"What do you think about doing a normal quest for a change?" Humphrey looked down at her. "It might be more productive than looking through the empty town."

Killing stuff might blow off some steam, and she needed to find some humanoids to regrow her little crop of zombies. Being able to raise and unsummon them as a group had been a game changer, but that didn't count for anything if she didn't actually have any at her beck and call. She had been keeping *[Summon Zombies]* in the back pocket, but perhaps this was the best time for it.

She held out her hand and cast it three times as fast as she was able. Seven zombies in total—a terrible roll, but you had to take what you were given. *[Endless Sleep]*—they sunk into the floor, ready to be recalled later on.

"It's much more impressive with twenty-five of them." She sighed.

"It should be thirty now that you have your keystone. Three per level." Humphrey stopped and shrugged.

Sally screwed her face up. As cool as that sounded, she didn't care to bring up her STAR and check. The System probably didn't even have a proper explanation for how it worked. That seemed pretty wild, if she got to Level Fifty and could have a horde of 150 zombies. She tried to manifest it and screwed her face up.

"My, those are some sad faces."

They both looked up to see a figure sitting atop one of the dark wooden houses. Light brown trousers and leather jerkin rose up to a red hooded cloak that obscured their face except for two circular red eyes.

In addition to their observant statement, they pointed a black-gloved finger into the air. Above it, a speech bubble appeared, with a round yellow sad face within it.

CHAPTER TWELVE

Wordless

The zombie stared as the bubble slowly vanished, her eyes widening. "Motherfuggin' emoticons," Sally whispered. "Or emojis. I don't know the difference."

"Who are you?" Humphrey folded his arms. "We've had quite enough strange demons turning up to—"

Lucius has joined the Party

"Sally!"

"What?" She shrugged. They needed a new friend, and despite the red eyes and hood, this demon didn't seem particularly annoying. *Emojis!*

"Thanks, friends!" A thumbs-up bubble appeared next to Lucius before he dropped down off the roof to the street. "This place has been pretty quiet lately."

"I didn't know we could emote, Humphrey." Sally kept her eyes narrowed at the new demon just in case he popped a new one up.

"Scrapped part of the System." Humphrey shook his head. "No points for guessing how you are glitched. Are you capable in a fight?"

Lucius shook his head, and a bubble with a red *X* popped up. "I prefer to talk my problems out."

"Shameful." The Death Knight deflated.

"I like talking!" Sally beamed. "Although, we are looking for some humanoid Monsters to punch for a bit to blow off some steam."

"Oh, I know just the place!" A joyous bubble popped up beside the demon's head as he pointed a finger into the air. "There's a barbarian tribe not too far to the north of here."

"Perfect!"

Humphrey sighed as the two started off along the street, only briefly looking behind to see if the tax collector had moved. Red flame flickered across the back of his helmet, as the body was no longer there.

Sally rolled her eyes. "I'm just saying there's nothing romantic about brain-eating, right? It's pretty gross no matter who the target is and the situation in which I am doing the deed, right?"

"I see what you're saying." A nodding emoji appeared next to the demon's head.

"But it's different for Theo because there is that media-based romanticism of vampires. He can bite and consume anyone on the battlefield, but if he is sucking on a pretty lady outside of a fight—there's an implication there."

"Even if you trust him, and there's nothing more to it than a meal, it's just the optics of it?"

"Yeah." She screwed her face up.

"Have you spoken to him about it?" A question bubble appeared beside Lucius as his hand entered the darkened shroud to rub at his chin, presumably.

"No, I don't want to appear clingy or jealous—and it's not something he has actually done." Sally deflated and looked out at the plains. "As if my unlife doesn't have enough problems, I have to make some up."

"It's important to set expectations and boundaries; he seems like he would understand and be accommodating if he really cares for you."

Humphrey slowly ground his metallic teeth together as he walked behind the pair, sending sparks off into the air.

"Thanks, Lucius. Theo is currently going through something—so after we help him with that, then I'll sit him down."

A thumbs-up appeared by the demon. "My pleasure, Sally. It's so rare to see a relationship with such promise out here; I wouldn't like it to go to *waste*—if you pardon the pun! Out here, such things require a little more care and cultivation to flourish against the odds."

Sally nodded thoughtfully. She knew better than to let what-ifs erode at the otherwise solid walls of her mental fortitude. It was just the nerves shaking her up, the ones still lingering from the morning. She hated that the tree of her worry now bore fruit. "What about you, Lucius? What's your story?"

"Oh, I'm just a demon that hangs around Bordertown to befriend and lure Players into a trap."

The sound of Humphrey's sword withdrawing from his back caused a sweat drop emoji to slide out from the demon's hood.

"Just kidding!" He waved his hands in the hope of cooling down the Death Knight. "I need to learn to read the room, huh?"

"We have had an . . . eventful day so far." Humphrey slowly returned the greatsword to his back as he kept his eye sockets narrowed at Lucius.

Sally looked out at the nearly completely barren plains around them. She had spent too much time worrying about the miserable blood bag. It had been fun to dance around the idea that they could be something more, but it just seemed to be dragging at the back of her brain too much. Annoying Humphrey about it had been fun, too, but maybe she was partly to blame for the Party falling apart.

They had gotten too comfortable with success and being the strongest around.

"Perhaps we should have brought the coffin with us." The Death Knight looked over his shoulder back to the slowly receding Bordertown.

"Eh, he can look after himself." Sally hardened her resolve. She had all the love in the world, or at least as much as her cold, dead heart could manage, for the members of her Party. But he was not among that select few currently. "Let's focus on getting more powerful."

Humphrey smiled but tilted his head.

"We are almost there!" A saluting emoji appeared beside Lucius. "Most remaining Monster groups are underground now, since the *incident*."

Sally gasped and raised her eyebrows at the Death Knight. "What *incident?*"

"There's a sandstorm that splits the Wastelands in two, appeared almost a month ago. This side of it got real dried out and barren, and it's hard to get resources from the other side." Sad face emoji.

"Hmm, I had not heard of this." Humphrey looked out into the distance with a furrowed brow. "Is there no way through the storm?"

Grimace emoji. "There are a couple routes, but they're maintained by chumps like Edward—tax collectors."

"You know *Eddy?* He keeps telling us he is unavailable or something." Sally cast a quick glance over her shoulder to see if the blue-eyed demon had shown back up.

"Know him?" An emoji of a rather contented-looking poop appeared. "Practically cousins, I think. He works for the dragon, though."

The Death Knight rubbed his chin. "The one who caused the sandstorm, no doubt."

"You're an astute one, Humphrey." Thumbs-up emoji. "You were an Observer before, correct? It must be quite the change to be disconnected from your purpose."

"I have a new purpose." The helmet flames flickered. "One much more suited to my beliefs and abilities."

Sally gave the Death Knight a smile. "Humphrey is my rock. He was there when I first awakened. Even made the decision to break from the System to save my life."

Heart emoji. "That brings me great joy to see such a strong bond." Lucius stopped and gestured around with his hands. "This whole area used to be barbarian tribes. Little villages, grazing bison and turtlecats, even some trees and the like."

"They do not respawn?" Humphrey frowned at the cracked earth.

"And did you say *turtlecats*?" Sally added, leaning toward the demon.

"I do not know how these things work, unfortunately. I am but a humble . . . demon." Sweat drop emoji.

"*Why* are you a demon?" She stopped and crossed her arms. "Other than the giant rats—"

"Mice." Humphrey sighed.

"—we have just seen two Unique demons and no Players."

Lucius shrugged and looked between the both of them with his two large crimson eyes in the darkness beneath his hood. "Look around, friends. There's not much here for Players. It was either turn to dust or buy their way into the second half of the Wastes."

The pair of undead continued to wait for a further explanation, causing him to emote another grimaced face.

"Demons are naturally fine with the heat . . . there's a portal or two where we can come through—or rather, there were."

The Death Knight nodded slowly. "An invasion event; you are one of the few remaining."

Lucius clapped his hands and pointed at Humphrey with finger guns. "Great having a guy in the know, huh? What do you know about the barbarians here?"

"Very little, if I am honest. I was stationed in the first area and never had much need to delve into the specifics of other areas. They should be around our level, mostly melee-based humanoids." Humphrey scratched at the side of his helmet.

"I'll assume that's correct—like I said, I'm no fighter, but you both look competent." The demon raised his own thumbs-up to pair with a smiling face emoji.

"Humanoids are my speciality, in fact." The zombie beamed. "We're a little on the softer side without . . . but I think we can handle some melee fighters, right, Humps?"

"Certainly. Continue to lead the way, Lucius."

The red-robed demon gave a low bow and then swiveled around and trudged onward across the dry plains.

Sally wasn't too sure whether she fully trusted the new Party member yet. He was cool and certainly friendly enough . . . but he was a demon—and from what she knew, they were either evil or manipulative in some manner usually. That said, her Party was meant to be bad guys. At least in the forest area, they had started that way. Now they were just morally gray, if you washed away all the Player blood from her clothes—which she should do more often.

As she ruminated about what the future may hold, they stopped at another hole in the ground, similar to where they had found the giant mice. Approaching, it looked as though it was smaller, perhaps only half the size, and covered with some manner of leather door.

"Ugh, if everything is going to be underground in gloomy tunnels, I will be annoyed." She sighed. "I hate it when they reuse assets so blatantly."

The head of a thickly muscled man popped out from the hole at the sound of her voice, his heavy brow set to a scowl at seeing the three standing there.

"Who are you?" he growled with a strong accent.

Lucius shrugged and started to step backward slowly. Humphrey started withdrawing his sword. Sally started salivating.

Two more heads popped up, another man and woman with long hair, both equally muscled and concerned about the new visitors.

Sally gasped. "Whack-a-meal!" With a wide grin, she leaped toward the barbarians, who started to emerge from their underground lair holding axes and swords.

CHAPTER THIRTEEN

Absolutely Barbaric

A warm and dry breeze ruffled Theo's hair. With a brief sigh, he stopped, his shoes crunching against the loose gravel.

"Why are you following me?" He looked over his shoulder, his eyes glowing bright red.

Archie stopped a few feet away and sat on the ground. The ginger cat tilted his head, a look of concern weighing on his bright emerald eyes. "I just wanted to make sure you're okay."

"They need you more than I do." The vampire looked back ahead. Nothing but rolling plains and the blurred shapes of structures in the distance. "What they need is to be safe—I can't guarantee that now." He worked his jaw but didn't move from where he was standing.

Archie stood and walked around in front of Theo. The man looked dire. Tired and even more gaunt than usual. His eyes constantly burned red, and his jaw clenched tight as though he wanted to grind his teeth to nothing.

"Perhaps I told you too much."

"It's not *that* . . . I'm . . . Archie, the System understands some pop culture references, right?" Theo kneeled to look into the cat's eyes better.

"To a degree, as far as I can understand it."

"So . . ." Theo brushed his dark hair back. "If I were to say that I could see a percentage figure slowly going up, the worse that I feel? Ring any bells?"

Archie waved his tail back and forth. "That isn't something I personally get, but I understand the implication."

"Great." Theo stood back up. "I don't want to be near any of my friends once it gets to one hundred."

The ginger cat furrowed his brow. "Current percentage?"

"Fifty-seven. It was forty-six when I left the Party. So, I'm continuing to leave."

"What if you don't have a choice about that?"

"Huh?" The vampire looked down at the cat, who was now pulsing with bands of green and yellow energy.

"I think you've . . ." Lucius gagged. "You've clogged up the entrance with their bodies."

Sally panted and rubbed the blood from her face. It seemed to be a common theme that the System-created had absolutely no brains when it came to choke points. Now they especially had no brains on account of her feasting on any that had tried to emerge.

With a shrug, she flexed her stiff stabbing shoulder. "I was kind of hoping that the Monsters in the second area wouldn't just yeet themselves at us. That's basic. Real basic."

"Stop complaining and at least loot the ones here." Humphrey huffed and planted the end of his sword into the viscera-soaked earth. "We aren't just here so that you could have a snack."

The zombie rolled her eyes. She had managed to get back her full thirty-strong zombie army thanks to the lack of tactics on display from the barbarians. A little too stereotypical, in her honest opinion. Even the orcs had been more fleshed out with the more interesting terrain and magic caster. Waves of these humans had just popped out in a frenzy to meet her knife, the Death Knight's sword, and over a dozen undead that could reach in.

"At least we didn't have to go in the tunnel," she relented and started looking through the bodies.

Lucius turned away, the unwell emoji appearing from the side of his head. "I'm both impressed and disgusted. Beats me why they are so stupid, though, I guess there isn't a Unique among them to lead."

"True." Sally nodded as she gathered what she could find in the mess of chopped-up corpses. The Uniques were often a huge boon, as they were capable of independent thought. These poor chumps were just . . . coded? To run in and hack and slash. But perhaps it was nice to not have been scorpions or snakes. Humanoids had the best brains if the giant mice were anything to go by. Too many System-created brains often made her unwell, like eating junk food constantly.

You couldn't beat a living, breathing *Player's* brain. Her stomach rumbled.

"So there's really no Players around this first section?" she asked, letting her appetite do the talking.

"Not as far as I've seen—but I only have the one pair of eyes. If there are, then they've been hiding out for a while." Lucius turned back and shrugged.

The zombie eyed up the Death Knight, who nodded.

Humphrey stowed his blade behind him. "There may be underground outposts of Players. It is unlikely all have leveled beyond or perished."

Sally sighed. "That would be pretty terrible if that were the case."

186 Gold
Dagger (3)
Skull (8)
Uncommon Weapon Chance Box (2)
Rare Armor Chance Box (1)

"Some neat things here, I guess? Is it worth pushing these gross ones out of the way to go inside? I really don't want to." She sighed and glared at the mass of dead bodies lining the tunnel exit.

Lucius put a finger to his chin in thought. "There might be treasure, but if you amass a bunch of wealth, you'll get Edward or one of the other cronies bugging you more often."

"Shoulda told me before I looted, punk." She turned her nose up at her Inventory. No chance she was going to drop it or hand it over to the demon. *The annoying one.* Theo had been right about not paying the tax; she didn't want their hard-earned cash going to some dragon who had messed up the Wastelands.

She walked around the pit and looked back to the shimmering dark buildings of Bordertown. "Humps, as part of the System, you're aware of certain pop culture references, right?"

The Death Knight shrugged. "To a degree, but not explicitly."

"There's a trope where zombie movies aren't really about the zombies but the struggles and choices of the surviving humans." Her head tilted to the side.

"So . . . you're saying we should go back and get the coffin?"

"Not yes, but *not* not yes."

". . . Okay."

Lucius watched them silently. A small bubble with three dots pulsed through the air. "Say, friends—do you even know where to begin in finding your pal?"

Sally scratched at her hair. The heat had already dried the blood in it, and it had become matted to her scalp. Combined with the mess from the fight with *Zero* and the swamp muck . . . she looked quite the part of a zombie. "Well, knowing Theo, he is probably going to grind for items or something—he can't level still?"

"*Yes*, correct." Humphrey nodded. "He will be stuck until he can nap."

With the vampire unable to complete his Keystone Quest, he would be stuck at his current level—and the experience gained would be wasted. If *anything* would be driving him mad, it must be that. Why he couldn't just nap was the real issue—it was something more than just it being daytime.

"So, how do you plan on finding him?" Question mark bubble.

Sally narrowed her eyes at the new Party member. Trust was something she had easily given, but questions quickly eroded away at her leniency. Perhaps being a queen now, she just didn't like people poking holes in her half-attempts at plans. Or maybe it was just odd how friendly this demon was—either way, seeing as he was so weak, there wasn't much to fear.

"Any ideas, Humps?" She spun on her heels to face the Death Knight.

"*Yes.*"

"Cool. Well, let's get the coffin first, yeah?" Sally deflated. Something about this oppressive heat was making her not want to argue. Whatever plan the Death Knight had could be squeezed from him on the walk back to the town. "Let's hope we don't run into the unassailable Edward again."

"I think we will." Lucius hopped after them as they set off. "I'd say that it is inevit—"

"*Don't.*" Sally shook her head and cast *[Endless Sleep]* to shadow away her zombie horde. It felt nice to have them all at full power. As if they weren't already overpowered enough.

Maybe that was why she had been feeling so glum. Party falling apart aside, after the Sanctuary fight they had all felt a little invincible. Growing stronger and working better as a team, without the need to strive for survival, everything had started to feel flat after gaining the acceptance of the Crown. Or the Council. It was never really clear what they were called, and they had agreed to steer clear of the Capital on this occasion. It would only be inviting trouble.

So, the question was, how could they now find some challenge? Firstly, getting the gang back together and in normal fighting form seemed like the hardest and most important thing. She was glad she could at least rely on Humphrey to stick around. Theo, she could understand some of his mania . . . it had happened before when he hadn't slept. But not this wild, and he had never run off. Archie was ever the wildcard, but he should still answer his messages.

She tapped the STAR.

Sally: answer me arch
Sally: worried about you and theonnn

Her feet caught on some loose stone as she stared at the screen, stumbling through her typing before she switched to direct messaging Chuck.

Sally: things okay, Chuck?
Chuck: this area sucks
Sally: right?
Sally: just me, humps, and a demon

> Sally: unending barren plains
> Chuck: demon?
> Sally: and chance boxes

Sally pouted as she closed the chat. There was a point where she thought that she had been friends with so many people. Jackie and the goblins seemed so far away now. All the weird Uniques they had fought alongside or helped had now settled into normal lives, where for the most part, they were outside of danger.

That was what she had wanted . . . but it wasn't for her. The short time they had spent not in constant struggle was pleasant enough—however, knowing that there was a bigger world out there kept her striving for something more. That and wanting to find the exit portal from this world or whatever they had. Sure, going back to being a normal human in the diner would be quite the downgrade, but—

She stopped and turned a scowl to the sky. Her hand raised, with her index finger outstretched.

"Lucius, what is *that?*"

In the air, fast approaching their location, was a sphere of darkness.

Sweat drop emoji.

CHAPTER FOURTEEN

Not a Scratch

The ball of dark matter dropped from the sky quickly and struck the parched earth around twenty feet from the pensive group. A wave of dusty air brushed against them from the aftershock, pelting them with loose sand. As Sally unshielded her eyes, her brow furrowed at the arrival.

A large, armored figure, similar to Humphrey, had unfurled from the rounded shape that had coursed through the sky. Obsidian plates of metal barely reflected the looming sunlight. Their face was an exaggerated caricature of laughter painted in silver. As the figure stretched out to stand tall, a second, more lithe one stepped out from behind it.

"*Edward*," the zombie seethed. "What now?"

"Well." The tax-collecting demon leaned against the larger figure and observed his fingernails. "It seems you are reluctant to give over your . . . donation, so I brought one of my more convincing friends to help you change your mind."

Sally knew well enough that she had just picked up some gold from the barbarians and would bet it all on the fact that Edward somehow knew this. Maybe even down to the exact amount. The excuse that Theo held all their money wouldn't work . . .

"I suggest you hand it over," Lucius whispered from behind, trying to hide away from the new entrants.

"Is that Lucius back there? My, you are persistent." Edward chuckled and stood up straight. He brushed some imaginary dust from his light purple suit. "Perhaps that should be your name. Lucius the Persistent."

"We don't *all* love clichés," Lucius hissed back, accompanied by an angry-looking bubble.

Giving the bad guys the money would probably save them a lot of trouble. Sally scratched at her nose. Still, it was *her* money that she found—what right did they have to take it? They were rendering her no goods or services, and taxation without anything to show for it just sounded like a shakedown with extra steps.

"What if I refuse?" She crossed her arms.

"Then Brutus here will show you the sharp end of his weapons. Which is both ends." Lucius gestured with his hand, and the large, armored figure withdrew some kind of spear that had silvered spikes at both ends.

"Then what if I kill Brutus?" She kind of wanted that spear thing, actually. She had been using the same dagger for too long. Something with a little more reach would be a nice boon.

Edward's glowing blue eyes twitched. "You cannot defeat him; why can't you just accept the inevitability?"

Sally shrugged and looked up at Humphrey. The Death Knight was mostly impassive, waiting to follow her lead on whatever the decision became. His eye sockets were narrowed at the new figure, possibly just trying to eye up whatever level it might be. Even if it was twenty, she thought she had a fair crack at it. They surely wouldn't be able to send something tougher just to rough up a couple of low levels for their meager cash.

"Does he have a brain?" Her fingers slowly crept down her outfit and toward the sheathed dagger.

"What does that have to—? Oh, you're a zombie." The demon rolled his eyes.

"I don't think this is a good idea, guys." Lucius recoiled farther behind the Death Knight.

Sally sighed. "You're right. It would be unfair to get you in danger for such an insignificant reason." She turned back to Edward. "One-on-one then? If I win, you leave me alone for a bit?"

She had some personal affairs to attend to, and giving money to this annoying demon ranked low on the importance list.

Her STAR *bloiped.*

Archie: =OwO=

"Well, at least the cat isn't dead." It wasn't the ideal time to show up, but then Archie did always play to his own tune. "Let's make this quick, yeah?"

Humphrey nodded and helped shuffle the emoting demon out of the way to give the fighters some space.

"Very well. We will just have to loot the gold from your corpse."

Sally bit her tongue to stop herself from reminding them that she was already a corpse, technically. Instead, she withdrew her *[Dagger of Luck]* and wiggled the fingers of her off hand in the air to limber them up.

She was about to ask when they should start when the armored figure burst forward, slamming into her and knocking her into a roll across the dried earth. As she groggily raised her head, the Monster was already in midair, descending downward with the spear.

"One of the collector golems was signed out for a job?" The robed man ran his fingers down a large ledger. The sparse candlelight barely touched the walls of the stone chamber.

"Yes," a coarse voice responded. "A new guild made it through the Swamps, apparently." The figure shifted on two large feet, their shadowed head almost scraping across the ceiling.

"Ah."

"Hopefully, whatever idiot took it will leave them alive. We get more gold putting them to work this side of the storm; you know how Ruben feels about it."

The first figure slowly closed the book and gently drummed wizened fingers on the burgundy leather cover. "It was Edward. The *Inevitable*, Edward."

Something akin to a long sigh escaped the mouth of the large, shadowed creature, responding as they slunk across the floor to rest.

Sally staggered backward and clutched at the gash in her side with broken fingers. Comparatively, the plated foe was not very damaged. She screwed up her eyes as the dust burned them. Perhaps she had been going about this all wrong. [Necroblasts] didn't seem to do anything other than scuff the matte armor, which reminded her briefly of the large swamp Toad. But surely he couldn't be *that* powerful.

Then what? His magic resist could be pretty high, certainly, if he was a few levels over her. It had been difficult to get close to him with his size and reach advantage, and she couldn't rely on luck to get an easy brain-eat as it was likely he didn't have one. He seemed more like a robot or golem than a functional, thinking person.

"Almost got me there," she said as she winced. Warm blood flowed down her hand, a testament to her lies.

"Aren't you going to do something?" Lucius prodded the Death Knight, practically gnawing on the edge of his armored plating as he nervously hid.

"If she asks me to. It would be rude to interfere without permission." Humphrey stood with arms crossed, a furrowed brow constant over his burning eye sockets.

"Did you need permission when you saved her life that one time?"

"Nobody likes an active listener, Lucius." The Death Knight looked down at the cloaked demon. "Sally makes her own choices, and I believe in them."

Lucius emoted a sweat drop and looked back at the battle.

Flipping the dagger around in her hand, Sally ran forward at the golem. Her broken-off hand raised as if to cast another *[Necroblast]* toward her opponent, readied in a defensive stance.

[Endless Dead]

Thirty zombies pooled forth from the ground, grasping at the thick obsidian legs of the Monster. Slightly caught off guard, he began to stab out at the walking corpses. Sally emerged from the horde and slammed her dagger into his knee joint.

Sparks flew up from the impact, and she rolled past, back into the group of zombies clambering atop the plated figure. Even with *[Hex: Slow]* on the golem, he had no trouble striking down the zombies one by one. With every other hit, Sally would dodge into range, level a slash of her weapon, and then almost vanish into the crowd. But the horde was thinning already.

With the golem's back turned, she leaped upon it, groaning in pain as her broken fingers tried to get a grip on the various plates. The obsidian figure tried to shake her loose, but the remaining zombies hung from his arms and weighed him down.

Making it to the pinnacle of the mountain, the zombie boss tried to jam the dagger into the back of the golem's neck. Sparks again, as her blade just slid across. In frustration, she grabbed forward, wrapping her arms around his head. She tried to gnaw down on the plate, to no effect. This was a tough nut to crack. "Just die already. *Unfair!*" she whined as he tried to shake her loose.

"How about now?" Lucius asked, a question bubble next to his head. "Running out of all those zombies you just farmed up?"

Humphrey sighed. Relaxing his arms, he looked over to Edward, who had been standing and watching the proceedings with a wide, shit-eating grin.

"Hey, Eddy the Untenable?" he growled out, flames at the back of his helmet flickering wildly.

The demon turned his gaze away from the fruitless attempts of the zombies to chew into the golem. "Yeah, what is it? Ready to relent and save her life?"

[Compelled Duel]

Humphrey whipped his greatsword from his back and stormed over to the tax collector, who was now frozen in brief fear.

"Looks like, blah, blah—" Humphrey's sword blazed brightly as it swung downward, cleaving the demon in half down the middle. "I won the duel, blah, blah." Dark crimson and chunks of gore splattered out in a long line across the dusty ground.

The golem paused in place, jostling Sally, who was trying to wrestle his head off. She fell forward, back onto the floor with a *thud*.

"Humphrey, you broke him," she whined, crossing her sore arms as she looked up at the now inert Monster.

"You clearly just won. Can we go now?"

She rolled to the side and pushed herself up with a groan. "It's much nicer with Theo's regenerative aura, huh?"

"It says 63 percent now. Maybe it will go down."

"Unlikely." Archie shook his head, despite the vampire being unable to see it. "I'm not changing my mind. This is for your own good."

CHAPTER FIFTEEN

Batting Cage

The sun was constant and made the return journey feel like it took twice as long to complete. Being covered in blood after the two fights in the oppressive heat certainly wasn't helping either. "So he is basically immortal, right?" Sally shrugged as they neared Bordertown once more. "That doesn't seem fair for a Unique Monster to have."

"I imagine there are some caveats," Humphrey said as he sighed. "Like with Bella." He looked out in the direction of the first area again, the darkened barrier of the Swamps on the horizon.

"Do *you* know, Lucius?" She prodded a finger toward the demon.

The crimson circles beneath the shade of his hood looked between the zombie and Death Knight. "I do not. Humphrey is right, however. There is something that keeps Edward coming back, but I'm sure there's a good reason."

"Other than him being *Inevitable*." Sally sighed and narrowed her eyes at the town. She half expected the tax collector to be there already, awaiting them with the golem again. "We need to level so we don't get stuck with a problem we can't chew."

They continued on in silence as they entered the outskirts of Bordertown. The dark wooden buildings seemed just as empty of life as earlier in the day. It felt a little odd to Sally that even her guild members hadn't hung around—but then again, there wasn't anything to do here other than sleep. Not much use in the middle of the day. Going out to find quests or Monsters would be a much better use of their time.

Dried blood from where Theo had maimed the demon remained on the street but was quickly being turned into dust from the constant heat drying the area.

"I swear the sun hasn't moved at all," she grumbled to the empty street.

"It hasn't." Humphrey glared into the sky.

Part of the reason it was so dry and devoid of life, no doubt. It was still hard to believe it could rend the spawns from the world and change the things that the System usually worked on keeping together. Even with the recent demise of the Architect, they had said the Wastes had been like this for weeks.

"Was this the inn we were in?" Sally exhaled again, reaching the maximum amount she was able to deflate without collapsing to the floor in a pile of sad undead.

"Yes." The Death Knight moved ahead of her and into the building.

"Cheer up, Sally." Lucius tilted his head to meet her gaze. "I bet we will find your friends in no time and get back on track."

"Ugh, I don't believe in miracles." She slunk in behind Humphrey and headed toward the stairs.

She continued to pout at his red cloak as she slowly followed him up the stairs, avoiding the splinters of wood spraying into the air as the large plates of his armor scraped along the walls again.

Humphrey pushed the bedroom door open as he squeezed through the door frame. "Oh," he said, with a momentary pause.

Sally squished beside him, trying to push him out of the way of the door.

Atop the coffin in the room still shrouded in darkness, sat Archie.

"Hi, Sally and Humphrey." He beamed, eyes glimmering bright green. "And a . . . demon."

"What demon? Let me out."

Sally frowned. "Is that Theo in the coffin?"

Beneath the cat, the wooden casket shook as the vampire tried to extract himself. Archie nodded. "Yes, he will say he is feeling fine and wants to get out, but we can't let him. He is very ill."

"I'm not ill . . . I feel fine. Just let me out . . . ah, damn."

"What's wrong with him?" Sally moved over to them and put her hand softly atop the wooden lid. "Will he be okay?"

"Perhaps." Archie wagged his tail back and forth.

"What is stopping him from getting out by himself?" Humphrey narrowed his eye sockets.

The ginger cat stood to stretch out and yawn. "Is *magic* a good enough answer?"

"Let me out! The number is going down!"

Sally turned and sat down on the coffin. She rubbed her eyes and tried to decide if she wanted to inquire further about what that meant or what even was going on. "Give us the facts, Arch. I've had enough of today already."

"Theo has been cursed with something. My assumption is when he struck the Toad, something transferred from his blades. It causes him to be exhausted but unable to sleep."

"Ah." Sally scrunched her eyes closed. That all made sense and was particularly bad. Not only did his grip on reality slip the less sleep he had, but they also didn't have a healer in the group. "How do we get rid of it?"

"It's something we'll have to wait out." Archie hopped down and waltzed over to the new demon to give him a sniff. "Eventually, it will pass . . . but he'll need to stay imprisoned. He doesn't want to hurt us."

"Silly ass." Sally sighed and knocked atop the lid. "Join the Party, jerkface. Take a break from being edgy for five minutes."

"I'm . . . yes, Boss . . ."

Theo has joined the Party

"There we go!" She hopped back to her feet. "Just like that, the miserable cloud has shifted from over me, and we are back at a full Party." Sally beamed at the group before the wide grin sagged a little at seeing Lucius. "You really have no combat abilities?"

"Ah, not really." The demon scratched the back of his hood as a sweat drop emoji appeared beside him.

"You can't see this, Theo, which is a real shame. You'd love it. But we have a fifth member, who is a demon, and he can make emoji appear." She raised her eyebrows and looked down at the coffin in expectation of his response.

"Uh-huh . . . I need to kill all demons."

"Good chat, *Eric Redd*." She rolled her eyes.

"Who's that?"

"What? So you know *Goreblaster*, but not . . . listen, it doesn't matter. You're not killing all the demons, and you're not getting out of the box." Sally waved her hands and sighed. "Line . . . Humps?"

"You want to know where we can go level up the quickest?" The Death Knight moved to pick up the coffin.

"Exactly!" The smile returned to her face. "Lucius, where can we go and grind the quickest?"

The demon thought for a second, accompanied by floating ellipses, before coming up with a decent answer. "There is one place . . . but it's pretty dangerous."

"*Danger* is our middle name. Or surname. I haven't decided." She smirked. "I'm pretty sure I put that out into the world this morning. It's basically canon."

"Okay." Lucius stretched out his shoulders. "There's a demon portal that has a bugged spawn rate; it's almost instant—or so I've heard. Naturally, it's not the sort of place I would hang out."

"The sort of place you hang out is the rooftops of derelict buildings," Humphrey interjected.

Lucius shrugged. "Yeah, away from any danger."

Danger was more than their middle name. Sally wrinkled up her nose as she watched the Death Knight lift the coffin and lumber toward the door. Archie scooted in the way between his plated legs, almost tripping him. Danger was also their headline. That's what it should say instead of "Wanted" atop their posters. She made a mental note to write that down for something later on, in case they found who had made them.

They clambered down the staircase after Humphrey; the coffin scraping the ceiling all the way down and causing loose dust to cover the rest of the Party. With Theo back in the group, his auras helped with her wound recovery. They saved a ton of money on not having to buy healing items, assuming they had enough downtime between fights. Thankfully, they were usually short affairs, and they could recover on their own time.

As they reached the lobby of the inn, she knocked on the back of the coffin.

"We fought Edward again. He had a golem that I couldn't even scratch."

"Sounds like something I could have dealt with."

She narrowed her eyes. Although she was well aware his snappy attitude was due to the curse, it still ruffled her feathers when he was rude. "Perhaps . . . We didn't give him any of our gold, and Humphrey cut him in half."

"Where'd you get gold from?"

"Eating barbarians. I got some Chance Boxes. Did you want me to open them and tell you what I get?"

There were a few seconds of silence.

Sally grinned. "I can hear your eyes twitching in there, pup."

Archie trotted up beside her. "It's not a good idea to antagonize him, Sally. He is not in a good state."

She pursed her lips but didn't press the vampire further. He must really be in tough shape if she couldn't even wind him up a little bit like usual. Theo was a lot more useful outside of the coffin than in it, but if he thought that he would be a danger to them . . . she would take that seriously. He may be a dork, but he was always competent enough when fighting. Could she one vs one him?

Perhaps not a good thought to entertain. If he were able to get out of his prison and had lost control, then they would really be in trouble. That would be a bloodied bridge to cross if it came to it. Sally had a lot of bridges in her future.

"How far away is this place, Lucius?" Many miles or kilometers, no doubt, depending on how you like to count.

"Oh, it's right here in Bordertown."

"*What?*" The group stopped, and all eyes turned to the demon.

"Not exactly—uh!" Sweat drop emoji. "There's a portal here that takes us to the underground part that has the bugged portal to hell."

"Portal to hell," Sally repeated quietly.

"So I can kill all demons."

Humphrey sighed. "It's not literal. You can't go through that portal into hell. That's just a spawning point for demons."

Sally shrugged. "Well, lead the way then, Lucius." Farming demons to get a couple of levels sounded like a reasonable plan. She would feel a little safer if they had an easy escape—but it didn't look like Bordertown would be able to offer up any portal scrolls without any System-created sellers around.

Ah, well. Danger *was* their collective name and title, anyway.

As the demon set off, she brought up her STAR and Inventory and withdrew the ChanceBoxes from earlier. This was fun; it had been a while since she had bothered to make a big deal about the suspense of getting random items.

She spun the locks of two uncommon weapon boxes and the rare armor box with eyes aglow.

CHAPTER SIXTEEN

Being Blunt

Uncommon Axe
Rare Hammer of Critical
Rare //Error Helm-.-/

Been a while since we had something like that." Sally huffed at the errored item. She looked through her Inventory at the new items gained from the now inert boxes. "Axe is whatever . . . but . . . why does the hammer look like a baseball bat?" She held it in the air.

"What's baseball?" Humphrey shrugged. "Just looks like a club."

"It's a bit reductive." Sally gave it a few test swings in the air. "I'm already manic enough to be compared to . . . oh, *rats!*"

"Mice."

"*No.* I forgot to get that spear thing from the golem." She sighed and stowed the bat on the back of her jacket somehow. "Hey, Theo, we've got a Mad Max thing going on here now."

"Are we allowed direct references?"

Sally looked around the derelict town to see if there was anyone nearby to stop them. "I guess we could play it cool; in honesty, I don't even remember most of them."

"Yeah, you don't even remember *Goreblaster.*"

She bore her red-eyed gaze into the side of the coffin. Perhaps he was more crazy than he sounded. The muffled tone of his voice didn't help much in giving the illusion that he was normal.

Archie padded out in front of her, almost tripping her up. "I can try to heal him."

"You hadn't already?" She frowned at the ginger cat.

"No, I don't exactly have a tight grip on what abilities I can cast, and I didn't want to make things worse."

Sally gazed over at the dark wooden coffin again. If he was going to get better eventually, then it might not be a great idea to allow the cat to risk something random. In all likelihood, it would just make the vampire more powerful or free him—the last thing they needed was some more inter-Party conflict. Especially if it involved sharp objects instead of words.

"Pass for now," she said as she waved her hand. "He seems stable—let's not rock the boat."

Archie smiled and half closed his eyes, an almost cartoony expression for the small but powerful cat.

The zombie turned to the demon, who had been leading them through the side streets of Bordertown. "Hey, Lucius. Want an axe to grind? Against bad guys." She pressed at her STAR and paused. "Bad guys that aren't us?"

"Uh . . . okay." A worried face popped up in a speech bubble next to him. "It probably would be a good idea to have something to defend myself with—not that you guys won't do a stellar job of it, I'm sure."

"Things can get confusing in the heat of the moment," Humphrey agreed stoically. "You're a demon, we are killing demons . . ."

"Don't wind him up, Humps." Sally withdrew the new axe from her Inventory and passed it over to the demon. It was actually pretty cool looking, now that she gave it half a chance. A dark iron metal, wrapped leather handle, and an etched pattern on the flat sides of the bladed head. Lucius buckled slightly under the weight of it.

"You guys aren't that bad, you know." A heart bubble appeared. "Like, for Monsters—you're certainly not as bad as Ruben and all his henchmen."

"Is the dragon going to send a series of increasingly tougher bodyguards that we will defeat barely and grow stronger until we can defeat him ourselves? Thus gaining entry to—"

"Shush, Theo." Sally knocked on the side of the coffin. "Don't plot out a narrative that we will have to fulfill. Focus on being less crazy and napping, so you can level up."

"I would like to level up."

"There you go." She grimaced toward the rest of the Party. It was a lot less uncomfortable when she was the slightly unhinged one. The vampire had his moments previously, but today had just been a complete drain.

Beating up the *Zeroes* had been fun and a good stretch out of their tired muscles. The Swamps had been a wash, and the Wastes were drab and dry. If anything, the area was just tougher on their emotional stability rather than their combat prowess. She should have expected it. If they were going to be super overpowered, then the System would find their weaknesses to exploit instead. It was more narratively interesting that way.

Silently, she cursed this world.

"Here we are." Lucius pointed dramatically at a house that looked reasonably the same as any other than they had passed. "It's in the basement—just in case I didn't make that clear from my reveal." A fireworks emoji faded away upon seeing their unimpressed faces.

"Alright, you take point, Humps." Partially because he was their designated tank, but also just in case his large body plus coffin got stuck, they would be able to push him through.

The doorway opened into a living room, dusty and cracked wooden furniture sitting atop a burned-out-looking rug. The opposite side had a doorway leading to a kitchen and some stairs leading up—probably to some bedrooms. Looking at the state of the place, Sally wouldn't trust the dried wood to carry the group of them up there without incident. On the side of the stairs, a smaller door looked as though it would lead to their destination.

"I'm not fitting through that." The Death Knight leveled a finger toward the intended route. Even Sally would have to duck to fit through it.

"Ah." Lucius rubbed his shadowed chin, accompanied by floating ellipses. "*That* I hadn't considered."

Humphrey tilted his head from side to side and looked around the room. "Is the basement directly below us?"

Sally gasped. "Don't you—"

The Death Knight had already gripped his greatsword handle and went to withdraw it from his back—but instead, he just hit it into the low ceiling and covered himself with dusty wooden shrapnel.

"Honestly." Archie padded across the room and sat in front of the door. The ginger cat closed his eyes, and silence fell across the Party.

Just as Sally opened her mouth to say something, the air burst, and a shockwave rocked the gathered *Outsiders*. Warm dust filled her nose, and vertigo brought her clattering down on ruined wooden planks and a torn rug.

As the dust settled, she looked up at the open ceiling—which had just been their floor.

"That's . . . that's no different from what I was going to do." Humphrey stumbled to his feet, shards of wood sliding off his plated figure. "Are you okay, Theo?"

"Mmhfg . . . yeah."

The vampire probably bounced around in his little prison and had a mouthful of the padding, Sally thought. It was a good amount of foresight that they had to make it nice and plush in there for him when they had it made. If there was only one way that he could sleep, then it was worth spending a little extra gold for the luxury. Especially when he went and farmed the necessary money himself.

"Archie? Lucius?" She stood and brushed sawdust from her shirt.

"I am okay," Archie confirmed, hopping atop the remains of the broken table that had fallen down.

A thumbs-up emoji popped up from a pile of rubble alongside the actual thumbs-up of the demon. "Yeah, I think I hit myself with the axe, though. The blunt side. Just give me a minute."

Sally beamed. Problem solved with only minor danger and zero injury. She made the mental note to add that to the wins for the day—the more they could add there, the less miserable she would feel. Across from her, just behind the Death Knight, a door of dim metal was in the wall of darkened stone.

"What time would it be normally? It feels like we have been adventuring all day long, not just in the morning. And how is the sun different here than in the forest area?"

Her words fell on deaf ears as Humphrey pulled the demon from the debris. The short answer was probably just System shenanigans.

Eventually, Archie looked up at her. "It would normally be time to eat now."

"Are you just saying that because you're a cat?" She eyed him up.

"I'm a what?"

"You know what, it doesn't matter. Humphrey, go open the door so we can go be dysfunctional in hell." She wagged a finger toward the metal door.

The Death Knight nodded and went over to it, obscuring her view of that corner of the room. A screech rang through the open space as he rubbed his chin with plated fingers.

"There is a lock, some kind of puzzle."

Sally found her eye twitching. As much as the previous version of her loved this kind of thing—delving into the unknown to solve riddles and bash in skulls—when you actually had to live it, the problems were just a distraction from your intended goal. An annoyance. Perhaps that was the intent.

"Well," she said as she deflated, "either solve it or put your sword through it. My brain is not able to even, right now."

Lucius watched calmly as Humphrey jostled with some manner of moveable pieces on the door. Archie sat and preened himself, one back leg extended out in the air. Theo seethed in his darkened temporary tomb. The roiling water that was Sally's mood started to come to a boil.

"May . . . I . . . *look*?" She stepped over to start jostling the Death Knight out of the way before he could answer.

"Ah—sure, *yes*." He awkwardly stepped away, stumbling on some loose wood.

Her tired eyes glazed over the panel of interlocking shapes. Maybe it was magical, as she felt her will to live draining from her face. "Lucius, you know the password, right?"

"I do."

Humphrey furrowed his brow and glared at the demon. "Then why didn't you say sooner?"

"I, uh, didn't want to seem rude. It always ruins the adventure if someone has seen all the answers already." He recoiled slowly away from the blazing flame of the Death Knight's helmet.

"Fair," Sally said and sighed. "But we are just here to—"

"Kill all demons."

"—to kill . . . to level up a little." She stretched out her fingers. The sooner she could start hitting Monsters, the better. She moved out of the way and gestured for the demon to do the needful.

Lucius sidestepped past Humphrey with a sweat drop emoji and then quickly went ahead to shuffle and adjust the small shapes on the door to the point where they made . . . a picture? It didn't look any different to Sally.

With a little fanfare, the door popped open.

Sally pushed through ahead of the rest of them, eager to just run into some manner of mess where she could blow off some steam—and stopped in awe of what lay before her.

An oval gateway of pulsing red and purple light, shimmering as if it was breathing, sat in the middle of a small room. Runes and sigils were carved into the floor, each one glowing with a similar red light.

"Neat," she whispered as the glow illuminated her face.

One by one, the *Outsiders* stepped into the portal to hell.

CHAPTER SEVENTEEN

Hell Spawn

The process of going through the portal was a little more underwhelming than Sally had expected. There could have been some tunnel extending through a hellscape or some infinite plane of fire—or even just a little elevator music would have been nice.

Instead, stepping through the glowing portal was just like going through a beaded curtain. Now, on the other side, the colors of red and purple were more apparent—as she had traded the sandy browns and ambers of the topside world for the glowing crimsons and fired oranges of hell.

It was also reasonably warm, but that had been pretty par for the course so far in the Wastelands. Briefly, she tried to consider if hell was actually cooler than outdoors.

A large cavern opened from the small alcove they had popped out into, and as each member joined her, they stood and took in the view. Across the walls of dark burgundy, cracks of amber-like lava veins ran across the rocky surface to the apex of the apparent cave, where a large orb of glowing menace illuminated the area. Opposite their entrance was another portal—this one kept in shape by a dark stone doorway that had engraved runic symbols upon it.

The cavern itself was filled with demons. Naughty System-created ones, by the looks of it. So far, they hadn't noticed the newcomers. Probably some form of teleportation immunity, Sally reasoned. Or they had terrible eyesight, which wasn't uncommon for the System's goons.

"Shall we?" She nudged the Death Knight. There were at least fourscore demons here, and if her intuition was right, the respawns would come in through the looming structure across the other side.

"My pleasure." Humphrey grinned and withdrew his sword.

"I will stay here and keep Lucius safe." Archie stretched out. The demon looked pleased with this suggestion, given the panicked smiley face next to him.

"Can I come out and kill all the demons, Sally?"

"No chance, bud." She sighed. It would be so nice if she could trust him; they fought so well together. Instead, she checked her STAR. Thirteen zombies left in the tank from after the golem fight. That'd have to do—once she got eating, then the demons would make up for it.

"Let's start with the group in the near right," the Death Knight said as he pointed the tip of his sword out. "Then circle around clockwise? Best we don't provoke the whole room."

"I can taste the reference."

"Sounds good, Humps." She gave a gesture for him to attack at will and withdrew the new bat with her dagger in her off hand.

With a short pause to limber up his shoulders, Humphrey pulsed in various shades as he buffed up with *[Adrenaline]* and *[Dead King's Court]*. Tensing his legs, he then ran forward.

Sally joined him, slightly slower, and raised a hand to cast *[Endless Dead]*. As soon as the Death Knight caught the attention of the demons, and they began to draw their weapons in anger, zombies burst out from the surrounding ground.

As Humphrey swung away with his wide attacks, Sally followed in, finishing off the ones that he wounded or tried to surround him. The bat struck a demon on their wrist, disarming them, which she followed up by pressing into them and slitting their throat. She spun from a sword swipe and stumbled backward into the coffin.

Behind them, the group of demons from the bottom left quarter of the chamber had taken offense at their presence and had started off toward them. A number of them had raised crossbows.

"We have company behind," she growled to the Death Knight.

She ducked to the floor as he swung a wide arc around himself with the flat of his blade, knocking three of the fired bolts from the air before slapping a slow demon in the side of the head with the blazing greatsword. Two other bolts clattered off his plated armor, with a final one embedding into a joint.

From their entrance portal, Archie sneezed, and a large globule of vibrating dull green energy flowed forth. It hovered a foot above the ground and slowly careened toward demonic group two. With half of them already on their way into the melee, the odd magic hit them unprepared—a wet burst spreading across them and causing them to be slowed or rooted in place.

Sally let the Death Knight and zombies contend with the first group as she leveled a *[Necroblast: Barrage]* into the approaching group. Two were wounded and two killed, the last blast dodged by the panicked target. She ran and blocked an axe with the bat, stabbing into the opponent's gut with her knife and then letting go of the blade to use her new weapon two-handed.

She swung, and a crackle of red energy ran down the weapon before it struck the demon in the head, shattering its skull. *[Eat Brains]*. She withdrew the blade from the corpse and sheathed it for now to put *[Hex: Slow]* on the nearest demon. Like a bloodied dance, she spun between all the enemies that Archie had managed to restrict, swinging the bat with both hands and cracking bones or blocking strikes.

Despite being made of wood, it held up to the damage pretty well. As she twirled from one demon to the next, she wondered if this was how Theo felt when using his skill. Her bat was blocked, and she kicked at the shin of the demon. As they recoiled, she jabbed forward at their face, knocking them backward. With a short leap, she brought the bat downward, another crackle of critical energy causing the weapon to burst through the bones of arms held up in defense. *[Eat Brains]*.

Her group had almost been cleared now, and in turning to look back at the Death Knight, it seemed he was mopping up too.

"Ahead, Sally!" Lucius called out.

The two other quarters of the cavern had now decided to join the fray. She dove and rolled across the floor slick with demonic blood to try to avoid the crossbow bolts of the ones pointed at her. One stuck into her shoulder, but the rest were rendered inert on the hard stone ground. She was thankful that the vampire was present for his auras, at least.

Clambering back to her feet, the outfit now marred with more blood and dust, she immediately had to be on the back foot as both a spear and a sword thrust against her. She blocked the sword, but the spear pierced her jacket and gashed at her side.

"Ass! I just healed that up!"

"You can talk?" One of the demons looked slightly taken aback.

She swung the bat around and struck their face, the crack of a broken jaw followed up by point-blank *[Necroblast]* to their chest. *[Eat Brains]*.

Combat was for fighting and witty banter only. Just because they were System-created, it didn't mean that they weren't capable of thought. They were just programmed to do a set thing. Respawn when they die with no memories. If her food started talking back now, it would give her an upset stomach.

Overhead, a dark cloud began forming, quickly followed by forked lighting cracking down into a handful of demons, the sound echoing around the cavern alongside their yelps of pain. Three of them dropped to the floor, charred and smoking—while two more looked seriously injured.

[Lord of the Damned]. Humphrey raised his Skeleton Warriors around him. While they might not be as numerous as the zombies or as flashy as causing a

night sky to appear over the area, they were an extra layer of defense. They were also buffed by the Party auras, and in keeping them in defense mode, they blocked additional hits so that he didn't have to. In their dark gray armor, they moved as if knowing his intended actions, ducking below his sword strikes or engaging where he was currently weakest.

Blunt force trauma wasn't really Sally's idea of fun. The bat was definitely a better choice in melee for blocking and dealing damage—but there was something about her dagger that felt more personal and effective. She sidestepped a wild overhead swing of a two-handed axe, wincing as a spark flew from the struck ground. Piercing or slashing was much more fun—perhaps she should ask Humphrey about crafting—if she could just duct-tape the dagger to the bat . . .

"More spawns!" The tiny voice of Archie rang out, only just reaching her dulled hearing. The day had been tiring, but this fighting was almost relaxing in a way. As she shoved the demon out of the way, *[Necroblast]* blew out part of their leg, and she caught the underside of their jaw with an upswing. *[Eat Brains]* from the snapped neck.

With a brief respite, her blazing red eyes looked up to the proper hell portal. More demons had been spilling forth, jogging over to the starting quadrants of the cavern as if in a set pattern. Well, in a way, they were. It looked like Lucius had been correct—the respawns were very quick. Usually, this kind of thing— she ducked and quickly withdrew the dagger to slice across an arm—would take—stabbed out again and cracked the bat down on an elbow—days.

Humphrey roved through the throng, a blaze of unholy energy as each sweep of the greatsword cleaved crimson sprays of demonic blood or knocked bodies flying if they attempted to block the wide strikes. Skeletons stabbed out with their shortswords to finish off the fallen and wounded.

She was slightly saddened that they filled her original purpose—but this way, she could go off and do other things. Being self-reliant was important. Humphrey was sure to drill that into them. You never knew when you'd be caught alone or away from the Party. Each of them was both strong and too stubborn to die. When the world wanted to kill you, it seemed like the smartest thing to be.

Despite her usual undead qualities, she found herself sweating in the humidity. A terrible mixture of battle and . . . hell. Plus, there was a weird, burned ozone smell that constantly bore down on her senses; it was no wonder Archie sneezed—

A black bolt crackled through the air and burst on her shoulder, rending the jacket and her shirt from the impact area. With pained anger, she turned to see a taller demon, a staff and a weird headdress denoting them as a magic user.

"Eighty-six percent," Theo murmured to himself.

CHAPTER EIGHTEEN

Sealed

S o . . ." Lucius sweat as his hands gripped the axe tightly. "What happens when the vampire gets to 100 percent?"

Archie looked up at him, his emerald eyes sparkling in the red hue of the chamber. "I'm not sure. This curse is . . . not as it should be, for a handful of reasons."

The demon watched as the zombie carved bloody carnage through the ranks of his System-created cousins. Humphrey was no less proficient either, his greatsword overpowering all that got in range, with severed limbs and broken bodies littering the floor in his wake.

"Handful of reasons?" His eyes drifted over to a new figure that had appeared from the respawning reinforcements.

"The Toad's curse was different as the Monster was too powerful, and Theo has an odd regenerative body."

Lucius nodded but frowned as this new demon shot a magic bolt and struck Sally.

Archie yawned and continued. "Normally, the curse lasts a week and is just minor sleep deprivation. Makes you grumpy and exhausted. Theo is peaking in less than a day, and he doesn't do very well with a lack of sleep."

"*Damon,*" Lucius murmured out loud in recognition. "That's a Unique demon, who works for the dragon. What are they doing here?"

Demons rushed past Sally, not even trying to attack her—as they went to their proper spawn positions. That was potentially bad, as now she was surrounded. As if the melee wasn't getting choppy enough, there was now some kind of spellcasting demon standing by the portal where the stream of replacements hadn't abated.

"Are you Unique?" she yelled as she ducked a club, stabbing the enemy in the foot before knocking them over.

The spellcaster grinned widely, their fangs showing and gleaming against the dim red glow of this hell cavern. They were not only taller than most of the other demons here, but their skin was more radiant—red, but as if they were filled with luminant light, like lava. Or magma? Sally always forgot which was which.

"I am," the figure replied, their hand crackling with dark energy.

"Then—" Sally took a cut from an outstretched dagger before she grappled with the opponent, headbutting them and following up with a wide bat swing— *[Eat Brains]*. "Why not talk this out?"

"You invade our home, slaughter us—and yet, you expect to parlay?"

"Boats, boats, boats," Theo murmured from across the room.

Sally growled. "At least, stop attacking me while I'm—" *[Necroblast]* hit a demon, and she turned and stabbed at the second. Arm, arm, neck, then eye socket. "When I'm in the middle of something."

The demon pointed their finger, and a crackle of dark energy zipped across the room and struck Sally in the thigh, rending a hole through her jeans and burning at her undead flesh.

"*Ow!* Seriously?" she hissed while blocking a sword, then turned from an axe. Things were getting complicated.

She rolled backward and withdrew a *[Crossbow]*, immediately firing a shot at the magic user. A flare of a dark barrier prevented the bolt from finding its target. Now she was at a disadvantage in the melee. With a kick out at the shins of the approaching demons, she raised her hands, dropping the crossbow. *[Necroblast: Barrage]*. As chunks of assailants sprayed the ground, she found her footing and retrieved her bat.

Two people versus all these demons was now turning into more trouble than it was worth. Especially with the spellcaster. If only they had Theo and a useful fifth. She shot a glance over to the original portal to see the cat speaking with Lucius. Reinforcements were still pouring from the larger portal—seemingly faster than they were killing them.

That just meant they would need to kill them faster. She became a dervish of undead energy. Most of her original zombies had been cut down by the horde of demons, but new ones were springing forth from the brains she had eaten. Not enough to turn the tide, but each one was a distraction that allowed them a slight breathing space.

She held the bat in her off hand and used it to block as she closed in on each demon, stabbing and slashing out with the *[Dagger of Luck]* in her right hand. For her efforts, she received damage of her own, but slowly she was healing thanks to Theo. Her feet stumbled over dead bodies, the cavern fast becoming filled with the corpses of those not rising to obey her command. *[Hex: Slow]* switched to the magic demon as they started to cast something new.

An orb of dark lightning crackled over their head, flickers of light briefly illuminating the chamber. With the point of a finger, the orb started to fly toward Sally. Even from the few dozen feet away, the hairs on her arms prickled upward from the amount of static energy the spell was generating.

[Impenetrable Defense]

The orb started to swerve in the air toward the Death Knight, who had cut a swath to almost the center of the room. A shield flared up as the demons tried to stab at him, the electric attack reached his arms, spread wide, and fizzled out. As his ability ended, he grabbed a demon by its shirt and pulled it in for a quick headbutt before using the limp body to block the attack from another.

"Things are looking a bit wild." Lucius had a sweat drop emoji almost permanently affixed to the side of his head. "Is there anything we can do?"

"You could attack?" Archie raised an eyebrow at the demon.

"Ah." Lucius seemed to sink further into the wall behind them. Not the most palatable of suggestions.

"Like this—" Archie narrowed his eyes as a circle of white light began to pulse from underneath him. Eight beams of light shot up into the air like wiggling snakes and beamed their way through the thick horde of enemies, piercing thin holes through dozens of demons before the white worms of holy energy dissipated most of the way through the room.

"I don't think I can do *that*." Lucius gulped.

Sally was starting to get tired. The constant block, strike, move, parry, block, and attack had begun to numb her arms. She almost wished she had *[Adrenaline]*— or at least wondered if it would have the effect that she craved. Bodies kept falling, and getting to use *[Eat Brains]* was becoming more of a liability—despite the ability being near instant, being left in that brief vulnerable position had earned her some injuries that the slow regeneration wasn't completely healing yet.

"Maybe we should call it?" she yelled at the Death Knight while trying to keep an eye both on the melee around her and the demon spellcaster.

Humphrey cleaved a demon almost in two and kicked away a second. "Respawns are not stopping. I concur."

"A simple yes would have sufficed," she said as she grinned, despite the pain. "Ninety-two."

Not a great time, all things considered. She ducked and wove through the demons, slashing out occasionally but mostly trying to move through the bodies and toward the exit portal. Experience, sure, but they did better when they could overwhelm a small force and then take time to recover.

The magic caster had mostly been watching them intently. She was all but certain that they were either just curious or trying to get a read on the group. That was never a good thing. Perhaps she should go back to the thoughtless System-created who just ran into melee with no concern for themselves. Barbarian did taste slightly nicer than the demon brains.

As she met up with the Death Knight at the small slope up toward the alcove, they turned back to fight off the approaching demons. There was now almost triple the number of Monsters in the room, not including the dead bodies.

"They can't follow us through, right?" She grimaced as her dagger hit bone, which sent a shock up her arm.

"No, they'll stay in here." Archie had backed up and looked like he was about to cast something.

"Alright, then on the count of—"

The magic caster raised up a hand, and his voice reverberated through the chamber. "I don't think so."

Beside Lucius, the glowing red portal shrunk and closed up. An emoji of a shocked, screaming face popped up.

Sally growled. "That isn't *allowed*, right, Humphrey?"

"No—well, not normally." The flames of his helmet flickered wildly as they continued to hack away at the constant assault.

"Ninety-five."

The spellcaster stepped forward among the throng of constantly spawning demons. "You are all quite interesting, so I have an offer to make you."

"No pyramid scheme! Kill all—"

"*Okay*, Theo!" Sally seethed; the melee unforgiving even though an attempt at discourse was in infancy. "What is the offer, demon?"

"Join the army of the great drag—"

"Pass." They were going to kill the dragon. Sure, the *Outsiders* were bad guys, but they weren't going to join organized crime—that made it both less cool and less fun.

"Then I suppose you will all die here unless you have a way to teleport."

"Duh." Sally rolled her eyes. "Theo, use whatever Party teleport we have, even if it takes us to the forest." She would love to do the honors, but the constant fighting made sifting through her Inventory a bit of a struggle.

"No, I must kill all demons."

"Theo!"

"Ninety-eight percent."

Sally narrowed her eyes at the demons still pouring forth from the portal opposite. Even if that were a way out, they'd never manage to cut through the dense crowd to get to it. This was their penance for the earlier hubris. Fighting until they physically couldn't. There hadn't even been time to check to see if they had leveled up yet. What a slice of misery this had become.

Lucius panicked. "I can open it, but I need time."

"Any cards hiding up your sleeve, Archie?" If ever Sally needed a small miracle, now would be the perfect time.

"Just one." Archie narrowed his eyes at the situation. "Big brother, *Operation Beyblade.*"

Without hesitation, the Death Knight swung his sword wide to give himself some space and then unclipped the tethers on the coffin, which struck the floor with a jolt. Growling out, Humphrey grasped the casket and spun, throwing it into the air.

Briefly, all eyes were on the large wooden box as it careened through the air.

A pair of unlucky demons took the brunt of it, crushed as the coffin clattered to the ground and split open in shards.

The air reverberated—shaking as if suddenly under waves pressure. Theo stood slowly and lethargically, his limbs relaxed and weak. Now in the midst of the onrushing tide of demons, a grin widened across his fanged mouth and he pushed his glasses up.

A snap of static electricity burst from around him as the chamber became awash with pitch-black darkness and crimson highlights.

"One hundred percent," he hissed.

CHAPTER NINETEEN

Daily Grind

A wave of silence buffeted the cavern, almost like a shockwave. And then Theo raised both his hands in the air as demons turned toward him. Black-metal punch blades popped into existence on his hands.

His face was unlike anything Sally had seen in him. Darkness had wrought his eyes into sunken pits of bright crimson, and a pained grimace sat widely on his face. It gave him the appearance of being older and much more sinister.

The vampire moved as if in a slideshow—his first strike impaling a demon through the face. Immediately he darted to the next one, his blade carving a chunk out of the throat of the shocked demon. A shadow of pink afterglow followed his every movement, not even in the same way as *[Sanguine Weapon]* or *[Novice Strike]*—it looked like the ability was following his whole body.

"How is this going to end?" Sally cut down one of the few still focused on the rest of the Party.

Archie shrugged and looked back over to Lucius, who was still trying to open the portal.

Somehow, the vampire had begun to move faster—as if slowly increasing momentum with each strike. As the demons tried to move closer or swing at him, a sudden burst of crimson would pop from parts of their body as he blurred past. It was not long before Theo was covered in their viscera, a trail of spattering blood painting the floor in the wake of his afterimage.

The gloom in the cave was oppressive—and didn't seem like *[Perfect Dark]* either. There was no crimson moon shadowing proceedings, though that might look odd being underground. Instead, everything was monochromatic and red.

Very red—not only the hellish surroundings, but between all the figures the ground had been stained by the blood of so many slain demons.

Even as the vampire flickered around, leaving arterial sprays and collapsing bodies in his wake, more demons continued to pour forth. Unrelenting and unphased by the constant carnage.

"It looks like . . ." she began, narrowing her eyes.

"The rate is increasing the more demons die." Humphrey nodded and twisted his blade from a demon.

"I'd advise not to intervene or get any closer." The ginger cat jumped up onto the Death Knight's shoulder pad as all the demons were now trying to focus on the vampire. "He isn't likely to be able to determine friendly or enemy targets at this stage."

"So we can't do the cliché thing of me talking him down from his crazed state because of our special bond?" Sally pouted and tapped some gore from the tip of the bat off on her shoe.

"No," Archie said with a yawn.

Theo began to hum. Tuneless, but it was . . . happy. Every time he received a charge for *[Blood Shift]*, he used the ability. And almost every other demon was slain in one strike. He became even more of a blur as he went from one edge of the chamber to the other, leaving crimson rain in his wake.

He had to kill all demons. But there were *so many*.

Damon had stopped gloating and had his brow furrowed at the proceedings ever since the vampire had started to attack. He must have known they had him stowed away—it was hard to mask that amount of power in a simple wooden box. But this was something else.

"You think if we kill the big bad over there, it'll help matters?" Sally scrunched up her nose as she regarded the spellcaster.

"I don't have anything to harm them from this range." Humphrey shrugged.

Her crossbow hadn't done much. Sometimes she really missed the mobster. Jackie was great at shooting things from afar. She considered the Party teleport . . . but with Theo acting this way, they'd fast become his targets—and fast become mincemeat, too, no doubt.

"Anything you can do, Archie? Can't you summon a gun or something?" She resisted the urge to sit down on the floor. Her next quest should be to nap, in her opinion. "Does this world even have guns?"

"Yes." Humphrey nodded.

"No." Archie shook his head.

Theo was now a constant streak of pink, and each demon was being struck multiple times each instead of once. Impossibly quick, his attacks crackled with energy as bodies began to pile up in excessive numbers.

"That's not an answer. I'll understand if it'd break the immersion of the fantasy setting—but where I'm from, some cultures, such as—"

"I think it is best we leave that for another day, Sally." Archie's emerald eyes twinkled in the crimson light of the cavern.

Perhaps. Personally, she didn't understand the difference between a repeating crossbow or a wand compared to a pistol. She wasn't exactly asking for a mini-gun or laser cannon. She put those on her mental list of things that she wanted. Although her recent acquisition of the not-a-baseball bat made that seem like an even further away prospect. Maybe a nicer dagger would be neat.

The hell portal was now overflowing, the demons respawning at a ridiculous rate, now struggling to fit through the opening as they squeezed and stumbled. Damon looked annoyed but also amused, in that odd way that demons managed to do.

"*Lucius?*" Sally prodded verbally.

"Getting there!" Sweat drop emojis constantly kept reappearing beside him. "I think Damon is keeping it closed—it's making it awkward."

"Awkward." She groaned and rolled her eyes. That's not exactly how she would describe the present situation where Theo was a rolling ball of instant murder, and the rest of them were left twiddling their thumbs in the audience. Well, actually, that *was* a little awkward now that she put it in context.

"We need to break the other portal, big brother." Archie pawed at the side of the Death Knight's head, causing his helmet flame to rise higher.

Humphrey narrowed his empty eye sockets. "Any suggestions? A special beam you could fire over there, or a way to erase it from existence?"

"I'm pretty tired, big brother." He yawned and stretched to emphasize the point. "I have maybe one more spell in me, and we might need that to deal with Theo."

Sally looked between the cat and the roving beam of bloodshed carving through the masses of demons. So Archie looked to have spell slots that recovered on a short rest. Not something she had come across in this System—that sounded like something else she couldn't remember the reference to. It was a glimpse into why he seemed useless sometimes, however.

She tilted her head. Normally it was nice to pull out a hidden ace card to save the day, but she wasn't sure she had any left—oh! There was something . . .

"Humps, if I open all my Daily Rewards now, do you think there will be an object that will get us out of our current conundrum?"

"Doubtful . . ." He grimaced at her, but there was the slightest hint of uncertainty in his tone.

It couldn't be worse than trying to put on the glitched hat that she received earlier. Imagine if that did something like making her really tall or capable of walking through walls. Most likely, it would just erase her head, or worse.

Theo had begun to beam his way closer to the larger portal but was slowing as the number of respawning demons—and their corpses—were delaying his progress physically. Damon looked to be trying to get a read on the vampire to levy some kind of attack, but he was beyond being able to be seen, let alone tracked.

"Is Theo taking damage?" She was worried that he was cheese-grating himself against the demons.

"Physically, he is fine." Archie looked out at the spectacle but didn't seem to be struggling to keep stock of Theo.

"*Ack*, the way you specify *physically*." She looked back at their demon. "Lucius?"

"Ah! So . . ." He spun around, hands clasped behind his back. "It turns out I cannot, in fact, open this with Damon there."

Sally exhaled through her nose. Looks like they were in this for the long haul then. She prodded at her STAR.

Sally: currently in hell
Sally: literally
Sally: theo has turned into the avatar of death
Chuck: bet that suits him
Sally: kinda
Sally:_

She let the cursor blink in front of her eyes for a few seconds, unsure what to say next. It wasn't so bad that she had to send some last goodbyes, right? Although the situation was dangerous and pretty dire, she didn't personally feel like she was in big trouble. Save for Theo turning on them or him dying and the gigantic crowd coming for them—they were just the audience for this show.

"You got a town scroll, just in case, Humps?"

"Yes. To one of the towns with people we don't care as much about."

Just in case Theo was still wild. Imagine going back to Jackie or the goblins and causing mass slaughter. That would be worse than just taking the loss here. Everything they worked for undone in one pink blaze. She was more annoyed at the vampire now, despite him not doing that yet.

"Alright, time for Daily Rewards."

"Are you sure you want to do that, Sally?" Archie raised an eyebrow.

"I'd rather know and not die than die and not know." She bopped the STAR and rolled over to the notification.

Daily Rewards Received
600 Gold
Error Experience
Rare Ranged Weapon Box (1)
Rare Melee Weapon Box (1)
Hearty Meal (10)

Basic Dagger (67)
Spell Scroll Box (3)
Stamp Card
Stamp Booster (5)
Error//stack misc detr-b

She hadn't realized it had been that many days that she hadn't retrieved the reward. Classic *error experience*.

"I got sixty-seven daggers." She shrugged at the gathered *Outsiders*. "Some nerd stuff like stamps, some gross food I'll never eat, gold which someone will soon come and try to extort from me—and Chance Boxes."

"Underwhelmed?" Humphrey grinned in the macabre crimson light.

"Completely whelmed." Sally worked her jaw and opened up the spell scroll boxes.

Spell Scroll: Summon Demon
Spell Scroll: Greater Firebolt
Spell Scroll: Savage Strike

Her jaw ached from how tense she was clenching her teeth. *Summon demon?* She opened the weapon chance boxes.

Rare Throwing Knives
Dagger of Luck

It probably wasn't worth opening the stamps now. She sighed as she watched Theo blend through the nonstop demon spawns.

So much for narrative fiat saving the day. The System could go stick these random items up its—

A flashing notification caught her attention. With all the weight of the situation weighing down on her, she pressed her finger on the flickering blue box.

Introductory Period Complete!
Welcome to the {System}!
500 Gold
Error Unlocked
////ss***__
Legendary Weapon Selection Box
Mark of the {unassigned}

Right eye twitching, she slowly withdrew the weapon selection box.

CHAPTER TWENTY

Power Spike

Instead of a puff of smoke and the reveal of a randomly disappointing weapon, the selection box instead brought up a list. Rectangles of orange denoted the legendary status of the weapons within.

"They're still *first area* items, but they—" Humphrey stood behind her, viewing the screens as she interrupted his train of thought with a wave of her hand.

"Don't rain on my parade." This would be her first legendary item, whether it was any good or not. "What do I pick, though? We really should have done the options reveal first."

"This is the . . . never mind." The Death Knight deflated.

"I don't know how you are all so calm during this—this is not a good time." Lucius grimaced and couldn't decide whether to stare at the blur of the vampire or not.

"Either being undead removes some of their fear, or they are just too traumatized to register such things." Archie turned to the demon with tired eyes.

"And you?" A question mark bubble appeared beside him.

"I'm the *Architect*." The cat yawned.

Sally rubbed her chin. All the basic weapon types were here—and either a crossbow or dagger seemed like obvious upgrades to what she already had. Melee was already pretty simple for her, and the few magic skills she had dealt pretty great damage. Maybe something ranged was the way to go. Although—she didn't really have the stats for it, as far as she knew.

"Wowzers, this is a difficult decision." She rubbed the back of her arm across her forehead. "Shame Theo isn't here to advise."

Humphrey pouted and looked over at the vampire. To Theo's credit, he had started to kill them quicker than they could fill the room back up, and he danced his bloody dance in the back third of the chamber. Damon was either interested to see what was about to play out or halfway to extracting himself from the situation.

Sally looked up from her window of unmade decisions to follow the Death Knight's gaze. "What's the range of your duel skill, Humps?"

"Not far enough, but I like the thought."

Even with the tasty orange treat awaiting her button press—none of the weapons were situation-changing. She winced as she considered leaving the decision for later.

"What's this mark thing?"

"It's usually a badge type thing that gives some minor stats depending on your class. More of an achievement thing than anything useful." Humphrey scratched the side of his head. "Theo is going to be very annoyed none of this experience counts for him."

"It does . . . for us, though?" She wailed internally at not being able to see her experience bar. Levels up often came after the area was clear or they were no longer in danger. Theo *was* the danger.

"*Yes.*"

"How long can he keep this up? With the curse, I mean." Despite him clearly being in charge of the situation, this was highly abnormal, and she was starting to worry about his well-being more than his well-doing.

"It is unclear," the cat answered. "Everything about this is beyond the scope that I . . . that the Architect envisioned."

Sally also didn't envision getting torn up in hell by her vampire companion. Not like *this*. The coffin was now destroyed, perhaps a shortsighted plan just for the added flair of—oh, she should have shouted, "*Theo, I choose you,*" as he was thrown out. Maybe next time, if there was one.

"What do you plan, Sally?" Lucius prodded at her shoulder.

"I'm tired of plans. Why don't we just wait—eventually, something will break, right?"

"As long as it isn't me," the demon said as he shrugged, leaning nervously on his axe.

Theo was about at the hell portal now, the demons only making it a few steps—some of them just tumbling from the clogged opening—before he rendered them full of puncture wounds. Damon had perhaps seen enough and turned to the *Outsiders*.

"Well, a lot has been learned here—perhaps you will change your mind about joining us once you—"

The pink blur of the vampire using *[Blood Shift]* over at the spellcaster, flares of dark energy flickering throughout the cavern as the shield activated and then failed—crimson marks shredding at him—twenty, no—thirty or more stab wounds appearing in just a brief two seconds.

Theo flickered back to the portal horde as the bloodied corpse of Damon dropped to the floor. Any zombie Sally had raised met the same fate under the determined blades of the vampire.

There was no more room for the hell portal to spawn new demons. Each one killed piled up before the glowing blur of his attacks was at the entrance itself—the bodies barely making it halfway through the gateway before being cored or decapitated. Eldritch sparks began to fizzle from the runes around the stone frame.

"Do you think—" Sally began before a burst of radiant purple light filled her vision, and a deafening ring stung her ears. It began to fade as her eyes filtered through the reds and crimsons of hell properly once more.

Theo stood among a small mound of corpses.

He was breathing heavily—panting, as his legs shook. From head to toe, he was absolutely drenched in blood and gore. Slowly, he lowered his arms as they shuddered.

"I . . . I did it . . ." He started to laugh to himself, quietly at first. "I did! *I killed all demons!*"

Lucius slowly sidled behind Humphrey as Sally ran out into the cavern.

Gingerly, she hopped over the piles of dead demons, slipping on some intestines and tripping on some bodies that were squishier than she had anticipated.

"Are you sane again, Theo? Don't stab me." Perhaps she should have exercised a bit more caution before going over to meet him. If the others didn't stop her, then . . . they had stayed at the back still. She didn't fail to notice their pensive stares, however.

"Not *sane*, no. I'm . . ." he said as he turned to watch her arrive, "I'm tired as shit, though."

"Uh, we kind of broke your bed." Her eye twitched at the implication. He had saved them by saving himself, or something, but without a proper bed to sleep in.

"I literally can't move my legs or arms. Even if I go *more* crazy, I couldn't hurt you."

Sally ran her tongue across her sharp teeth. "Promise?"

His mouth opened and closed, and tears began to clear thin trails down his face. "I didn't . . . I didn't get any of that . . . experience, did I?"

"No, pup." She gave him a glum smile. "But we have a lot of loot to dig through. You killed so many demons, you broke hell. Really did *Redd* proud."

"*I don't know who that is,*" Theo wailed, head hanging forward as tears and blood dripped from his face to the cavern floor—or at least atop the corpses blocking the ground.

"Alright." She spun on her feet and started giving orders. "Humphrey, come carry Theo. Archie, help me to find any good loot among all these corpses. Lucius, fix that *damn* portal."

They all nodded and voiced their agreement. Sally even folded her arms to look a little more commanding before the Death Knight rolled his lack of eyes.

"Hey, Sally." Archie came up and brushed against her legs as she tried to decide how best to start looting these . . . potentially hundreds of bodies. "Is it okay if I take a nap after we loot all these bodies?"

"Of course, Arch." She kneeled to give him a pet. The ginger cat didn't get enough limelight on the best of days; the least she could do was give him some rubs and a well-earned nap.

"Okay, put your hand on my back, then. This might work." He waited for her to do so, and then closed his emerald eyes and opened his mouth.

He felt warm beneath her dead hand, but that perhaps wasn't unusual. Then, there was a vibration of energy, some kind of power, as he opened his mouth.

"I hope you like Inventory management," he growled as a pulse of white light briefly flooded the room.

7534 Gold
Basic Shortsword (23)
Basic Axe (44)
Basic Crossbow (53)
Basic Spear (23)
Basic Greataxe (26)
Basic Club (36)
Basic Dagger (76)
Basic Leather Armor (42)
Basic Leather Leggings (67)
Basic Leather Boots (71)
Basic Leather Helm (44)
Demon Horns (231)
Skull (127)
Cooked Meat (85)
Demon Coin (12)
Crimson Key (17)
Crimson Treasure Box (6)
Mount Feed (45)
Lower Demon Card (14)
Uncommon Weapon Chance Box (24)

> Rare Weapon Chance Box (6)
> Uncommon Armor Chance Box (38)
> Rare Armor Chance Box (8)
> Demonkiller Blade (1)
> Healing Potion (31)
> Greater Health Potion (21)
> Mana Potion (34)
> Campfire (16)

"*Ahhh*," Sally said, her eyes wide and unblinking as the stream of text messages passed through the side of the System. "That's a lot of . . . *everything*."

Archie burped. "Sucks that I can only use my abilities once, huh?"

"Yeah." She nodded slowly, her voice distant as the messages started to give her a headache. "I think that would be somewhat overwhelming most of the time."

"*Anything for meeeee?*" Theo wailed from atop the Death Knight.

She continued to slowly nod. This would take a while to parse through and understand. Probably in a moment of downtime when they weren't sitting in a huge pit of corpses and oppressive heat.

"Portal is done!" Lucius beamed, as a little firework emoji popped beside his head.

"Let's get out of this hell and back into the other." Sally got to her feet and scrunched up her eyes. Overwhelming. She now had hundreds and hundreds of useless weapons inside her Inventory—alongside some things that actually sounded useful. Perhaps it was time for that crafting tutorial, or maybe just finding a room where she could dump a lot of them in.

She picked up Archie and cradled the cat as he began to drift off to sleep. Walking up to the Death Knight, she gave Theo—who was now hanging limply over the shoulder plate of Humphrey—a little bop with her nose. "Come on, dumbass. Let's get you a new coffin."

They trudged across the damp floor and up into the alcove, not even giving the place a second look before they passed through the portal and back into the normal Wastelands drudgery—still in the ruined basement. At least the sun seemed to be getting lower in the sky now.

Just as she was about to ask how they were going to get up through the doorway, she almost dropped the sleeping cat as her STAR *bloiped*.

Arranging Archie so that she could reach it, her eyes lit up, and all the exhaustion from the day washed away from her tired body.

They had leveled up *twice*.

CHAPTER TWENTY-ONE

Double Trouble

After a few minutes of grumbling, Sally hopped up the broken furniture they had arranged and rolled onto the dry street outside. She gave Lucius a hand up, and then, after Theo's battered body was unceremoniously hauled up, they both struggled to assist the Death Knight.

"So, what did we learn today?" Archie sat and wiggled the tip of his tail as they all collapsed to the ground.

"Huh?" Sally rolled into a sitting position. "I'm not made for learning."

Theo exhaled as his face lay mushed into the ground. "I learned I could kill all demons."

The zombie put her hand on his gore-matted hair. "And how does that make you feel?"

"Sad." He groaned and deflated.

"Enough with annoying Theo," Humphrey said as he shooed her away. "He is in a state of calm now, but without a way to get him to sleep, we only have so many last straws to tug on."

She blew air out of her mouth but swiveled around to face the demon. "You leveled too, Lucius?"

"Yeah. First time for everything, right?" He was looking up at the sky, probably focusing on his options.

Sally shrugged and pressed her STAR again. She remembered Humphrey saying that Level Eleven was another improvement skill selection, but she was more excited about Level Twelve and getting something new.

> **Pick One**
> [Improved Mighty Aura] Increased Bonuses the lower your % HP is
> [Improved Summon Zombies] Zombies Summoned are higher Level
> [Improved Zombie Curse] The chance for kills to turn into Zombies is doubled

The curse one was pretty weak—thanks to *[Eat Brains]*. The only time she bit someone was when she was getting the guaranteed turn, anyway. And as neat as their auras were, her small army could do with a level boost to suit the new area. For once, she didn't deliberate over the selection for too long.

> **[Improved Summon Zombies]**

It would have been nice if it gave additional uses or increased the numbers summoned . . . but she would take what the System could give her. It's not like there was an Architect to complain to now, anyway. She sighed and brought up the golden STAR once more.

> **[Pick One]**
> [Gravewalker] Movement and Attack speed increased when near undead allies
> [Desecrate Life] 30ft Area Curse. Targets have lowered STR and CON
> [Foul Breath] 15ft Cone Attack, Necrotic Damage

For starters, she wasn't going to pick *[Foul Breath]* even if it was overpowered because she wouldn't be able to live down the skill name. It was easy to imagine Theo giggling every time she used it. With a different name, it may have been in the running. Then again, she also didn't want to foul up her potential meals with . . . whatever a necrotic damage spray might look like.

[Gravewalker] seemed good on the surface. She was practically always around undead allies with Theo and Humphrey—even if her zombies were currently absent. It only affected her, though, and as much as she enjoyed being powerful, things that could benefit the group took preference.

[Desecrate Life]

More interesting than another aura, she shrugged to herself. A thirty-foot area was a decent spread when it came to melee and would soften up enemies for the whole Party. When their defenses were already stacked high, lowered target Strength just made them even more effective. Not flashy, but living was preferable to exploding into sparkly body parts.

"What are you picking, Humps?" She turned back to the Death Knight, who had now wrestled the floppy vampire back over his shoulder. "Oh, you didn't tell me about your keystone still?"

"Yes. I went for *[Improved Compelled Duel]* and *[Decimate]*."

"Gnarly. Care to enlighten on what they do?" She stretched her back out and fought back a yawn.

"This sucksss," Theo whined from behind Humphrey. "I didn't level, and now I have to listen to all thisss."

The Death Knight grinned. "*[Decimate]* gives me a powerful strike every time I take ten hits."

"I guess that's roughly paired with the true meaning, then. I would have thought it'd do 10 percent of their health or something." Sally rubbed her chin and briefly considered getting up off the floor. While they risked cooking themselves by languishing in the sunshine, it also took a lot of effort to move after such a stressful fight.

"I'm not sure what to pick," Lucius said as he continued to stare above. "I didn't really have skills before."

"Any ranged damage options or healing?" Sally cooed hopefully.

"I chose *[Improved Emoji]*." A more animated, higher-quality sweat drop appeared beside his head.

Sally blinked. Somehow she should have expected that, yet didn't. It had been a long day, and she was a little off-kilter from everything she had witnessed. Maybe it would be a bad idea to ask the demon what his other skill would be.

"Oh, here you go—*[Inspirational Word]*. It doesn't do any damage, but it gives a boost to stats or something." He now turned to look at them and shot them two thumbs-up.

"It's support." Humphrey shrugged. "As long as it's not too annoying."

"Are you a deeeemon?" Theo whispered from the back again.

With a yawn, Sally stood on her feet. "No point asking you, Archie? No offense," she continued as the cat nodded, "but we need to get some sleep and then work out what to do with our boneless vamp."

"We'll need to hold watches, old school adventuring style." A twinkle radiated from within the Death Knight's eye sockets. "Not only to make sure Theo doesn't try to murder us, but Ed the Witless will surely turn up soon."

"Especially after coming into so many riches." Sally made the show of patting her side pouch, despite the gold being held in the abstract nether of the Inventory. She wondered why it was just gold and not other valuable things, but perhaps the dragon preferred cash to stocking up on assets.

"Can I count it?"

"You can count yourself lucky we didn't leave you down there." She wagged a finger at the back of Theo. "You've been very rude lately and . . . and . . . don't be an ass anymore." Her lecture faltered, remembering how mind-numbingly awesome it was for him to kill hundreds of demons in such a short time. She couldn't help but be impressed, even if he was being annoying about the whole thing.

[Inspirational Word]—"Great leadership, Sally!"

She smiled and felt better with the weak attempt at admonishing the out-of-control vampire. "Thanks, Lucius. Very kind of you to say."

The demon gave her a pair of finger guns, despite the narrowed glare of Humphrey from the side.

"Right meow, there isn't anywhere we can get a coffin." Archie looked up at them with emerald eyes. "With the town destitute, our travels tomorrow should prioritize helping Theo."

Sally nodded. "Let's head to a house that still has a floor. Are there any other towns nearby?"

They began walking down the street to find a building with a big enough ground floor for them all to sleep in a circle, as if by a campfire.

Lucius thumbed at his belt. "There's a town to the north and to the east, but they're in a similar state to this one."

Sally sighed as they pushed into a building. The coolness of the inside was instantly relaxing. "So how far do we have to go to get Mr. Crazy Pants a sanity box?"

A thoughtful emoji rubbing his chin appeared. "Well . . . from a System-created . . . unless there are some underground towns I don't know about, then we are looking at past the storm." He shrugged apologetically.

The zombie slumped against the wall with a groan and flopped on the floor. "Unfair." *How could there be nowhere else that had boxes to bury people in?* She supposed the System didn't really care much for that side of things, unless it was thematically relevant.

"We could always go back to Sanctuary now that Theo has . . . calmed," Humphrey offered. "It would mean travel back through the Swamps without an easy way to teleport."

"Not quickly, anyway," Archie added. "But remember what we had discussed, big brother?"

"Ah. *Yes.*" The Death Knight rubbed his chin in contemplation, ignoring the narrowed glare of Sally.

Eventually, she tired of the scratching sound. "Spill it, you two."

"The power to unlock our . . . other memories." Humphrey folded his arms. "There is a location to the west that has the object we seek."

"And . . ."

"It would have coffins, of a sort."

"Oh!" Lucius snapped his fingers. "The pyramid, right? You're thinking sarcophagus' . . . sarcophagi?"

Sally righted herself and pointed an accusatory finger between the two ex-Observers. "You mean to tell me there's a big undead place, and you weren't going to say anything?"

"Well . . ." Humphrey turned to place the limp vampire down against the wall. "We wanted to get a couple levels first—which Theo has now done."

"I didn't get any levels." He moped sadly.

"You'll catch up, pup. Don't fret." She looked at him, concerned. Mopey Theo was definitely preferable to the bloodthirsty killer Theo, but she would like him to be somewhere in the middle. All he needed was some rest. You wouldn't have thought that it'd be such a hardship to overcome.

"I'll take the first watch." Humphrey nodded as he observed them both.

"I'd prefer it if you didn't kill him when I was asleep, though, Humps." She turned her concerned glare toward him.

"My disdain for the bloodsucker is only banter; I would not really harm him unless *necessary*." He grinned in a manner almost convincing.

"I propose we should watch in pairs," Lucius chimed in. "Just for a little accountability?"

Sally shrugged and looked back toward the Death Knight.

"*Yes*. You're with me, demon. Sally and Archie can have the next watch." Humphrey waited for them to nod their acknowledgment, which they did.

"I'll watch too," Theo whispered.

They each took up a position and used a *[Campfire]* to soothe their remaining aches of the day. Somehow, it didn't seem to clog the enclosed hall with smoke, which would have been a reasonably anticlimactic way for them to go out.

Sally stared at the wooden wall, unable to sleep. Their first day in the Wastelands had been . . . well, it was certainly different. Same old killing and oddball antics. But something else was nagging at her. The whole thing with Edward and the dragon was—

Death approaches.

She frowned at the wood. Voices in her head weren't very welcome. Just because it was a long day, that was no reason to go a little crazy. A few screws loose was already her normal state of being if she started—

Death approaches.

Slowly, she twisted over. Humphrey was turned away from the fire, staring at the doorway in his statuesque pose. Lucius was on the other side of the almost inert *[Campfire]*, and she couldn't see him. Her eyes ran up the wall further down to see the vampire staring back at her.

"Death approaches," Theo whispered, his face slack and impassive.

CHAPTER TWENTY-TWO

Some Actual Loot

She narrowed her eyes at the vampire. "I don't appreciate your tone, sir," Sally whispered back.

Theo seemed to close his eyes at the admonishment but wasn't falling asleep, even if he looked half dead. Or half undead—which he was. Instead, he just stayed slumped against the wall, and his tongue lolled out of his mouth as he relented to being shushed.

Well, if she couldn't sleep, then she had other things she could be doing. Quietly, she sat up and stretched out her arms. Things like sifting through all that loot that she had managed to fit in her Inventory. Mostly, she was thankful that there were no encumbrance rules—or at least she was strong enough to where it might not come into effect yet.

"If you are up, I will rest now," Humphrey said in a hushed tone, not moving from his position.

"Go for it," she whispered back, causing Lucius to startle. The demon made the show of definitely being awake, despite his crimson eyes being half closed.

She rotated through her STAR and thought she should at least update Chuck on them not dying. More than they already were. Not since the *incident.* She smiled to herself.

Sally: we are okay.
Sally: heading to pyramid 2moro
Sally: theo is_

She scrunched up her face as she looked at the mess of a man. It would be a stretch to say that he was okay, but he wasn't also trying to tear their faces off, so . . .

Sally: theo is unwell but stable

Until he regained his stamina, he shouldn't be a problem—although it was odd it was taking so long. Perhaps part of the curse made recovery slower. She exhaled through her nose and switched around to the Inventory.

Masses of daggers, swords, and whatever else grossed her out. All those numbers of stacked boring weapons—but at least she got a sizeable boost to her skull collection. She almost gagged at the thought of opening all the Chance Boxes too. There were three things that were marginally interesting now that she had some time to look at them. Finger in the air, she rearranged them so they were beside each other in the Inventory grid.

Lower Demon Card (14)
Crimson Treasure Box (6)
Demonkiller Blade (1)

She had more keys than treasure boxes, which seemed like a bit of a scam. Normally if there were actual Players around, she imagined she would be able to sell the spares to those who couldn't delve into the hells themselves for whatever reason. Or just had bad luck.

The cards didn't seem too useful—only giving a fire damage bonus. She didn't deal any fire damage—aside from her witty burns. Her face wrinkled up in not being able to level that brag at any of her Party members. The set bonus for five of the cards gave fire resistance or something—but she was pretty tied to using the Cyclops Card. And not just because the picture on it was cute.

Saving the chests for last, she then brought up the information for the blade.

Demonkiller Blade
Rare Sword - Requires Reputation with {Burning Sun} to wield.

That brought rise to more questions than it answered. A rare sword might be better than the baseball bat, but she had no idea who the Burning Sun was—other than in the literal sense. Options included: something to do with the dragon due to the current malady ailing the Wastelands, a specific guild, or perhaps a System-created faction that was dead, or they had not met yet.

Either way, that just meant the blade would be taking up a slot in her Inventory and be no more useful than the stacks of clubs or normal swords.

Briefly, she considered discarding all the trash, but then realized how bizarre it would be to start dropping hundreds of weapons. And then she wondered if there was any combat advantage to doing so.

With nothing interesting left to prod at, she turned her attention to the crimson treasure boxes. Rather than bringing the large chests out into real space, she was briefly amused to see that she could open them from inside the Inventory—saving the necessary hassle of box animation and having to hold and store the retrieved item. That would have been nicer to know at the start.

> Item will bind to you once opened.
> Accept? Yes/No

Yes, she thought as she pressed the yes button. There couldn't be anything terrible in them that the items being bound would be a problem. Although, in saying that, a dozen ideas for cursed items popped into her brain. Sucks that she was getting all the loot for herself, but that's what the rest of them got for being asleep. Plus, only Theo had a proper Inventory, and he didn't seem too interested in the loot.

> Open All?

Even more useful—she didn't have to do it one at a time. Something in the back of her head tried to convince her she should properly learn more about the System that she found herself stuck in. But that was also Theo's thing. At once, she used six keys to open the chests.

> Crimson Dawn Helm
> Crimson Dawn Chest Armor
> Crimson Dawn Leggings
> Crimson Dawn Boots
> Crimson Dawn Bracers
> Crimson Dawn Shoulder Pads

She puckered her lips as she looked at the new icons in her equipment Inventory. Despite all the growth she had achieved in the last area, she was still unable to see the basic stats on things. This armor set must be an upgrade, though. Either through luck or design, she received no duplicate pieces—but then, that did make sense if they were bound to her. It must be a coincidence that she found six chests, and the set had six parts too. Either that or the System had someone more competent at the helm when designing this part of the . . . experience.

Actually, that was another question for the gang in the morning. Silently, she yawned. Looking at items always sapped away her strength. Maybe if she just rested her eyes for a minute, she'd feel a little better.

"Edward?"

The demon stopped as he passed the open doorway and deflated.

"Yes, High Master?" He slowly stepped backward into view of the illuminated room.

The robed figure ran their fingers slowly down the page of a large tome—more to feel the texture than to find a spot to read from. "Ruben would like to see you."

Edward grimaced. "Of course, I had a feeling that would be—"

"Inevitable?"

"—on the agenda soon." The demon gave a low bow and then carried on back down the passageway. Exhaling half the way, he eventually stopped at a pair of wide double doors. The sand-colored brickwork around the burgundy wood was engraved with various symbols he didn't much care for. It was magical but did nothing to him—good or bad.

Eye twitching, he gave the smooth wood a knock.

"*Enter.*" A deep voice vibrated through the floor and into his bones.

Two doors parted to reveal a large chamber, wide and with a tall, peaked ceiling. Everything was the color of sandstone or rust. *Very drab*, Edward thought—although he daren't say it in anything louder than a whisper within his head.

The reason for the large room sat before him, shrouded in darkness due to the almost total absence of lighting. Two large eyes of amber watching him enter, and the shifting shape as large as a house rose and fell with large breaths.

"You return empty-handed again, Edward." Even the weight of the words from the dragon felt like it could crush his bones.

"Yes, sire. A new Party has entered the Wastes, and they are . . . stubborn." He bowed as low as he was able. It wasn't required, but it seemed the smart thing to do when you were liable to be eaten—and could respawn to experience it more than once.

"Scribe tells me you have lost a golem to this Party."

Edward's right eye twitched again. "Not lost, but they saw fit to—"

"To kill you, yes. You must be smart enough to know that such a thing would be . . . inevitable."

"Sire." The demon winced. "So too is the acquisition of their tithe."

"See that it is so, Edward. I would hate to be disappointed . . . when we are so close." The creature lumbered forward slightly toward the demon, the brief lighting illuminating sandy-yellow scales and large leathery wings. "Try something more convincing than the golem this time."

*   *   *

"*Sally.*" Humphrey shook the zombie.

"Hmfs?" Her eyes opened blearily, part of her jacket in her mouth. "What, oh, is it my turn for . . ." Sunlight illuminated the hall from the side windows. "*Ah.*"

The Death Knight stood up straight and gestured with his head.

Theo was not where he had been. She blinked to make sure it wasn't some trick of the light. "*System damn it.*" She scowled. "Where has he gotten to?"

"Not very far," Archie called from the slightly ajar front door. "He is trying to run away in the way that a worm does. *Wriggling.*"

Sally stood up and stretched. The sleep was not great—in fact, it was terrible, and she felt just as grumpy as yesterday morning. Then again, it had been a while since she had eaten some Player brains. They seemed to be a rare commodity this side of the sandstorm. A far cry from the comfortable forest area where tasty meals couldn't wait to feed themselves to her.

She walked across the hall to the doorway, almost tripping over the cat, and glared down the road. There the vampire lay, trying to move his legs and then torso in a fluid motion to push himself along the road. A trail of dark crimson gave his travel away because of the dried blood from the hell fight rubbing off on the cobbled road.

"He has been singing something about being a maniac and dancing," Humphrey said as he shrugged and moved up behind her. "There is a determination for something, but I do not know what."

"If it's to kill someone, then I guess we are lucky he moved farther away from us." She shrugged. "Weren't you meant to be watching with me, Arch?"

"Probably," the cat said as he looked up at them with emerald eyes. "But I didn't."

"Clearly."

She turned to see Lucius still asleep. How anyone could sleep through the rest of them stomping around, she didn't know. A job half done and fully remembered, she brought up her Inventory and equipped the new armor set beneath her casual clothing.

It felt . . . pretty good, actually. It was slightly heavier, and it reduced some movement, but it definitely had more *armor* to it.

Humphrey narrowed his eye sockets. "What did you just do?"

"New armor. Why?"

"That is not meant for *you.*" The flames behind his helmet rose higher.

CHAPTER TWENTY-THREE

Against the Grain

Under the watchful glare of the Death Knight, her eyes grew tired. "What do you mean?" Sally pouted. She had found the armor fair and square. If you ignored the skill that Archie used so that she got all the loot. And that she didn't *share*.

"Did you even read the effects of it?" Humphrey crossed his arms as they stepped out into the road to stop awkwardly crowding the doorway.

Theo had shuffled along about another foot in the time they had spent watching, so keeping an eye on him was easy enough while they had time for discourse.

"Big brother is right, Sally." Archie stretched out in the morning sun.

"Right about what?"

"It's nothing terrible, but the armor is meant for someone else." Humphrey tilted his head but looked no less perturbed.

"But . . ." She pinched the bridge of her nose. "The armor is *bound* to me; nobody else could have it. It came straight from a box."

"Hmm." The Death Knight exhaled and looked down at the cat. "What do you think, little brother?"

"If what she says is true, then that makes sense, surely?"

Sally felt like her head might pop. She was still groggy from having just woken up, and they were going to berate her about her armor because they didn't understand how bound items worked? Even as ex-Observers?

"Let me get this straight." She waved her hands in the air to get their attention. "There are lots of items in the System that belong to someone—but you are unable to tell me the specific person or persons. You just know that the items *belong*?"

"*Yes*," the Death Knight said as he nodded in tandem with Archie.

She deflated and turned to catch up to Theo. She had always known they were fallible, but to have such a gross misunderstanding of a core concept of these types of things was . . . wow, she really wished she had the normal vampire to gripe about this thing with.

"Hey, pudding." She gave his legs a little kick, and whatever tune he had been humming along to ceased. "You got somewhere to be?"

"No." He rolled onto his back and looked up at her.

If she didn't know any better, she would have assumed that he had died in the night. Of course, he was already undead—but now he looked rougher than some of her summoned zombies. She managed to give him a polite smile. "Then where are you going?"

"Away from you." He tried to shuffle backward slightly.

"Away from me specifically? Or from the whole group?" She crossed her arms.

"Yes."

She spun around and wagged a finger at the Death Knight. "You're a bad influence! Also, we must have some rope and something to gag him with, right?"

Humphrey shrugged. "Depends on what we are planning." On catching the intense glare of the zombie, he grinned and continued, "But we could probably wrap him in my cloak if you have no rope in your Inventory."

Sally didn't even bother looking through it to check. "Yeah, wrap him up."

As the Death Knight approached, the vampire tried to squirm away. He was unable to get far before the red cloak encircled him like a swaddled baby. Unceremoniously, he was then slung over the Death Knight's shoulder, his glaring eyes the only thing peeking out behind the back of the plated figure.

Sally sighed. "That's one thing taken care of; now let's check the list."

"Oh, morning everyone—sorry I overslept." Lucius stepped out of the hall, rubbing his neck.

"It's fine." Sally waved him off. "We have just been bickering about semantics and grabbing our little lunatic here."

The demon nodded, but he just stared impassively.

Next on the agenda was getting to the pyramid to get the Observer magic object and hopefully somewhere for Theo to have a nap. Even if they could just reset his mania temporarily, that'd be great—at least then they should have a couple of days of normal Theo to help them fight or farm items for her.

"You said it was Level Fifteen for mounts, Humps? How are we going to get to the pyramid without turning to dust under this sun?"

On the map, it looked like a couple of days of walking. Why the System made everything so far apart was still beyond her. She cursed it once again.

Archie rolled over on the ground, rubbing his back against the warming cobbled road. "I could do something, but it could go wrong."

She wasn't too keen on trying out whatever random skill the cat could conjure up. It could be something as banal as summoning a horse-drawn cart—or he could turn into a hot-air balloon that popped over the desert and dropped them to their doom. If there was some method to his madness, it might have made it a more palatable option.

As she shook her head, she looked around at the rest of the buildings on the street. Nothing untoward, but the empty town still put her on edge. It should be bustling with Players and System-created, just like Sanctuary or any of the other villages. It became a pinprick of anger within her—a hatred for the dragon that had scoured the System of the rightful life in this area.

She had thought the System oppressive in the forest, where Uniques had no place among the Players—but here it was just as bad, in a different way. Nothing was allowed to flourish. No doubt countless Players and Uniques had died in rebellion against the harsh rules imposed by the greedy Monster. Even the System-created couldn't function and had been forced into living underground. Everything was ruined, and she was too tired to abide by that.

"I know of some ways—we can get about a third of the way there through the tunnels." Lucius slowly moved into her eyeline as she stared intently into the distance. "But then it'd be mostly above ground after that."

Sally sighed and shook the frustration from her head. All things came to be eaten by her wanting maw, eventually; the dragon was no exception. The important thing was getting her Party fixed up.

"Alright, Lucius—can I call you Lucy?"

"I don't . . . sure, I could live with that." The demon shrugged and was accompanied by an emoji of a yellow face doing a similar motion.

"Lucy, Humps, Arch—let's go into the tunnels again and . . . stuff." She deflated as her rallying cry lost its luster.

"*Mmf bffts.*"

"I'm not calling you that, Theo. Don't be reductive." She shook her head and followed the demon as he led them onward.

Two hours had passed since the troupe had left Bordertown, and things were drab.

Sally sighed for possibly the three hundredth time. Theo could probably tell her the exact number of times—if he wasn't constantly glaring at the floor in some kind of catatonic state. The tunnels were a miserable expanse of boring rock and little else. None of the alleged hidden-away Monsters or Player groups to break up the monotony of just walking.

It was tiring, and even the group had become quiet and morose. The slight benefit of not being under the constant glare of sunlight was nice, but they still had to make the distance to the pyramid. And then they had to hope that Theo could sleep in a sarcophagus. If not . . . that was a couple of days away, and who knew what he'd be like.

"You still got a percentage thing, Theo?" She hung back to be closer to him. "*Urf.*"

"He doesn't at the moment." Archie translated. "He doesn't have the curse, so he isn't on a downward spiral—but the exhaustion and not sleeping has his level of . . . troublemaking up."

Sally wouldn't exactly call it troublemaking. Corpse-making, maybe. The last time he had gotten this bad, they were luckily in the midst of the System-created, and the carnage he wrought—although terrible—had been to their brief benefit. Theo-100 was something else: unrelenting carnage, unstoppable, and chaotic. His normal exhaustion still had some sensibilities to it; he was just bloodthirsty. Literally and figuratively.

"You could tell him to be less heavy," Humphrey grumbled.

"Aw, you could carry a truck, Humps. You're strong." He might not know what a truck was, but he perked up a little at the compliment. She turned to the demon. "How did all these tunnels get made?"

Lucius tilted his head back and forth in thought. "It's like . . . all the areas that had a System presence were shunted down beneath the surface. That is the best way I can describe it."

"Oh." Sally wrinkled her face and looked back and forward along their route. So it was either somewhere where Monsters spawned or a quest location or route, possibly. "That explains how the barbarians had a tunnel—it would take far too long to actually dig something like that out."

"Especially without the direction of a Unique," Humphrey added. "I assume a lot of System-created would have been too stubborn to move and perished completely under whatever ability the dragon has."

"Right on the money, Humphrey." Lucius had a thumbs-up emoji appear. "If you excuse the expression, of course."

"I will allow it."

If anything, this reveal just ruined Sally's mood further. She was already annoyed at the dragon for messing up so much of the Wastelands and her progression. Would this be what it would be like if someone evil became the new Architect—if that was possible? In the weeks since their apparent death, there had been nothing to show that the mantle had been picked up, and some of the System was still broken or full of errors.

It gave the slight possibility that she could still put that crown on her head—although, at this rate, it would be months before they even got to Level Fifty. By that time, anything could happen. Part of her still wanted to return to the real world, if that was even achievable. Part of her liked it here. But then, part of her was a Monster, so that checked out.

Lucius stopped at the front and waved his torch around a bit. "Hmm." A question mark bubble appeared. "That is new."

Sally squinted her eyes to see a ladder scaling the cavern wall. Across the rock, someone had painted a phrase—no, a sign—with an upward arrow, which read: Last Chance Saloon.

CHAPTER TWENTY-FOUR

Unquenchable

Sally rolled her eyes at the name of the supposed tavern above them. "That's a little cliché."

"I wonder how literal it is?" Humphrey rubbed his chin with his free hand.

It could just be some manner of trap. Though, a trap for who? Sally tilted her head at the ladder, which led up to a hole in the top of the cave. A brief hint of light could be seen at the edge. At this stage, anything would be preferable to wandering the boring caves for a minute longer. Even if it just led to more sunlight, a change of scenery would allow her brain a chance to refresh.

"Let's check it out, gang. There may be clues!" She hopped forward and began to climb up the ladder.

"Er, okay." Lucius shrugged. "I don't believe I know of this place."

Sally burst through the top, the slats of thick wood pinned into place through the rock as it emerged back into the outside world. The sun overhead burned at her eyes as she stumbled onto the sandy ground. As she turned, behind her sat a wide, wooden building. Dark wood planks and carved edges. A sign stood atop the swinging doorway, stating very simply, Saloon. Didn't even have the full name, so she rolled her eyes in contempt.

Archie hopped up beside her next, having ridden awkwardly across the Death Knight's face and shoulders. Humphrey came up next, a glower in his empty sockets as he hefted the limp vampire up beside him, dumping Theo unceremoniously onto the floor so that he could fully pull himself up.

"Hey, don't scuff the merchandise," Sally tutted.

Lucius was the last and didn't look too pleased at having to follow the large plated figure up—probably figuring he would be crushed if the Death Knight had fallen. The repeated sweat drop emojis followed along beside him until he collapsed on the hot earth and sighed.

"Well, that looks as advertised, I suppose." Humphrey tilted his head with a sigh. "It says they have rooms to let. Maybe I can try getting Theo to sleep."

"Like, wedge him between two beds like a sandwich?" Sally licked her lips. "My mouth is dry; I'll start drinking for clues at the bar."

Lucius remained on the floor like a pancake. "I may need a minute."

Archie hopped atop the demon's chest and began to alternate pawing on his cloak. "I'll keep Lucius company; we haven't had much chance to talk, anyway."

Sally snapped her fingers with a smile. "Alright—that almost sounds like a plan where we all know our places, and nothing can go wrong."

"Almost," Humphrey agreed, lifting the vampire back up with a grin.

Immediately, the shade of the overhanging upper floor was a delight, and the zombie paused at the swinging doors. Music could be heard inside—a piano if clichés were anything to go by. The low murmuring of voices accompanied it, and for a second, she was worried about whether it could be Players or Monsters in there. In the end, it didn't matter too greatly.

She pushed the doors wide and strode into the saloon, soon followed by the Death Knight. Just as she expected, aside from the piano, everyone in the room went silent and looked their way. She made the show of tipping a hat that she didn't have. Nothing quite like a good cliché.

Around twenty figures sat among groupings of tables and chairs. Even with a brief glance, she took the educated guess that these were mostly System-created Monsters—in that a few of them weren't humanoid. Straight ahead of them was the bar itself, where the barkeep stood cleaning out a glass. A wide mirror extended across the wall behind him, and the shelf just below it was stacked with mugs and tankards.

The barkeep himself was a slim man, tall and with a huge beard—almost excessively so. His tiny eyes sat behind large glasses, and his purple robe seemed more fitting for a mage than someone running a bar.

As the general chatter resumed, Sally stomped up to the counter and gave the man a nod. "Howdy. Ah, sorry—is that a bit reductive?"

"It's fine, little lady; we accept all types here." He gestured as if a wink followed that statement, but his eyes were too small for her to properly make out the action.

"Could we get a room for my buds here? Maybe a drink for myself?" She squinted at the taps on the other side of the bar, but none of them looked to be fresh Player-Brains flavor.

"Certainly, that'll be fifty gold for the room—and the first ale is on the house." He turned to grab a key for room number two and slid it across the counter for Humphrey.

"It's a medical thing." The Death Knight narrowed his eyes at the barkeep, who was staring at the bound vampire inquisitively.

"Of course. Name's Duncan, by the by." A small grin appeared from within the massive beard.

"Sally," Sally said. "You had this place long?" She watched Humphrey meander off to the staircase to attempt to put Theo to bed. A lot cuter said in her head than the visual reality of the situation, although she was glad she had gotten out of that duty.

"About a week, actually. It's a little refuge for those of us still around after . . . well, you're new to the area, correct?" He grabbed a mug and began filling it with some ale.

Sally wasn't much of a drinker, but she could hold it and look the part. "Yeah, couple of days, actually." She pulled a face. It seemed like forever that they had left the verdant greens and soft grasses of the first area.

"Don't get many new Uniques. Ruben either puts them to work, or the dust bowl takes them." He placed the filled mug in front of her. "Best keep your head down and don't invoke the ire of the tax collectors."

"Definitely." Sally nodded slowly, cupping the mug with a smile as Duncan moved away to talk to another patron. It would be like her to get into any trouble, of that she was sure. Discounting the times they had already killed Edward, of course.

She focused on the frothy liquid in front of her. There was zero desire in her heart, or her stomach, to actually drink it. It just seemed like the done thing to order up a beer or mead or whatever they drank in this world. Perhaps if she just stared at it long enough, it would either vanish or she would have an excuse to throw it at—

"Hey, you're pretty strong for a woman."

Slowly, her glare turned to meet the man who was now standing beside her, leaning against the wooden bar. He looked human but, for some reason, was not wearing a shirt. Undoubtedly to show off his six-pack and chiseled physique. His bright hazel eyes matched his trim haircut.

Her brow furrowed further. "What?"

"Sorry, I get tongue-tied. I meant you look strong, and you're a pretty woman." The man scrunched up his almost perfect face in awkwardness.

"That's barely any better; what do you want?" She was tired of the conversation already, but her glare bore into him.

"We just don't meet many Uniques. It's always good to get . . . acquainted." He pouted.

"No offense, but I'm more attracted to brains." She started to wonder where slaughtering the saloon occupants would fall on her morality scale. Surely it wouldn't matter if she didn't leave any witnesses.

The sound of shuffling, followed by a deep *thud*, came from the rooms above, knocking down a brief cloud of dust from the wooden planks across the ceiling.

"I'm not asking for much, just a little of your time. I can change, you know." He flexed his muscles and made the show of looking . . . cute? It came off more pathetic than anything.

Sally worked her jaw—both in frustration and in preparation for attempted violence. "You seem pretty misogynistic—and I'm guessing you're a werewolf?"

The man looked slightly taken aback but posed dramatically to show off his jawline. "Correct, but how did you guess?"

From above them, the continued sound of scraping wood was accompanied by a raised, deep voice.

Her eye twitched. "The smell of wet dog, for one. Also, you're a walking cliché. You literally disgust me. I can't believe you haven't gotten the hint yet. If you like, I can beat your skull in to leave the impression of my disdain on your barely functional brain."

"I . . . uh, perhaps we got off on the wrong foot. My name is—"

A hideous creak reverberated through the saloon, and the ceiling burst. Shattered wood and plumes of dust struck the middle of the floor, accompanied by the *thud* of half of a bed. A figure silhouetted in pure black, crimson electricity crackling across their body stood up from the wreckage.

Eyes of bright red scoured the room before resting on Sally and the werewolf.

"Where is he?" the vampire hissed.

The werewolf started to slide along the bar, away from her. "Is . . . is that your boyfriend?"

"Sure." Sally rolled her eyes. "Theo, what are you doing? Go to bed."

"I heard someone talking sssssssshittttt." His mouth opened wide, and his fangs caught the light despite the rest of him still being shrouded in darkness.

Loud stomping came from the staircase as a very annoyed Death Knight came back into the saloon proper, his own helmet blazing with red fire and a determined scowl across his empty skeletal face.

Whatever the werewolf was called, he now recoiled as far from the situation as possible—continuously making an *eep* sound as he did so.

Theo's head snapped to the doorway, and he ran toward it. Sally and Humphrey followed suit.

"Get back here!" the Death Knight growled, the slashed red cloak still in his hands.

The vampire made it through the doorway just before they did. Bursting through the door straight after, they almost slammed into the back of him as he had only stopped just beyond the porch, still under the awning.

"Too late. He was here, but we were too late, toolatetoolatetoolate." Theo held his head and growled, sinking to his knees as the other two looked ahead.

Where they had left the other two, Archie now sat encased in an ice cube. Lucius was gone.

CHAPTER TWENTY-FIVE

No Emotion

Panic and confusion washed over the zombie. "What the . . ."

Humphrey interrupted anything further that she could say as he pushed past and struck the cube of ice with his blazing sword.

It cracked and split, aided by the constant heat from the sun above. The cat jumped out as the two halves slid across the heated rock. Shivering and wet, he shook himself before turning to the Party.

"Hello."

"What happened?" Humphrey growled.

"Oh. It was Edward; he came and took Lucius." Archie continued shivering as he slowly warmed up.

Sally kicked up some dust. "But why? Just because we wouldn't give him some gold?"

"We wouldn't bend the knee," Theo slurred from behind them, still collapsed on the floor like a wet towel. He looked miserable and slack, as if the heat was sapping his energy away. "Dragon gonna get us. Gonna get ussss."

"Bed thing not a good idea, then?" She sighed at Humphrey with tired eyes. "Oh, what's this, Theo? A clue to Edward?" She pointed at the floor where Lucius had been laying previously.

The vampire crawled across the floor on all fours, dusting up his suit. He sniffed around the area indicated, where some dark crimson lay drying in the light. With a shaking finger, he scooped up the bloodied sand and stuck it in his mouth.

"I was about to say that is super gross," Sally said with a grimace, "but I've done that a few times, so who am I to judge?"

"No, you are correct," Archie said. "That *is* super gross."

Theo sat down and crossed his legs. Running his tongue around in his mouth with a furrowed brow, as if trying to taste it like a sommelier.

Sally rubbed her eyes, too tired for all this. "It's a good thing you guys came when you did. Otherwise, Theo would have had to fight a werewolf for my hand or something." She stuck her tongue out as if she were about to throw up. It was much cooler when Lucius emoted it.

"I'll kill him. Kill'em all. Haha." Theo nodded to himself, but his eyes remained glazed over as he thought.

"As fun as that would be . . .'" Humphrey sighed and scratched at the side of his head. "It's better we have some allies for the struggles ahead, right?"

Sally wasn't so sure. It did help them out in the fight for Sanctuary, but then the other two villages were mostly just her Party alongside whatever Uniques fancied becoming a Leader—if even they were combat-orientated. If their success depended on a narcissistic werewolf, then they had failed already. Maybe they should kill him now just to make sure that never came to pass. It always paid to not give fate the chance.

"I think this is . . . *blood*." Theo shrugged and laid back on the ground.

"Oh. I'm not sure what I was expecting, really." Sally exhaled. It's not like he was a tracking hound or even mentally stable currently. She drummed her fingers on her dagger sheath. Theo had known that Edward was nearby—like he did in Bordertown. There was some way he was able to be aware of his presence.

She walked over to him and crouched beside his head. "Hey, pup. Warm day out, huh? Did you know that *Edward* was a demon?"

"Yes." He remained impassive; his eyes closed.

"Didn't you want to kill all demons?"

He lay there for a handful of seconds in silence. Eventually, he opened his eyes and turned to her—slight confusion across his brow. "I killed . . . all demons?"

"You left *one*, pup. Just a single one."

"Fuuc—" He was silenced as the zombie put a finger on his lips.

"Language. First, he has taken our friend, who we need to save, and second, we need to locate where he is. Can you help with either without going crazy?" She removed her finger.

"It's possible." He frowned and rolled up to his feet as Sally stood too. "Or not impossible. Or plausible—but not—"

"Shhh. Or you have to be wrapped up again." She sighed. "Why does the saloon not have a coffin?"

Humphrey shrugged. "It's not exactly something that—*Theo!*"

The vampire had begun to jog away from them and slid across the sand to a stop, turning dramatically with eyes wide. "WHAT?"

"What did I *just* say?" Sally put her hands on her hips. This was getting ridiculous, like trying to train a naughty puppy. "Get back here." Putting him on a lead was out of the question; they already got enough weird looks as it was. Part of her was tempted to find out how long it'd take to learn carpentry and make their own place for him to sleep. Her own sanity was feeling the strain.

Archie sat preening himself, seemingly not too bothered about current events.

With a sudden flash of blue light, the familiar figure of Edward appeared atop the awning of the saloon, catching their glares immediately.

"Hello again, friends! I thought I best put a little distance between us so your pet bat doesn't attack me before I—"

Theo growled and ran toward the building in an attempt to climb up one of the supporting pillars.

Edward sighed. "I guess I should be quick, then. Kidnapped your boy, won't give him back until you meet our demands. The meeting place is the Eternal Sands, and—"

He vanished in another flash of blue as the vampire slid across the top of the awning to where he had stood, Theo almost tripping over the tiles. He paused and was tense, waiting just in case the demon suddenly reappeared.

"Well, that sucked." Sally rubbed her forehead. "He didn't say Lucius was at the meeting place, so that wasn't exactly too informative."

"Nor what the demands are," Humphrey agreed.

She watched the vampire twitch in place for a while. Although Lucius was a relatively fresh addition to their roster, they should still try to rescue him. The plot to grip at her heartstrings would have been more effective if Edward had taken Theo or Archie—but neither of them were easily contained. If anything, it was a shame there were no System-created around to have helped them get a teleport stone bound to the demon. Then they could just pop to the location and have fun.

Though, if Edward had any brains, then they'd be prepared for that. He hadn't shown much evidence of having any common sense—but perhaps it was just his inevitable nature that caused him to be lazy. If only he could . . .

"Theo, get down from the roof already!" She sighed and tapped her foot. This wasn't going to work. As she eyed up the Death Knight, he nodded in understanding.

It took a little coercion, but once they had coaxed the vampire down from the roof and over to them, Humphrey had pounced and wrapped him up. Sally knew part of Theo accepted and wanted it, as he didn't fight it as much as he was able to. If he really didn't want to be contained, he could turn into a flurried assault of crimson and light pink. But he did not, and now he was bundled upon the plated shoulder of the ex-Observer. Still had the look of annoyance in his eyes but was contented enough to stay.

She brushed her face and groaned. Where to even start? At least venting to some third party might help her aching mind.

> Sally: now my demon was stolen by the other demon
> Sally: all the problems coming to a boil
> Chuck: we got to eleven, but it's hard to find mobs
> Sally: noobs, we are level twelve

The STAR span closed, and she didn't wait for his response. There wasn't a great deal of point in harassing Chuck about things, but sometimes it was nice to expel some steam to an outside source rather than keeping it building around the Party.

On the map, it appeared that the meeting place was somewhat close to—but not quite in the direction of—the pyramid.

"Why can't they be narratively useful and put things in the same place?" she whined to the Death Knight, who was reading over her shoulder.

"It could have easily been in the opposite direction, so we are somewhat lucky." He shrugged.

Luck didn't seem to have much of a factor in it. Ever since stepping in the second area, she had felt cursed, and she would repeatedly complain about it until she escaped or things got better. Neither seemed currently likely.

She kneeled to give Archie some pets. "Do you know what kind of magic they used to break the weather?"

He purred briefly and then looked up into the sky. "Something big and bad. If it has been going on before the Archie-tect died, then that seems odd."

"Surely." She nodded, not quite understanding. If things were broken when the Architect was still in control, then they would have tried to fix it. Unless they couldn't? Lots of information far beyond their knowledge.

There were definitely a lot of missing puzzle pieces that they were trying to work with and guess at the intended final picture. It would be nice if there was just a reset button somewhere that could be pressed to bring about a proper weather system here—some rain or a nice cloud cover—even a dramatic storm would be lovely.

"So what's the plan, then? Just walk in that direction until something bad happens?" She folded her arms and looked between the two members of her Party who could actually talk.

They both shrugged in response, causing her to deflate. It may have to be something that rested on her shoulders. Time seemed to be ticking by as they stood out in the heat, frozen with indecision.

Finally, she threw up her hands with a sigh. "Let's ask around in the saloon; maybe someone in there has something useful between the ears. And the ceiling repair money is coming out of your counting stash, Theo!"

"*Hmmf bff.*"

CHAPTER TWENTY-SIX

Mist Already

Sally kicked through the saloon doors, one side snapping from the hinges and clattering to the floor.

"Alright," she yelled, "we need information! Also, Duncan, so sorry for all the property damage; let me pay you."

"No, no, that's quite alright!" The heavily bearded man behind the bar practically recoiled from the offer.

She shrugged and walked up to the bar, followed by the rest of the group. "Why not? I feel bad about it—even though it wasn't me. I mean, the door definitely was—I wouldn't lie to your face-beard so brazenly."

"If you give us a lot of gold, it'll draw the attention of the tax collectors."

"Oh. I mean, Edhead the Inquisitor was just here on the roof, actually." She looked up at the hole in the ceiling where one half of a bed was threatening to slide down into the saloon proper. Theo must have gotten his blades out and burst through as Humphrey was trying to sandwich him. She wished she could have seen that; it sounded hilarious.

"He was?" The beard quivered across his face, a shimmering curtain of differing browns. "Was he after you?"

Immediately, the atmosphere of the saloon dipped as all eyes were now on them.

Humphrey turned to face them, almost hitting the zombie in the head with Theo's wrapped up noggin as he spun. "Try it if you think you can; they will be peeling your remnants from the woodwork for days after."

The gathered oddities turned back to their own business, unable to meet his glare. As he turned again, Sally ducked the spinning vampire.

"No—well, he kidnapped our friend," she said with a sigh and leaned on the bar. It almost reminded her of the diner—if it was vaguely Western-themed instead of vaguely fifties-themed. "We just wanted some information or help so we can go rescue them."

She caught the side-eye of the werewolf hiding in the corner and trying to avoid the Party. "Hey, wolf-boy, come here. Here, boy." She patted the stool nearest them.

"You can ask around, but I'm not sure what most of us could do." Duncan shrugged and went back into some default routine of cleaning out a mug. "We don't carry much money, and most of us practically live here in fear of the goons taking us to work in the . . . mines."

Humphrey narrowed his empty eye sockets. "You say *mines* as though it was something other than what immediately comes to mind at the phrase."

"It's gold farming, essentially." The barkeep moved away from potential questions as the werewolf came and sat awkwardly beside them.

"How can I help you, my lady?" He grinned with perfect teeth but looked like he wanted to be anywhere else but here.

"First, I'm not your lady. I'm not really even *his* lady." She prodded a finger into Theo's wrapped legs.

"*Mmff.*"

"*Later.* Second, what is your name, and what do you do other than creep me out?" She crossed her arms and glared at him.

"My name is Barthelemy. I used to be the wealthy owner of a large estate here, but I was cursed to become a werewolf on the full moon."

Humphrey looked out the window. "Isn't it daytime 90 percent of the time here?"

Barthelemy puckered his lips and avoided answering.

Sally sighed. "So you must know the area, then? We need to get to the, uhh . . ."

"Eternal Sands," Archie interjected, curled up in the sunlight atop one of the empty tables.

"That's it. Yeah, we have no mounts and hate walking. Give me options here, furball. Not you, Archie." She waved off the glare of the ginger cat.

The man's mouth moved as if he had a few cheesy one-liners to spout, but part of his self-preservation kicked in and didn't allow any sound to come to fruition. "Ah. There's one place nearby—but it's not guaranteed."

"Spill it."

"There used to be a form of chariot racing, not too far from the massive expanse of land that I owned—and still do *technically.* Although it is mostly sand now, and—"

The zombie growled.

"Yes, as I was saying! Chariot racing—but they are powered by magic. There's a chance some may still be there and functional. But aside from that, there are no animals or beasts of burden left alive. Aside from yours truly, of course."

"*Mff bff mfmfm.*"

"Yeah, and that would be fun to watch, Theo—but you're staying there." She tilted her head and closed her eyes. If only things could be simple. "Humphrey, get the map location from our bud here. I need some fresh . . . some air that isn't so full of itself."

She slunk out of the saloon and sat in the shade of the awning against one of the walls. Some days the mania just couldn't even, and she felt tired of the constant stress and conflict. It wasn't fair that Lucius had been taken; he wasn't even a combatant, really.

With tired eyes, she spun the STAR around to bring up private messages and started writing to Dent.

Sally: We made it to the Wastelands.
Sally: It's garbage—did you see it before the sandstorm?
Sally: Would be nice to call in that favor, but I don't know what to ask for.

She paused and briefly wondered if the Swordsman was working for the dragon. They had made it sound like Players were forced to gather gold, so him being able to jump around the areas didn't seem plausible unless he had gotten those teleports before the constant sunshine had scoured away everything from the area.

After a few minutes, she closed the STAR. He wasn't dead yet; she was pretty sure that the System would decline to deliver the messages if he no longer existed. Perhaps he was knee-deep in his own peril. There was plenty to go around.

Humphrey pushed through the single door and once out into the open, turned to notice her sitting there. "I got the details, and then I had a little fun pointing Theo at the werewolf like a weapon."

"Thanks, Humps. That makes me feel a little better." She gave him a glum smile and tried to imagine the panic on the jerk's face.

"For a brief moment, you had us all back together." The Death Knight looked out to the barren wasteland as he spoke calmly. "Whatever you decide, we are with you."

"*Mrrf.*"

Humphrey shook the bound vampire. "We are *not* doing that."

Archie came strolling out and stretched his back, clawing at the dark wood. "Everyone okay?" He tilted his head, eyeing the Party up with his emerald eyes.

"Just struggling a little." Sally deflated. "We need to get to Lucius. We need to get Theo some sleep. We need to get your magical thing."

The cat sighed. "There is one thing I can try, but it will mean both Theo and I will be unavailable for an unknown amount of time."

Humphrey kneeled beside Archie. "How unknown are we talking? There's a stark difference between hours and months."

The response wasn't immediate, but eventually, the ginger cat relented. "Days. Could be one day, could be a week."

"It'll fix Theo, though?" Sally raised an eyebrow as she looked at the vampire.

"Yes and no. It could be as good as a long sleep. It could irreparably change him in unknown ways."

"This seems risky, Sally." The Death Knight exhaled. "Can he not survive a few more days as he is?"

"*Mgfg mfmfmmm.*"

Sally gasped as tears welled in her eyes. "That's . . . it's up to Theo. I know you're not in your right mind, but you have to accept what Archie is offering."

"*Mfbmm.*"

"You too, pup." She wiped her eyes with the back of her forearm. "Go ahead, Archie. How does this work?"

"No idea," the cat said with a smile. "Please put him down, big brother."

The Death Knight laid the vampire on the wooden floor and stepped back.

"Well, good luck." Archie looked up at them, a glimmer reflecting in his emerald eyes. "All things going to plan, we will *probably* see you again."

He opened his mouth, facing Theo. With a burst of energy, the cat evaporated into a radiant beam of light that briefly blinded the zombie. Archie spun around the prone form of the vampire, creating a casket made of magical light.

Just as the illusion had completed and Theo was fully entombed, they both vanished. A puff of ginger hair and magical energy fizzed through the air in the space left.

"What?" Sally felt lost for words. Except for the word *what.* "What?" she repeated.

Humphrey rubbed his chin, the scraping of metal echoing over the dull sounds of chatter from inside the saloon. "He has become a coffin in some manner and taken Theo to someplace in the System where they can be in stasis in this form."

"Really?" Sally stood on her feet shakily, now the proud owner of two words.

"Yes. That is my best approximation. It may not be the sleep that he requires, and they may not exist in that space without issue—but without other options, it is a good chance."

"Ass." Sally scratched her head. In some ways, it was a weight off her shoulders—now just her and Humphrey again. It was easier to focus on their tasks at hand and push forward. It was also double as worrying not to know where the pair were or what would happen to them. Plus, with Lucius being kidnapped, their Party was just down to two *again.*

"Classic Sally and Humphrey adventure?" The Death Knight grinned.

"I don't think our classic adventures were this messed up." She sighed and leaned against the plated figure.

"I know. But you want to have an undead dragon mount, right?"

"Even better than that," she said as she closed her eyes. "I want to fix this area to be fair for everyone."

"Classic adventure." Humphrey nodded, his helmet flames flickering.

CHAPTER TWENTY-SEVEN

Throwing Shade

The only thing more miserable than stomping away on the dried plains of the Wastelands was doing it without all your friends. Actually, Sally could think of several more miserable things than that. Or rather, she could have if the constant sunshine wasn't melting through her skull and threatening to turn her head in a cauldron of soupy brains.

"You know," she gasped, "I was never much of a hat gal, but perhaps I should carry one, just for these sorts of situations."

"Yes. Try being made out of metal." Humphrey lowered his gaze to the zombie and sighed. "Apologies. This was perhaps an ill-thought-out plan."

"All our plans are." She shrugged in response. If they had good plans that made sense, they'd probably be too sensible and safe, and they'd be back in that luscious and cool forest. Oh, how she missed it.

She missed Theo and Archie already too. It had seemed a bit extreme to take them both into some other . . . plane? Humphrey couldn't quite explain it, but she assumed it was something beyond normal space—like Henkk's ability. Theo had seemed manageable—but if they had to struggle through this overbearing heat, then it probably would have made him worse. Especially if salvation was days away.

A reflection of the previous day, it was now just her and Humphrey again. At least she knew where everyone was this time, to some degree. With a huge sigh, she at least relented to the fact that things couldn't get much worse.

Destiny appeared to be listening in on her inner monologue. With a sudden flash of blue, Edward appeared slightly ahead of them.

"Hello, friends!"

"What do you want?" She scowled, the pair of them not even bothering to draw their weapons.

Edward gave an exaggerated bow. "I learned recently that you came into quite the sum of gold and wondered if you'd like to make a donation of—"

"No!" Sally growled at him. "Give me a good reason to! You just kidnapped our friend!"

"Ah—apologies. That is an entirely different business matter." He shrugged and looked out at the distant roving plains. "You are going in the wrong direction, though."

She glared at him as she opened up the map. "Shit. Humps—we've been curving to the left."

"Neither of you look too well." Edward's face fell. "Is this the best option for you? Where are the other two from your Party?"

"They are currently not a large, super-heated, and furious titan of metal with a sharp weapon." Humphrey's helmet fire blazed higher. "So consider your intentions here."

"It's not my intention to . . ." The demon paused and furrowed his brow. "I've never met Uniques so headstrong. Even most Players give up by this point. What is it that drives you?"

"Spite." Sally stood and stretched her back out. "What drives you to vacuum up other people's hard-earned money for the dragon?"

For a moment, Edward paused, his tongue rolling around inside his mouth. With tiredness hitting his eyes, he shrugged. "I have my reasons—that is beyond the point."

"Can we just buy Lucius back? Or a way to kill Ruben?" She was sweating, or at least she hoped it was sweat—the usual antics hadn't prompted her body to fulfill the necessity on account of her being undead.

"That you would suggest the latter shows how little you truly know." The demon deflated slightly but turned to rub his chin. "As for the former—keep me company for a while, and I will see what I can do."

"You want our company?" Humphrey twitched his plated hand in readiness to draw his blade.

Edward turned back to them with a grin. "I may be a pawn of the dragon, but the whole organization is full of bores. If it weren't for my . . . employment, I wouldn't care to spend a second in their presence."

"Get us some shade, and you have a deal." Sally narrowed her eyes at him. As a demon, he probably had no issue with sitting about in the constant heat, but if he could provide them some brief relief from the oppressive overhead sun—then that'd earn him a stay of her wanton violence.

He snapped his fingers and then withdrew something from his pocket. With a quick flick of his hand, it struck the dried stone and burst up into a handful of deck chairs beneath an oversized parasol.

"It only lasts fifteen minutes," he said as he again bowed, "but that should quench both our desires."

Sally immediately went and collapsed into the shade, lying face down on the deck chair to absorb any mote of cool that was available. Humphrey tested the chair to see if it'd take his weight and was surprised to see it did. He sat with hands on his knees and deflated with a sigh.

Edward hopped onto a third one and laid down, sunglasses coming from nowhere and falling over his eyes. "I'll admit it's nice to relax once in a while."

"You know," Sally began, turning slowly to glare at the demon, "it's hard for us to be friends when you have taken Lucius away."

"I never considered the possibility of us being friends." Edward idly tapped on his long leg. "So much bloodshed."

She shrugged in response. "We can let that slide—we very much live in the present rather than hold grudges."

"Really? Your vampire friend doesn't seem so keen on me."

That was true, and partially it had something to do with his sleepless mania. There was another thing there too that she wasn't too sure about. Theo could sense Edward, and his desire to kill all demons had sprung from that—but why didn't he like this particular demon?

"He isn't normally like that; it's a curse thing." She frowned and swung her legs around so she could sit and glare at Edward properly. "But there is something odd about you, more than just being a jerk."

He raised his eyebrows and tried to read her face. It was hard to see what he was doing behind the sunglasses, but any retort did not come immediately. Eventually, he sighed and sunk into the deck chair to look upward.

"Do you always attempt to disarm your opponents by being so affable?"

"I hardly ever *aff* people, and you're the one that wanted our company. You can see it, though, can't you, Edward?" She grinned wildly.

"I see nothing, zombie girl."

"Fine, whenever you're ready, let us know. But until you give Lucius back, you're in the top five of our bad guy list."

He was deflecting, but she could see it clear as day. The demon was in some kind of bind and wanted out of whatever job he had with the dragon. There was no way he would admit it to her, but he saw them as the key to unlocking those chains. If nothing else, the *Outsiders* were a wrecking ball for the System—and if he had gotten a whiff of what they had achieved in the forest, then perhaps it had sparked the hope that they could do the same in the Wastes.

"Flattered," he said, the hint of a wry smile on his face. "Even if I had the desire to give you the demon back, I cannot. He is not my prisoner; I was just the messenger."

Humphrey grunted. "A terrible one. You told us neither the conditions of his release nor exactly where he was being held."

"In fairness . . ." Edward held a finger in the air. "I was avoiding getting cored by the vampire for a third time. Dying isn't pleasant, even if I can come back from it."

Sally desperately wanted to ask how he managed that—but perhaps his Unique glitch was maintaining the ability to respawn that the System-created had. More important was the information on Lucius. "Spill it now, Edward."

He opened his mouth as if to protest, but the use of his proper name softened his response. "Eternal Sands has a dungeon; he is being held there. The intention is you'll die in the attempt or survive by a thread and have no option but to join alongside Ruben."

She bit her tongue at how much information he was willing to divulge. It was briefly surprising. "What does Ruben want?"

"Gold." Edward sat up and removed his sunglasses, turning his burning blue eyes toward her. "Dragons get more powerful the more gold they have; he wants to ascend past the Wastelands. Rule the world and all that boring stuff."

She nodded. It made some degree of sense—motivations aside, Players wanted to gather strength and move on, so it wasn't a stretch to imagine a powerful dragon would feel that they could do the same thing.

"Though . . ." Edward stood and brushed his lavender suit down. "Now that I have told you this, I *will* need to kill you."

Sally stood too, but she didn't believe him. Well, he was slowly drawing his sword—but there was no anger or malicious intent in his eyes. She frowned as she tried to read him.

"Better not loot my corpse after this, either." He gave them a grim smile. "Now perish."

He swung out with his sword, but Humphrey was already there—having leaped over the deck chairs to block the attack aimed at the zombie.

With a flash of crimson, he scored a deep gash across the demon's chest—blood spraying over the unarmed Sally.

[Eat Brains]

Edward's emptied body dropped to the floor, spilling more demonic blood among the small area of shade.

"Oh no!" She looked at her marred hands. "I did that by reflex; I feel kinda bad."

"Don't worry," Humphrey said as he grinned. "I'm sure he felt worse."

CHAPTER TWENTY-EIGHT

Split Apart

Sally wiped the rest of the gore from her mouth. "I hope that doesn't hamper his ability to come back."

Humphrey sighed and looked out at the expansive plains beyond their brief shade. "You don't have to befriend every walking oddity we meet, you know?"

She scowled at him and kneeled by the body of the dead demon. "I most definitely do, Humps. That's like my whole shtick. Bringing the whole System together like friendly glue. Or clumps of viscera." Wiping her hands off on Edward's suit, she began to rifle through his Inventory.

"I thought it was *destroy the System*—or *eat the Architect. Make the System fair.* What exactly was your mission objective?"

"Don't . . ." She glared up at the Death Knight. "Don't you start having a *Theo moment.* I'm hot and bothered, too, but I'm not being an ass about it."

"You just ate that man's brain."

"It was an *accident.*" Sally rolled her eyes.

Humphrey ground his teeth together but then sighed. "What does he have on him, then?"

"Well, for some reason, I can loot his underwear—but I think he probably wanted us to take *[Water]* and *[Summer Hat].* There's five of each, how thoughtful."

"I'm not wearing a . . ." He paused as the deck chairs and parasol vanished, and they were again blasted by the unrelenting heat. "Okay, pass one here."

Sally hummed to herself. She felt a little better that she had eroded at the evil of Edward. Generally, she had a good read on people, and as annoying as he constantly was, he was mostly unthreatening. That they had killed him in one strike each time proved this fact. He must be pretty miserable to end up coming to them for a slice of solace.

She put her hat on—a wide-brimmed straw bonnet with a red ribbon around it and passed the Death Knight one similar to hers that had a purple band. "Why'd he attack, though? Under observation?"

Humphrey sighed again as he popped his hat on, somehow avoiding his helmet-flames burning through the item. "Yes, most likely. It would be odd for him to be seen fraternizing with those he is attempting to extort."

"Huh." Sally tilted her head and gestured for them to continue their journey. "People sure are complicated, aren't they?"

"Back so soon, Edward?"

The demon rolled his eyes. "Have you ever had to fight someone to the death?"

"No."

"Well, let me tell you—it's usually a fifty-fifty thing. That new Party is one of the more powerful ones I've had the displeasure of dealing with."

The shadowed figure turned to eye him lazily. "But will they help Ruben?"

"In time." Edward shook his head. "They are quite cold but have a weakness for their Party members—with one of them kidnapped away in the dungeon, it's only a matter—"

"It will be *inevitable*, I'm sure, Edward." The man turned back to the ledger. "They could be what we need to push productivity up 3 percent for the following weeks. Do not mess this up, or the case will be reassigned. You have two days."

The demon gave a low bow and turned for the doorway, a scowl dominating his face.

"And then she said—*pancakes*! Ha!" Sally beamed at the Death Knight.

Humphrey glared down at her from beneath the sun hat. "I'm not sure I understand the joke; perhaps there is a—"

"*Never mind.*" She pouted out toward the emptiness before them. The hat and water definitely helped, but the journey was still a slog.

Her STAR *bloiped*, and she lifted her arm to see the private message.

Dent: Wastelands pretty bad.
Dent: I'm . . . I can't say.
Dent: Stay safe, stay away from the dragon.
Dent: Will be in touch.

"That Swordmaster is still in the Wastes—though if Ruben is forcing everyone to stay put . . . it didn't sound like he was working for the dragon, though." She idly tapped on her arm before lowering it.

"Sounds . . ." Humphrey paused and furrowed his brow. Slowly, he reached for his sword—and then gravity took them both.

The area of sandy rock they were walking across collapsed inward to a hollow area shrouded in darkness. A waterfall of warm sand poured down around the rough circle of light above as the pair extracted themselves from the debris.

"*Blech.*" Sally spat out a mouthful of dry rock. She dusted down her clothes and looked around. "Seems we found a tunnel system."

"Yes." Humphrey righted himself, picking his summer hat from the floor and placing it back on his helmet. "*Joy.*"

"At least it is cooler—and as long as it is heading in the right direction, it'll make traveling easier."

"What about when it changes direction? We can't exactly dig upward." The Death Knight glared into the darkness surrounding them. He turned to see the zombie had already started off down one of the passageways. With a sigh, he followed.

"You worry too much, Humps." She turned with a grin that quickly vanished. The Death Knight was no longer behind her.

Humphrey scratched his chin; he was sure he had seen the zombie just ahead of him a moment ago.

A giggling noise off to the left caught his attention.

Humphrey: What are you doing?
Sally: walking, where r u?
Humphrey: I was right behind you.

She looked up from the STAR. The amber light pooling down from where the roof had collapsed was still very visible—yet no sign of the Death Knight.

Sally: something foul is a feet
Sally: afoot*
Humphrey: Continue with caution?
Sally: yes

With a sigh, she drew her bat. Just what she needed—to be alone. Even at the start of the adventure, it hadn't been this way. Humphrey was there from the moment she awoke. The thought brought back memories of the diner—and that of her life from before. Archie said they came here through magic but was unable to elaborate further, even when pestered after he got his voice back.

A great wizard that made a video-game-esque world and populated it with young people from her world, wiping their memories . . . for what? It seemed egotistical and short-sighted. Although, she did imagine a great wizard would be those things. Did her previous life still exist, or was the old her dead? If she could return to that life, she wouldn't be half zombie, surely. So what would happen?

The odd caverns had dulled her mood. She almost wished she was back up, trudging through the bland, hot sand and constant sunlight. At least she still had Humphrey back in those days. How long had it been? Days? Years? Bringing up the STAR, she checked the timestamps on the chat logs. Oh, just two minutes.

There was still an odd feeling to it. Like the Death Knight was still around her somewhere; she just couldn't see him. Eyes narrowed, she took the bat and spun around in a quick circle with it extended. She completed the movement without any interruption, the crackling of critical energy along the edge of the bat the only sound. It dissipated, and she wondered where crits had been before this.

Perhaps it was part of how the forest area was supposed to have more realism, and now more game effects were in the Wastelands. Maybe they would appear randomly, outside of skills or magical items. She found it hard to grasp on to some reason to care about them.

With an exhaled sigh, she deflated and continued.

A slight corner bore nothing but more tunnels—although something didn't feel quite right. She kneeled and checked the ground. The dust had been disturbed at some point, and there were multiple sets of footprints. That's about where her detective skills ended, but one of the tracks did look suspiciously like the large plated boots of the Death Knight.

She took another dozen steps and then froze as something caused the hair to prickle along the back of her neck. With her off hand, she slowly withdrew her [*Dagger of Luck*].

One farther step forward, and then the walls collapsed ahead of her. No— it wasn't the walls; there were figures camouflaged in dark brown and gray to blend into the cavern. Six of them rolled out into her path and raised repeating crossbows.

Sally opened her mouth as their fingers clicked the triggers.

Humphrey furrowed his brow as he ground his metallic teeth together. As Sally's bodyguard—as far as the System was concerned—he could tell she was in danger. Being her close friend, he believed he had such a sense of trouble when it came to her naturally, even without the process of her being his boss.

But he just couldn't see her. Even if he concentrated, there wasn't even the barest shuffle of sound anywhere else down this tunnel. It was infuriating—yet he did not believe this was the work of magic or any monstrous group.

The part of him that still held a grasp on being an Observer could feel the pains of the System. Whatever strain the dragon had put on the workings of this area had effects that he couldn't quite explain. Things had been strange—but still made sense in some twisted way. This current situation did not, and if his experience told him anything . . .

This would just be the start.

Growling to himself, he continued onward, the flames from his helmet illuminating his path.

CHAPTER TWENTY-NINE

Less Than the Whole

Several bolts slammed into Sally as all six figures opened fire. After the first volley, they paused.

"*Ow*," she grunted in response, pulling one from her shoulder. "That's not too nice."

Not that she wasn't hurting from the assault, but her armor had managed to absorb most of the damage and even deflect a couple of the bolts. Again, this must be the System becoming more game-like in this area. If that were to happen in the forest area—well, six bolts would probably have killed her or at least put her in a terrible situation.

They raised their weapons again to fire once more.

"*Ah-ah.*" She held up a hand and wagged a finger. "I'm giving you a chance to give up before I kill you all." She grinned as her eyes blazed crimson. Maybe eating a few brains would cheer her up.

One of the figures in the center brought down the cover from their face to reveal a woman with tan skin and deep brown hair tied up in a bun. "Who or *what* are you?" she asked, her tone apprehensive but stern.

"Tired and hungry. And Sally," she added. "The other way around. Uh. Are you . . . Players?" She narrowed her eyes in return—the woman didn't look like a Unique.

"We are. You . . . seem like you are too? My name is Lana." She lowered her weapon, but the other five did not.

Sally's eye twitched. Player brains would be even nicer to consume—plus that was extra stats depending on what class they were—most likely advanced classes by now. She wiped the drool from her mouth. "I'm a bit of a mixed bag. The System broke me—half Monster, half Player. Super friendly, though, unless you want to try to fill me with more bolts." She hoped they did.

"That sounds . . . unfortunate." Lana narrowed her eyes and didn't seem to know what to make of the zombie. "You've made it this far, though . . . alone?"

"Not alone. I have an equally odd Party, but their whereabouts are a bit of a long story." As much as she enjoyed talking, finding at least Humphrey was top of her priority list. Right after potentially eating six brains.

One of the cloaked figures moved to whisper into Lana's ear, and she nodded to them. "If you were traveling with a Death Knight, then he is in one of the fractured tunnels."

"Fractured tunnels?" she repeated, half expecting the obvious answer based on the name.

"The System is a bit . . . fucky." Lana shrugged. "Especially down in some of these tunnels where everything has been forced underground." She paused and wrinkled up her nose. "Say, you're not working for the dragon, are you?"

"Far from it." Sally shook her head. "Want to eat him or turn him into a mount, hopefully."

"Okay. That seems unlikely, yet I fully believe that is your intent." Lana shrugged. "Some of the tunnels, the System errored when trying to place them— that is my assumption—and they have been fractured into . . . different planes of reality, if that makes sense?"

Sally looked around. Mostly, she wondered why the group of six had been hiding in the wall to jump out and surprise her—that seemed like an odd thing to do since she was down here randomly. It was suspicious, in fact. But there was something else that she could almost . . . taste in the air.

"It does make sense," she eventually concluded. "So why are you . . . all of *you*, down here lying in wait?"

Lana narrowed her eyes at the choice of phrasing. "I get a notion when someone is down here."

"All of you?" Sally grinned and wagged her eyebrows.

The woman sighed in response and rubbed her face. "Smart little shit, aren't you?" Resigning to the reveal, she gestured for the group to lower their disguises.

One after another, the dark clothing used to blend into the cavern was removed to reveal—they were all Lana.

"Neat." Sally nodded. "So you glitched through the tunnels in certain ways, and the System duplicated you?" That seemed super odd for a Player, but who was she to talk?

"Something to that effect." Lana hooked her crossbow to her belt and crossed her arms. "They are me, but they're not me—I'm the one with the soul, still. If that's what you call it."

A couple of glares from the other Lanas gave the hint that they might not all believe that, but the woman continued.

"It's not all great—my effective power is actually split. As one Lana, I would be Level Sixteen, but as six, I'm—well, it's about Level Five or Six, I reckon."

"Aw." Sally pouted. She had hoped that absorbing all those attacks was because of how useful her new armor was, not because her opponent was weak. Still, crossbow bolts had proved pretty fatal regardless of level, so maybe she shouldn't be so sad. "Oh!" Her train of thought switched tracks. "Does that mean my friend might duplicate?"

"Based on his current travel route . . ." She closed her eyes to focus on something. "No."

"Are you in a Party of all your clones? Oh, but there's six of you."

"We figured that it wouldn't be fair to exclude one of us, so no."

Sally licked her lips. "I could help with that."

"You have a free space in your Party?" Lana tilted her head.

Free space in my stomach. Sally grinned to herself. Although it might not be polite to ask to eat your new friend's clone. Even if it was a spare one. Or at least the one not currently in charge. She briefly considered if the talking Lana was a decoy and the real one sat to the side to observe with less personal danger. That would be smart. Shame they had just taken on Lucius, otherwise she would adopt one of the Lana clones.

"No," she eventually relented. "Part of my long story is me and Big Boots were heading to the Eternal Sands dungeon to rescue a friend that the tax collector kidnapped."

Lana nodded. "Sounds like a Player thing to do. You didn't seem like much of a hero on account of being . . . what I assume is a zombie? Do you eat brains?"

Sally narrowed her eyes. Not that she had the moral high ground or anything, but if the woman turned on her because of her penchant for consuming smart Jell-O then—well, Lana was pretty weak. It would make for a short meal, but perhaps then she would become lost and unable to find Humphrey.

"*Some.* Usually just Monsters. A handful of Players have taken offense to my existence, and I've had to defend myself." She shrugged. That was mostly the truth.

"Defend yourself by eating their brains?"

"Waste not, want not. They clearly weren't using them." She grinned and crossed her arms. "Look, at the start, my desire was for wanton destruction of the System—eat everything that opposed me. But in finding my friends and how the System truly was, I became a bit more nuanced in what I chose to consume. It's still pretty evil to eat Player brains, but I give them a chance to be friends or run away." *Usually,* she added inside her head.

"Like you are with me?" Lana tapped her foot and smiled.

"You shot me first. I'd be well within my rights." Sally grinned to show off her sharp teeth.

"Fair." The woman turned and looked farther down in the tunnel. "Been awhile since I've had someone . . . else to talk to, to be honest. You said there was just you and your one friend?"

"Yeah, why?" Sally furrowed her brow.

"Something else is approaching the Death Knight."

Humphrey exhaled through his nose. Or, at least, the holes where his nose would be if he didn't have a skeletal face. The pang of danger sense had faded, so whatever had threatened Sally was no longer an issue. Whether that meant she had killed it or befriended it—no, it was much more likely that she had made friends with whatever it was.

Briefly, he considered how she had that effect on people. He supposed that since she was a half-human Player and half-zombie Monster, she could see both sides of the coin. Either something was a threat, or if not, then why not get along? Plated fingers ground across his chin. He didn't quite see it that way, but it had worked out well for them so far.

If they could ally up with Edward, or at least find a way to stop him from annoying them constantly, then . . .

The Death Knight paused and turned slowly.

Shadows and rock. His grip tensed on the handle of the greatsword. Humphrey knew when something was afoot. But this wasn't just a demon to bug him for loose change. The air had cooled in anticipation of the reveal.

"Show yourself," he growled out, his deep voice carrying down into the pitch-black of the cavern.

Three eyes of burning green energy popped up among the shadows, a good dozen feet in the air.

<Why? What will you do once you see me?>

The voice carried like the wind yet coursed through the Death Knight's hearing like sandpaper. He winced and leveled his blade in preparation.

"Depends. Are you friend or foe?" He was not as good as Sally at the small talk and could feel the imminent fight looming his way already.

<Oh-ho-ho>

The eyes came closer, as the radiant crimson pulsing from the Death Knight began to illuminate the massive shape of a creature that shouldn't exist. A horror beyond comprehension sent a chill down Humphrey's spine. As a wide maw filled with hundreds of reflective teeth caught the bloodied light filling the area, he spoke again.

<I am much worse than both, Humphrey.>

CHAPTER THIRTY

Soloed It

an you take me to him?" Sally's eyes searched the face of the main Lana.

The woman held a hand over her eyes and turned to the side as if she was trying to think—or perhaps read something only she could see or understand.

Sally tapped her foot on the floor as the woman thought. "Lana? . . . Laaaanaaa?"

The cloned woman tensed up and turned back to the zombie with a glare. "*What?*"

"Can you take me to him or not? I feel as though he is in some manner of danger. Like an entire *area* of it—if you will." She grinned to herself, wishing Theo was here.

"I can, but it will take time." Lana deflated. "Things have to be crossed in a certain order, and—"

"I won't get cloned, will I?" Sally interrupted, screwing her face up. There were definitely some things that would be more fun with a body double, but the prospect of being weaker, to any degree, put her off more than anything.

"Unlikely—again, it's only certain movements that can do that." With a nod to her fellow clones, she gestured for Sally to follow. "Come on, we will get there as fast as I am able."

With grim determination, she returned the nod and jogged after the Lana group.

Humphrey slid backward across the dusty ground and dropped to one knee. He raised his empty sockets to see one of his Skeletal Warriors get ground into dust beneath a large foot.

The Death Knight growled as he stood, the tears in his plated armor vibrant silver in contrast to the dark crimson of the outer parts. His helmet flame flickered wildly, as if fighting not to be put to rest.

<Do you see now the futility? This is what will come to pass.>

"I cannot allow it," Humphrey hissed, leveling his greatsword into a defensive stance. "It ends here."

<Ho-ho-ho. Something certainly will, Humphrey.>

With a burst of energy, he ran forth toward the waiting maw, activating his keystone ability.

[Endless Knight]

"What do you do for food down here? Or water? Do you just sleep on the floor? Do you usually just shoot visitors? What's your endgame plan with this setup?" Sally barraged the woman with questions. More out of worry than needing to know.

"Could you *please?*" the main Lana growled, as the rest rubbed at their respective temples.

The zombie closed her mouth. She had been away from Humphrey for long periods before—usually when adventuring with Theo or sleeping—but now he wasn't even responding to her messages. As much as she annoyed him, he wouldn't leave her worrying.

"You said there was someone else. Do you know what?"

Lana shot her another glare but then softened at seeing the expression on the zombie's face. "Some kind of enormous Monster—I imagine it was something Unique to have wandered down here this far. They are usually allied with the dragon, but . . ."

They ran in silence for a handful of seconds before she continued.

"But something was odd. Nothing I can really explain—but it was overwhelming, in a way. Trouble with a capital *T.*"

Sally knew when things started to require proper grammar, then it was important. Especially when it came to nouns. Humphrey was pretty tough, though—the most defensively proficient out of all of them. If anyone could hold out against an unknown assailant, then she'd bet all her chips on him.

That didn't stop her from worrying. They were a Party, after all—and part of their ridiculous strength was being together and supporting each other. Of course, that was going *super well*. A sour expression crossed her face. With Theo and Archie in some nether space, and Lucius kidnapped—with Humphrey gone, things seemed to crumble apart again.

They took a right turn and then, after a while, a left. Lana and her group of Lanas then stopped, and the real one put her hand on the wall and closed her eyes.

Sally said nothing, a rarity in times of quiet. In truth, the running had tired her out a little more than she had expected, and combined with the lack of Player brains in her stomach, she felt a little ill. Nerves rarely got the best of her, but she tried to draw focus away from inner turmoil to stare at the back of the round cranium of the other woman.

"Alright," Lana said, turning. "We go back now."

Sally sighed and made to jog behind the group once more. It looked as though the planes of . . . reality? If that's what you could even call it. They shifted on a schedule, and the Death Knight must have been split from her as they crossed over the junction as it changed destination. *That was surprisingly smart*, she thought; she should use her brain more often.

"There are three splits there," Lana called back, a little out of breath herself. "You went on number one, and your friend went number two."

With a wide grin, the zombie struggled to keep the giggles to herself. Things may be serious—but the Death Knight would have appreciated the joke. Probably not, actually, but Theo would have. Perhaps not in his current condition . . . she sighed again.

The tunnel turned slightly to the left; the curve blocking off her sight farther down—until they came across it.

Sally gasped.

Humphrey was kneeling, his sword planted into the ground before him. A tiny flame, no more than what a candle would emit, was wavering slowly from the back of his helmet. His armor had been pierced straight through, and several places had wide and deep gashes, exposing bright silver metal within. He didn't acknowledge the newcomers.

She ran toward him. "Humphrey!" Dirt had been moved around—there were also gashes in the stone, crushed skeletons, and dark patches of something akin to blood. All blurred in her vision as her eyes filled with tears.

With her feet sliding to a stop, she immediately opened up her Inventory to withdraw a Healing Potion and poured it into his open skeletal maw. Part of the magical liquid dripped from the open gaps in his armor—but most seemed to settle.

Gradually, the flames at the back of his helmet grew a little brighter, and he lifted his head to observe her.

"Humps!" she called again and wrapped her arms around his plated form, her shirt catching on some of the twisted metal parts of his armor.

"Good to see you again, Sally." He sighed warmly. "I wasn't planning on dying here. I was just resting my eyes."

"My ass," she said, stepping back and giving him a light punch on the shoulder. "Couldn't go ten minutes without me before you fell apart."

"Yes, *ha-ha*."

She wiped her eyes with the back of her arm. "So, you wanna tell me what happened here?"

"Not particularly. It is safe to say that I won. Could we not leave it at that?"

Sally looked back at Lana, who was investigating the aftermath of the fight, and put her hands on her hips. She gave the Death Knight her best scowl. "No—we cannot. I've just been worried about you, and you almost died; we need to know what it was, surely."

Humphrey slowly stood, his right leg shaking as he tried to put weight on it. Eventually, he straightened up fully and placed his sword over his shoulders. He looked over the zombie's head to look at the group of women inspecting the area.

"New friend already?"

"She is pretty weak but knows that these tunnels are wonky. Like—the System has split them into different paths. Fragments of different planes? You know, like Henkk's stuff?"

"Hmm." The Death Knight tilted his head, absorbing this information. Already, some of his holes and gashes had begun to slowly bend back into their right places.

"Don't change the subject, though." She jabbed a finger at his chest.

"She is one Player? All of them?"

"Yeah. She found a way through the split paths that somehow also split her. There's the main one, and then clones—but each time, it lowers her power, like it is shared between them to a degree."

Humphrey nodded. "And you didn't ask to be duplicated?"

"Could you imagine two of me running amok?" She smirked and crossed her arms. "The System wouldn't know what hit it. I'm not really interested in being less powerful, though, only *more*. Much more." She cast her eyes back to the ruined cavern and then growled at the Death Knight again. "Why won't you tell me?"

He shrugged. "Why must you know? If it is not something easily given, then there must be a reason. You trust me, correct?"

Her mouth opened and then closed. *Dick move.* Certainly, she trusted him more than anyone—even Theo. But it made little sense that he couldn't tell her what he had seen and had to fight—there's no Monster that could be that bad. Plus, now that they were together, a second one would be no issue. Plus, plus, if he had defeated the creature, then the trouble with a lowercase *t* should be in the past now.

"I trust you," she relented. "If you can't tell me, that is okay—but you know I'm here for you if you ever feel you can, right?"

"Yes." He grinned.

"Hey, uh?" Lana waved a hand over to them to get their attention. They turned to see her crouched by the wall, hands on her knees, with her nose wrinkled up.

"Why is there so much ginger fur here?"

CHAPTER THIRTY-ONE

Dungeon Fun

Sally walked along with her arms folded. A scowl leveled at the wall.

Humphrey slowly regenerated, his armor gradually repairing himself as his health rose.

Lana and her clones awkwardly followed along behind them, not wanting to be part of the argument.

The pathway ahead of them hadn't changed much. It was still just a dim tunnel, roughly circular, but with a flat floor. It was dusty, dry, and drab. The zombie sighed. "I just don't know why you can't tell me if it was Archie or not."

"I've already told you it wasn't."

"But you're *lying*," she growled. Her eyes flared crimson, and she glared at him. "I can read you like a book, Humphrey."

"Then you should know that I do not want to tell you for your own good." He looked down at her, his face impassive.

"Pah." Sally deflated. She could definitely see he was being stubborn. It wasn't like him to be so tight-lipped about something like that, though. The claw marks were huge, and although she was sure there were other Monsters in the world with ginger fur . . . it was all too convenient. His silence told her more than his stupid skeletal face did.

"There should be an exit coming up soon," Lana offered from the back, hoping to change the conversation.

Helmet flames flickered wildly, and Humphrey leveled a finger forward. "I disagree."

They stopped and stared ahead. Just beyond the gloom, only just coming into their view, was a dead end.

Lana ran forward to get a better look before slowing to a stop. "That's not right . . ." She turned back around, her confusion melting straight into worry.

Sally and Humphrey both turned around to look behind them—to see it was a dead end too.

"Huh." The zombie shrugged. "Hope you brought a shovel, Humps."

"I have no Inventory to store garbage." He grinned as she glared at him.

"No, no, no, no, this shouldn't be happening." Lana walked back toward them, hands over her eyes. "We went the correct route . . ."

"At least we can just go back to Sanctuary." Sally shrugged. "We aren't going to die here." She pressed her STAR in preparation, and it just returned a flicker of light—nothing further happened. "Ah."

"The floor isn't supposed to be this soft, I imagine." Humphrey made a show of moving his plated boots up and down as the rock beneath him bent and squished like it was made of cake.

"Shit." Sally frowned, glancing over to Lana for advice—to which the woman just responded with a panicked shrug. The System seemed to be melting away.

Out of Bounds Warning

"Oh, hey, System messages—neat." Sally's eyes widened as the message blared into her pupils.

Players Stuck - Reconfiguring
Locating Appropriate Landmark
[Searching . . .]

"What's this, Humps?" She grimaced at the thought of the System trying to fix something large and wholesale like her position within it. It might look too closely and realize she wasn't normal.

"One of the few fail-safes. Honestly, I'm almost surprised the Architect thought about the situation." He crossed his arms and grinned at her as he slowly sank into the floor.

Certainly, the Architect had cut some corners when it came to . . . creating this world. The alternative was unthinkable, though. Either they would have been stuck down here and would have had to try to dig out—if that was even possible should they have been split from the main plane—or they would have fallen into some unimaginable void that would have put Henkk's area to shame.

Teleporting. Please Stand By

Blue enveloped them, and vertigo rushed through Sally. Something about it felt different from the other teleportation she had previously used. It wasn't stronger or quicker, but . . . deeper? That didn't make much sense to her brain rattling around her skull as she stumbled into the heat of the overworld again.

Humphrey appeared next to her, stumbling across the loose sandy rocks. Lana didn't appear.

"Where is she?" Sally jabbed at her STAR, and with a brief flicker, it then resumed normal functionality.

Sally: you okay?
Lana: Yeah, back to . . . my home down here, I guess.
Lana: What about you?

Sally looked up. Empty plains of overheated rock. *Hell.* Humphrey coughed from behind her, and she turned around. A large structure loomed behind them. Ruddy brickwork and carved details showed off detailed suns and barren landscapes. A waterfall of sand ran from the domed peak of the building, covering a wide entrance with a constant warm curtain.

Sally: right where I needed to be
Sally: be safe, stay in touch
Lana: You too, Sally.

She closed the STAR and tilted her head. "It put us right in front of the dungeon? The Eternal Sands?"

He nodded. "There aren't many landmarks in the Wastes now; our quest was here, so it pushed us forward rather than back."

"You say *quest* as if it was something official and not just us bumbling about trying to save our friends while we beat up Monsters and steal their lunch money."

Humphrey smiled and gestured toward the doorway pelted by flowing sand. "The best kind of quest, then."

Sally sighed. Sure, it was most convenient that the System had decided to put them right in front of where they had wanted to be—but now that the dungeon lay before them . . . she had a little anxiety about the whole process. She wanted Theo and Archie back—but they couldn't exactly wait when Lucius was apparently right in front of them.

Plus, dungeons often required a sharp mind and consideration to avoid traps and puzzles. Not many things she could just stick in her maw and chew through to win the day. However, given the company that she kept, intelligence wasn't exactly in abundance.

Two steps closer to the dungeon, another flash of blue lit up beside them. The slim figure of purple with bright blue eyes gave them a bow.

"Welcome to the dungeon," Edward said with a wide grin.

"I guess it was *inevitable* you'd show up again." Sally glared at him.

"You know, it's a lot less fun when other people say it." The demon stood up straight, and his eyes dimmed.

Humphrey shrugged. "I suppose if you say it all the time, tiring of it becomes inev—"

"Point made." Edward held up his hand. "Nice hats, by the way." He gave them a wink, and then a bit of stoicism returned to his face. "I recently heard you dispatched Damon; that is quite a . . . *shame*."

"Not a big fan?" Sally raised an eyebrow.

The demon looked around the area as if expecting someone crouched among the wide-open plains with their ear wide open to spy on his thoughts. "We had our disagreements, sure. It was more of a shock—I knew you all were competent, but . . ."

Sally smiled, but her gaze fell back toward the dungeon where her friend was being kept. "Is this a business or pleasure visit, Edward?"

"Hmm. It is a warning, if you will. Apparently, they grow tired of my inability to extract funds from you, so they will soon assign someone else to the task." He adjusted his suit jacket.

She bit the inside of her mouth. "Are they as edible as you were?"

"No. Also, that was unpleasant—next time, just stab me in the heart or decapitate me, please." His face pulled up into a grimace.

Humphrey stretched out his sword arm. "How do you keep coming back, though? You can respawn?"

Edward raised an eyebrow and paused as if he was unsure whether that was information he wanted to give out willingly. "There are stipulations, but yes."

"Neat." Sally began to walk toward the dungeon. "What *I* would do with that sort of power."

The demon shrugged and looked away toward the sandstorm. "Indeed."

"Got any plans for the day?" Humphrey slapped him on the back as he walked past. "We could use a bit more mania while we die in the dungeon."

Edward clucked his tongue and frowned at the Death Knight before looking over at the zombie, who was eagerly nodding. He deflated. "Fine—but I'm not helping or getting involved."

"You're pretty weak anyway." Sally winked. "How do you keep dying in one hit? You're not under-leveled, are you?"

"That's my business. I . . ." Edward wrinkled his nose up. "How about you just go ahead? You can have my life story later."

"Deal!" She jumped and punched into the air. "Can you give us clues, though? Who has Lucius now? Is there a boss Monster? Should I prepare any specific resistances for the dungeon? What kind of puzzles are there? We're kind of dumb, so can we just bypass those? Or can we just start breaking through any of the walls? I don't want to ruin the experience, but we are kinda in a hurry, so . . ." She paused as she reached the curtain of falling sand.

"Is she always like this?" Edward murmured to the Death Knight.

"Yes, *ha-ha*. Although she has been filling the silence more now that the Party is split." Humphrey held out his sword so that the flat side would block some of the falling sand, creating a small gap of empty space so they could see beyond.

"Ha! There's already a trap right there!" Sally pointed excitedly at a slightly raised platform just beyond the waterfall of sand. "Sneaky, huh? I kind of want to see what kind it is, though . . ."

"*Sally.*" Humphrey shook his head as the zombie slowly moved her foot toward the pressure plate.

She pouted and instead hopped over it wildly, causing the demon to wince.

"You know, I almost want to help you now. You look like you'd need it."

Humphrey grinned and gestured for the tax collector to go next.

As he stepped over, too, they took one last breath of the outside air before they delved into the dungeon.

CHAPTER THIRTY-TWO

Rats to This

After descending a short staircase, the zombie sighed. "I'm getting pretty tired of amber hues." Sally rubbed her eyes as they entered the first room of the dungeon. When she had thought about the Wastelands, she had expected more gray or marshy conditions, muddy greens, and pale browns. Not bright sand, constant sunlight, and everything being made of the yellow-to-red spectrum of the color wheel.

Flickering torches sporadically illuminated the chamber. She didn't even care how long they had been there or who had lit them. Passing things off as System shenanigans had become an easy way to smooth over the bumps. If it indeed was meant to be some kind of game, then she should allow it some suspension of disbelief.

A stone doorway sat both on the right and left sides of the room, where the far wall had a big carving upon it. The text was surprisingly legible despite the dungeon looking like it had been here for centuries—even as she kicked her boots across the floor, small plumes of dust rose up.

She narrowed her eyes to read the engraving that sat among what looked like some Monster with googly eyes and teeth set too far apart.

Welcome to the Eternal Sands
Rest while you can
But don't take too long
Lest you start to sink below
Choose the Right Path
"Aw, *shit*." Sally covered her eyes. "It's trying reverse psychology on me."

Edward leaned against the back wall and crossed his arms. "And that physically hurts you?"

"You don't understand." She shook her head and glared at him. "I'm not meant to make the right decision—I'm a little out of control. But is the right decision the right, or not right because the writing writes right as right—to mean left?"

"We're going left," Humphrey said with a sigh. "If we start listening to walls, we'll be here all day."

"The walls have no ears of mine." Sally nodded, relenting to the Death Knight's logic.

The demon just stood with a blank expression on his face, blinking slowly as he watched the pair.

If Sally's memories were correct, she had never actually played through a dungeon in the real world. Certainly, she had thought about them—even rolled some dice by herself to simulate the experience—but when you held all the cards, it was a little easier. Death could loom in every room. Hopefully, the treasure could too. She tried to remember the protocol.

"Check for traps!" She punched the Death Knight on the shoulder as he moved past to open the door.

He paused, hand an inch away from the smooth stone surface. "How?"

"I don't know, just look?" She turned to face the demon. "Hey, Edward? I have darkvision."

Edward remained impassive. "Do you?"

"*No.* Theo does, though. He would have loved it here—maybe." She began to hum to herself. Humphrey was observing the door the best he was able, but after ten seconds, he deemed the job done.

"Safe." He shrugged and pushed the stone door open.

Immediately, the twang of air-propelled projectiles burst from inside the room and clattered against his metallic body. The arrows fell to the floor by his feet, and he looked down. "I disarmed the trap, Sally."

"Neat! Were they poisoned? Probably, if they weren't strong enough to pierce you?" She hopped over closer and leaned down to get a better look at them. She was acting a little extra; as much as she knew it, she wasn't sure if it was due to the pressure of the dungeon or the fact that they had someone watching them make their inevitable series of mistakes. Heh, *inevitable.*

Edward shifted himself from the wall and began to walk over, hands now in his trouser pockets. "Do you guys always fail upward?"

"Sometimes we fail downward too." She righted herself. "But on the whole, we mostly get lucky or violent, and that sees us through."

"Uh-huh." The tax collector seemed neither surprised nor particularly understanding of the answer. He certainly had the poker face of a casual observer, at least.

Humphrey stepped into the room that had assaulted him to find a small chamber with a single exit. Other than the torch on the wall, there were no other interesting facets to the room.

"Just here to poison us, huh?" Sally tutted to the dungeon. "Bit of an ego there, wasting this space for one trap."

"Don't taunt the dungeon, Sally." Humphrey scowled at her.

"Why not? You just told me it has no ears." She crossed her arms and began to tap her foot, awaiting the Death Knight to check for traps at the next door.

"That's not what . . ." He sighed and put his hand against the next door. "I almost wish Theo was here, too, so you had someone else to annoy."

Sally pouted and looked toward the demon standing in the first doorway. "I'm not annoying," she whispered.

Edward just nodded, his blank stare slowly beginning to become a furrowed brow.

The Death Knight pushed the door open, a waft of damp fur blowing back to where they were. "Giant rats," he reported. "Not mice, this time."

"Dibs!" Sally squeezed past him, jostling him to the side as she ran into the room with her dagger drawn.

There were six of the gigantic beasts in the room—though they were smaller than the giant mice, which was disappointing. Oddly, they were all an albino white, and their red eyes turned to meet her as she approached. The room was dirty, with nests in each corner, scrabbled claw marks across the stone, and a large ball that—*wait, a ball?*

She slid and turned her free hand to the sphere of almost white stone. *[Necroblast]*. The dark energy pulsed through the air and shattered the orb into dozens of broken parts. A wave of static energy passed through the room, and the rats shuddered.

Her nose wrinkled up as each of them squirmed and pulsed—before they each stood on their back legs, oddly bipedal as they mutated into muscled figures with rat heads. The crackling static energy continued to pulse around them as they flexed and stood in martial poses to greet her. Muscles that looked like shining rubber burst from beneath their fur to reveal pectoral slabs and defined abs.

"Why did you do that?" Humphrey sighed from the doorway as he strode in.

"I thought it was their toy—a rubber ball." She shrugged, glancing over her shoulder. "They might have just wanted to play."

A rush of air signaled they had begun to attack, and she rolled to the side as a haired leg brushed past her. With a grin, she blocked a second ratman—the force sending her feet sliding back across the floor.

"At last, something with strength," she growled, as Humphrey pulsed with his activated skills.

Edward tilted his head from the doorway as he watched them, the rats seemingly uninterested in the passive observer.

Sally blocked a punch and slashed her blade across the offending arm, drawing a slim line of crimson. The enemies were fast outgrowing the range of her *[Dagger of Luck]*—perhaps it was about time she opened that legendary box . . .

The *clang* of metal signaled that Humphrey had taken a hit, but from her peripheral, she could see that he was doing fine—blocking a kick with the flat of his blade and then lashing out with his pommel.

She swerved and twisted away from the constant assault, flicking her blade at an onrushing ratman and drawing her bat as he knocked the dagger away. An overhead fist knocked her to her knees, and she rolled away to avoid the follow-up. A third strike connected with her side, sending her stumbling over to where the Death Knight was.

"New combo time!" She beamed as the combatants surged toward them.

[Desecrate Life]
[Will of the Dark Lord]

Now weakened, they would be easier to stun with the Death Knight's area ability. Two of the nearest ratmen to her became stunned, and she held out her hand as Humphrey drove his blade into a third dazed enemy.

[Necroblast: Barrage]

The first three projectiles struck the first immobile ratman, each one blowing a layer from skin to bone to brain. The second took two of the same—then she jumped into *[Eat Brains]*.

"Gross," she spat, taking a blow to the arm from the ratman unaffected by the stun. It numbed her muscle, but it definitely felt like it was weaker than it should have been. She blocked the follow-up punch with the bat and then swung downward. Crackling energy surged around the weapon as it struck the knee of her assailant, the critical hit shattering the bone. As it dropped to its good knee, she grabbed the furred throat. *[Necroblast]*. She swung the bat to clock the ratman across the head, dropping it.

She turned to see Humphrey skewer the final ratman with *[Grave Strike]*, the dark energy mixing with the crimson flame of his blade as he slashed outward, withdrawing the sword. The entrails of the creature fell to the floor, the individual clutching at them, until it collapsed.

Sally sighed and tried to rub her tongue across her jacket to get the taste off.

Edward slowly clapped from the doorway. "You took a combined five or six hits, I believe. That is despite immediately changing the encounter to the worst possible version. I'm not sure whether to be impressed or disgusted."

"Be both." Sally winked at him. "As we are only getting warmed up."

She turned and vomited up the rat's brains across the stone floor.

CHAPTER THIRTY-THREE

Become Legendary

Sally took a deep breath and wiped her mouth, slightly shaken at the sudden expulsion of her stomach contents. "Maybe they were poisonous or something." Sally flexed to check all around herself. "Do I have any status effects?"

"That's not how you check." Humphrey sighed. "You know this."

"Knowledge is a burden for the empty mind." She brushed her hands off. "I feel better now, anyway. Did you want to check the next door?"

The Death Knight looked up at the doorway leading to the supposed next room. "I think it's your turn."

Sally exhaled through her nose for far longer than necessary. She glanced at Edward, who remained watching from afar, a hint of amusement on his face. He seemed to have gotten past the shock over the fact they were somehow competent, and he was now enjoying the show.

"Actually, why don't I open my legendary box now?" She shrugged. "I know it's not a key moment where I could build suspense, but it's been sitting around for a while, and I don't want to forget about it."

"Wasn't that only yesterday?" Humphrey rubbed his chin.

"If they aren't going to give me Daily Rewards anymore, then I'm not going to keep track of days. We'll see how the System likes *that*." She spun her STAR around and brought up the Inventory, prodding at the box to open it. Again, a list of all the weapon types popped up.

"I know you said it was first area stuff, but legendary should be good damage. Compared to my rare one, at least?" She wrinkled her nose up. Picking a dagger seemed rather cliché, but there wasn't really much else she cared to use.

"Depending on the random enchantment rolled, yes." Humphrey crossed his arms.

"They just give these out to anyone who finishes the Daily Reward chain? We didn't find any legendary weapons on the *Zeroes* we killed." She narrowed her eyes at the Death Knight, who just shrugged in response.

With a sigh, she selected *dagger*.

Error

She ground her sharp teeth together as nothing happened. She pressed *dagger* again a few times, each attempt bringing up an error message.

"Can you see this? *Honestly!*" she hissed at the intangible screen, and Humphrey walked over to watch.

Sally tried pressing faster. She tried pushing down harder on the button— more deliberately—even though it was just a hovering screen. Each time, the same result. There was a hesitation to try anything else in case she received something she didn't really want.

"Why is this so hard to understand, System?" She withdrew her *[Dagger of Luck]*. "Look, I want the dagger!" She jabbed at the button with her dagger, and the screen flickered away.

". . . Ah, crap. I think I killed the System."

Err-
Legendary/y/y Weapon Rec%d
Dagger of [Dagger]

She winced. Typical—something she should have expected. Dare she even have a look? A nested weapon sounded like it could be a problem.

"*Ha-ha.* What is it with you and daggers?" Humphrey beamed as he stepped away. "*And* with errors. You really are a problem."

"Save it." She waved him away as she tried to focus on her Inventory— picking the dagger out to try to view the description.

Dagger of [Dagger]
Legendary Dagger - Ignores Target Defense depending on how many [Dagger]s you own. Subtype ERROR//reference overflow:

"Okay. So it's both broken *and* busted." She half grinned but was half confused. "I could literally use this one weapon forever if I had enough daggers to hand."

"Let me see?" He stepped behind her and narrowed his eye sockets at the description. "Ah. That is not meant to do *any* of that."

"Right?" She held it in her hand. It was a reasonably plain weapon, with smooth silver and soft curves to the handle. The grip was wrapped in a leather dyed orange, and there was a reflective sheen to the blade—almost like a polished mirror.

"Hey, Edward?" She turned with a grin and waved the weapon in the air. "Look at me failing upward again."

He raised his eyebrows and shrugged, not sure what they were really up to.

She flipped the dagger in her hand and gave the air a few test swipes. Pretty much standard. Theo would definitely be jealous of this. "I need to find a merchant where I can exchange all these junk items for more daggers," she murmured to herself.

"No, what you need is to go through the door." Humphrey wiped his sword off on his cloak.

Sally turned her nose up at the stone door. Knowing her luck, it would be something even worse than the last two. Trying to juggle her new weapon, she walked over to the door. At least there weren't multiple choices; she would hate to get lost. She placed her hand on it. Not too cold, not especially warm. It didn't scream out danger—but then, she would probably ignore it if it did.

She pushed through and walked into the room beyond.

And stopped with a furrowed brow.

This was the starting chamber again—but they were entering from the doorway that was on the right. From their movement, the rooms definitely hadn't been able to circle all the way around. She hummed to herself as she continued to the middle, allowing the other two to pass through behind her.

"Interesting," Humphrey added, tilting his head. The demon said nothing.

"The silly poem thing hasn't changed." Sally waved at the wall, mostly thankful that it wasn't going to be that sort of puzzle. The grinding of stone prompted them to turn to the door behind them, now closed. "Very interesting." She nodded.

The original left side door was also closed again—unless Edward had shut it. If not, then that was the dungeon itself. Sally rubbed at her forehead. If they went left again, would it be the same rooms, and they'd loop again? So maybe the right path was the right path. They felt unfair, though—the one she had chosen should have been correct no matter which it was.

"What are your thoughts, Sally?" Humphrey looked rather nonplussed.

She wasn't sure whether he had some insider knowledge or, rather, he just had an idea of how the world would have come to comprise this dungeon. Maybe that's why he let her go through that door and have the revelation for herself.

Looking around the room again, she exhaled. What would Sally, the Queen of the Dead—or *Undead*—really do in this situation? With the carving trying to trick her into which path to take. Was she really a path taker?

With a flip of the dagger, her brow furrowed, and she walked straight at the carving. At first, there was some brief resistance from the wall—before she pushed through into a darkened chamber beyond.

"Heck yeah," she hissed to herself. Two different paths? She would barrel through and make her own way. The magical barrier behind her shimmered as Humphrey and then Edward walked through.

"Didn't even need to use detection magic," the demon commented. Neither complimentary nor judgmental—just an observation.

"It was obvious, really." Sally rolled her eyes. "I just wanted to get warmed up before we headed into the dungeon proper."

Humphrey narrowed his eye sockets at her but said nothing.

The surrounding room was plain—aside from the layer of dirt and dust, it seemed like just a way through from the main chamber to whatever lay beyond the doorway ahead. It was similar to the other stone doors—but this one had carvings in the corners. Four suns, as if they hadn't had enough of the heat in their time in the Wastelands.

"Your turn again, Humps," she said as she gestured forward.

The Death Knight approached the door and glanced around the edges. The faintest bit of amber light was visible around the cracks—showing that at least the room beyond was better lit than this dim chamber.

"There is a trap." He pushed the door open and immediately a burst of flame engulfed him fully, the constant barrage of fire illuminating their chamber.

Sally shielded her eyes from the light as the superheated air billowed around her. After three seconds, the fire petered out, and the smell of charred cloth and hot metal permeated the air.

Humphrey brushed off his shoulder plate. "I've had worse burns from *Theo*."

The zombie rolled her eyes. Despite the armor smoldering slightly, he didn't seem that much worse for wear. She looked over at the demon, whose stoic face had sunk into a little surprise. She smiled at him.

"It's nice when they make the beginning really easy, huh?"

He licked his lips as the words caught in his mouth. "I . . . uh, it's not really meant to be . . . such an easy dungeon."

A *crunch* came from the other room. "Disabled the trap."

"Eh, I don't think you really realize who we are, Edward." She shook her head. "You should've seen us take over the forest villages."

He nodded but didn't have much to add.

"Glad you opened that one," she said as she smiled at Humphrey and walked into the room. "I smell a lot worse when I'm cooked."

The Death Knight gestured with his head to the other side of the room. Two doors, each engraved in a similar fashion—but much more importantly, against the wall was a treasure chest.

"Dang! Our first dungeon treasure." She crouched down to stare at it. It looked to be made of sandstone, with polished metal struts and bracing. It wasn't large, by any measure—but any size chests were valid. "This one is all yours, Humps."

"I cannot . . ." He sighed and gave her a smile. "Fine."

She smiled back. Humphrey wasn't able to enjoy the looting experience without a proper STAR or Inventory. He had the same sword since he was bound to that body—and it was doubtful he would find one as cool. The least she could do was to allow him a little suspense and reward for a change.

Kneeling to the small container, the Death Knight gripped the lid and, with a slight dramatic pause, opened it wide to see the contents within.

CHAPTER THIRTY-FOUR

Dusted Off

A jet of dark, foul-smelling liquid immediately sprayed into the skeletal face of the Death Knight. He paused, as the dark drops ran from his face and down onto the floor.

"*Ah,*" he intoned. "That probably would have hurt if I had any eyes, in the traditional sense."

"How do you see things with empty sockets?" Sally crossed her arms, once again glad not to be on the receiving end of another dungeon trap.

"Mostly by suspension of belief." He wiped away the errant liquid from his face with his cloak. "Same way as you are undead, yet not exactly."

"My belief is basically on the end of a bungee cord with how suspended it is." She wrinkled her nose up and turned to Edward. "How about yours?"

He paused as he looked between them. "I think I'm starting to learn."

"You're not very talkative; you need to constantly blab about all sorts of inane crap if you want to fit in with us." She beamed at him. "Shame we have no more Party space for you—though I think I can have a third minion now. Humps? Not that I'd ever ask that of you, Edward."

"*Bodyguard,* Sally." Humphrey sighed. "Not minion. But yes, you can have three now."

Edward tilted his head. "Huh, so you're like a boss Monster mixed with a Player?"

"We're all a bit like that," she said with a nod. "Theo is the same as me, but a vampire, obviously. Humps used to be an Observer; Archie . . . has part of an Observer in him. Uh, Lucius, you kidnapped." Her smile turned into a scowl.

"I did." He smiled sheepishly. "But in fairness, the rest of you I wouldn't have had the chance to."

"True, but that's not exactly an excuse." She wagged a finger at him before turning back to the Death Knight. "Any loot in there?"

"Yes, but I can't access it." He shrugged and allowed the zombie to come retrieve the items.

Sun Disc
80 Gold
Healing Potion

"Neat—what's this disc for?" She glanced around the room as if the solution would be immediately present.

"Probably a puzzle or door." Humphrey looked between the two doorways—one to the north, one to the west. "Which direction do you wish me to absorb danger in?"

"Let's let the disc decide!" She took it from her Inventory. It was around three inches across, one side engraved with one of the sun pictograms that decorated the area, and the back side was blank. "Sun goes north; blank goes west?"

She flipped it into the air, spinning it wildly. "Call it Edward!"

The demon stumbled on his words at being called on unexpectedly. "Ah—Sun!"

With a slap, she caught it from the air between her hands and then revealed it, palm up. "Sun it is! Looks like luck is on your side, Edward."

He grimaced and gave her a nod.

"You're an accomplice now." Humphrey grinned. "You have diverted the tides of destiny and become part of the unending sea."

"*Poetic.*" Sally nodded and gestured with her hand. "Open the door, bud."

The Death Knight exhaled and turned toward the door, placing his hand on it. "Hmm, I reckon this one will be combat." The door opened slowly, the stale air pushing through and cooling the previously flame-touched room.

They filtered through to a large and dark room with a high ceiling, the main source of light seemingly to be the doorway on the wall opposite—a good sixty or so feet away. In the middle of the room stood a large statue. A four-armed man with an angered, toothy expression engraved on his face.

"Ooh, we have to fight that?" She winced as the door behind them closed.

Torches lit up around the room from one end to the other, gradually illuminating the area. As the final ones burst into flame, the statue began to shift, shedding dust and loose pebbles to the floor. He was a good twenty feet tall—and now, brightly lit, Sally could see the sun-shaped clubs he wielded in each of his hands.

"No brains," she tutted. "But a good chance to use my new dagger!" She flipped it in the air and caught the handle, ready to run forth.

The statue crouched and brought his four weapons to bear.

"Hey, Sally." Humphrey grinned as he watched her eagerly handle the new blade. "Guess what?"

"What?"

[Compelled Duel]

"Oh, come on!" She deflated and glared at him. "Kill stealer."

The Death Knight narrowed his eye sockets. "Never mind, he seems to be immune to—"

A large mace clattered into the stone where they had both stood, cracking the floor and sending a puff of dust into the air. Immediately, a follow-up from another sun mace was in motion—sending them running in opposite directions to avoid the constant blows.

Sally hated golem-type Monsters. *[Hex: Slow]*. Not only could she not bite them, but they often didn't have the consideration to have a brain, either. Fighting rock with a knife seemed like something totally not in her wheelhouse. She jumped as a mace swung wide and struck the wall—and she jumped upon it, wrapping her arms and legs around the long handle of the stone weapon.

At the risk of getting squished against the wall, she stabbed at the weapon, surprised at how easily the dagger pierced the stone. Almost as though it were butter. While there was too much resistance to slash through the grip of the mace, with enough stabs, she had weakened it. When the statue tried to clash two of his weapons together, the one she was on snapped off from the impact and fell to the floor.

Sally rolled away, nursing her leg with a hobble. She had disarmed a quarter of the arms, but one of the spiked rocks of the sun mace had stabbed into her leg. With a raised empty hand—now marred with her blood—she went to cast right before a swinging club struck her. Blood flicked across the dusty floor as the golem knocked her back a dozen feet, a new gash across her collarbone.

"*Ass,*" she spat. *[Necroblast: Barrage]*.

Each of the five bolts scoured the air as they struck the body of the statue. Everywhere they hit, a fist-sized hole in the stone blasted away, sending shards across the chamber. Not enough to truly hurt him, but he was becoming weaker.

Sparks flew around the Death Knight as he was fully on the defensive. Each strike blocked or deflected made a sharp grinding sound, and likewise, any attack he attempted against the golem just resulted in a heavy *clang* wherever he struck.

Sally ran up, sliding to avoid the swing of a mace, and jabbed the Monster in his thick legs. She doubted he could feel pain, but she jumped and dove, repeatedly stabbing him over and over despite the cramps of her own injured leg. Eventually, the statue got lucky and caught her where she didn't have the movement to dodge—but then Humphrey was above her to stop the strike. A second mace then swung in and knocked the Death Knight to the floor with a loud *thud* that reverberated around the room.

As much as the ground was now littered with dust and stone from the statue, he showed no attempt at ceasing the assault. If only they had the full Party, then something like this would probably be easy. They had enough overpowered abilities between them that usually one of them would have something for every occasion.

She shot herself backward and slid across the floor, avoiding the plumes of dust from where the sun maces struck the stone. *[Necroblast]* struck the most injured leg, blowing a larger chunk from where he had already suffered some damage. The Monster buckled slightly, briefly off guard, which gave Humphrey time to right himself.

"Sally," he growled, gesturing with his free hand.

With a nod, she ran toward him instead of the statue. As the Death Knight bent low, she put a foot atop his hand, and with a grunt, he launched her into the air.

She reached her arms out and grappled around the head of the statue, scrabbling to get a purchase with her feet—and then she started stabbing. "Let's see your lil rock brain then," she growled, as the dagger drew lines of dust in the air every time it stabbed back and forth into the Monster.

He tried to slam a mace into her to remove her from the tightly gripped position, and the zombie growled in pain as one of the stone prongs pierced through her. But she did not relent, continuing the assault even as her blood ran down the statue's face. He twisted and slowed as he went to perform the same attack—but Humphrey had grabbed onto that arm and weighed it down.

And then something popped up that she didn't think was possible.

[Eat Brains]

The statue paused for a brief moment and then dropped to the floor as if whatever magic had been powering it had suddenly disappeared.

Sally fell to the floor with a crack, rolling over and coughing out blood and stone dust.

Humphrey lent a hand down, which she took and stood on her feet, still choking with her face covered in light powdered rock and crimson. Pausing to hold her breath—since she didn't technically need to breathe—she withdrew a Healing Potion and popped the cork, gulping it down with wide eyes.

"Oh, shit." She eventually gasped. "Never doing that again, so gross." She retched and covered her eyes. "Oh my god, why does everything here taste so bad?"

"I'm not sure you are meant to eat everything," Edward said as he rolled his eyes.

"Why not," she said as she smirked, "when you can earn cool new abilities from it?"

Passive Unlocked: Rock Bottom

CHAPTER THIRTY-FIVE

Three Hundred

Edward narrowed his eyes as the zombie shuddered from the aftertaste of the golem. "What does that even do?"

"It's like, earth resistance or something?" Sally closed her eyes and leaned over, still struggling to recover from the violence. "What is even earth damage? Like fire or ice, I can understand—but mud doesn't usually hurt."

"Are you not hurt now?" The demon raised an eyebrow.

"Yeah, from the trauma to my body from being pierced by big ass spiked maces. The stone just tasted gross." She withdrew a medicine kit and passed it to the Death Knight.

"It doesn't even have brains," Humphrey mused.

"Right?" She stood up and stretched. Her spine and possibly some of her ribs cracked back into place. From the holes in her shirt, it looked like one of the hits might have gone all the way through her. "Glad I can arbitrarily fix my clothes," she murmured to herself, finding the option on her STAR.

Edward crossed his arms. "It surprises me that you are able to overcome such obstacles. This dungeon is meant for a full Party of Level Fourteen plus."

"Levels don't mean anything." Sally grinned back at the demon. "It's what's up here that counts." She winced as her arm clicked as she tried to tap the side of her head.

"You say that now," Humphrey said as he healed himself, "but wait until you get your first ultimate skill."

"What? *What?* What's that? Why do you not tell me about these things sooner?" She glared at the Death Knight. "What level is that? Thirty? Fifty?"

"Fifteen," he said with a grin. "Though you do get a second at thirty and a third at fifty—so, very astute as always."

"Ultimate skill," she whispered to herself, looking around the room. There didn't seem to be any chests to spray goop at Humphrey, but there should be *some* reward for winning against the big lump of rock, though. She wondered if Theo knew about ultimate skills? Maybe that was why he was in such a rush to level up.

"You know, you *can* loot bodies?" Edward frowned and walked over closer to them. "Like you did to me?"

"Ah, damn it—the one thing I always forget." Sally kicked up some dust and then turned to the statue. "This one. I can't loot his underwear, though." She didn't turn around but could hear the demon shuffling awkwardly.

Powdered Stone (12)
Coarse Stone (5)
Loose Gravel (16)
Plain Stone (6)

"*Neat.* I noticed that I say *neat* a lot when we receive loot, or I don't generally know how else to process an interaction."

"It could be some trauma related to you being half undead." Humphrey shrugged glumly.

"*Neat.* So, Edward." She turned back to the tax collector. "How close are we to our friend?"

He raised an eyebrow and folded his arms tighter across his lavender suit. "I am unable to say."

"What about if I use the *[Summon Demon]* scroll and think really hard about Lucius? Will that bring him back to us?" She leaned toward him and narrowed her eyes.

"No, I don't . . . I'm not sure how the spell works, but I doubt it." The demon shrugged.

Sally exhaled through her nose. She wanted this leg of the journey over with already. As much fun as it was to have some classic Sally and Humphrey adventures, being stuck in an underground dungeon was not as cool without the rest of the Party. Other than getting Lucius back—which was partly Edward's fault in the first place—this whole side quest wasn't really furthering their main goal.

Which was . . . making everything equal and balanced for everyone? That all seemed more clear-cut in the forest, where Uniques didn't have it anywhere as easy as Players, despite also having the one life to live. The solution there was just to kill the right people, and enough of them, that the System allowed them to live and thrive.

But what about the Wastes? Other than Lana and her guild members, she hadn't seen any other Players. If they were all on the other side of the sandstorm, then she would be hungry for a while. By the time she got there, would any really be morally okay to eat? From what she gathered, they'd all been put to work in service to the dragon—it didn't seem fair to free them from that and then eat them.

She exhaled. Too many problems that weren't affecting her current position. There was nothing to do but continue—carve what path she could and hope that everyone could rejoin soon and they'd have a better taste of what was going on in this terrible place.

"Ready to move on, Humps?" She shot him a smile, but there was clearly worry written across her face.

"As you wish, my queen." The Death Knight feigned an over-the-top bow.

"Ass, go open doors." She waved him off, but a genuine smile had crossed her face.

They moved over to the doorway at the opposite end of the chamber, and once again, Humphrey put his hand on the carved stone door to gauge what lay next for them. "I do not detect anything untoward."

Sally winced and moved slightly farther away from the door.

With a deep grumble, the door opened, vibrating as if not set on the hinges properly. A well-lit room was beyond, and it didn't immediately pelt the Death Knight with anything dangerous. He tilted his head as he stood in the way of her being able to see more.

"Looks like . . . a room to rest?" He stepped forth, allowing them to follow him in.

Another smaller room—this one seemed to have a handful of beds aligned in the room equally. A table with two chairs. Sally wasn't sure how long they had been up now—but after that fight, she sure did feel sleepy. She yawned and stretched her arms out, regarding the plain beds for the one that looked *just right*.

A grinding came from the Death Knight as he rubbed his chin with his plated hand. "I suggest we move on."

"Aw, but I'm so sleeee . . . hmm. You might be right." She shook her head and glared at the room again. There was something about it that didn't settle with her. Maybe the arrangement of the furniture, or the textures of the linen . . . there was something that was just slightly off—like an uncanny valley—but for places to sleep.

Another door to the north and one to the west.

"Flip time." She yawned, swaying slightly. "Your turn to call it, Humps."

"Blank."

"I haven't even . . . you do it when it's in the air." She frowned, and her vision became slightly blurry. "Actually, yeah, blank wins. Choose a door."

The Death Knight turned and leveled his boot, a dull crunch of the stone door to the north shifting open and bringing a cool breeze into the chamber—briefly giving Sally a little energy.

"Ack, something is off here—don't fall asleep, Edward!" She hopped around the room, avoiding touching anything.

Edward said nothing but sighed, a hand holding his nose as he walked through the room. Once in the next chamber, he stopped, as the greatsword rose up to meet his neck.

"Ah—hello?"

Humphrey narrowed his eye sockets. "I know you do not fear death, but how are we so sure you are not just collecting information on us for the dragon?"

"Hmm?" Edward recoiled slightly from the edge of the sword, and it followed him.

Sally stood in front of him with her arms crossed, tapping her foot on the floor. "Damon was mostly watching us to report back. You guys don't just collect money but are prospecting out your next big gold farmers."

"That's not . . . how did you even decide to jump me together like this?"

The zombie smirked. "You see us talking a bunch of rubbish constantly, but there's a lot of unsaid communication."

"No, I'm not gathering information to report back." The demon shook his head slowly, trying not to saw his own head off.

Humphrey moved closer, his skeletal face looming into that of Edward's. "How can we believe you? Caution would dictate we send you back, anyway; you're not exactly helping."

His eye twitched, and his luminous blue eyes switched between the hard glares of Sally and the plated figure. Eventually, he sighed. "I'll tell you my secret to earn your trust. But it has to stay between you two."

Humphrey tilted his head toward her, and Sally gave him a nod. The Death Knight moved away and relaxed the sword.

Edward licked his lips and looked to be trying to reconsider his honesty. "I'm . . . every time that I die . . . I lose a level."

Both *Outsiders* nodded slowly.

"Ah." Sally snapped her fingers. "That's why you are so weak. We've dropped you by three levels alone."

"Yes," Edward said as he grimaced. "In doing so, I am now far below the power needed to effectively level up again. Due to my duties, I am unable to travel to the first area."

"Have you tried asking nicely for help?" Sally glared at him, to which the demon just returned a shrug. "What about leaving your job? What will happen?"

"Probably one of the Level Twenty goons will come and twist my arm—or my head—off." Edward placed his hands in his trouser pockets.

Humphrey grinned and turned to observe the new room. "Shame you were not more pleasant from the start. You could have joined us and leveled up."

"We got two whole levels from Damon and the broken portal." Sally beamed. "Theo didn't, though."

Humphrey dropped his sword with a loud *clang* and held his hands over his face.

"You okay, Humps?" Sally moved over to him, concern on her face. "I know it's terrible, but Theo will get over it, he always—"

"No." Humphrey shook his head, and his voice sounded strained. "You cannot see this System message, but for some reason, I can."

Her eyes darted between his empty sockets. "What does it say?"

Humphrey looked up at her with his eye sockets wide—confusion and apprehension across his skeletal face, but he seemed hesitant to respond.

Sally put her hands on him. "*What does it say?*"

"Please welcome three hundred new Players to the System."

CHAPTER THIRTY-SIX

Safety in Numbers

Sally stood there in shock, her mouth opening and closing as she tried to process the statement. "Are you . . . sure?"

"It's as clear as the System can be." Humphrey rubbed the side of his head as he stood.

"But how? Without the Architect . . ."

The Death Knight shrugged and shook his head.

A large lump had settled in Sally's throat. More people from the real world had just been pulled into whatever this place was, somehow. Even without the Architect being alive to do the necessary deed. They had considered the possibility of waves of new Players, but it had slipped from her mind, like so many other things.

"I can't . . ." She covered her face with her hands. It was a lot to take in. More food for her stomach. Or . . . lost souls brought to this terrible place that needed saving? She took a deep breath. "We need to fix the Wastes before they try to come through—the Toad! Shit. With the System not even working properly, how are they . . . how are we . . ."

Humphrey opened his skeletal maw, about to say something, but then closed it.

"I know what you're thinking. You were about to say that it isn't our problem, right? Well, who else, Humps? Who else is going to do it?" She started pacing. Time was against them—it might only take newbies two weeks—maybe even one before they tried venturing through the Swamps. Assuming *Zeroes* or some other group weren't gatekeeping, then the nigh immune Toad would kill anyone.

She stopped and deflated. Here she was, trying to play the hero—when she was supposed to be a self-styled villain. Instead of being overjoyed at there now being a banquet of fresh brains to consume, she was worried for their survival. Perhaps just because they were new, behind the curve. It was conflicting.

"I seem to be out of the loop here." Edward leaned toward them with his brow furrowed. "What are you talking about?"

"Long story short." Sally waved her hands in exasperation. "Players come from somewhere else, like another world. There's just been a new group brought into the forest like there was about . . . two months ago?"

Humphrey nodded.

"Ah." Edward tilted his head and looked off, unfocused, while he thought.

"That's quite a big thing to drop out of the blue." She sighed and pinched the bridge of her nose. "We'll need to kill the dragon as soon as possible—then the Toad?"

The demon snorted but then retracted the humor he had found in her statement. "Normally, I'd think you mad—and certainly you're not powerful enough to do what you dream of . . . but watching you in this dungeon, with training, then you might be the best ones to stand a chance."

"Flattery," Sally said with a smile. "Hopefully, once we are all back together, we can get some more levels. Right, Humphrey?"

"Of course. Let's focus on the task at hand for now and hope Archie returns soon . . . without breaking anything."

Sally narrowed her eyes at him, trying to scrape the truth from him with her glare. Despite being in the room for a generous handful of minutes, she hadn't really given it a proper look. Social issues took precedence when the room itself hadn't tried to kill her.

The room was a similar square shape to the rest—in fact; she was fast becoming tired of the dungeon. Where was the multi-level, varied terrain, true exploration experience? These were just boring rooms with danger in them, connected in a way that eventually led to the boss, or Lucius, hopefully.

In the middle of this bland cube of space was an altar with some shapes on it. She almost didn't want to get any closer in case it was a puzzle—in fact, she was pretty sure that it was. She didn't have the stomach for it currently.

"Humphrey, go look at the puzzle thing, please. I am too exhausted now. This place has terrible food."

The Death Knight would have rolled his eyes if he had them but relented to go do what she requested.

"How serious is this new Player thing?" Edward sidled up to her.

"Depends on what you mean by serious." Sally sighed and rubbed her forehead. "It's kind of a lot to process right now. You ever think . . . about how you got here?"

The demon shrugged. "I suppose not. There are memories there, but no physical evidence of any of it having happened. I'm here *now*, though."

"You are." She gave him a smile. "You're a lot cooler when you're not being an annoying henchman."

Edward closed his eyes and then looked up at the ceiling. He exhaled and shook his head. "I bet you've met plenty of assholes that you eventually charm to your side?"

"No," she said. "Some of them I kill and eat." A grin spread across her face as she began to walk over to the Death Knight. "I have more patience for Uniques, but if Players don't want to bend the knee, then I always have dinner reservations open."

She left the demon to quietly consider this as he stood with his eyebrows raised.

"What's the damage, Humps?"

"None, yet." He scratched at the side of his head. There were three exits to this room, and the altar had a series of stars engraved into stones arranged in a jumbled order.

"It is like . . . a constellation thing? Do you have those here?" Her eyes burned as she stared intently at the mixture of tiles.

Humphrey shrugged.

"Edwaaaard. Can we not just pay you to help us?" Sally whined and leaned across the altar. It was nice and cool, and she was feeling overheated from doing too much thinking.

"Any gold you give me, I'd have to take back to Ruben."

"What about . . ." Her STAR lit up her wrinkled face as she opened her Inventory. "You want a demon coin? Or is that reductive to ask? I don't mean to be offensive."

"You have a *coin?*" The demon narrowed his bright blue eyes and rubbed his chin.

"Good sir, I have more than one." There was a look on Edward's face that told Sally she should be a little coy about the total number—if one had pulled such a reaction from him.

"More than one? Those are very useful for demons . . . but even for a handful, Ruben would not look kindly on my betrayal. I should probably remain impartial."

"What could we get for twelve?" Sally raised her eyebrows, putting her figurative cards on the table.

Edward licked his lips. "Twelve? Uh . . . you should know there is a cost to making a deal with a demon."

She looked back to the Death Knight, who shrugged again. Making a deal with a demon sounded a lot different from her intent to just trade some of her items for some help. Although her mind was lagging, she tried to imagine what kind of cost he might be expecting. "Surely you dictate the cost if I'm making the deal; why not just *not be an ass* about it?"

He smiled and shook his head. "It's not always a direct deal—we aren't making a contract. Call it fate, if you will. An ill omen for your troubles."

Humphrey shuffled on the stone floor. "Perhaps not a good idea to invite further malady on ourselves."

"True." She sighed. It didn't sound like it would be a problem, but they shouldn't add to their problems while they were already on the back foot. "I suppose you'll have to share with Lucius; he might like some."

Edward nodded and crossed his arms, not intending to interrupt them further.

"I have an idea." Sally stretched out and went toward the door to the east. "Does the door count as an enemy?"

"Only to your progress, *ha-ha*."

"I mean like an entity that has defense." She rolled her eyes, then withdrew her dagger. With a stiff jab, she struck the carved stone—the blade sinking into the surface as if butter.

"Normally no, but in a dungeon . . ."

"Yeah, alright, Humps. I've already stabbed it and worked the answer out. There's no need for the extra exposition." She waved her free hand at him. "Sorry."

With a few additional stabs, she managed to strike whatever counted as a lock mechanism within the door and, with a groan, it started to open up.

"Puzzles can suck it." She turned to stick her tongue out at the altar.

"Sally! Behind—" the Death Knight began.

Something shot out from the room, striking her in the back. Pain and warmth flared up her torso as she looked down to see the tip of a metal spike protruding from beneath her ribs.

With a metallic screech, the chain attached to the pole yanked her backward into the room as the door shut itself—plunging her into darkness.

Humphrey slid up to the wall and slammed his sword into the door, the only effect being a white line of dust upon the unmoving stone. He spun back to the demon with the fire behind his helmet blazing wildly.

"Fix the puzzle, *now*."

"I . . . cannot."

Crimson flame flickered in the eye sockets of the Death Knight as he stomped back to the center of the chamber.

"You do not want to know what I will do to you if you do not."

Edward gulped.

CHAPTER THIRTY-SEVEN

Taste of Metal

Sally was no stranger to pain. Although, with how overpowered they were, fights often ended without too much injury. These traps hurt quite a bit, though. Perhaps she was underselling it to herself so that she didn't panic.

The harpoon that had pierced her torso had dragged her back through rising floor spikes. Her armor had deflected most of the damage, but enough had gone through to shred her legs pretty badly. After she had stumbled back through these, the end of the trap had greeted her. She imagined it was supposed to be some form of iron maiden—old metal that pierced right through her.

It was perhaps designed for Adventurers slightly thicker than her, however—and utilizing the baseball bat, she had been able to wedge the two metal parts far enough apart so that the end tips of the toothed maw of the trap were the only part piercing her. She should have chosen the left door.

Theo's regenerative aura would be really nice about now. She had heard Humphrey bash at the door and then argue with the demon. Assuming the bat didn't break, she could hold out here long enough for the Death Knight to solve the puzzle. In fact, she *did* feel like having a nap. She shivered, her body convulsing against the spikes, a painful expression of how the contrast of her warm blood felt against her cold skin. Why was her blood even warm?

Actually, she didn't feel like waiting. Slowly, she blinked. Oof, sleep would be nice. But saving herself would be even better. Gritting her teeth as one of the pointed metal parts dug gradually deeper into her muscles, she moved her arm to press the STAR.

She growled as blood coursed down her arm, and the trap groaned, pressing a spike against her forehead. From the intangible space of the System, a sword dropped to the floor in front of her, landing at an awkward angle due to the plated lip of the trap. And then a second and a third clattered down, getting stuck between the spikes.

"You are under the impression that I know how to work this." Sweat ran down Edward's face as his light blue eyes darted over the mix of tiles.

Humphrey was gripping the edges of the altar so tightly his plated fingers had dug into the stone, his helmet flame becoming a blaze that illuminated the chamber in bright crimson.

"I've never been here before, you understand. I just handed over your friend to . . . to the boss here." His eyes darted between the Death Knight and the puzzle.

"You better do it," Humphrey seethed. "Sally is your only chance of freedom from the dragon."

Edward licked his lips and renewed his efforts. Tentatively, he moved one of the tiles.

Behind them, the door rumbled open—followed by the clattering of metal as Sally slid out of the trap chamber atop a small wave of weaponry.

"I yet live!" she gurgled, her body unresponsive on a bed of dropped metals, as blood ran from her mouth.

Humphrey stomped over and lifted her gently to place her sitting against one of the walls. "You are injured."

"Only physically," she said with a smirk, her eyes staring off at the ceiling. "There are floor spikes and then a big mouth trap—it tried to eat me, Humps."

"You are not that palatable." He grinned. "I will set up a *[Campfire]*, but I do not have an Inventory, so I can't—"

"Urghhh, I get it." She closed her eyes and exhaled. "You only have a few items."

Edward hovered in the distance as the Death Knight began setting up the *[Campfire]* to slowly heal them all. "Is she . . . are you okay, Sally?"

"What, you don't think I can survive being cored and impaled? I'm not . . . I'm not . . . ah, you wouldn't get the reference, anyway." She sighed. "Where's my stupid vampire guy?"

"I would hope that he is at least having more rest than us." Humphrey turned to her as he sat beside the lit *[Campfire]*. "I do wish for his recovery and not just for his regenerative assistance."

"You're a chunk of soft metal, Humps. I'm not sure he could have stopped me, either." She exhaled and relaxed against the wall as the warmth of the fire made her feel comforted.

Quietly, Edward came over and sat around the fire with them, crossing his long legs.

"It's been awhile since I've been humbled," Sally murmured. "Sucks that it was to an uncaring room."

"I can see your internal organs." Edward narrowed his eyes, unable to take them off the injured zombie. "I'm not sure how I feel about that."

"Probably better than I do." She grinned before coughing up blood in the place of a chuckle.

For a few minutes, they sat in silence, until Sally was able to move her arms to open up the STAR and remove two Healing Potions. The first one was a struggle to get down, as her arm shuddered, acting as if it was opposed to rising to her mouth. After the wave of magical healing went through her, the second was much easier to down.

"Ah, nothing like a bit of magic, huh?" She pulled her knees up to her chest and wrapped her arms around her legs. "Doesn't quite heal the trauma, but hopefully the undead part of my brain will cope with it."

Edward rubbed his fingers together, seemingly withdrawn. "Sometimes I wonder what the last death will be like. When I run out of levels. Dying hasn't been fun so far, but I can glaze over it because I know I'll come back. What about when I don't?" He looked up at the zombie, who was now beaming at him.

"Gotcha! This whole thing was a ruse to get you to open up. Stole your heart; now you belong to us." She stuck her tongue out and felt pleased with herself.

The demon opened and closed his mouth, trying to process, and looked at the Death Knight.

Despite the grin also on Humphrey's face, he shook his head. "No, she didn't really get maimed for the reaction. But all rivers come from the mountain or something."

"Honestly." The zombie rubbed at her hair. "I just wanted to make sure you were okay on the inside and you weren't just a hacky two-dimensional B-plot villain."

The Death Knight nodded. "We have standards."

"Yeah," Sally continued, "you should have seen the antagonist for the first area. Cliché *and* a hypocrite." She made a face as if she was retching.

"I'm not specifically your antagonist." Edward leaned back on his palms. "I'm just doing a job that happens to be assigned to your Party and happens to be something you don't agree with."

Sally shook her head. "*You* don't agree with it either. When was the last time you even asked for gold? Plus, you said we were getting reassigned to someone else more capable soon."

"I'm not sure I said more *capable*," he grumbled. "But sure—you caught me. I want out of the schemes of this sandpit to have my own life to live. Several lives."

"Just think of all the good you could do with all those lives," she said with a wink.

"Once the dragon is out of the way, I'm all ears."

"That would be pretty creepy." Sally stood from the floor, stretching her arms out and then brushing the dust and blood from her clothes. "Wow, we had a heart-to-heart with you before Lucius. Should we swap which demon we take with us?"

"I would prefer no demons." Humphrey stood and rolled out his shoulders. "Both irritate me in a manner, but this one is weak, and Theo doesn't like him for some reason."

"Hmm, yeah. True." She narrowed her eyes at the sitting demon. "Theo could sense when you were nearby. Why is that?"

Edward looked blankly up at the pair. "I have no idea."

Sally exchanged a quick glance with the Death Knight before extending her hand down to help the demon up. With a brief pause, he grasped onto her and lifted himself up, dusting off his suit.

"If it's something *bad*, you'll soon find out what happens when you run out of levels." Sally glared at him; her finger raised. "Theo is a goof, but he is my only reasonable ship—so I trust him more than most."

Edward furrowed his brow. "I'm not sure I understand the—"

"We'll cross that bridge when it requires decapitating." She smiled. With a quick turn, she put her hands on her hips and glared at the doorways. "Now, to get on with this terrible event."

The demon stood and watched the woman walk around the chamber, her clothing still matted with blood, as she withdrew her dagger. He was perplexed, and it was taking awhile to fully absorb what had happened in the last fifteen minutes.

"You get used to it." The Death Knight grinned at him as he passed. "Or you don't. Some just get dead. You should think about that."

Sally stabbed the middle of the puzzle with the dagger, and a screech of agony hissed from within as if a magical spell had been dispelled and was unhappy about the fact. The shunting sound of doors becoming unlocked around the room immediately followed.

"*Ta-da!*" She bowed before them. "I shall now give my dagger a name."

"Skeleton Key?" Humphrey grinned and crossed his arms.

"Ah—oh, yeah! That would be much better than what I was thinking, huh?" She tilted her head in thought and then flipped the blade in her hand. "Skeleton Key, it is!"

Edward shivered and followed them toward the next door they intended to pick.

CHAPTER THIRTY-EIGHT

Monetary Loss

Sally slid down an inclined slope and then leaped across a pit to roll on the floor beyond. As she coughed out dust, she peered back over the edge. Looked like acid . . . or maybe some apple juice. Not the kind of fifty-fifty she should be entertaining right now. She struggled to remember how many different rooms it had been now, each as boring as they could be. Had she always been living in this dungeon? Maybe.

"There's a pit to jump over, Humps."

A rough screech followed from above where the slope began, and she took a few steps backward as it drew closer. Sparks lit up the dim corridor as the plated figure of the Death Knight came into view, using both his heels and greatsword as an anchor to slow his descent. Once he reached the last few feet of the decline, he launched forward, landing surprisingly deftly over the other side of the pit.

"I am beginning to detest the dungeon." He exhaled, looking back over the edge.

"Join the club; I've been simmering since a stupid poem tried to tell me what to do." Sally rubbed her arm across her forehead. They must be nearing the end soon, surely? There were only so many fatal traps and inedible Monsters the System could throw at them before the dungeon became unfair. This sort of place would be a horror for normal Players.

Edward slid down and easily hopped over the pit with his long limbs, only wobbling slightly as he tried to find a place to land that wasn't too close to the wide Death Knight.

"Can you at least tell us how far we've gone, Edward?" Sally glared from the side of Humphrey.

"No. Well, I don't think so." The demon pinched the bridge of his nose. "It's not like me to get a headache—and I'm not sure if it's just the dungeon or having to listen to you two constantly prattle on."

"We don't prattle." Humphrey crossed his arms.

Sally agreed. "Not *constantly*. But that is rather rude, Edward, after all that we've been through."

Edward deflated. "You ever have the taste of the future in your mouth? Something rueful that pains you so much that it affects the present you?"

"I'm barely cognizant half the time." Sally sighed. "That sounds like something Theo would say, though. We'll ask him when he is back."

She turned back to the passage. It just went on farther until it became shrouded in darkness. Perfect place for a whole bunch of traps. "Why don't you go first, Edward?"

"I'm . . . not the one that has to complete the dungeon."

"Did the terms of our return of Lucius actually involve us completing the dungeon?" She crossed her arms and spun back to glare at him again, mostly blocked by the large form of the Death Knight.

Edward's bright eyes blinked slowly a few times. "He is being held here, so you would have to find him, at least."

"Or die trying, I believe you had told us?" Humphrey would have turned back to the demon, but maneuvering in the corridor was enough of a struggle with how wide his shoulder plates were.

"You don't seem capable of that." He shrugged back in return.

It wasn't enough to reassure Sally, and she briefly seethed before looking back to the darkened alley before them. She withdrew a skull from her Inventory and bowled it down the hallway. Not exactly the most consistent of projectiles, it at least bounced a few times before the odd shape of it wore out any of the momentum.

As it laid to rest for a second, the floor dropped away to be replaced by a bright amber glow.

"Ah." She rubbed at her eyes. "Pit drops into lava. Or magma." The slight time delay made it a problem, but she would have to use one of her most secretly guarded and rarely used skills—patience.

"Humps, go in front and probe the floor with your sword. We'll go spaced apart in case there is a weight limit."

"If I can pass, I doubt either of you would tip the scales." The Death Knight glanced between the two of them. "But, as you wish."

She watched as he squeezed past her and began to strike the floor with his sword—waiting a few seconds to take a step forward and then repeating the action.

It took them sixty years to make it to the next door—at least, so Sally thought. They had uncovered three other pit drops along the path and had avoided them using their painstakingly slow plan. Perhaps it was a good thing the others weren't here—she seemed to show off and be more reckless with more of an audience.

"Pretty good, huh?" She turned back to grin at Edward.

"Yes, I'm increasingly worried that you might actually pull this off."

"Aha! So we are getting closer?"

He deflated. "I don't actually know; I've told you several times I haven't been through here before. Your friend could be in the very next room, for all I know—"

"Quick, Humps! Victory draws near!" She pointed her finger out at the doorway before them, much to the anguish of the demon.

The Death Knight approached the door and tilted his head. "This one has a barred window."

"Like a prison door, perhaps?" She hopped up and down in hopes of seeing something past him.

"No, looks like a combat area." Humphrey pushed the door open and stepped inside, followed shortly by the other two.

Sally narrowed her eyes. The wide chamber was of similar design to the statue room, except this one had no statue—and was lit by four waterfalls of lava or magma that fell slowly from the ceiling and into recessed pools encircling the room. There was no other doorway out of here, but the center of the room held a small altar and a pattern of runes in a circle across the floor.

"Bah!" She shook her fist at the plain domed ceiling. "This better not be another puzzle."

The Death Knight walked up to the altar, eyeing the surroundings for any traps or untoward shapes among the well-lit walls. Nothing prevented him from reaching his target, and he tilted his head in observation of the square stone shape that rose from the floor.

"What is it?" Sally called, still standing at the door end of the room. If it was a puzzle, then she didn't want to take a step closer, lest she throw up over everything as her brain took a vacation.

"Looks like . . . a coin slot." Humphrey turned to her with a grin.

"My favorite sort of puzzle." She gasped and discarded any previous worries to run over. "Putting the right shape in the correct hole."

She slid across the stone as she reached the Death Knight and peered at the surface of the altar. Indeed, in the middle of the polished sandstone, there appeared to be a slot—just slightly slimmer than her finger, but as long as her hand.

"Why was your first instinct to try to fit your hand down it?" Humphrey narrowed his eye sockets.

"In case there were coins already in there, we could steal them, duh." She rolled her eyes and moved her hand away. Humphrey probably had no idea when it came to vending machines or claw machines or really any manner of machines—half of which she could barely recall.

There was a brief line of text beside the hungry coin maw, but it wasn't in a language she knew. "What's this say, then?"

"You would think that as an ex-Observer, I would have the capability to read and understand all languages present in the System, and that—"

"Just say you don't know." Sally emptied her lungs through her nose. "Edward? Can you read it?"

With tired eyes, the demon walked over, standing around the other side and tilting his head at the muddy crimson lettering engraved in the stone.

"Unfortunately, I do not. It's certainly odd, though." He seemed genuinely perplexed and not just playing the part about not wanting to meddle.

Sally glanced around the room again. The runes on the floor she didn't recall—although they bore some similarity to the demonic portal runes they had seen previously. Just the day before, perhaps? It felt like longer.

"My best guess is . . ." she said as she rubbed at her chin. "If we stick the sun coin thing in, then either it opens a portal to somewhere else in the dungeon—or summons a big baddie to fight."

"Fifty-fifty." Humphrey nodded.

She hummed to herself as she went to open up her Inventory—pausing briefly to open chat.

Sally: now in a dungeon
Sally: 1/5 stars do not recommend
Sally:_

She waited a few seconds for Chuck to respond, but he did not. A little shrug to herself, and she continued to hum and open up the right menu to withdraw the coin found earlier in the dungeon.

Gently, she placed it flat on the altar beside the ridges of the slot.

"See! But my question is . . ."

She then withdrew a second item to place beside the first.

Edward winced as he eyed up the demon coin she put down.

"What if we put this one in instead?" She wagged her eyebrows at the pair.

Humphrey shrugged. "Most likely, nothing would occur if whatever magic or mechanism is used to detect the right coin is not—"

Sally slowly slid the demon coin into the slot while maintaining eye contact with the still talking Death Knight.

A wicked hiss filled the air as the lava falls turned a dark crimson, shadowing the chamber in a red hue.

Before them, the runes began to spark into life—white hot at first and then fading to a pulsing amber.

"Fifty-fifty," Sally whispered, slowly withdrawing her dagger.

CHAPTER THIRTY-NINE

Raising the Stakes

The chamber shook as energy flooded around them. From the center of the runes, an orb of electricity formed—deep purple in color and crackling out wildly. Where the reaching tendrils struck the stone, blackened marks remained.

"We've just fought a bunch of demons," Sally groaned as she slowly stepped backward, away from the maelstrom. "Can't we have something different?"

"Be careful what you wish for." Humphrey stood in a defensive stance, crimson fire flickering down his blade and buffeted by the energy whipping around the room.

"You know, normally I would have gone by now, but something is restricting my teleportation ability." Edward looked even more worn out and fed up now and had just allowed himself to be slowly pushed back across the ground by the barrage of wind and foul energy.

Sally briefly considered if she had made a mistake. Surely not, however. It wasn't really something she made a habit of. If the silly magic machine didn't want to be powered by the demon coin, then it would have rejected it or become inert. Maybe if she could put a second one in, the effects would be reversed? Her eyes narrowed—probably not the best plan she had come up with. Maybe all twelve of the coins would have been better.

With a flash of bright white light, the surrounding storm ceased, and everything came to a standstill. As their eyes adjusted, the runes had now become inert—and a figure now stood in the midst of them. Enveloped in a dark robe that appeared to wave and flickered as if it were made of mist, bright yellow eyes peered out from the shadow of a hood. Two horns of ivory twisted out from the top of their head through convenient holes in the hood. In one hand, they held a book of bright purple, the cover of which shifted hues slightly. The other hand held a long staff made of silver, the top of which was a pulsating orb of amber light.

Why hath thou summoned me?

Sally snorted. Someone needed to tell the Architect that people didn't really talk like that. Well, they should have gotten the memo before they had died— that'd be more useful than knowing currently.

"Who are you?" she yelled, though her voice came out muted as if the energy in the room was dampening the sound.

I am Natus, the Eternal Horizon.

"Okay. We don't really want to fight right now; want to make a deal or something?" Not that she didn't think they could take whatever this being was, but she was feeling pretty sleepy, and their brains probably tasted bad. She considered asking if that was the case, but that may be impolite.

The figure wavered for a moment as if in consideration, their misty robes buffeted by an unseen wind in the chamber.

What doth thou have to offer a being such as I?

She furrowed her brow and looked at the Death Knight. The spectacle of their arrival and archaic language was just fanciful dressing over the fact they were still a part of the System. Some being created a short time ago, following a set path—unless they were Unique. Shame she had no more room in the Party. Knowing what she did, it kind of took the magic out of the whole encounter.

"What do you seek? Power? Souls?" She checked her Inventory quickly. "Mount feed?"

I am the collector of abilities. For every two I consume, I can grant you a boon in return.

"*Oh.*" Well, now that they had put it in game terms, the wet blanket had fully smothered her. Couldn't she just meet all powerful entities without it being part of the on-rails experience? She tapped her ability sheet to review what she had. "Give me a minute then. Sounds good."

Edward sidled up to her, his movements slowed by the power in the room. "Are you sure you are willing to do that so easily? Everything has a cost—"

"Yeah, duh. Cost is two abilities. I get one back." She turned back to Natus with a wrinkled-up nose. "The boon is an ability I can *use*, right—something good and not a curse?"

If your gift pleases me, then—

Right, right. Sally ignored the rest of the sentence. It was just a yes with more words than required. She had missed out on being able to replace a skill when Dent had stolen the shrine out from under her nose. She wasn't about to lose the chance to reroll something else.

But what? Most of her skills had some use; after the System had finally set her on the right path for a zombie boss or necromancer, most of her choices had been in the right vein. There was no telling what Natus would give her . . . and what they would even want. Just based on appearance, they were some kind of spellcaster—with the book and staff.

"Here." She waved her hand in the air. "I give you *[Necroblast]* and *[Necroblast: Barrage]*." Partially a risk to give away her two ranged attacks, but she wasn't really much of a spellcaster herself. She wasn't sure if her lack of intelligence, stats-wise not actual, would cause it to drop off once enemies with magic resist became more common.

This is an . . . acceptable gift.

"What do I get?" She crossed her arms, ready to be disappointed.

The path thou walk is littered with the dead. You receive [Error].

Sally exchanged glances with Humphrey. "Did you just say error?"

It seems I am unable to provide [Error]. Fortune must favor you; as such, I will have to provide you a stronger boon with the fated [Error].

Natus paused again and rubbed the side of their head with the glowing tip of the staff, illuminating their shadowed head and revealing no features—just further shadowed mist.

"Maybe it's just playing up?" Sally shrugged. "Just try out the highest tier next and see if that works?" She shot Humphrey a not-very-sly wink.

"I'm not sure that will work," he grumbled back, knowing full well he had doomed it to become reality.

I do not usually have such issues. I doubt I'd even be able to give you [Zombie Apocalypse]. *Ah*, curses.

Sally watched the skill filter onto her list.

Edward stepped forward. "Could I have the same deal, please?"

No.

The pressure in the room dropped, and any residual movement of air halted as the large figure looming above them froze and turned to ash. Slowly, parts of them broke off and dissipated, as if they were a burning piece of paper now made two-dimensional.

"Damn it," Edward growled. "Put another demon coin in." He turned to the zombie.

Sally stood staring at her new ability with lips pouted. Reading the vague System description over and over again.

"Everything okay, Sally?" Humphrey walked over to her, positioning behind so that he could read her windows. After a few moments, he stood up straight. "*Oh.*"

"That's like . . . an ultimate, right?" She blinked slowly, unsure how to think.

Humphrey scratched at his chin, causing her to wince. "It isn't something a Player would get, or even high-level bosses, really."

Edward fidgeted, unable to see the messages in front of the zombie's face. "What does it do? Why are you both so pensive about it? Was it worth the cost? Give me a demon coin."

Sally exhaled and closed the STAR down. Her eyes also closed, and she rubbed them with her fingers. "Man, no wonder Theo gets so grouchy. Being tired sucks." She lifted her head, a wide grin across her face as her eyes sparkled.

"It has limitations." Humphrey put his hand on her shoulder. "So do not go wasting it."

She rolled her eyes but couldn't wipe the smile from her face. "The conditionals aren't even active, so don't worry. I'll actually keep the horses in the barn for this one."

"I'm not sure what that means."

"Me neither," she said as she continued to beam at him.

The demon worked his jaw. "Can we please summon the spooky god thing again? I'd like to trade some of my skills."

"No." Sally shook her head. "You are not taking part in this dungeon, remember? No pain, no spoils. Did you want a turn, Humps?"

"I am content with what I have available, but thank you." The Death Knight walked around, back to the altar, and gave her a brief nod.

"Alright, let's pop the proper thing in and play by the rules for a change!" She shot Humphrey some finger guns. "Like *that* ever worked out for us."

Edward trembled with anger, tensing as if he were considering drawing his blade. After a few seconds, he sighed and relaxed. His hands found his pockets, and he strode off toward them as they peered at the coin slot once more.

"Don't look so glum, Edward," she said with a smile, noticing his face. "I'm sure you have great things in your very near future."

It looked more like he had an upset stomach, but it wouldn't hurt trying to pep him up a little. The sun coin slid into the slot, and a warm energy filled the room.

"You didn't even explain your new ability," he grumbled.

"Nope! I want to keep it a secret. Trust me, it'll be worth the wait."

The demon rolled his light blue eyes as a pulse of amber rose up from the runes, a swirling vortex appearing and shimmering. After a few volatile seconds, it became flat and inert.

"*Neat*. A portal." Sally hopped around to stand before it.

With one last chance to take a deep breath, she stepped into it, followed by the two others.

CHAPTER FORTY

Dance with the Demon

Light washed over them as they stepped through—a brief sense of vertigo before their feet found solid ground again.

They now found themselves in a massive chamber, easily double that of the statue or lava rooms. The sides of the walls were slanted to meet the floor, giving the effect that they were in a large pool. Far above them, darkness shrouded the high ceiling. Around 120 feet in front of them, a pair of wall torches flanked a small figure. A figure of red and brown, chained to two posts on either side of them.

"Lucius!" Sally called, her voice echoing down the room.

A small bubble with an exclamation mark popped up beside the figure, and he raised his head. "Sally? It's a trap!" His voice echoed back.

"Duh," she murmured. "Hey, Humps, you think after this, we could go back through the dungeon?"

He deflated and narrowed his eye sockets. "*No.* Why?"

"I kinda left my bat in that room that almost killed me." It had saved her life, and she hadn't even considered saving it in return. How cruel she truly was.

"We'll find you a new one." The Death Knight sighed and looked back at the open expanse in front of them.

Slowly, they approached the slightly raised dais where the demon sat restrained. Sally checked the floor, awaiting something to burst from the stonework. Humphrey checked the ceiling, expecting something to drop down upon them. But gradually, they made it across the whole room without incident.

"Sorry we weren't here sooner; what was the trap?" She stabbed at the chains with her dagger, splitting them.

"Ah!" A heart appeared beside his head as his shadowed crimson eyes flooded with joy. "Thank you for even coming! I don't know what the trap is—only that they will be expecting you here."

"Ah, that's pretty simple then." Sally shrugged. "We weren't ever not going to be here, so—"

A flashing shard of light blinded them as something seemed to unravel from the very air itself. As quickly as it started, it blinked out, and two figures dropped to the floor.

One was unmistakably a cat, and the other appeared to be a Theo.

"You're back!" Sally beamed, resisting the urge to leap atop them both.

"Yes." Archie stretched out and yawned. "Good news and bad news."

Theo groaned and rolled onto his back.

"Theo successfully had a proper sleep," the cat continued, "however . . . he . . ."

The vampire sat up and rubbed his eyes as Sally walked over and put her hand atop his head.

"Wow," he said, "what a difference a bit of sleep can have. I feel like a new . . ." He paused his train of thought to open up his STAR, giving the zombie a brief scowl for the presence of her holding his brain container.

"Archie." Sally narrowed her eyes and put her hands on her hips. The cat gave a sheepish grin and tried to sink into the floor.

"So, first—" Theo sighed as he pushed himself to his feet. "—I am Level One again. I have absorbed everything, *once again.*"

Humphrey shuffled awkwardly. "Was that the good or bad news?"

"We already went over the good news," Sally snapped. "Are you a Novice again, Theo?"

"No. I am *Unknown*, apparently." Theo slowly turned around. "Second, what is *he* doing here?" He leveled a finger toward the tall, blue-eyed demon.

"I see having a nap didn't shake the rocks from your head." Edward tilted his head with a grin.

"Play nice!" Sally waved her hands in the air. "Edward is mostly a reasonable demon that has recently opened up to us and hasn't tried to extort or kill us."

"I don't trust him." Theo narrowed his crimson eyes. "And I *know* why."

Edward said nothing but furrowed his brow at the vampire.

"He is acting as a beacon to signal when we get to this room. There would be no other way for the other henchmen to get close to us. But now we have been led to this area to be preyed upon. Either they will kill us all or try and get us to bend the knee and join with Ruben."

Silence fell across the Party. Sally's right eye twitched. "*Deny it* then, Edward."

The demon didn't respond, seemingly too stuck on chewing on something unpleasant. Eventually, his eyes dropped. "I truly am sorry. They know how many lives I have left. I couldn't . . . even if I wanted to help . . ."

Theo spat on the floor. "Then there's one way to settle this. Duel to the death."

"Don't be an ass, Theo—you've only just—"

"I accept." Edward bowed. "May fate guide us to the destined outcome."

"We both know it already has." Theo bowed in return.

Sally shot an exasperated look at the Death Knight and raised her hands in the air. "Humps! Are we just going to allow this?"

"Yes. If it is what brings Theo some peace, it will be for the best."

Lucius sidled along beside him. "But what if he *dies*? Edward has less to worry about." A plated shrug was the only response.

Theo stretched out his tired muscles and yawned. "Oh. I don't have any weapons anymore; could I borrow one?"

Sally glared at him, half tempted to let him suffer without. "*Fiiine.* Honestly, what is it with you and duels? You don't need to impress me, you know. It's the one reckless thing about the normal you I don't understand or enjoy."

The vampire walked up and gave her a hug. "You talk too much, Sally Danger."

"*Ass.*" She pushed him away gently, slightly flustered. "It hasn't even been a day; no need for that." She shook her head. "You can have a proper hug when you stop being a dingus."

"You've been here about three days, actually." Edward withdrew his thin sword and gave the air a few test slices.

That somehow seemed very likely given how tired they were, even if it hadn't felt that long. Sally sighed. "Here, can you use this?" She passed him the [Demonkiller Blade], expecting to have to stow it away right away.

"Oh, yeah—perfect. That's pretty apt, too, huh?" He tested the weight of it in his grip.

"When did you get the reputation for that? What even *is* reputation?"

"Probably when I killed hundreds of demons." He walked across the room a little to give them both some space, giving her a brief wink. The blade was a dark metal with symbols glowing down the flat sides—pulsing between amber and crimson.

"You realize I have . . . quite some levels on you? If you have just been reset . . ." Edward tilted his head.

"Yeah. I might not even be able to damage you." Theo pushed his glasses up.

"Then why do this? Why risk your life when your Party could easily kill me?"

"Oh, I'm not going to kill you." The vampire grinned, his fangs reflecting in the light. "I'm going to humble you, and then when the other lackeys arrive, we will slaughter them in front of you. Then you can run back to your boss and tell the tale."

A sweat drop appeared beside Lucius. "Wow, he is a lot different when he is well-rested."

Sally kneeled beside the cat. "Arch, did he retain all his vamp skills?"

Archie just shrugged in return, an odd movement for a cat.

If he didn't, then he was getting himself into more trouble than she thought him capable of. Not that she truly doubted him—his stats should hopefully still be incredibly overpowered . . . but with the unknown level difference . . .

Edward licked his lips as he used some of his abilities. *[Quick Footed] [Last Laugh] [Sword Dance]*.

Theo just stood there, looking rather uncomfortable.

Immediately, the demon lashed forward. Theo blocked the attack, the metallic clang filling the chamber, but the follow-through as the blade slipped past cut across his arm. He turned away as the next strike was already on the way, and he barely jumped back to avoid being impaled.

Edward was quick, even if he was lower level than most of them. Every sword attack already had a second and third planned in advance—as if he knew the best choice of action, whether or not his blade would land—and many of them did. Blood flicked to the ground as gashes sliced through Theo. His health slowly regenerating, but with his reduced pool, it wasn't giving him a great buffer to absorb a lot of damage.

In return, he had done zero damage to the demon. Barely even attempted an attack, as he was constantly on the back foot. Clumsily he slashed forward, but Edward had already spun around the side, winding two new crimson lines across the vampire's arm.

"Are you toying with me?" The demon grinned. "Feel I'm not worthy of your time?"

"I'm just worried if I hit you, you'll die in one hit again." Theo dodged an attack, but the blade of his opponent snaked around and stabbed into his side.

"If the blade is too heavy to carry, then—here." With a lunge, Edward impaled Theo's shoulder, and the sword clattered to the ground as his arm twitched.

"*Idiot*," Sally murmured to herself. Why they had to stand around and accommodate these duels, she had no idea. She would hear no end of it if she interfered, though. Plus, Theo always had a plan for these things.

Humphrey kneeled to Archie. "Anything else happen in . . . wherever you were?"

"No." Archie stared blankly at the Death Knight before turning back to the fight, unblinking. "*No*."

The vampire stumbled backward as he avoided being struck through the heart, his left arm instead taking damage as he held his bleeding shoulder.

"Well, looks like destiny was on my side, after all." Edward chuckled. "Guess you shouldn't bite off more than you can chew?"

[Inevitable End]

As energy pulsed through the demon's blade, it flickered through the air straight for the neck of the vampire.

Theo paused, frozen, as the attack careened toward him.

A wry smile curled at the side of his fanged mouth.

CHAPTER FORTY-ONE

Goodbye, Theo

[Dread Counter]

The attack from the demon flexed ineffectively against the vampire. A grin flashed across Edward's face—this was not the first time he had seen this skill—and had been expecting it. Immediately, he was twirling into a follow-up strike.

[Blood Shift]

But then, Theo wasn't there anymore. The sword struck through empty air as the vampire rose up behind him, mouth crackling with critical energy. Pain and blood, as fangs sunk into the demon's neck. Edward tried to move, but his limbs became lethargic and slack.

"Interesting." Humphrey rubbed his chin. "Theo figured that only a critical would have damaged the demon because of the level difference, so he bet it all on one attack that could debilitate him."

Sally narrowed her eyes and watched the vampire continue to drink from the weakening demon. "I thought *[Vampire Bite]* only lasted two or three seconds?"

"He is doing it the old-fashioned way," the Death Knight said with a grin.

Eventually, Theo dropped Edward with a gasp. The demon collapsed to the floor with dim eyes. He looked dried up, with his skin sunken to his bones.

Humphrey kneeled beside him and gave him a prod. "This was supposed to be a duel to the death, Theo. Finish the job, otherwise, you are desecrating the sanctity of—"

"*Humphrey!*" Sally scowled. "Theo did as he said he would."

Theo raised a finger as if to say something, then immediately threw up blood. A lot of blood. "Oh, boy." He gasped between retches. "I'll stick to the skill n—*urp*—next time."

The Death Knight stood back up and shook his head. "I'm getting rather tired of watching people empty their stomachs." Archie looked up at him, but then immediately avoided the empty-socket gaze.

"Alright." Theo sighed, wiping his mouth off on the back of his arm. "We'll call that even, then. Water under the bridge, Edward?"

". . . Okay . . ." the demon gurgled from the floor.

"You can notify your friends now to come kill us." The vampire walked back over to pick up the dropped sword.

"I . . . refuse."

Sally squatted down. "Why not? You'll get in trouble, right?"

"I'll be fine."

She rubbed her face. So much had happened recently; she needed to get everyone on the same page. With a hop to her feet, she turned to the gathered *Outsiders*. "Right, so . . . the System has . . . invited another three hundred Players to the forest."

Their collective confusion and surprise were like bees in her ears. "Alright, settle down." She sighed deeply. "So Theo, I suppose you will be heading back there to go level up again?"

He nodded slowly and brought up his STAR interface. "I've no teleport, though . . . but it would be safer than hanging out here."

"I've got one for Sanctuary still." She smiled. "You can get the goblins to make you a new casket. I'll trade you some of this armor and gold too."

Humphrey walked over to them as they made the trade. "May I see your stats, Theo?"

"Depends." The vampire looked up at him. "How good is your poker face?"

The Death Knight stared at him impassively.

"Alright, good enough for me." He swiped the menus across and waited for the plated figure to stand behind him.

After a handful of seconds of staring, Humphrey stood up straight again and looked away. "*Fuck.*"

"Yep." Theo stood to his feet groggily and tried to brush off some of the demon blood. "So, these new Players—what's our take? Kill, cultivate, avoid, or befriend?"

Sally sighed and walked up to throw her arms around him. "Do whatever. You're still a dingus, but you can have your hug. Just come back *alive*, okay?"

He held her in return, and they were quiet for a few moments.

"Demon blood vomit smells horrible, by the way," she whispered in his ear.

"I can smell brain vomit on you too."

She gently pushed him away and shuddered, slightly breathless. "That's something I'm going to file away mentally and not address. Uh . . ." She turned to the *Outsiders*. "Why are you all standing around watching? This isn't a *show*." With the addition of a growl, they all seemed to have small talk among themselves.

"Keep me updated, okay?" She turned back to the vampire. "Wish I could see what classes or abilities you get. Oh, and we don't have a teleport stone for you to find us again."

"Don't worry, I'll find my way back to you." He looked past her to give a brief wave to the rest of the group and then vanished in a wave of blue light.

Theo has left the Party

Sally stared out at the blank space where he was just standing for a few seconds before spinning around to the group with a snap of her fingers. "See, that werewolf guy could take a lesson or two from Theo." She yawned and sat down on the floor.

"You know he will be back within days." Humphrey grinned. "You needn't worry about him."

"Who's worried?" She rolled her eyes. "We can just wait here till he returns, right?"

A heart emoji appeared beside Lucius, which promptly split in half. "Now that I've seen how he is when rested, I appreciate your bond a lot more."

". . . Having to listen to this . . . is agony . . ."

"Oh, please." The zombie sighed. "Like you've never had a close platonic companionship that wasn't quite bound by traditional romance or love."

". . . Well . . . no."

She withdrew a Healing Potion from her Inventory and threw it over to Humphrey to feed to the desiccated demon. "How about you, quiet pair? Anything to add to the current situation?"

Lucius and Archie exchanged glances, a question mark appearing beside the demon before he spoke. "No, I'm happy to be a passive observer."

"Ah! I have something for *you*, maybe? Do you want a demon coin?"

The emotive demon just gave her a blank stare.

With a groan, Edward righted himself into a seated position—now a bit healthier looking from the magical effect of the potion. He rubbed at his neck and winced as the bloodied wound was still raw. "Ack. The coins will help you unlock your hidden potential. An ability that you don't have if you've space for it."

"In that case," a smiley face appeared, "yes, please, Sally! I only have two skills out of a possible . . . twelve?"

"They are once per day or something too." Edward yawned and covered his eyes. "Never had one, so I'm not sure."

Sally withdrew one and flipped it through the air toward her Party demon, not failing to notice the blue eyes of the tax collector follow it through the air. Lucius caught it and immediately placed it into the shadow, where his mouth probably was.

"Ah!" A fire emoji played beside him. "I have a new ability—it's an aura for increasing speed and dodge."

The zombie hissed a celebration to herself. Auras were great for the group, and those were great stats to increase. She had more than enough coins to max out Lucius and make him a proper part of the *Outsiders* . . . her eyes then narrowed at the other demon.

"What are we going to do with you, Edward?"

"A coin would be nice." He turned to her with a grin, but a lot of his usual pomp and flair had drained from his face.

"I'm sorry that Theo drank all your blood and stuff, must have sucked . . ." She winced at her poor choice of words.

He tilted his head. "It was a mercy. He could have killed me, and I him. He made well on his promise to humble me—and for that, I respect him and hold no grudge."

"Yet you didn't end up summoning the other goons?"

Edward shuffled awkwardly before deflating. "A Level One defeated me. Were they to come here and see that, I would be as good as dead anyway. I might as well ally myself with you now."

Humphrey grinned. "More self-preservation than getting used to our companionship, though?"

The demon gave them a wry grin. "I wouldn't mind failing upward for a change." He paused as he received a notification. "Are you sure?"

"You already have experience in being a manic asshole; you just have to trust us as much as we trust you." She beamed at him and stood on her feet.

Edward opened his mouth, then closed it to look at the floor. After a few seconds, he sighed and scrunched his eyes closed.

Edward has joined the Party

"This is just a temporary thing until Theo comes back." She wagged a finger at him. "But the least we can do is get you a couple of levels, so you aren't going to die to trash."

He stood to his feet and tried to straighten his dusty and blood-soaked suit. Facing the Party, he gave a low bow. "I hope to make you all proud and hope my previous transgressions can be ignored." Straightening up again, his confidence fell from his face. "Although it is only a matter of time now before they send someone to punish us all."

"Pfft, not worried." Sally waved her hand and then looked down at the ginger cat. "Archie, you don't feel like a giant eldritch Monster, do you?"

The Death Knight narrowed his eye sockets, as the cat tilted his head.

"I don't believe so. The time in the . . . beyond was odd. Peaceful, but I believe it gave both myself and Theo time to think." He looked up at Humphrey. "I am more eager than ever to find the artifact we require, big brother."

Sally snapped her fingers and turned to point at the expansive cavern. "To the pyramid then!"

A few moments of silence passed before she turned back around. "Actually, how do we get out of here?"

CHAPTER FORTY-TWO

Gatekeeping

The Death Knight sighed. "There is usually a boss, and defeating it will open up an exit portal."

"That's pretty handy," she said, shrugging. "But where is the boss?"

They all looked around the empty chamber, briefly narrowing their eyes at the massive space, which didn't seem to hold anything whatsoever. The zombie turned around and put her hands on her hips. "Lucius, are you secretly the boss in hiding?"

A sweat drop emoji appeared next to the demon's head. "What? No. I've just been a prisoner here for, well, it seems like days."

Sally rubbed her chin. "Edward did say it's been three days. It hasn't felt like it. But you know what that means?" She wiggled her eyebrows at Humphrey. "We must have been having *fun*."

Humphrey slowly shook his head while the tax collector looked in the other direction, trying to avoid eye contact and acknowledge her statement.

Sally turned her attention once again to the empty room. "It's no wonder we've been feeling a little crazy, if we haven't slept in a couple of days too. Maybe our first port of call once we escape should be to have a little rest." She wasn't yet sure where they'd go to acquire this desired rest, with everything being a desert, but that was a problem for future Sally.

"Sounds reasonable." Archie yawned. "I feel a bit tired myself."

"Weren't you just sleeping for the three days as well?" She wagged her finger at him. It was an assumption, but it seemed reasonable that they had both been in a state of rest in the nether. Otherwise, that would have been pretty boring and undoubtedly would have led to mischief.

"Maybe," he answered and started looking in a different direction before he caught the glare of the Death Knight and drifted his emerald gaze instead to the emptiness above them.

She looked around to see who should get a prod of her questioning next. "Perhaps there's a way for us to summon the boss. What do *you* think, Edward?"

The demon shrugged. "I'm not too sure. As I said, I haven't been here before either, so this is all relatively new to me."

Sally feigned prodding at her STAR. "How about if you tell us, then I'll give you a demon coin as a treat?"

"I don't think trying to tempt me with the coin is going to make the answer appear. However, I will take a coin if it's on offer." Edward's eyes lit up a brighter blue as he leaned in her direction.

Sally shook her head. "We defeat the boss, then you can have one."

The demon crossed his arms in retaliation. A narrowed gaze leveled at her.

Lucius cleared his throat. "Actually, I think there's some writing on the back of this dais. Would you help me have a look?" The Party turned to him, the glare across their faces causing a sweat bubble to appear beside him.

"Is it in that silly language again?" Sally started walking over to where the demon had been chained up. "There was some writing on the portal device we played with before entering here, but none of us could read it." She hopped over the slack chains and squatted down at the back of the raised platform. "Yep, looks to be that way. Can you read this, Lucius?"

Another sweat drop emoji appeared next to the demon's head as he kneeled beside her to get a better view. "No, it's not something I know, unfortunately."

Sally turned her head to him and narrowed her eyes. "What's going on underneath that hood of yours?" It wasn't that she particularly minded some secrecy, but the demon had been covered in shadow from the moment they had met. Just a heads-up if they were someone in disguise or important and on the run. Maybe they weren't even a demon—her mind started unraveling at the possibilities.

Lucius practically leaped from where he was standing. "*Nothing*, it's just my face."

Sally nodded enthusiastically with a blank expression as Archie walked over and rubbed himself against her legs.

"I can read it, Sally," he said.

"Okay." She waited for a handful of seconds, staring at the cat as he looked back at her with his emerald eyes. "So, *are* you going to do it, then?" Internally, she sighed. If she had a demon coin for every time one of the *Outsiders* couldn't follow-through with a sentence, then she would have—

"I suppose," he said with a nod. Briefly, he ran his eyes along the odd, deep-red runes engraved along the smooth stone. "It says there needs to be a sacrifice to summon the boss."

Sally furrowed her brow. "What does it mean by sacrifice? They can't expect groups to come down here and kill one of their own Party members to summon the boss. Nobody would do the dungeon." Well, now that they had Edward, she might entertain such an idea—although it would be unfair this early in their grouping to designate him as the sacrifice.

"Is there like a low indentation here?" The cat jumped down from the side of the raised dais to sniff around the brickwork behind it. "It's like a bowl shape, but it has no food in it."

She bit her lip and then stepped down beside him, squatting down to have a look herself. "It looks like a receptacle," she agreed. "Maybe *blood* goes in there." She grinned. "Shame that Theo didn't vomit over here instead."

Humphrey sighed and rubbed the side of his head. "It's a shame he had to throw up at all. I find it most concerning that neither of you seems to find that a bit problematic. As someone who doesn't eat, I certainly have seen enough food come back up out of people."

Edward bared his sharp teeth as he continued to hold his arms crossed. "Seeing as it was my blood that, you know, he threw up all across the floor here. *I* could have used that. I *was* using it."

"Alright, alright." Sally waved her hand. "Enough of the back-and-forth banter. You're not paid per hot take."

The tax collector tilted his head. "We get paid?" He caught the glare of the Death Knight and deflated.

"What do you think, Archie?" Sally continued. "Should we try blood first, or do we have anything else that we could try to pour in? It looks like there's a little grate down at the bottom." She narrowed her eyes at the slightly recessed area behind the dais—it was a slightly different color than the rest of the brickwork and smooth like a bowl. In fact, if it weren't for the odd positioning, she would almost assume that it was some kind of basin and had been placed on the floor. But instead of the plughole, there's just a small grate of tiny holes, almost like pinpricks, at the very bottom of the indent.

"Actually," said the ginger cat, tilting his head, "I prefer for it to be filled with food. But in the event that isn't possible, then perhaps blood might work. Do you have any volunteers?"

Sally surveyed the group of *Outsiders* as they tried to avoid her glare. Edward had already done enough bleeding for one day, she thought, and Humphrey didn't really have any blood that she could think of. Lucius had spent several days chained here, so it seemed a bit unfair to prompt him to bleed when he'd been a prisoner and only just freed, and Archie was too small. Barely had any blood in him at all. "I wish Theo were still here." She sighed. "He wouldn't mind bleeding a little."

She withdrew her dagger and held it by the blade, pointing the handle toward Lucius. "Lucius, you have to *cut* me."

"I don't want to cut you, Sally," he murmured uncomfortably, trying to edge away from where she was now crouched.

"Fine, I have to do *everything* myself." She placed the tip of the blade against the back of her hand and slid it across, briefly surprised at how easily it cut through her skin. As crimson began to well and drip from the wound, she held it over the basin. Gradually, one drip after another, they plopped down to seemingly no effect. Fully engaged with the spectacle, they all stood watching her as drip after drip landed in the basin and formed a small collection. She raised her head and caught their impatient glances.

"What did you expect? I'm not going to cut my whole hand off just to do this. It would be a waste of a good Healing Potion." She was tired of the dungeon and exhausted from the days spent wandering around the halls, getting prodded by sharp things and bested by simple puzzles. It was a wonder that they couldn't tell so much time had passed, but the day/night cycle was strange in the Wastelands, so it might have something to do with that.

"I half expected Theo to have messaged me already." She sat down to be more comfortable beside the basin. "Just to brag about leveling up already. But I guess he might be socializing or something." The thought made her a little glum. Perhaps after saving the world, she could go back for a little victory tour and see the goblins and Jackie again.

Archie pawed at her non-bleeding hand. "I might be able to help this along." A ripple of energy ruffled his fur from his tail down to his head as he opened his mouth. A wriggling worm of energy pulsed forth, shimmering between yellow and green, and fell into the basin. As it touched the drips of blood, they expanded to ten times their size.

Now, with the bowl almost full, the blood began to seep down into the small holes. "Huh." Sally grinned. "I guess I don't have to do everything my—"

Before she could finish that thought, a crackle of energy ran around the dais and interrupted her. A yellow light emanated from around the cracks in the rock and vibrations pulsed through the floor. The *Outsiders* scrambled away from the platform as it rose into the air, golden light illuminating their faces as a figure came into view.

Archie's emerald eyes grew wide as the form of the boss rose above them.

CHAPTER FORTY-THREE

Bossy Boots

Sally shielded her eyes as the golden light blinded her.

"The Eternal Sands shall consume you. Wear you down until you are one among us." The voice reverberated around the large chamber.

As the immediate glow faded, the *Outsiders* turned to look at the figure that had risen from the floor. A tall humanoid, male in appearance but with a bird-like head, either fully composed of gold or perhaps illuminated by some radiant power.

"I reject your threatening and substitute my own," Sally yelled back. "Come a little closer so that I may eat your brain!"

The golden, bird-like figure, muscular and wielding a long spear, turned his head down to leer at her. His eyes were blank circles of golden hue. Briefly, she became lost within them as the boss slowly drew his arm backward.

With a rush of air, the pointed end of the weapon flashed forward as she dodged, and the zombie narrowly missed being impaled as the golden spear dug a groove into the stone floor.

Light illuminating the area alongside a pulse of energy, the Party activated all their buffing skills.

[Inspirational Word]—"Sally, you can do it!" said Lucius.

At the same time as their skills were being cast, the boss raised his hand, and crackles of golden lightning rained down from the ceiling. Instead of being able to launch directly into an attack, the Party found themselves having to avoid the sudden downpour of electrical energy. Where each bolt struck, it scorched the sandstone flooring, leaving a scar of charred black across the battlefield.

Hopping spot to spot in brief panic, the Party avoided all the attacks.

Eventually, the spell ceased, and the boss lowered his spear to prepare for the renewed assault.

Sally raised her left hand as the right held Skeleton Key. Confusion flashed through her face at the realization that she didn't have *[Necroblast]* anymore, and her attack just didn't come out. She rolled beneath a wide arc of the long spear as both Edward and Archie dropped below it too.

Humphrey blocked the swing with the flat of his blade, the force sliding him several feet across the stone floor before coming to a stop. He slid his greatsword down the metal shaft of the spear and ran forward, *[Grave Strike]* pulsing dark energy through his weapon.

[Hex: Slow]. Sally winced as it didn't seem to hold very well on the creature—perhaps his level reduced the effectiveness? If it had been three days, then she should have her zombie pals waiting in the wings. *[Summon Zombies]*. Five of the undead began to crawl from the floor around her as the Death Knight struck the boss in the leg.

A hiss rang through the chamber as a mark remained across where the large blade had struck, as if he had bruised the metallic figure. In response, the boss jabbed the blunt end of the spear down toward Humphrey—who buckled beneath it as he barely blocked the strike.

[Summon Zombies]—Another five rose up, this group in the midpoint between her and the boss.

Edward looked pained, as if angered at the sudden assault of the statuesque creature, yet also panicked into not wanting to lose a level and his life in the attempt. He stood in place, frozen with indecision.

Likewise, Lucius had slowly recoiled away from the melee as far as possible, almost up against the back wall now as he occasionally murmured out encouragements too weak for them to hear over the thumping adrenaline battle.

The golden boss kicked out at the Death Knight, sending him stumbling backward, and raised a hand out to cast another skill. Farther down near the entrance, small whirlwinds of dust started to form—bright amber eyes bursting into view as the living storms began to work their way toward the Party.

"Don't stand in the red stuff!" Sally yelled, casting the final *[Summon Zombies]* right up close to the boss. Another five—a decent roll at last. Now she had a loose train of walking corpses from her current position to the large figure focused on Humphrey.

"There *isn't* any red." Edward narrowed his eyes as he growled back.

"There will be if you don't move it, buster." She nodded toward the approaching tornados—three in total—before she started off for her attack.

As the boss whipped the spear around to dislodge the Death Knight further, he sensed her approach and turned to level a quick jab at her.

Sally weaved between her summoned pals, dodging behind them and using them as cover on her approach. The sharp tip of the spear surged forth and impaled the corpse next to her, breaking the body clean in half. The boss withdrew his weapon to sweep forward with the blunt end—but again, she spun to the side between the next zombie, which was flung dozens of feet into the air from the missed blow.

A couple more steps and she had made it close enough. Her dagger found purchase in the leg of the boss, sinking deep into the golden skin where Humphrey's sword had just made a blunt dent. As she rolled through the legs, she saw that the Death Knight had engaged one of the tornados, Edward was trying to bait out an attack from the second, and the third was trying to chase after Archie.

The cat had decided it was finally time for the zoomies and was rushing around the more open space of the other end of the chamber. He stopped occasionally to change direction abruptly whenever his assailant got closer. Distracted by how he looked with his ears back and a wild look in his eyes, Sally would have found it amusing to continue to watch him were she not kicked in the stomach by the boss.

She tumbled across the floor, righting herself just in time to see the closed golden fist come down upon her. With no time to react, she held the dagger up to block and was crushed into the ground.

The crimson greatsword flashed a bright blue as Humphrey was able to use *[Decimate]* for the first time, the strike passing straight through the dust storm elemental but seeming to destroy whatever core held it together. As the Monster faded away, he spun around to see the golden bird-man looming over the prone zombie. *[Compelled Duel]*.

The impassive eyes of the boss looked up at the Death Knight briefly before ignoring the challenge. Instead, the spear flickered forward and crashed into the stone floor, cracks forming from where it struck.

Sally rolled back up to her feet, dizzied. It would take more than that to keep her down; she was *overpowered*. She spat her own blood on the floor and tried to remember how to reset a dislocated shoulder. Thankfully, it wasn't her dagger-wielding arm. Though her dagger wasn't even being wielded currently, as it was still lodged in the boss's hand.

[Desecrate Life]. She briefly regretted not picking more active attack skills while leveling. Giving some away wasn't super smart either—but the look on Theo's face when she used her new skill would—

She leaped backward, falling onto her back, causing a sharp pain to flare through her inert arm as a plume of dust erupted from where the boss tried to strike her with the spear.

The weapon caused sparks to shoot into the air as he pushed it forward, slicing across the sandstone and just catching Sally in the upswing—a large gash immediately flooding with crimson along her thigh.

Clouds gathered in the high ceiling chamber as the golden bird raised a hand up to cast the lighting skill again. Humphrey made it back to her and was trying to help her up. Edward had just about finished off his opponent but looked rather bloodied himself. How the swirling wind had caused him to bleed would have to be a question for later.

Archie was . . . well, there were now five Archies sprinting around erratically, causing the tornado to become . . . confused, if that was even possible.

"You need to move," Humphrey growled, partially lifting her and then pushing her out of the way as a shock of golden light snapped to the floor between them.

She fumbled for a Healing Potion as she hopped on one leg, the other numb and unresponsive. The Party really needed to get a healer as soon as possible. Being overwhelmingly powerful was no use when the Monsters were glitched or high level. The cork popped from the glass bottle as she cast a nervous glance upward to the ceiling for any incoming lighting. She raised the potion to her lips and—

"*Sally!*" Humphrey yelled.

A blunt force struck her, and the attack sent her tumbling across the room, slamming into the far wall. The healing item fell and shattered on the floor. Something cracked inside her, and a flood of cold ran through her body. As her eyes stopped rolling around, she regained focus to see the boss briefly harried by the throng of zombies who had managed to clump around the golden feet.

She found she couldn't move her legs and only one arm. Not ideal—so much for the armor being any use. Oddly, she felt . . . good. Obviously, she wasn't in very good shape, and the pool of blood from her leg that didn't seem to want to stop was less than ideal . . . a notification popped up.

Crimson Armor Set Bonus Passive
Low Health Threshold Reached - Temporary Bonus Stat Buff Activated

---

The Death Knight slid across the floor in front of her to protect her. Archie had become a tornado of his own, a literally spinning dervish of multiple copies of himself. Edward was cautiously circling around the boss, watching and waiting for an opportunity to strike. She could still hear the encouraging words of Lucius in the distance, his emoticons switching between panicked sweat drops and jubilant fireworks.

She popped the cork of another Healing Potion as her stash dwindled.

"Help me up, Humps." Her arm extended toward the Death Knight, and he lifted her to her feet as bones cracked back into position and her severed arteries sealed up.

"There's only room enough for one boss in this chamber."

CHAPTER FORTY-FOUR

Worth Less

You know, I'm kind of okay with Theo being the more powerful fighter."
Sally gave the Death Knight a pat on the shoulder as they watched the boss
try to stomp and stab through the rest of the zombies.

"Oh?" Humphrey raised a wary eyebrow. He seemed to be more intent on
focusing on the current battle than she was.

"Like, I can be the main character but not be the best at *everything*." She
shrugged, a wave of exhaustion passing through her as the healing magic put
her back together. "I went for the melee powerhouse stuff to keep myself alive—
but . . . you know—maybe I should have chosen that *puppy* skill."

"I think you have hit your head a bit too hard." He grinned at her. "I
understand, though. Theo has . . . Depending on how the System treats his class
advancement now, he would be hard to keep up with."

"That's fine. A queen isn't supposed to do all the dirty work, anyway. I'll have
you as my shield and Theo as my sword." She narrowed her eyes. "*Golden ass* still
has my dagger. I hope we level up from this."

"Just to warn you . . ." Humphrey rolled out his shoulders as the boss looked
to be finishing up with the last handful of zombies. "Thirteen is a passive ability
choice. Fourteen is an active, then at fifteen, you get an ultimate and class
change . . . if you're normal."

"Normal." Sally rolled her eyes and brought up her STAR.

Sally: level ten yet?
Theo: still one :*
Theo: goblins are well

Theo: new players are . . .
Theo: a temptation

She shuddered and closed the chat, wiping the drool from her mouth. "Some people get all the fun," she murmured.

He just rolled his empty eye sockets, an impressive skill. "If you could rub the heart shapes from your eyes, we have business to attend to."

With a tut, she nudged him on the arm as she brought out her *[Dagger of Luck]*. "Don't be jealous, Humps. We'll find you someone to have a cute but platonic companionship with in no time."

Humphrey opened his mouth to say something, but a gathering of energy drew their attention as the boss began charging up a beam attack after having finished destroying all the zombies.

Perhaps next time, she would use them for something a bit more efficient than having a conversation. It had allowed her limbs time to recover their proper function, however.

A fifteen-foot-wide beam burst from the golden boss—a radiant circle of white-gold energy—and flashed toward them in an instant.

[Impenetrable Defense]

The silhouette of the Death Knight was the only thing Sally could see as the bright light washed over them. His arms outstretched. A fizzling noise crackled in her ears, almost loud enough to miss hearing Edward make his move on the channeling boss.

[Inevitable End]

As soon as the light had blinded them, it dissipated, as the powerful skill ended. The golden figure turned away to strike out at the demon, his block not strong enough. With a thud, his body rolled across the floor. The muttered curses were enough to signal that he was wounded but not dead.

There was a growing crack running up the leg of the boss where he had struck, a deep purple that pulsed like a vein. Sally didn't know what it did exactly, but the golden bird-man didn't seem too happy about it. She turned to Humphrey. "Fling me."

With his free hand, Humphrey grabbed a hold of the zombie, and she held his arm so that he didn't just wrench her socket out. Turning a quick circle, he launched her into the air toward the Monster.

As she flew, she swapped to her crossbow, firing off the bolt before dropping the weapon, her old dagger popping back into her hand. Thankfully, Theo wasn't around to see her quick swap. She landed atop her target at shoulder height, clambering to get a grip on the smooth metallic form of the boss. The hand holding the spear went to raise to jostle her away, but the Archie cat-nado swirled up the weapon and weighed it down.

Her attempted stabs did little more than leave small indentations in the body of her opponent, and with a deep growl that vibrated through her whole body, the boss reached for her with his other hand.

[Inspirational Word]—"Just as planned!"

Sally leaped through the air just as the hand came for her, as hers wrapped around the handle of Skeleton Key, plucking it from the wound it had become lodged in. She fell to the floor and rolled to absorb the impact, turning to see that the boss had attempted to come for her, but Archie had begun to pull the weapon away, and the purple decay had almost filled the whole leg of the Monster, leaving it sluggish.

She spun through the STAR to grab something more useful for her off hand than the luck dagger, and mis-clicked on the [////ss***__] item she had hoped to ignore. Immediately, System messages flooded her vision.

> Type Error: Missing Skill {Necroblast}
> Incorrect parameters. Analyzing . . .
> Attempting override. Please stand by.

Humphrey came up behind her. His eye sockets narrowed at the messages as the boss continued to be inconvenienced by the cat.

"Did you touch an *error?*"

"It was an accident!" She scrunched up her eyes in trying to get the messages to move out of the way of the battle, the blue boxes flickering slightly.

> Skill granted [Necro[Necroblast]blast[Barrageblast]]

"Ah, that doesn't seem much better." She waved her wrist around as if she could shake the ill omens straight out of the STAR.

"I'm not sure you should—" Humphrey began as Sally raised her arm toward the boss.

[Necro[Necroblast]blast[Barrageblast]Necroblast[[blast]Necrobarrage] blast[blastblast]]

Sally blinked. Warm blood ran down her arm from cracks in her hand, as a stinging sensation started to burn at the end of her nerves. A hiss pierced the silence in the air. At first, it was the dusty atmosphere in the chamber moving to fill in the gaps of reality rent from existence. Then, it was the sand slowly filtering in from the hole in the ceiling where the skill had pierced all the way out into the unknown.

The golden boss faltered, the impassive eyes on the bird's face glaring at the floor as it toppled over. The fist-size gap cored through his head had become detrimental to him being alive.

She took a deep breath and then another. The process unnecessary but also draining.

> Error - Skill Use Out of Intended Bounds
> Restricting [Necro*st]
> System Granted: Skill Reset Points (2)

Sally dropped to her knees, her arm still extended. Apparently, she couldn't move it or feel much other than the burning sensation ravaging her fingers and palm.

Humphrey kneeled beside her to glance between the System messages and the wide panic in her eyes.

"What lesson did we learn?"

"Don't . . . don't mess with errors." She breathed.

The rest of the *Outsiders* moved over to them, concern and shock across their faces. An emoji of a little face sat screaming beside Lucius.

"You should have just done that at the start." Edward smirked, hand holding his ribs where some crimson had soaked his suit.

"What happened, big brother?" Archie wobbled as his eyes still spun, dizzied from the constant tornado attack.

The Death Knight sighed, relenting to how convoluted the answer was. "Sally had a bugged item that referred to a skill she no longer had because she made a deal with an eldritch entity to remove it. The System gave her the skill in an attempt to fix the mismatch, but it also became errored, and after she tried to use it, the System realized it was wrong so took it away."

"Oh." Archie yawned. "I didn't mean *that*."

Humphrey narrowed his eye sockets, and his plated hands tensed and flexed.

"Are you okay, Sally? You did great!" Lucius gave her two thumbs-up. "You could . . . put your hand down now, though?"

"That *would* be nice." Sally continued staring off into the distance. "I can't seem to move, though. I feel like I just killed every atom in that direction."

They all turned to look up into the darkness of the ceiling, where a light stream of sand continued to pour down. It certainly looked like she had done something of the sort.

"I've got some medicine kits for those that need it," she continued, wincing as her arm slowly became limp gradually. "Just as soon as I can hit the button."

"Just you and Edward." Humphrey nodded.

As Sally struggled against her complaining muscles, she managed to get into her Inventory and carefully bring out the right items. "I hope the boss dropped some potions—we are running low since I've been chugging them like gamer fuel."

The Death Knight shrugged. "You're the only Player here, so be our guest."

"Heck yeah, I am," she whispered to herself.

As she said this, a *pop* of magical energy burst from where the dais had once stood—and a portal came into being. Sally relaxed somewhat, both as the warmth of the healing flooded through her and from the relief of having an easy way out of this dungeon.

Humphrey helped her to her feet, and she stumbled over to the golden corpse. "Sorry that I didn't get to eat your brains," she whispered to the boss as she looted it.

3618 Gold
Dungeon Reward Chest (1)
Greater Healing Potion (3)
Tornado Wand (3 charges)
Lightning Resist Potion (2)
Golden Tome
Emblem of Eternity
Dungeon Clear!

Her hand hovered over the items, not really wanting to get into any loot theatrics until it was really needed. The emblem piqued her interest, however.

[Emblem of Eternity] +2 STR, +2 CON, Increased Defenses

Well, that seemed rather arbitrary, but she seemed to be able to equip it without replacing anything else, so free stats were free stats. It looked like the engraving that had the poem under it, in miniature form, which was almost as disappointing as not making her immune to time or something.

"Neat," she eventually declared. With a glum shrug to the group, the exhaustion of three manic days finally greeting her with the spent power of the bugged skill, she led them out through the portal in the amber heat of beyond.

CHAPTER FORTY-FIVE

Three Days Grimace

The heat was unbearable.

After stepping through the portal, the Party found themselves right outside the dungeon, back among the sun-bleached stone and sandy desert of the Wastelands. Despite how stuffy the boss's room had gotten after the battle, the fresh air did little to relieve the group since it was heated beneath the constant sun.

"We can just go into the starting room again to sleep?" Sally held her arm over her eyes. "I can't move through this without rest."

"Not the most ideal place to have a nap." Edward shrugged. "But the next potential place is a good walk away."

Humphrey held his sword in the midst of the falling sand so that they could step over the door trap again. With a collective sigh, they walked down into the shaded chamber and slunk against the walls. Sally shot a glare at the poem on the faux side again, before she too sat down.

Dungeon Completed: Reset in Eight Hours

"Time enough for a sleep," she said and sighed. "Edward, tell us some bedtime stories about the other half of the Wastes. I think our main goal is to get through the storm, right?"

Humphrey nodded. Killing the dragon was a lofty goal for their current position, and just getting through to the more inhabited areas of the second zone would be something to aspire to after they had visited the pyramids.

"Okay." Edward tilted his head in thought as he sat against one of the stone walls. "Player-wise, there are three groups: gold, silver, and bronze. Each wears a tabard showing the colors of the rank they belong to. Bronze and silver both farm all the Monster spawns in the second area to gain money for Ruben. Silver rank has more allowances and freedom . . ."

"But they still have to make money for the dragon?" Sally yawned and rubbed her eyes.

"Correct. The gold ranks are more of enforcers working for the dragon's council. They make sure the other ranks are playing nicely and are usually Players who have earned out from the previous ranks to earn favor."

Humphrey scratched his chin. "What about Uniques?"

"Five tax collectors. Five Champions. Five council members. Then there's Ruben above all." Edward sighed, his face sinking with exhaustion as the last few days took hold of his normal disposition. "Anyone else is farming alongside the Players . . . or killed."

Humphrey grimaced at the tired demon and shook his head. "Lucius and I will take the first watch."

Silence drifted throughout the chamber as the rest of the *Outsiders* fell into an easy sleep.

Sally rolled to her side and spat out a mouthful of dust. She felt like someone had been using her skull as an anvil, and they were a really shitty smith. With aching limbs, she got to her feet and stretched out. Everyone else seemed to be asleep still, aside from Archie. The cat was staring up at the corner of the room.

She whispered to get his attention. "Everything okay, Arch?"

He turned and nodded, his focus on whatever invisible thing loomed in that part of the chamber now eradicated. "Yes, they all fell asleep after awhile, so I have been watching."

She glanced at the empty corner, then back to the cat. Well, they were all alive, and nothing untoward had happened, so there wasn't much to complain about. Her STAR had pending chat notifications, which she opened up.

Theo: level 2
Theo: level 3
Theo: level 8
Theo: just kidding, level 5 now tho.

Judging by the timestamps, it looked like he had been grinding most of the night. The most annoying thing was he hadn't mentioned anything about new skills or his class. Was he a Vampire Lord still? Would he get a second pick at an overpowered Monster class and have two classes? The greedy ass.

Sally: Skills? Class? You have a bed, right?

A reply didn't come straight away. He might be sleeping still. Chuck hadn't been in touch for a few days . . . that shouldn't be worrying, but with how weird things were, it certainly ground at her empty stomach. Oh—but there was a new mail message. She always forgot to check those.

[From Chuck] [Sally, I know you don't check these—but it seems that nobody else does, so this might be the best way to warn you. They have taken us to the other side. We are being put to work as a "bronze," which sounds like enforced adventuring. I don't know what you can do, but be safe—we at least won't die, I don't think. Have to go. Take care.]

Sally kicked up some dust and balled her fists. They dared kidnap Chuck? She had half a mind to barge straight through the sandstorm and free or eat all the Players.

"Everything okay?" Humphrey rose from his seated position.

"The dragon has Chuck and his Party!" She shuddered as the anger found solace in venting out to the Death Knight. "Even more reason we need to murder our way through the second area."

Humphrey gave a gentle kick to Edward, who woke up rubbing his shin. "Huh? Danger?"

"There will be. We will have to fight our way through one of the checkpoints, correct?"

The tall demon stood and brushed down his suit. "Correct. There will be a tax collector, Champion, and Party of gold Players at the least. If we are to be expected, then . . ."

"We *will* be expected." Sally stomped around as she paced, fuming. "They will come check on Edward, and we'll kill them. They'll track us and get in the way at the pyramid, and we'll kill them again. They'll know we want to come through, and they'll send an army."

"That's not . . ." Edward rubbed his forehead. "Okay, some of that is possible. But Ruben doesn't exactly like his resources being wasted or diverted away from gaining gold unless the situation is dire."

Lucius had now awoken and rubbed at his supposed face beneath the shadowed hood.

The Death Knight walked over to the bubbling zombie and put a plated hand on her shoulder to keep her still. "It is best we focus on what is directly in front of us. If the Druid is in no current danger, then there is no need to fret. The artifact in the pyramid will give us some boons for the coming conflict."

Sally allowed her frustrations to melt away and deflated. Perhaps it was just too long since she had been able to eat some proper Player brains. If all the Parties were now on the other side, then that meant another age still before she could satisfy her empty stomach. It was no wonder she was skin and bones.

"As nice as your sun hats were, Edward . . ." She slunk against the wall and sighed. "I don't think I could walk all the way to the pyramid under this heat."

He smiled and crossed his arms. "I can't promise a straightforward route, but I can get us both closer—and to a place that has brains you can . . . eat." The sentence seemed to lose its luster once he realized what he was saying.

She narrowed her eyes at him. "I knew there was a good reason we were destined to be friends. Spill the details."

The demon rolled his eyes. "There are a few locations I can teleport in order to aid my previous duties. The pyramid is unfortunately not one of these—but there is a village of hostile lizard-people nearby that I can. They have persisted through the heat."

"Neat." She snapped her fingers. "So, we drop in, get a quick bite to eat, and then it'll be a short stroll over to our main objective?"

"*Shorter*, yes."

Humphrey stretched out his shoulders. "The dungeon brought you close to leveling. Hopefully, a bit of combat will push you over the edge."

"Hopefully, there will be some edges to push the lizard kin over and into my mouth." She grinned and looked at the gathered Party.

Sure, they were less effective without the powerhouse of Theo with them, but she knew he would turn up just when things were dire once again. While she was no damsel in distress, she was willing to let him be the knight in shining armor if it made her life more convenient and less traumatic. She glanced at Humphrey with a little guilt in her eyes over the literal knight in . . . crimson and black armor who had saved her life plenty of times.

"Alright." She shook the thoughts from her head. "Any objections to getting started on our bloody path toward . . . answers or something?"

Edward cleared his throat. "Ah, how about one of those *demon coins*?"

"Of course." She gave him a bow in apology. "How inconsiderate of me to forget. Don't spend them all at once!" She withdrew two coins and flung one at each demon.

Sally watched as Edward shoved the coin into his mouth, eating it down like it was a tasty meal. "Wow, you really *do* just—when I saw Lucius do it, I thought maybe it was . . . never mind."

An emoji of fireworks appeared next to Lucius. "I now have *[Soothe Spirits]*, which doubles passive regeneration outside of combat."

"Neat." She smiled. Some in-combat healing would have been the golden ticket, or even some ranged damage could have rounded the team out better. Still, you couldn't argue with more buffs. She felt better about it already. "What about you, Edward?"

"Oh, mine is called . . ."—A smirk curled up at the corner of his mouth—"*[Betray Trust]*."

"Alright, well, we aren't ending on that suspicious tone." She shook her head. Humphrey looked around the room. "Ending what?"

"The conversation before we teleport out, of course." She tilted her head with a frown. Maybe the Death Knight had taken more hits in the boss battle than she thought. "Instead, I just remembered with my smart brain that I was given two skill reset points!"

"So what are you going to reset?" he responded, deflating slightly.

Her eyes shone with bright crimson.

"See, now *that* is a good question."

CHAPTER FORTY-SIX

Behind the Veil

Sally beamed as she rolled her STAR around to bring up her skills tab. There was now a reset button to press beside each ability—but what was giving her the cause for the wide grin was where the System had messed up again.

"It lets me reset the one that was taken by the spooky dude." She raised an eyebrow up at the Death Knight.

"That might have . . . implications," he replied.

If anything, it would be foolish not to take that opportunity. After all, being an ability short was no fun when everyone else had their maximum. They still needed to find Skill Books, too, but that was neither here nor there. Definitely not *here*.

She pressed the button. *Error*—it replied, then it filled in the missing skill.

"No fair, I didn't even get a choice!" She sighed and pressed to see the details.

[Mortis Bomb] Ranged Magic attack that summons 3 to 5 zombies if the strike is successful. Consumes Skull (1) on use.

Humphrey moved around behind her to read the System messages too. "Conveniently, that seems to be more useful than even Necroblast had been."

"Perhaps," she said and shrugged. "Good thing I've been stocking up on skulls, I suppose." Now she had to pick the second skill to get rid of. It was more of a risk if she didn't get to pick what she wanted, but then that's maybe what the shrines were for—like that which Dent stole out from right in front of her back in the forest.

She decided to reset *[Hex: Slow]*. When she wasn't forgetting to use it, either there were too many enemies that it was a hassle to switch it, or against strong solo monsters, it seemed to have less effect—if any at all. The System had finally agreed to treat her as some kind of necromancer, so hopefully the reward for giving up the skill that had saved her a few times would be worth it.

> **[Living Dead]** Area Buff. Undead targets recover 15% HP over five seconds and receive STR and Speed boost for the duration.

"That seems useful." Sally tilted her head at the description. Things were *really* starting to come together now. "We just need some stability rather than bouncing between odd encounters, and maybe some cloud cover, and *then* we'll be back on top of things." She grinned at the rest of the Party.

"I'll prepare the teleport out front." Edward gave a brief bow. "Dungeons can be a bit grumpy when you try to do that kind of magic."

"Theo got out fine." Sally crossed her arms.

"Good for him." The demon shrugged and walked toward the exit, the rest of the Party following along after Sally's nod of approval.

She held out a hand. "One second, Lucius, hang back so we can have a little chat."

Humphrey shot a glance back to her but said nothing as he and Archie headed out with the tax collector. Lucius looked nervous, even without the sweat drop emoji appearing beside his head. Sally waited until the shuffling sound of their movements was silent and she was alone with the demon.

"Everything okay, Sally?"

She clucked her tongue. "Don't you go thinking because I've got a few screws loose that I don't notice things."

"W-what?"

"What are your motivations for staying with us? You're not much of a combatant." Her arms crossed across her chest as she glared into the crimson eyes under the shadow of the red hood.

"You seemed . . . fun? I was pretty alone, so being around people made a pleasant change." There was no accompanying emoji to his statement.

Sally tried to read his lack of face. She paused as she weighed her next thought. "You're allowed to have secrets. Hiding your identity or true purpose is something we can forgive. But . . ." She leaned closer as Lucius recoiled away. "Do *not* betray us. I will not hesitate to kill and eat you."

This time, a sweat drop followed by a screaming face emoji appeared beside the demon's head. "No! I wouldn't do that. What has brought this up all of a sudden?"

She smiled. "We all have something to fight for. Even Eddy had some depth and wasn't just a ridiculous foil to our progress. You've been nothing but affable and agreeable."

"That's a bad thing?" Lucius took a step backward to be farther from the zombie's looming presence.

"It's something I don't trust. Everyone has an agenda." Sally snapped her fingers and grinned. "So come up with something neat. That's a little homework for you."

With that, she turned and walked out toward the dungeon exit, leaving the demon frozen for a second before he followed along.

"I hate this constant sun," she grumbled as she stepped through the waterfall of sand, placing the sun hat atop her head. "Hats on, team."

The small straw bonnet looked especially cute on Archie, and Edward relented to joining in despite his tangible disdain for how it looked.

"Good thing I didn't give Theo his hat yet, so we have enough." She passed the last one to Lucius, who was hanging at the back, very slowly and purposefully placing it in his open hands as she maintained eye contact.

"Need I ask?" Humphrey murmured after she turned back around.

She shrugged in return and gave him a wink. "Alright, Edward. Let's go eat some lizard brains!"

The demon rolled his eyes. With a flash of blue, vertigo enveloped the Party and after a brief moment, they were inside a house.

Edward's blade slashed through the air, a crackle of energy as he struck the seated figure turning to acknowledge them. A lizardman clutched at his gashed throat and collapsed to the floor from the chair.

"Normally, I could decapitate him." The tax collector sighed. "Probably shouldn't have my spawn point set in a building, but it's a safe enough place where we won't pull any aggro until we leave."

[Eat Brains]

"Ha!" Sally wiped her mouth and rose from the body. "You didn't finish him off. What an odd tasting brain."

The creature wasn't much like the Unique crocodile Theo had fought back at Sanctuary. These Monsters had short, squat faces more like a Komodo dragon. Their scales were a mix of soft greens and pale yellows. And currently, bright red blood.

She looked around the room. It was a small building where one side was slightly raised and held several filing cabinets. Like an office or data collection place—oh, maybe some kind of lizard tax office. That would make some sense, in a manner that she wasn't too convinced by.

"That reminds me, Sally." Edward put his thin sword back in its scabbard. "May I see your dagger, please?"

"Is this for *[Betray Trust]*?" she asked, narrowing her eyes.

"Yes, yes, it is." A wide grin spread across his face.

She nodded. "Oh, okay then." Withdrawing Skeleton Key, she handed it over to him. "That reminds me. I know of a way you can get to Level Eleven easy, but you're not going to like it."

He grimaced and ran his hand down the blade, a sheen of light green energy surrounding the dagger. "What is it?" Edward passed the weapon back to her. "The enchantment is dormant until I activate it."

"Become my bodyguard." She wagged her eyebrows at him. Despite having the ability to have three now, they hadn't found many willing candidates. As far as she understood it, it would allow him to become a level below hers every time she leveled up.

"What . . . would be the benefit for me?" He didn't immediately reject the idea, but there was a healthy amount of skepticism in his tone.

Humphrey looked down at Archie, who had already curled up on the floor as if to nap. "It may make you nigh immortal." The Death Knight rubbed his chin. "Or at least have enough levels that death wasn't so dire. There are stat bonuses for being around Sally, and as a Unique you wouldn't be forced to be around her forever."

Sally nodded. "You do get a tingly feeling whenever I'm in danger, which is *a lot* of the time, but every time I level up, you'd get all your lives reset back to max."

"So I have a vested interest in keeping you safe and alive." Edward rubbed his chin as he narrowed his bright blue eyes. "But you wouldn't force me to follow your merry band around?"

"Nope." She shook her head and smiled. "I imagine you want to see Ruben humbled, so you're not going anywhere too soon—but as long as you're on our side still, you can have whatever freedom you wanted." Sally cast a brief glance at Lucius before looking back at the tax collector.

"Well . . ." The demon looked around the room. "Let me think about it. While it is a most generous offer, I am only just unlatching myself from the shackles of subservience, and I'm not keen to jump into something else too soon."

Sally bowed. "I appreciate your honesty and respect your decision." She smiled between each of the *Outsiders*, only lingering on Lucius for a brief extra half second. "Anyone with any last words before we get started?"

They all shook their heads as Humphrey withdrew his greatsword.

"Allow me to go first. That doorway is too small. I will need to make a new one."

Sally took a skull from her Inventory to hold in her off hand, the slightly glowing Skeleton Key in her main. *Now* she was feeling like things were coming together.

"Be my guest, Humps. Let's give them *hell*."

The two demons groaned.

CHAPTER FORTY-SEVEN

[Living Dead] Girl

Humphrey blasted through the doorway and sent shards of wood from the broken wall scattering onto the open road of the town. Immediately he ran into a group of six Monsters just outside and used his area ability to stun. All surrounding foes failed the check and became stunned. He then swung his greatsword in a dark arc, striking two of them across the neck. Across the street atop a balcony overlooking the road, three lizardmen held bows and were drawing arrows in preparation to fire down at the Death Knight.

Sally, holding a skull in her left hand, stepped out into the sunlight. A dark green energy enveloped the skull as it soared from her grasp, eye sockets ablaze with intensity as it flew like a rocket—to explode against the middle archer. The creature stumbled back as its scaled skin sizzled from the attack, and four zombies emerged from the ground around the archers, disrupting their shots.

"I could get used to that," she said with a wicked grin across her face.

They were in the middle of the town, with several groups of lizardmen wielding swords and halberds advancing from both the left and right among the various houses and buildings. Farther past these groups, even more lizardmen who hadn't noticed the Party's arrival were present and just idly walking about absentmindedly.

Sally held out her hand, casting *[Summon Zombies]*, as Edward swiftly moved to thrust his thin sword into the head of one of the stunned Monsters. He moved backward immediately, avoiding any retaliation. Archie and Lucius stayed back in the somewhat shaded area of the broken building, waiting to support when needed.

Sally withdrew another skull from her Inventory, flipping around her Skeleton Key. She spotted a small group of mace-wielding lizardmen approaching from the left. With a pulse of green energy that swirled around her feet, she cast *[Living Dead]* to further confront the approaching threat.

A surge of energy pulsed through the zombies, and they attacked with even greater fervor against the lizardmen and recovered some of their health. Sally swiftly dodged to the side, avoiding the downswing of a lizardman's halberd, and stabbed the Monster in the thigh with her dagger. She kicked out at her opponent and turned away, pointing her held skull at the floor to cast another *[Summon Dead]* around herself. While her Constitution and Strength should have been much higher than any normal Player of her level, she was now more interested in taking a backseat and observing how her new zombie abilities played out. The cooldown on her new skills was quite high but helped in providing extra zombies for when she could not summon any more normally.

In fact, as they looked up at the balcony from the building across the street, those who had risen around the three archers had managed to overcome their adversaries with only one loss of their own. The three remaining were attempting to find a way to clamber down from the balcony without dropping and injuring themselves. Sally narrowed her eyes at them and used *[Command Dead]* to prompt them to go inside the building and work their way down, avoiding the more direct route.

Humphrey seemed to have no issue engaging the additional lizardmen in the melee. The clash of metal against metal rang out as he blocked or was struck by their weapons. However, for each blow he took, he cut bloody swaths through the green-scaled Monsters. Every so often, the Death Knight would pulse with dark energy as he executed a *[Grave Strike]*—his sword blazing a bright crimson.

If there was one drawback to hanging back and letting the zombies do the job, it was that Sally wouldn't get to feast on as many brains by not being in the thick of the battle. She swerved among her summoned friends and assisted them, trading blows with one of the approaching lizardmen. While the new zombies were of a higher level, they still weren't especially combat proficient, relying on greater numbers and their damage resistance to wear down their foes, much like zombies in pop culture.

Her blade found the exposed back of one lizardman, who was trying to push away a couple of zombies, and then she devoured its brains. It wasn't the best meal she had ever had, but having been a bit starved of brain matter in the past three days or so, it was a relief. In such dire circumstances, anything would have to do.

Edward cautiously advanced behind her. Much like Sally, he aimed to jump in and finish off any lizardmen struggling against the mass of undead. Despite the fact that he would get his share of the experience whether or not he contributed, just by being in their Party, it seemed he didn't want to be seen as not contributing to the battle.

If only everyone could be so useful, Sally thought. Both Lucius and Archie were still in the office building. Although the cat could be relied upon to bring out some odd skill at opportune times, she had less confidence in the supposedly supportive demon. If anything, he seemed to be doing even less work now after she had chastised him. Perhaps she had been a bit too overeager to admonish him when he did seem like a nice enough chap. For a demon. It was odd that he had so few skills too. Perhaps the System had given him the short end of the stick, and she should press him to find out more.

There would be time enough for that after the battle. She spun and ducked as the swing of a blade narrowly missed her head. The attack instead embedded into one of the zombies beside her. She barreled into the assailant, stabbing twice in their chest before tripping to the floor over the dead body of one of its comrades, ready to feast on its brains.

She rose from the body and cast *[Living Dead]* again, the necromantic magic rejuvenating the zombies that had been wounded.

"Fresh meat," a deep voice yelled out from down the street.

An eyebrow raised across Sally's blood-flecked face as she turned to see who was yelling. Down the left side of the lizardman town, a much larger Monster of albino scales and heavy armor stood illuminated by the constant barrage of the overhead sun. Quite possibly the boss of the area, she considered. She held up her gore-splattered arm to wave at the approaching boss.

"Oh, that meat's not fresh." The Monster now looked disappointed and shrugged at the three bodyguards he had been approaching with. "Half of them don't even look edible."

Sally felt offended. She narrowed her eyes and slowly lowered her hand in the wave to grip at her dagger tighter. Not that she wanted to be the next meal for these Monsters, but it sure seemed like an insult more than anything. The assumption, then, was that they were just going to fight rather than try to make a meal out of her.

"On the other hand, I'm pretty sure I could eat all of you," she shouted back. With a deep breath she held out the skull, which illuminated the dark green light for shooting across the crowded melee straight toward the boss. One bodyguard with a shield that had a reddish hue to it leaped in front of the attack, the blast of green energy screaming as it scoured a dark mark against the defensive item. Zombies began to crawl out from the surrounding ground, but two of the five were felled before they had even stood on their feet.

The crackle of lightning drew her attention briefly as the smell of burning meat and charred scales struck her senses. Archie was sauntering through the melee near Humphrey, his fur on end and an illuminant yellow glow pulsing around him as arcs of bright lightning flickered from his body and struck the lizardmen near him.

"You all right at this end Humphrey? I'm going after the boss." She rubbed her head as the Death Knight was maneuvering through his combat with expert proficiency. He wasn't particularly fast, but every movement was carefully considered either to block or to strike out at the lizardmen. Some hits he just ignored—his armor was too dense to be injured past a scratch from their attacks.

"Yes," Humphrey grinned as he replied. As another group of twelve combatants surged forth from his end of the village, he slammed his greatsword into the floor and five skeletons rose out from the darkness with swords and shields in their hands.

Sally didn't bother to ask the two demons how they were doing. One of them she did not trust, and the other could come back to life if he died, anyway. They may be members of the *Outsiders*, but they hadn't earned the last name Danger yet. She dodged her way through another handful of Monsters, occasionally stabbing out with a dagger or eating the brains of those that were already weakened. Eventually, she came face-to-face with the boss and his three bodyguards after they had destroyed her zombies with little injury themselves.

"Who are you that you feel you may come to our village and slaughter our people?" The albino boss was large and muscular and peered down at her with bright crimson eyes.

"I'm Sally, and I'm Sally," she said with a grin. "Who are *you*?"

"I am Gorax, the Human-Eater." He flexed his arms wide as if just his title alone deserved some manner of fanfare.

Sally snorted. "Bet I have eaten more humans than you have." She mimicked a yawn as she finished her sentence.

The boss snarled. "Dead or not, I will add you to my list." He leaped toward her, a spear of swirling blue energy held in his hand. His bodyguard took the cue to rush toward her as well.

The zombie smiled to herself and hummed a little tune, the sound of dozens of undead feasting among the battle behind her like music to her ears.

CHAPTER FORTY-EIGHT

Golden Star

The last of the lizardmen bodyguards dropped to the floor, their heads emptied of the usual things you'd expect to find cluttering up a skull.

Sally yawned and resisted the urge to empty her stomach again. Turned out the lizardmen hadn't been worthy of much attention. The stakes just weren't there, even with the supposed boss. Her right arm ached, both from stabbing so much and also the amount of damage that she had taken was not negligible. She was briefly amused that *[Living Dead]* could also heal herself. In wanting to find a supporting Unique for their Party, it turns out she had become one herself.

The cooldown was a few minutes long, so it wasn't something that could be relied on in a pinch—but it was a guaranteed top up every so often that extended the lives of her undead Party members as well as the horde of summons she could command now.

Fighting the boss had been somewhat underwhelming. Sure, they had put up a much better fight than the rest of the lizardmen here, but between her gaining stats from eating their brains and the last of her summoning skill, it had only been a matter of time before she wore them down and feasted on them too. Whether they had even been worth eating was another question, as they didn't seem to settle in her stomach well. Perhaps some poison still lingered from the rat brains.

"Any good loot? I didn't even see you fight him; it went by so quickly." Humphrey affixed his greatsword to his back and strode over to her, past the milling undead among the corpses of the lizardmen. Some zombies were eating at the fallen foes, whereas some were content just to idly stand about and stare off into the distance.

"I *hate* looting," Sally whined. Even after getting rid of most of the hundreds of weapons she had been labored with thanks to Archie, her Inventory was still way too cluttered. Oh, that was a good point.

Sally: hey Theo
Sally: give me any and all daggers you can find
Sally: no time to explain

She closed the STAR and rubbed her chin. The vampire hadn't responded to her for a while, and as much as she knew he was capable, she hoped that nothing bad had happened to him. Although it seemed rather impossible that he could die from anything in the forest area with his broken stats.

"Humphrey, I'd know if Theo died, right?" Her face contorted into a grimace.

"He's not in the Party currently. But you would see in the guild notifications." The Death Knight stopped beside the corpses on the floor and put his plated hands on his hips.

"Oh." Sally scrunched up her nose and prodded at the STAR. "I turned those off awhile back."

Her brow continued to furrow as she scrolled through the updates that she had missed out on. Eventually, she closed the System messages and clasped her hands behind her back with a weak smile to the Death Knight. "Well, the good news is that Theo hasn't died yet."

Humphrey narrowed his eyes sockets. "And the bad news?"

"One of the other Parties is completely wiped out." She exhaled through her nose and looked out to the empty planes beyond the reach of the village. While she didn't exactly hold any love for the Player groups apart from Chuck's, it was still somewhat sobering that another group of people that she had known was now dead. And she didn't even get to eat their brains.

The Death Knight nodded and followed her gaze. "It's not surprising given how harsh this area is. Even more so than intended." He scratched the side of his head in thought. "I wonder how all the new Players are doing now."

If Theo would actually answer his messages, then maybe she would find out. Not that she needed him to be constantly updating her of his progress, but it would be nice to know *something* occasionally. While part of her did envy that he got to go back to the forest and see all their old friends and become more powerful with more System errors, she knew she had to press on and get things fixed here.

"I'm surprised we didn't level up actually." She pouted, brushing away the thoughts of the vampire to focus on the current situation. There had been a sizeable number of Monsters they had killed, and if they were pretty close after having completed the dungeon then she thought that would've pushed them over the edge.

Humphrey pointed back farther into the town near the office where they had teleported in. "There are still one or two that Lucius and Edward are fighting."

"Are they okay?" While she was content to not carry them on the adventures, it seemed a little coldhearted to leave them stranded and struggling against an enemy. Especially when it was holding up their experience gain.

The Death Knight shrugged, and they both relented to going and seeing what was going on. Sally used *[Endless Rest]* to put the zombies away, ready for later. She had already used all her summoning abilities for the day, so other than the—*oh!* She should be looting all these lizardmen for their skulls. Even if she didn't run out soon, it always paid to have more than she needed. But first, the demons.

By the office they passed Archie, who was curled up asleep in the sunshine. Although the ginger cat was technically one of her bodyguards, he didn't seem to show the same amount of consideration for the two newer members of the Party. She rolled her eyes, but it didn't feel like it would be fair to wake the cat up.

In an alleyway beside the next building, two lizardmen had cornered the two demons. Lucius was at the back, pushed against the wall as he tried to give inspirational words to the tax collector, who stood in front of him bleeding, as the two opponents jeered on.

The Monster at the back turned his head as the bulking figure of the Death Knight blocked out the light. Sally plunged her dagger up into his ribs, stabbing again with the *[Dagger of Luck]* that she had withdrawn into her off hand. *[Eat brains]*. As the second lizardman now turned to face the more capable foe, Edward blazed forward, cutting a gash across the Monster's side, quickly following up with a jab to the underside of the jaw of the Monster. *[Eat brains]*.

"Thanks," Edward growled, before turning around and glaring at the cowering Lucius. "Could you be any *less* useful?"

"No?" The demon had a constant emoji bubble beside him of sweat drops, one of the most common ones he seemed to portray in adventuring with Sally and the gang. "I'm sorry, Edward."

"You need to cool it, Edward," Sally interjected. "Everything is fine. Everybody's fine now."

The tax collector sighed and rubbed his temples. "Right, I apologize. That's kind of on me. I don't mean to be so sharp—I'm just frustrated at my lower level, in part, *thanks to you guys*." He gave Sally a smirk and shrugged his shoulders.

"Look here now. We've leveled up, haven't we?" The zombie raised her hand in the air to show off the golden light emanating from her STAR.

Edward paused, finally realizing that he too had received the experience from their attack on the village. He didn't look ecstatic—but at least contented, and it mellowed his fury at the other demon.

"Let's go back into the office and into the shade. Get this sorted out," Sally ordered, crossing her arms. Infighting was one of the few things she couldn't tolerate when it came to the Party. Not that she expected them to obey her every whim, but they at least had to get along and trust each other for the whole thing to work out.

They both relented by agreeing to her suggestion, and they all left the only way to circle back around to the office building, now very open-plan after Humphrey had knocked most of the front wall down. Sally picked Archie up on the way. The cat continued to sleep and flopped loosely in her grasp.

She went and sat on the raised ledge of the area with the filing cabinets and put the cat on her lap. With a sigh, she watched the rest of the Party filter into the room and find their own places to awkwardly sit or stand, the two demons avoiding eye contact with each other. Perhaps part of this was her fault for being too harsh on Lucius and too trusting of Edward. Her dagger still had the green sheen of his enchantment on it, and she wondered what his intention was with that.

"Edward, do you know anything about how the weather here was broken, or how we might go about fixing the constant sunshine?" She wiped the sweat and blood off her forehead with her forearm, which was equally bloody and grimy from the battle.

"Some." The demon worked his jaw and narrowed his eyes at the ceiling as if trying to will the thoughts or memories back into his skull. "Not really enough to know what to do, especially in our current situation."

That was a shame. Although part of her knew everything was joined in some manner to the dragon, she had hoped that some things could be fixed without having to resort to having to fell that one figure to end it all. Still, it was generally how these things seemed to work. Should everything go well at the pyramid, they might find something else to assist them on the journey.

Relenting to the guaranteed disappointment, she pressed her golden STAR to select which of the passives the system was going to offer her for being Level Thirteen.

CHAPTER FORTY-NINE

Breaking Bard

Pick One
[Crack in Fate] Your Melee Dodge chance now applies to Spell Avoidance.
[Unavoidable Horde] Undead Allies may pass on your Zombie Curse.
[Death's Mirror] Your Critical Strikes afflicts targets with Doom.

Tough choice for a change. She ruminated over the three choices for longer than she usually would. Passives weren't as exciting as active skills usually, but some of them could definitely change things more than most.

Although the other two were equally interesting, she decided on *[Unavoidable Horde]*. Even thinking back to the fight that they just had against lizardmen, if her zombies had been able to cause the fallen Monsters to rise up on her side, then that would have been an even easier wash for their side. In fact, with the amount of summoning she was now able to do, it would be even quicker to maintain a large horde for any fight they would come up against.

Thanks to the error of the System in giving her the bugged Necroblast and then the reset points, it seemed she had finally lucked into being the necromancer that she had always hoped to be—even way back in the starting town of Hillan. Thankfully, these summoning skills didn't seem to be dependent on intelligence or any kind of spellcasting stat, otherwise she would have been in a lot of trouble. With the auras the three of them had, it turned all her summons into individual powerhouses despite their lack of combat proficiency and simple-mindedness.

"What did everybody else choose or get?" she asked the room as she stroked the cat's head. There wasn't much point in asking Archie, but the ginger fur ball didn't seem much like answering, anyway.

Humphrey shrugged and grinned. "Nothing exciting, just further defensive stuff for me."

Although she knew the Death Knight liked to hide away some of his skills so he could pop them up as a surprise, she believed that he was being mostly up front about the reveal. Defenses were his kind of thing so, it made sense.

"I actually leveled twice," Edward said with a smile, "and I have *[Avoiding Responsibility]* and *[Shared Despair]*, a defensive buff and an offensive aura."

"Neat." If there's one thing Sally did like, it was auras. Her opinion of the tax collector raised a couple of degrees. Hopefully, that's not what the aura did.

"I just got a stat passive." Lucius shrugged, trying to look away from the group. There was no emoji bubble that accompanied his statement. "Nothing particularly useful for the Party."

Sally tilted her head. It looked to her like she was losing the demon. Although it had been a bit much to accost him as she did, the way that he was acting now was a bit unexpected. Either he was more sensitive than she had thought or truly had something to hide. She was betting on the latter.

"Well, I chose something that is going to make our lives a lot easier. Or *unlives*. More. Beautiful. Zombies." She raised her eyebrows as she beamed at the rest of the Party.

The reception was lukewarm. Humphrey seemed contented enough, but the other two didn't seem to care much for her undead companions. Theo couldn't come back soon enough. She brought up the chat window to see if he had replied yet, but there were no notifications. Neither from Chuck nor Dent. She needed a few more pen friends.

"All right, I'm going to set us up a *[Campfire]* to soothe our aches, and then we can decide what we are doing next." She shuffled the cat awkwardly off her lap and onto the wooden flooring where he just slumped down further continuing to sleep. From her Inventory, she withdrew the item and placed it farther into the room in the middle of the floor. "I'm glad we found so many of these."

"It is odd." Humphrey smiled. "Despite the atmosphere being hot enough as it is, the heat of the *[Campfire]* soothes rather than makes it more uncomfortable."

"Magic!" Sally beamed back at him as she set the object up. With a short burst of flames, the *[Campfire]* became lit, and she sat back to find what comfort she could on the empty floor. Although she could quite easily heal up everybody with either the Living Dead skill or medicinal kits, there was something about campfire items that was just more relaxing.

The rest of the *Outsiders* gathered round, and even Archie groggily woke up to saunter even closer to the flame. There was still tension in the air between the two demons, and it was probably part of why Lucius had started to feel out of place. He was already far below the rest of the Party in terms of combat ability, and now that he felt he had put Edward in danger, he was overthinking his choices.

"Can you play any instruments, Lucius?" Sally tilted her head, watching as the demon jumped with a start.

"Ah, no, well actually . . ." He looked nervously between the gathered Party as an emoji bubble appeared next to him, one of an embarrassed face. "I do a little, but I'm not very good yet."

Sally snapped her fingers at him. "Perfect, that's just what we need for a campfire—a little music, and maybe some food we can put on sticks to heat."

The Death Knight sighed. "You didn't even loot the boss yet. How do you expect us to have food at the ready if you never pick anything up?"

She scrunched her face up. Although she had immediately forgotten about doing that—especially the important gathering of skulls—that was something that could be done after the campfire, so she wasn't too worried about that. As far as she knew, the bodies wouldn't disappear anytime soon, and the respawns would be at least a day away.

If you played by too many of the System's rules, that's how they got you. She had resigned herself to being as untenable as possible. Make the System work hard to put her in the right box, seeing as it had started her off with one foot in the grave already. It had been working out for her partially well. If you ignored the *hardship*, then they'd actually been doing pretty great in the grand scheme of things.

If anything, overthrowing the dragon would just cement the fact that she was on the right track and was definitely in the running to becoming one of the greatest Players in this world. It did make her wonder whether there were any more glitched Players in the new batch that joined a couple of days ago. Whether there were any kindred spirits yet to be found — or even those that might rise up themselves to be a self-designated villain as she had done originally.

"Well . . . okay." Lucius shrugged and withdrew a harmonica from a pocket under his cloak. The demon moved it up with both hands, into the shadows under his hood.

There was a metallic clink, and his eyes went wide, as a demon coin fell from the darkened recess and clattered onto the floor—spinning around dramatically for longer than necessary.

The group slowly moved their eyes from the coin as it finally came to rest and up to the demon.

"Play the song, Lucius," Sally asked calmly.

The demon was shaking as he put the instrument back to his mouth. It did little to improve the tune. Several off-key notes punctuated his attempted song awkwardly. Without having anything to slowly sip, Sally instead withdrew the closest consumable item from her Inventory to chew on as they watched the supposed demon in silence.

After an abrupt ending, Lucius slowly brought the harmonica away from his mouth and lowered it to the floor alongside his gaze.

Sally could see the others wanting to speak up—especially Edward—but they were giving her the option of asking first. It was tough being the leader sometimes, especially when you realized you were absentmindedly chewing on [Mount Feed].

She stood and brushed herself down, the suspicious demon remaining frozen in place and daring not to look at her. So nervous, perhaps, that he didn't even have the capacity to emote it. "Well then," she eventually said, her voice cutting through the dead silence and causing him to flinch, "there's a decision to be made here . . ." She crossed her arms and tapped her foot. "Are you with us, or against us?"

At first, there was no response, as the demon continued to avoid engaging with anything past the patch of wooden floor right in front of him. Then, slowly, he raised his head to meet her gaze.

"I can't . . . not now . . ." His voice was quiet and without the upbeat flair he usually exhibited.

"Who are you working for? The dragon?" Edward seethed and tensed as if he wanted to leap up from his position to strike the other demon.

Lucius looked between the enraged tax collector and the zombie, before looking at the floor again. ". . . for one of the Champions."

Humphrey shook his head. "This is why you don't just invite any oddball we come across to the Party."

Sally didn't say anything but continued to tap her foot on the floor. He had been so nice at first, full of advice and positivity. Was that just something to gain their trust? It had worked to a degree. She would be the first to admit she was happiest when people were straightforward with their intentions.

"So, what now? Did you want us to kill you, or are you going to turncoat like Edward?" She narrowed her eyes.

"It's probably too late now . . . now that my cover is blown, I—"

"Lucius." Sally withdrew Skeleton Key and pointed it at him. "*With us or against us?*"

Any response that the demon was trying to formulate was interrupted, as a sound caught the attention of everyone.

Through the large hole Humphrey had made through the wall, the constant patter of . . . rain could be heard. Even now, as they stared in disbelief, the raindrops became visible, and the dry ground started to darken as the downpour increased.

"It's too late now," Lucius whispered; his head hung low.

CHAPTER FIFTY

Wet Wipe

Sally looked at the demon, dragging her gaze away from the surprise shower outside briefly. "What do you mean?"

Unable to wait for an explanation, the Party stood on their feet and went to stand outside. The first rainfall they'd seen in weeks could go without some explanation. With how hot it had been, it was a miracle that any rain could fall at all considering they had not seen a cloud in the sky for several days.

As soon as Sally stepped out into the lizardman street alongside them, the rain was instantly cooling. She paused to close her eyes and then looked up toward the downpour. Only slightly concerning was the fact that there was only one enormous cloud in the sky, which seemed to be only hanging over the village itself. She closed her eyes and tried to enjoy it. Something gnawed at her insides, and it wasn't just bad brains.

"This is going to be a bad thing, right?" She turned with a grimace to Humphrey. He was also looking at the sky with a furrowed brow.

"Yes."

Edward shielded his eyes from the rain as his light blue eyes glared around. His head snapped back to Lucius, who was standing idly within the building still, looking sorry for himself. "It's *her*? Really?"

The tax collector looked tense and clearly knew what was about to happen. Sally looked around the village, wondering if she had time to loot before they had to evacuate from whatever was to arrive. Most likely not. This is what she got for being so lazy about it. Gripping her dagger tightly, she turned to Edward.

"Who is it? Should we be worried?"

He turned to her with clenched teeth and narrowed his eyes. "Make me a bodyguard *now*. Quickly."

Sally sent him over the request immediately, and he accepted. If he was willing to make such an important choice on a whim like that, then it didn't spell too well for them. She wondered what the rain could bring to cause him to be so worried.

"Okay, I got a few new skills but will discuss that later. If we still live." He gave her a sour grin, clearly still not 100 percent on board with the decision.

She withdrew another skull from her Inventory and clipped it onto the side of her belt, ready for when needed. Actually, she had enough room to put three—and she did so—which not only made things convenient but also looked pretty fitting for her blossoming role as a proper necromancer.

"Any heads up, then?" Humphrey withdrew his sword and rolled out his shoulders.

"Champion—" Edward began, before being immediately interrupted as a darkened shape fell from the cloud in a flash of lightning.

The large figure, shadowed in dark blue, crashed down onto the stone ahead of them as tidal waves of water washed across the road and sunk into the dry ground. Stretching out to be revealed from this crash of falling liquid was a tall woman in a slick looking dark blue dress. With pale blue skin and curved ivory horns, her black eyes regarded them over a wide smile. Lightning crackled along her arms as a trident of bright gold filtered into her hand.

"*Maeve*," Edward seethed.

Sally felt tense. Although they were no longer able to see the levels of other Players and Monsters, there was still an aura about this Champion where she could tell that the woman's power was way above her own. It stood to reason that the dragon would have Level Twenty Champions or bodyguards given that it was the maximum for this area. If Theo was here and at his full potential, she might be a bit more confident about the standoff against such a powerful foe.

As the small wave of water was absorbed into the thirsty surroundings, a second figure slammed down into the damp ground just ahead of the new demon. A rounded shape of obsidian metal that was familiar to Sally and Humphrey— the golem from before. It unraveled from its ball-like shape and withdrew the long, double pointed spear. It stood to attention, awaiting commands from its controller.

"Well then, it looks like I'm the one who will pick up your mess, Edward," she hissed her words softly, a coy smile rising at the side of her mouth. "You seem to have forgotten where your loyalties lie as well. Ruben will be so disappointed . . ." she tutted and shook her head slowly.

"How about you leave the dragon and join us too?" Sally grinned. "Wouldn't you rather a free area than be under the control of Ruben forever?"

The demon smiled even wider, then her dark eyes met the zombie's, exposing far more sharp teeth than necessary. "Your little tricks won't work on me, small girl. Ruben offers far more than you could ever hope to."

Sally shrugged. She tried. They were going to have to eat the Champion's brains somehow as well, if that's how it was going to be. She couldn't win them all, but she could at least eat half of them.

"And you all have Lucius here to thank," she continued, "for keeping track of you and being good bait to draw you to the dungeon. Good thing we weren't just relying on you, Edward."

Lucius had remained staring at the floor, partly to dissociate from what was happening but also not feeling ready to accept his place at the event. Archie sat beside him, looking mildly interested in the new demon but mostly annoyed at the rainfall.

The tax collector didn't say anything but looked furious. Whether this was because he was regretting his choice to abandon the dragon, or he was now coming to terms with what he would have to face, Sally wasn't sure. He intended to fight and survive with them, hence his acceptance of being her bodyguard.

Maeve must have a lot of self-confidence to arrive here with just a golem and herself. She must know what the Party was capable of if Lucius had been keeping an eye on them. Just Sally alone had an instant forty zombies that she could pop into existence and buff up. She didn't do the battle planning thing as well as Theo, but it was a safe bet that the Champion either had some area attacks, something against the undead, or just was defensible enough to not worry about the zombies.

The demon would be more powerful than the dungeon boss. She could definitely assume that. Even with her higher than normal stats, she took quite a beating in that fight—so she wasn't too keen on having an encore so soon.

"Ruben is impressed with your ability to overcome all the challenges in the Wastelands, and thus, has granted me the allowance of giving you one last chance to surrender and join under his banner. You have proven yourselves so much that he is willing to promote you straight to silver rank immediately." The demon bobbed up and down on feet that seemed to be constantly riding an unseen wave.

Sally looked over at the rest of the Party. Although she was the leader, it didn't seem right to always be making life or death decisions for all of them. She raised her eyebrows and gestured for them to let her know their thoughts. Although Humphrey's face didn't change much, she could read it perfectly. He'd be on her side. Edward looked pensive but had made his choice to follow her long as a bodyguard. Archie did nothing but yawn.

She waited for Lucius to answer. Despite his betrayal, he had not left the Party. If there was a time where he could make his move and leave them in safety, then this was it. Instead, he seemed reluctant and guilty. Still, she *needed* to know. He *needed* to say it.

"Make a choice," she asked him quietly as the rain continued to fall down around them lightly.

"How could you trust him, after—" Edward began, before Sally held her hand up.

"The same way which we trust you."

Lucius clearly did not like to be put on the spot and was having a troubling time making any sort of decision. Sally could understand, to some degree. He was not a strong fighter and without their help, he'd be easy to pick off. Joining up with the dragon was probably something he had to do for his own well-being and was acting as a spy for the Champion to pick up on new Players in the area.

She had coerced goblins into making dangerous decisions back when they intended to take over Sanctuary, and although it had worked out in that instance, she couldn't guarantee that it always would work out in their favor. In fact, as the disparity in levels got higher, it was even more likely that they would bite off more trouble than they could chew, eventually.

Archie pawed at the legs of the demon, and Lucius kneeled so that Archie could murmur something to him she couldn't overhear with the constant rainfall. A question mark emoji bubble popped up beside his head, before a sad face, and then exclamation mark one.

The demon stood back up and turned to the expectant Party.

"If you will still have me, I wish to ally myself with the *Outsiders*," he said, still some shakiness in his voice.

Lucius lifted his hand up and pulled back his hood.

CHAPTER FIFTY-ONE

Sanctified

The rest of the Party paused and looked at the supposed demon as he made his reveal. For a few awkward moments, there was just silence except for the raindrops beating on the rocky ground.

"Not sure what I expected." Sally rolled her eyes. "But it's good to have you on board, Lucius." A smile widened across her face.

Now, with his hood down, the apparent demon's true form was clear for all to see. His head was nothing more than a shadowy mist with two crimson eyes affixed, looking a bit ashamed of himself.

"A Shade," Edward said, deflating. "Not *quite* a demon."

"Would you all stop bickering?" Lightning flashed as Maeve roared in anger. Swirls of water surrounded her feet with greater intensity as her temper rose.

"Probably not," Sally murmured. She rubbed the side of her head as she looked between the golem and Champion. "Hey, Humps, monologue for a bit, would ya?"

"Certain . . . ly," he replied, somewhat confused. He cleared his throat and then began yelling at the Unique. "Foul demon! It is you who shall rue the day, for you have approached the—"

Sally turned her attention away from the ramblings and opened up her STAR.

Sally: level ten yet?
Sally: could really use some help
Theo: in danger? Can be there in two hours.

She looked between the Death Knight and the increasing amount of ire growing on Maeve's face.

Sally: two minutes, or no deal
Theo: . . . I can't
Theo: co-ords pls

With a sigh and a weight filling her stomach, she sent over the map location to him. He didn't reply. Window closed, she turned back to the looming battle. It was perhaps unfair to expect the vampire to come bail them out—he had only been gone two days. She could surely deal with her own problems.

"—and furthermore, we weren't even ready for this yet, so I'm not sure why you've—"

"Enough!" Maeve held out a hand.

The golem lurched forward, immediately sprinting toward the group.

Sally tutted. "Dibs." She flipped Skeleton Key around in her grip and ran forward to meet the monstrosity. It leaped into the air, the arm holding the large spear pulled back, ready to strike. She jumped up to greet it, her dagger arcing through the light rain.

[Betray Trust]

The dagger burst into green flame as they collided, the spear narrowly missing the zombie, as her blade found a place in the domed head of the golem. True to form, it pierced the previously impervious skin of the Monster.

Sally dropped to the floor and rolled backward as they landed after their clash, readying herself for the follow-up attack. The golem, however, stayed still and didn't prepare a follow-up attack. A halo of green energy now encircled its head.

After a few seconds, it slowly turned and leveled the spear toward the Champion.

"Neat, Edward." The zombie shot the demon a thumbs-up. His enchantment seemed to allow him control over a System-created, which perhaps was a lot spookier than she cared to think about right now.

"First Lucius, and now the golem." Maeve rolled her eyes and twirled the trident in her hand. "Ruben is going to be very unhappy today."

Sally hoped he would be very dead soon too. Maybe with the golem on their side, she could call off whatever Theo had planned. Things might be looking in their favor. "Hey, Ed—you don't have a teleport just in case?"

The demon worked his jaw, his eyes not leaving the Champion opposite them. "Only one, but I am only using it for selfish, self-serving reasons. I am sor—"

"It's fine," she said as she nodded at him. "If you die, you go back to dragon castle or whatever, and you'll want to teleport away from that as soon as possible before you get in trouble, right?"

He opened and closed his mouth and shot her a quick furrowed glare. "Yes, but . . ."

"That's just pragmatic, not selfish. You *can* be a little bit of a jerk sometimes, like Humphrey, because we are villains after all." She gave him a wink and flipped her dagger around.

"What?" The Death Knight deflated. "When am I ever a—"

[High Tide]

They turned from their disagreements to see a wave building beneath the demon as she hovered in the air. At three feet tall it surged forth, soon shrinking as it crossed the distance to the Party. The water itself didn't appear to be the main point of the attack, as just when Sally was about to scoff at it, figures loomed out from the shallow water.

Large pincers rose up in front of thick bodied crabs, their legs long and dripping with sea water. Each was around five feet tall and eight feet wide, their dark, beady eyes scouring the Party with cold intent.

"Giant enemy crabs." Sally shook her head and smiled. "Theo wishes he could be here now."

"I'm not so sure." Humphrey narrowed his eyes. "There's fifteen of them. If they are also Level Twenty, then . . ."

"You worry too much, Humps." She looked past him to the Shade and the cat. "You guys want to play too? I have a neat formation thing planned."

"It's raining," Archie complained, while Lucius just nodded.

"Perfect." She clapped her hands together at the lukewarm response as the crabs finished rising up. "Humps, you are my shield, so stand on my left. Edward, you can fill in for Theo and be my sword on my right. Lucy and Arch stand at the back and don't get eaten by crabs." Sally gave them all jazz hands.

"Okay." Edward rolled his eyes at being the stand-in for the vampire. The rest of them had fewer arguments and stood in place—even Archie played along despite his scowl at the precipitation.

Sally looked at the golem, who was still standing at the ready. "Fido, you can just go ham. Run amok. Kill the crabs or whatever. Humphrey, don't you dare compel duel that woman. *Forbidden.*"

The crabs started to march toward them, probably slower than she had anticipated, but then they were going forward and not sideward. It probably felt awkward and unnatural, perhaps the default flavor of the System.

"No promises." Humphrey grinned as he began to cast his defensive skills.

Lucius put his hand on her shoulder. "I'm sorry for everything, Sally." A sad emoticon appeared beside her face. *[Shadows Embrace].*

For a brief moment, she thought he was doing a double-double cross. But now he wasn't standing behind her. A confused scowl on her face, she then noticed her shadow—a gloomy thing against the wet floor in the darkened sky—had crimson eyes. It waved at her and raised up a shadowed dagger that looked like her own.

And then they were upon them. Humphrey immediately jumped ahead and swung his sword around in a wide arc, clashing against a pincer as if it was made out of metal. Sally chucked a green skull out into the throng and hit *[Endless Dead]*—her own army of summons emerging from the puddled floor to clutch at the approaching Monsters.

Edward moved in to assist the Death Knight. Every time the plated figure had to block or was pushed back, the demon would dart in to strike with glowing skills to prevent follow-ups or waylay reinforcements. Archie sat at the back, looking damp and miserable, but seemed to be gathering energy for something.

The zombies weren't much of a match for the crabs—probably even half their level. While they were causing little damage, they at least clogged up the melee and slowed the roving tide of giant Monsters from getting to attack them.

She ran to catch up to the Death Knight, hitting the nearest clump of undead with *[Living Dead]*. While she had definitely taken on more support skills recently, she was still a powerhouse in the melee, and where her zombies couldn't cut the mustard—or through crab shells—she was certainly capable and willing.

With a duck under the widely swung greatsword, which illuminated the area in deep crimson, she slid across the slick floor and stabbed the closest opponent in one of its legs. With a loud snap, the chitinous limb cracked off, and the creature stumbled slightly. It was times like these she missed having Necroblast—or any kind of melee skill would be nice. Still, she was being a team player by having all these buffing skills—

She rolled to the side to avoid the piercing stomp of one of the other legs—and then another crack as her shadow-Lucius struck out at the offending limb.

"Shoulda said you could do that earlier," she grunted as she stood beneath the Monster and rammed the dagger into the underbelly. The crab screeched in pain but was quickly silenced by a heavy strike of the Death Knight's sword.

Sally rolled from the collapsing body into the throng of three more, trying to get past her grouped zombies. One of her pals had been pierced through with a leg but had just used the opportunity to wrap themselves around the limb and weigh it down.

[Desecrate Life]

Now the undead had a slightly easier time of holding the crabs back—three of them even managing to pull one to the ground and pile on top. She heard Humphrey use his area stun and the resulting cracks and snaps told her they had felled a couple from his success.

Archie vibrated with energy and spat out his next skill, the ground cracking around him. Earthen spikes cracked the earth, jutting out three times in succession, just past the Party and carrying on down toward the Champion. Crabs were knocked into the air before the demon absorbed the final blow with a magical shield around her.

The golem was having a bit of a fun time too—with faint scratches along its body; it had felled one crab and was working on a second.

Sally ducked the snapping of an oversized pincer and slashed upward, cutting into the extended arm. As the crab withdrew its injured appendage, her shadow leaped up to strike it in the same place—the large claw falling from the Monster. She rolled and used *[Eat Brains]*, picking the claw up in her off hand and using it like a sticky, gross glove.

The brains weren't the worst—a little saltier, so she shouldn't try to eat too many. Two zombie crabs now rose behind her. Things had the chance of going their way. As much as she wanted to taunt the Champion, looking past the army of crabs ahead of her, there seemed to be more than when they had started the fight.

Blue arced beside her as Humphrey used *[Decimate]* and cracked a large gash through the shell of a crab. She had lost a dozen zombies, gained two, and the Champion had lost maybe seven crabs. Not great odds if there were now more crabs.

Maeve raised her fist.

[Aquatic Guardians]

Sally clenched her teeth as two pillars rose up, flanking the demon. Atop them, two colossal figures—goliaths with heads like seahorses—appeared in a splash of water. Each held an oversized bow, and they began to draw three arrows to fire at once.

A pulse of electricity began to swirl around the trident, and the weapon was leveled toward Sally. The two archers following suit with their aim.

Sally took a step backward as all the pitch-black eyes of the moving crabs turned to her.

"Ah, nuts."

CHAPTER FIFTY-TWO

Crab Sticks

As the arrows and lighting arced through the air, Sally dropped to the floor. The crabs gave her some cover, and the first volley slammed into the surrounding ground—two of them cracking into the Monster right in front of her. She turned over and stabbed upward into the sinking beast. *[Eat Brains]*.

The lightning bolt fizzled over her, and Archie ate it straight from the air, leaping up to catch it as if it was a hovering toy. With a quick spin, he then spat it back out—but this time it was green and split into three.

Each crackling energy ball surged toward the standing Party members and enveloped them in the crackling energy—critical strikes. Sally pulled a skull from her belt as the zombie crab rose back to its feet, and she flung it out toward the mass of gathering enemies. It burst with the arcing green energy, paralyzing the Monsters as more undead bodies rose around them.

With a screech of metal, Humphrey stumbled back from the blow of a claw. Edward stepped in to block the follow-up attack of the enemy, and then withdrew as the Death Knight recovered.

"We are soon to be overwhelmed." The demon licked his lips as his bright blue eyes observed around them.

"Have some faith," Humphrey said with a grin, his sword now blazing blue with the energy that *[Decimate]* gave it. "We are yet to be—"

He recoiled as he was struck by the volley of arrows, two of them breaking on impact, two missing, but two embedding into his armor.

"You were saying?" Edward rolled his eyes.

Sally used *[Living Dead]* over by the Death Knight, healing him and a couple of zombies. A sudden blow knocked her to the floor as a large pincer slammed into her. She rolled and stuck the dagger upward to stop the follow-up from crushing her. Lucius added his strength as the claw cracked itself on her blade, numbing her arm.

Lightning began to arc around the trident head.

While they weren't losing, Sally could definitely see where this was heading. Getting chewed up by the constant melee while the Champion and archers could just pelt them from afar was just going to wear them down. The number of zombies was slowly dwindling just as the number of crabs was increasing.

Their group, being mostly melee again, was seriously cramping their ability to fight effectively in this battle. Other than the occasional skull, they couldn't really do much to the demon from behind a wall of giant enemy crabs. They couldn't kill them quick enough to advance. They were losing to the eventual attrition of combat.

Perhaps they should try to flee. Would it make more sense to wait until one of them was seriously injured? Or for Edward to die? She casually blocked and backtracked away from the crabs. No, there was no need for unwanted injury. She needed to find a way to . . .

She looked down at her shadow-Lucius as the flare of Humphry's skills illuminated the surrounding puddles.

"Archie!" Sally called for the cat to run over—which, to his credit, he did without his usual tired indifference.

"Yes?"

"How bright can you go? Like a sun?" She nearly tripped over him as she dodged the wide arc of a giant pincer, the ginger cat weaving between her ankles.

"I could probably go pretty bright. I would have thought you'd have had enough of—"

"Do it now!" She leaped forward to jam her dagger into the surprised mouth of the attacking crab, her shadow following up with an attack to the neck, to the sound of a splitting shell.

Archie focused and began to glow—dimly at first, but he increased in intensity, soon lighting up this half of the melee. The enemies paused for a second, shocked at the sudden glow. He didn't stop there, and as she finished off her assailant, she picked up the cat.

"Don't stop!" She held him in her lap and turned away from the melee.

The cat flared pure white, blinding all foolish enough to look straight his way. Sally scrunched her eyes shut, but it still burned. She held him farther away and closer to her feet.

"A little lower," Archie purred. "I see what's happening, but I can't hold on this much longer."

She did as he said. A scream came from down at the end of the battle, followed by cursing and growled threats.

The light pulsed away as Archie yawned. Sally blinked her eyes, but they were still blinded.

"Not bad," Humphrey said from close to where the scream came from. *[Compelled Duel]*.

"Dammit, Humps." She spun, trying to locate everyone while her vision was slowly restored. All the crabs were currently slunk low and being feasted on by zombies or beaten up by the golem. One of the archers was hunched over, his skin pulsating with a purple energy that had cracked and grown along his body—Edward's power. The other archer held his bow somewhat dazed still and confused about not being able to shoot the tax collector, who was hiding behind the Death Knight, who was apparently no longer a valid target.

Maeve was clutching at a bleeding stab wound in her stomach, her blue dress darkening around her hand. She looked pained and annoyed. Now very furious at Humphrey, especially.

That had worked better than Sally had anticipated. Lucius was acting like a shadow, so the best way he could reach them was to use the light to have him stretch across the battle. The fact that the harsh illumination had not affected the Death Knight, and he had managed to drag Edward along with him, was a stroke of luck.

"You are fools," Maeve sputtered, blood running from her mouth. "Even if you defeat me, there's no—"

"*Even if* I defeat you?" Humphrey beamed crimson fire from the back of his helmet. "Let me tell you about my dueling record."

It was slightly better than Theo's, kinda. Sally stretched out and started to hopscotch across the dead crab shells to get closer. She sent a skull at the confused archer trying to pick out a target—the blast knocking him from his pillar and into the rising zombies below.

Lucius melted away from her and back into his normal form with a *pop*. "Very ingenious, Sally."

"You did all the hard work, bud." She looked back at the pouting cat. "You and Archie."

"How did you know that would work?" A slightly panicked-face emoji appeared beside him.

Sally raised an eyebrow. "I didn't. If you want to fail upward with us, you have to make all the one in a million shots." For all she knew, the bright light could have rendered his shadow form useless, or he might not have reached or been strong enough to attack.

They paused and looked up at the dark clouds. A portal of black edged with green opened up and a wooden crate fell from the sky. It quickly dropped to the ground, crushing one of her zombies.

As Humphrey dragged out the intro to his next duel, Sally went to inspect it. It had her name atop it, painted on in large letters.

The Death Knight flourished his sword. "Are you ready, demon?"

Maeve spat a glob of blood, which landed in one of the puddles. "I'm no melee fighter. If it weren't for your skill, I would have teleported away by now."

He chuckled. "One little scratch and ready to turn tail home?"

"I kinda use my intestines for digesting, so the wound is pretty inconvenient." Lightning arced around the trident, held loosely in her hand. "Why don't we make a deal?"

Humphrey leaped forward, *[Grave Strike]* glowing dark energy along his greatsword as he swung it around. She blocked the attack and sparks flew out of the impact. He grinned and leaned into the blow.

"I don't make deals with losers," he hissed as five skeletal warriors erupted from the surrounding earth.

"It's from Theo." Sally tilted her head as Lucius helped her pop the lid off. Edward had come over to join them but had his eyes on the duel.

She peered inside and lifted a note from the top.

"Sally, sorry I couldn't be there in person. Things are swell here down in the forest. I have committed unspeakable horrors. In my absence please find the enclosed, and I hope that you don't die so I can be there soon. Theo."

As much as she rolled her eyes, she couldn't help but smile at the note. The dumb pup couldn't message her on the System thing but had the time to write something out by hand. She folded the paper and tucked it away in a pocket. *Keepsake.* Too precious for the error-prone Inventory.

She withdrew the tarp covering the crate's contents and gasped. A screaming emoji appeared next to Lucius. Even Edward raised his eyebrows.

Maeve stepped back as the skeletons gathered around the Death Knight. Her hands pulsed with deep blue, and a slick shell of energy started to form around her.

"*Defensive skills* are my thing," Humphrey said with a grin. "That won't win you a duel."

The demon growled. "I just need to wait out the timer and survive your weak attacks, then I'll teleport away."

"Oh, dear me, Champion. I had thought you wouldn't have been so soft." The Death Knight held his sword up, and his five skeletal warriors turned to him—stabbing him with their swords.

"What are you—" the demon began—before the bone protectors did it a second time.

The bright blue flame of *[Decimate]* flickered along the long greatsword.

Humphrey tutted as waves of power pulsed around his feet.

"The System sure is silly, isn't it?"

CHAPTER FIFTY-THREE

Care Package

Sally peered down into the crate. "Oh, I guess I can just *loot all*. That'd be easier."

Healing Potion (10)
Dagger (37)
Personal Beacon (1)
Teleportation Stone (2)
Scroll of Mass Healing
Card Chance Box (3)

Archie went to jump atop the wooden crate but just fell straight in as everything disappeared.

A blast of blue energy illuminated the area as Humphrey broke through the shield of the demon, his skeletons stabbing at him to generate a second *[Decimate]* attack—this one severing the head of Maeve clean from her shoulders.

"This makes me the winner." The Death Knight grinned as he flourished his sword into a resting position. He turned and deflated in seeing that nobody was watching.

"Anything good?" Edward asked the zombie.

As she cycled through the notifications, the gloomy clouds started to fade away and part. She wrinkled up her nose as the bright sun washed over the battlefield. "Humphrey." She pouted at him as he walked up to the group. "You should have kept her alive so we can get rain more frequently."

The Death Knight shrugged and turned around to glare at the single skeleton still occasionally stabbing him.

"That was pretty cool, Lucius." Sally tapped at her STAR to open up the menu. "Next time you should do that with Humphrey, that would be pretty neat."

"Sure," the Shade said as he scratched at his misty head. "Though, I'm kind of worried I made myself the target of lots of strong opponents now."

"Eh, you get used to it." She hummed to herself. "There's a beacon here, so Theo can teleport to me when he is competent enough. Enough potions for all since I have been greedy with mine . . ."

"Didn't you have a bunch?" Humphrey crossed his arms.

"They just taste nice, okay? I'm pretty sure we have had this conversation before." She leaned out from behind her Inventory screen to glare at the Death Knight. "I'm not sure how Theo thought he would save us with a big care package, but I suppose it worked out. I should let him know we are okay before I divide up the spoils."

> Sally: ty for gifts
> Sally: we are alive, fyi
> Theo: good. Need me there still?
> Sally:_

Hmm, probably not *need*. She did want him around, but they could survive without him. The Party was a bit full now, and it would be awkward to have to ask somebody to leave. If only one of them could have died in the battle, that would have made things easier. Next time she wouldn't have *bright* ideas so quickly.

> Sally: not yet
> Theo: use the beacon when you need me.
> Theo: and I'll be there asap.

She smiled and closed the chat. Still no clue on what leveling had done to the vampire, but she was willing to wait out the suspense for him to be their last-minute savior at some point in the future. Although, they had managed to kill a Level Twenty Champion with little damage of their own. Mostly by being smart rather than tough, but the brain was a muscle too. A tasty muscle.

"You okay, Sally?" Lucius tilted his misty head as a question mark appeared in the air. "Thinking about Theo too hard?"

"No!" She scowled at the Shade. "You're certainly more sparky now that you're not hiding your true self."

"Guilt is a wet blanket over the flickering flame of my zest for life." A large, grinning face popped up beside him.

Sally handed two potion bottles to him and then withdrew another two for the tax collector. "You demons don't have to stick around, you know. It means a lot that you're proud Team Sally supporters—but things will be dangerous going against the dragon." She paused as she watched the demon attach a bottle to his belt. "So being *ride or die* isn't a requirement for you two."

"I'm good to stay for now." Lucius shot her some finger guns. "Now that I can be myself, I will be a bit more useful in combat too."

Edward grimaced and looked away. "I will leave at some point. Probably soon—not to say it hasn't been an absolute joy . . ." He rolled his eyes and grinned at Sally. "Once the vampire takes his rightful place, then you shouldn't need me hanging about. I still hold some grudge against him, and I wouldn't want to jeopardize this . . . ensemble."

"Astute and pragmatic." She nodded back at him in return. "There's a reason you're my favorite tax collector. You'll know when I'm in danger—so if ever you want to drop in and get massacred by something new . . ."

"My one dream." He bowed to her. "We will get one of my teleportation stones bound to you, so that I can come replenish my lives too."

"Neat idea. Now that both of you are playing nice, it's time to spill some details." She tapped the side of the crate. "Once we are done with the pyramid, we'll probably want to zoom to the endgame as quickly as possible."

"I'd recommend getting a few levels," Humphrey added. "I'm sure they have much worse than the watery demon."

"They do." Lucius rubbed the mist where his chin would be. "I only know two of the other Champions though, and they were better suited to combat than Maeve. There's Sidiv, the King of Snakes, and Lady Greenfinger—though I haven't met her."

"There's also the Golemancer, Brakenfold," Edward added. "Not sure about the last one."

"Is Sidiv a snake man or a man who likes snakes a lot?" Sally narrowed her eyes.

"I guess both?" Lucius shrugged and was accompanied by an emoticon reflecting the same gesture.

"Perfect." She grinned. Looking back around them, the blazing sun had already started to dry all but the most puddled areas of the street. Her dozen or so remaining zombies seemed to now be joined by a handful of undead crabs, all standing idly around awaiting something to do. She waved them back away with *[Endless Rest]*, contented that she seemed to be able to save the beasts that had turned. The golem sat idle, its controller now dead.

In seeing her gaze, the demon went over to the corpse of the Champion and removed the device for taking possession of the golem. "I'm taking this for myself, for when I leave."

She shrugged. "Oh, snap, I still haven't looted anything."

Humphrey sighed. "Make it quick. I'd like to move from this area before anybody else finds us, and Archie has fallen asleep in the crate."

Sally hopped around, grabbing everything she could from the fallen lizards, as well as the Champion. The Party started preparing to depart as she did so.

489 Gold
Skull (28)
Dagger (5)
Campfire (3)
Uncommon Armor Chance Box (3)
Unknown Chance Box (2)
Healing Potion (2)

"Not a bad haul." She eventually rubbed her eyes and sighed. "Everyone good?"

Their murmured replies leaned toward the positive. Nothing like a post-battle lull to dampen the mood. With one last look at the town, they headed out toward the rock and sand that eventually would take them to the pyramid—in fact, if she narrowed her eyes, Sally could see the peak of it on the hazy horizon.

"Make us Level Fifteen already, Humphrey, so we can get mounts." She deflated just thinking about the distance they'd need to walk.

"I am unable to do that."

"I could," Archie piped up from the Death Knight's shoulder. "But there's a caveat."

Sally narrowed her eyes and tripped on a dead lizardman's arm as she waited for the ginger cat to continue.

"I can cultivate my own experience. With enough time, you could kill me and level up a few times."

As tempting as that sounded, she wasn't about to murder one of her core Party members—especially not one who was her bodyguard. Doubly, especially as he was so cute. She shook her head and pouted toward the horizon.

"Just think of something amusing, and we will be there in no time," Lucius offered.

She tilted her head to him. "What's the limit on your shadow ability?"

The Shade pulled his hood back over his misty head and pondered for a second, ellipses appearing by his head. "I believe I can do it indefinitely, but certain damage types knock me out of it. Also, it can't be anyone too large or small—generally humanoid size is fine."

That probably ruled out Archie and the dragon. Both Humphrey and Theo would be amazing with a shadow ally, though. She drummed her fingers on her dagger sheath. If she was honest with herself, she was not looking forward to what lay beyond the sandstorm.

As much as she wanted a few Player brains in her stomach, fighting through another area seemed like a tall order. Getting to Level Twenty themselves might take more time than they had, and there was no telling how tough Ruben himself was. Unless Theo had become a walking demigod, then they'd have their work cut out for them.

She sighed, missing the simple life of the forest. Eating brains and making friends. Not that they weren't making friends now, but the fight for Sanctuary definitely had more weight and draw to it. The Wastelands had been them bouncing from encounter to encounter, just getting by on errors and her magnetic personality.

"What made you decide to join us, Lucy?" She raised an eyebrow at the Shade.

"All Ruben and Maeve had to offer me was power and fear . . ." He tilted his head and looked out to the desert. "I knew my chances of dying were higher being on your side, but so were my chances of living."

She smiled, feeling a little more upbeat about their progress.

"You guys are strange but willing to accept me and treat me as a friend. Even after the lies . . . you haven't turned your back on me."

"Just be yourself and be willing to fail upward." Sally snapped her fingers. "Say, you're still demonic, right, not undead?"

Lucius shrugged.

"His alignment is out of . . . alignment." Archie yawned and stretched out. "Shades are usually chaotic evil, so masquerading as a demon probably held some reality. If you want, I can nudge you one way or the other?"

A question mark bubble appeared next to the Shade's face, followed by narrowed eyes deep in thought. "You could make me undead or a demon?"

"It shouldn't change much about your physiology or abilities, it's just about what you're more comfortable with." Archie slid down the Death Knight's arm with a scrape of claw against metal as he dropped to the ground.

"Huh." Lucius once again rubbed at the mist where his chin would be. "I have some locked skills. Perhaps being true to what I really am will unlock them?" He stopped, and the Party paused to observe.

He kneeled in front of the cat. "Archie, please make me undead."

Sally raised her eyebrows to the other two, both of them returning shrugs. This was good for the group but came as a slight surprise.

"Okay," the cat replied, and tapped him on the knee with his paw. "Done."

"Oh." Ellipses dotted the air. "I thought it would . . . OH WOW!" The Shade jumped to his feet, exclamation marks popping into the air before bursting like bubbles.

"Now *this* is living!"

CHAPTER FIFTY-FOUR

A Good Point

Sally thought of many amusing things while they strode across the desert—occasionally one of the other Party members found it worthy of a chuckle as well and didn't just roll their eyes or exhale.

Did it make the journey any less of a slog? Not particularly, but before long, what had been a blurred peak on the horizon had turned into the looming structure of the massive pyramid, almost within tasting distance. Other than the constant presence of the hot sun, there had been no sighting of any Monster, Unique, or Player along the journey.

"—and then she said, *pancakes*!" Sally beamed.

"I think you've told that one before." Humphrey worked his skeletal jaw.

"Impossible." She stopped to look behind them, putting her hand over her eyes. "My memory is impeccable."

The Death Knight winced, second-guessing his desire to open that can of worms. Ultimately, he stayed silent and just exhaled slowly.

"What's going on?" Edward rubbed at his ears. "I've had my ears blocked for the last couple of hours."

"No wonder you didn't laugh at the pancake joke," Sally grumbled. "I was just thinking things have been too easy since the lizardman village. I expected some drama or menace to rear its ugly head our way."

"Do you want there to be trouble?" The demon rolled his bright blue eyes. "I would rather we found somewhere to sleep, and then we get whatever it is you're after from the pyramid with no stress."

Sally snorted. "You should know by now it doesn't work that way. Humps, what's the chance of something going wrong very soon?"

"It is..."—The Death Knight tilted his skeletal head toward Edward—"*inevitable*."

"Sometimes I regret my life choices." The demon covered his face and groaned. "More so since I met you and the vampire."

The zombie grinned to herself but turned back to face the large pyramid now only half a mile or so away. There was no time for regrets, only pushing forward into unknown danger. If anything, the short reprieve during their long walk only meant the coming problems were going to be even worse. They had gone past the easy win stage and now were full tilt into falling into the void.

As if hearing her thoughts on a slight delay, the ground rumbled.

"Inevitable," Humphrey whispered, as the demon physically cringed.

They turned to see the sands shift behind them. Around forty feet away, a large circle vibrated. Anticipating danger, they withdrew their assorted weapons at the ready.

With an explosive plume of sand, a huge shape burst from the dried landscape. Looming around thirty feet into the air, loose sand ran down the solid shape like waterfalls to reveal a huge maw made of yellowed rock. Two eye sockets illuminated in golden light as the head atop a short neck looked down at them.

"Ruben." Edward sighed. "Or at least the apparition of him."

"I'm not eating him if he is really made of sand." Sally balked.

"Well, If It Isn't The Troublesome Party." The voice was deep but came out coarse and scratchy, the projection taking on the quality of the rock it had been built from.

"Hi." Sally waved, not particularly liking the stilted tone he was talking with. "That's us."

"I Have Received A Report That One Of My Champions Has Been Slain."

"Yeah, that was us." She crossed her arms. Her expectation was that the dragon would have been more imposing. He could have at least had the decency to come and appear before them in person.

"Impressive, As Much As It Is Frustrating."

"This is where he offers us a deal we can't refuse or something, right?" she raised an eyebrow at the Death Knight as she murmured to the Party.

"I Am Hereby Closing Crossings One And Three. Crossing Two Will Be Bolstered. You Are Not Welcome In My Domain."

With that, the light in his eyes faded away and whatever magic was holding the figure together collapsed to the ground in a cloud of dust.

"Yes," Edward said as he held his hand up to silence the zombie, "he is always that rude."

Lucius tilted his head. "I only really know crossing one. What about you, Edward?"

The tax collector worked his jaw. "Two is the middle one, generally you could say it had the least security as it is comparatively a wider entrance than one or three. But with those closed, even if Ruben only diverts those forces to two, then it'll be . . ."

"A tough nut to crack." Sally nodded and cupped her chin. "What are we talking? Twenty Players, ten Uniques, and maybe some groups of System-created wrangled there somehow? All Level Twenty?"

"Probably triple that." Edward grinned humorlessly. "More if he *really* doesn't want you going in."

"Ack. Can you teleport us in? You, Lucius?"

They both shook their heads.

"Single person only."

"Same."

That seemed unfair. Ruben must be really tight with his security. Could they really take on hundreds just to get into the rest of the Wastes? She started imagining some convoluted plan where they'd go back to the forest and get Henkk—or whoever had dropped the care package—to air drop them over enemy lines. It probably didn't work that way.

She turned to see the rest of the Party patiently waiting for her and shook her head. "We'll demolish that bridge when we get to it. It is a bridge, right? For now, let's focus on the doom right before us."

"Yes, it's a bridge." The tax collector sighed and deflated.

Sally snapped her fingers. As good as done then, if she got that much of it correct. All that was left was finding a way to murder scores of people unharmed, and then just a quick waltz up to the palace, or castle—wherever the dragon lived. One quick brain meal later and they'd be on to area three.

Humphrey kneeled beside the cat. "Are you going to relent the truth to me yet, little brother?"

Archie opened his mouth but seemed to melt slightly at the Death Knight, referring to him as such. He glanced at the captive Party and sighed. "When I was away with Theo, I may have gotten a little bored . . . and . . ."

"*And?*" Humphrey loomed his skeletal face closer.

"I may have coughed up a hairball into the void." He looked at the floor.

Edward raised an eyebrow. "You do that when you're bored?"

"Read between the lines, Ed." Sally jostled him out of the way. "He was just preening himself or something."

Humphrey exhaled and stood up. "So that explains the big monster version of you that almost killed me."

"I knew it!" The zombie punched him on the arm.

Archie looked up at them with his wide, emerald eyes. "It helped me learn something, though. There are other Archie's out there. One in each zone."

"Good thing I absorbed that one, then. I hope the others are less *like that.*" The Death Knight shrugged.

Silence fell over the Party, as half didn't quite understand any of it, and half understood too much. Sally stared between them, her tired brain beneath the straw bonnet trying to make some sense of it all. "There's five Archies . . . is that because the Architect split something of themselves into five parts? If we have to turn this into a quest to rescue all five . . ."

"We don't know for certain." Archie tilted his head. "That's why we are here."

Sally flipped her dagger around a few times as she looked up at the looming pyramid. She hoped the thing they wanted wasn't right at the top. The dragon might die of old age before they got all the way up and then out again. That's only if it wasn't full of terrible things, which it probably was. She flicked her STAR open.

Sally: going into the pyramid now
Sally: hope to find answers
Sally:_

She pouted at the flickering text boxes, unsure what to add. He didn't reply right away, which she assumed meant he was now grinding twice as hard, knowing how eager they were to dive into trouble.

"Alright, troops." She cleared her throat. "Rules for the pyramid. Do not split up. That's mostly it . . . uh, don't die? Edward can if he wants."

"I do not want to."

Humphrey grinned. "We *will* totally split up."

She sighed. "We will find a safe room to take a break. It has been sunny for infinite hours, but I bet it should be time to sleep soon." Hopefully, the darkened interior of the structure could allow their internal rhythm to accept sleep. "Dibs on any daggers too."

"You're the only one with an Inventory, so . . ." Edward put his sword away, his blazing blue eyes eager for the shade and rest of the pyramid.

Without further need for distraction or ceremony, she stomped off ahead of them to lead to the pyramid. Even without their constant grumbles, she was getting tired of the day. If anything, the exhaustion just helped with making the trek feel like it took less time.

Then they were there. The stonework of the pyramid was smooth, rather than the large, jutting steps that she had expected. There were no windows she could see, or ways out of the pyramid higher up, so using it as a large slide was out of the question. Plus, hitting the ground at that speed would do nothing but break her legs, anyway. Design flaw.

A small entrance, barely a spec against the otherwise gigantic pyramid, sat before them. An open doorway with a stone awning over it, both covered in some ancient text she had not seen before. "Anyone read this?"

"I can," Archie offered, after the rest shook their heads. "It says, 'Tomb of the Great King.' Except the *king* is crossed out and *queen* has been written over it. And then king over that, and then queen again."

"Must change ownership quicker than a . . . than a . . ." Sally snapped her fingers and let the jab sink away. It was difficult to make pop culture references when most of your brain was zombie mush and you couldn't remember the real world.

"I'll check for traps," Humphrey offered, walking toward the opening.

Edward moved a couple of steps backward away from him.

CHAPTER FIFTY-FIVE

Entrapment

Archie yawned and stretched out.

"Yeah, this looks like a suitable spot." Sally rubbed at her neck. The first room of the pyramid seemed devoid of any danger and only had a small entrance on either side. Humphrey had gone through and checked everywhere for traps, places Monsters could climb through, or ports for gas or lava to flow from. It was just a room of wide stone blocks and plain décor.

Which made it all the more suspicious.

Sally was tired, though. It would have been nice to have been able to eat the Champion's brain, but it probably wouldn't have sat well in her stomach. It was a good thing they were no longer allied with any nearby normal Players, otherwise she would be tempted to break bad. What was the point of being a villain otherwise?

She let her stomach continue to grumble as the rest of the Party collapsed against the walls. The inside of the pyramid was surprisingly less run-down than she had expected. The stonework was half a soft yellow paint, and dark brown coursed from the floor tiles up to about midway on the walls in blocky, rectangular designs.

"I'll take first watch," Humphrey offered, placing himself facing the open doorway to farther into the pyramid.

There wasn't even time for her to argue or bring out a *[Campfire]* before she was asleep. A sleep without dreams, but an odd feeling. Not exactly being watched, just an uncomfortable feeling of . . . change. She awoke and blinked the blur from her eyes.

"We were about to wake you." Lucius waved from across the room. "You must have really needed that."

"You mean she doesn't always sleep like the *dead*?" Edward rolled his eyes.

"Laugh it up, suits." Sally stood up and groaned. "It takes a lot of effort to herd you weirdo cats. No offense, Archie."

Archie was either still asleep or didn't pay her comment any heed.

She stretched her back out and then withdrew her dagger. It would probably be bad form to drink one of the Healing Potion bottles just to get rid of the stiff muscles from sleeping awkwardly on the stone. Maybe she could just throw herself at the first danger and get a little injured for the excuse.

After rallying the troops and prodding the cat awake, she led them toward the next room.

"I should probably go first," Humphrey offered, pointing at the slightly arched doorway. The room beyond looked pretty plain and unassuming.

She hesitated at first, before allowing the Death Knight the honors. After all, he was her shield, so he'd need to—

Just as he stepped into the doorway, a large axe head slammed into him from one side of the wall like a pendulum—the clang and resulting squeal of metal as it squeezed him against the opposite side, echoing around the chambers. Humphrey growled and pulled the shaft of the trap with him, bending and eventually snapping the sharp metal pole off.

"Disarmed," he stated impassively, dropping the axe head to the floor to inspect the inch-deep gash running up the side of his armored body.

"Point made, no need to show off." Sally deflated and walked through the doorway, followed by the pensive Shade and demon.

The new chamber had a doorway on each right and left wall, right at the end corners. On the far wall was more text that only Archie could read.

"Left is to go up the pyramid, right is to go down."

"There's a down?" Sally sighed and pinched the bridge of her nose. As if things couldn't get any more complicated, she would have to consider things in another dimension. "Do we know which way has your magical item?"

Archie and Humphrey exchanged glances before the Death Knight shrugged.

"Aren't you just going to flip a coin?" Edward verbally jabbed from behind.

Sally rubbed her face in thought. It was too early in the day, or whatever manner of time it was, to be stuck with such an issue. Where would she go if she was a magical item of some importance? Probably right at the apex. Harder to reach. But depending on the nature of the item and whatever was below them, it might also be hidden away somewhere dark and dangerous.

"Well . . . we always fail upward," she eventually concluded. "So if we go downward and it's the wrong way, we'll eventually end up on top, right?"

After a couple of seconds of silence, Humphrey shrugged with a wide, skeletal grin. "Sure."

The others gave some manner of acknowledgment for her plan, either accepting her odd decision-making skills, or too tired to argue with the logic. Not that she wanted them to be pliable yes-men, but it helped get the ball rolling and stopped her from wanting to eat their brains.

Without ceremony, they continued to the door on the right, immediately leading to shallow steps and torch-lit walls. After a ninety-degree turn to the left, it went farther down until it reached the first floor. The brickwork became less yellow and brown and more amber and black as they descended—as if the decor was darkening to signify they were moving below ground.

They stopped by the door and allowed the Death Knight to shuffle to the front. Sally looked at the engraving beside the closed stone door. It said B1, which was somewhat immersion breaking.

"That means this is the first basement floor," Archie added helpfully after clambering up Edward's suit to sit on his shoulder.

"You know, I'm not a fan of *cats*." Edward narrowed his eyes at the encroaching creature.

"*I'm the Architect.*"

"Focus, people." Sally felt like she needed a nap already. Back to five oddballs again, and it was sucking the air out of the room. Not that she didn't enjoy their company, but the bickering made her feel Theo's absence more. If only her Party could be larger than five members. She crossed her fingers as she thought that out into the world, just in case the System was listening to her inner monologue. Or they should set up a second Party—but who would join which . . .

"Ready when you are, Sally." Humphrey grinned from the doorway.

She nodded and turned to the Shade. "Assuming there's no trap, but there are enemies, then go ahead and shadow form with Humps, okay?"

Lucius nodded, a thumbs-up appearing beside him.

Although it had been fun in having him help her out, with the Death Knight stomping into the room first, he would be a powerhouse with a shadow wielding a second greatsword. One big ball of metal and a swinging sword. The perfect defense.

Humphrey pulled the doorway to the side, the stone grinding heavily against the floor. With the flames on his helmet flickering higher, he stepped into what lay beyond. Silence followed, before there was the long escaping of air.

"It's a puzzle room." His voice echoed out into the hallway.

With a groan, Sally slunk into the new chamber, followed by the others. There was an odd red lighting to the room that wasn't just coming from the Death Knight. Six statues stood equal feet apart in a grid. Each held an item and had a hand pointing in a certain direction. They were all faced differently, as though they were trying to find a hidden focal point and disagreed on where it was.

"This is impossible," she said as she slunk against the wall. "I left my thinking brain at home."

"Don't be so eager to give up." Humphrey grinned. "I think I have worked it out."

She tilted her head and then turned to raise her eyebrows at the rest of the Party. Edward looked as drained as she felt, probably having dungeon flashbacks. Lucius had a question mark bubble twitching beside his head as he cupped his misty chin—so who knew what he was feeling. Archie was facing the wrong direction.

The statues were all relatively humanoid but weren't detailed enough to determine if they were human or specific genders. Whether they were worn by time or meant to look this way, she wasn't sure, but—

Humphrey swung his sword around at the closest statue—the subject immediately cracking and splintering into dozens of powdery chunks. The only thing left atop the stand was a stumpy torso.

A few seconds of silence, and he lowered his sword. "Ah." The Death Knight scratched at his chin. "Perhaps not then."

"Now we don't know what that one was supposed to be doing." Edward worked his jaw, his right eye slightly twitching.

Sally looked over at the supposedly locked door on the other wall. "Do the statues rotate, Humps?"

He turned his attention to the next one that he hadn't battered. Placing his sword down, he took a wide grip around the lip of the base the statue was positioned atop. With a grunt, he tensed and made the attempt. At first, nothing—but then with a deep grinding, the base started to rotate.

And then tipped slightly as the Death Knight became unbalanced. The statue fell off the podium and burst across the floor. "Ah," he repeated. "I do not seem to be the right one of us to be attempting puzzles."

"Humphrey." Sally slowly walked across the room. "Did you think of checking the door first?"

He turned to her as she stood before it, and as she gripped it, it ground across the floor and opened. She gestured with her hand and raised her eyebrows.

"So you've just destroyed someone's art collection," Edward tutted.

Lucius pulled his hood over his non-face a little more. "It's fine, it wasn't exactly good art . . ."

"Hey now!" Sally wagged her finger. "No need to be a critic. True art is about the joy of expressing yourself. Even if the results are . . . lackluster."

She shrugged and walked into the next room.

Though she seemed to stop about a foot into it as she met some kind of resistance. As she forced her way farther, her feet somehow stepped upon the thick air. She opened her mouth, but it became filled with something.

The floating skull just to her right said nothing, as a burning sensation began to flare up across her whole body.

CHAPTER FIFTY-SIX

This Is the Pits

Sally moved sluggishly through the air, her body now on fire—before a heavy weight shoved her. Her trajectory started with resistance, and then she dropped to the floor as gravity took proper hold.

Immediately, she threw up some kind of gel. Her insides were burning as much as her skin against the suddenly cooler air. She turned with bleary eyes to see the rest of the gang stabbing into the slightly opaque air between them. Rising to her shaking legs and rasping at the air, she then stumbled back. With a click, the floor beneath her shunted down to a sloped angle, and she spun to face the danger.

As a pit of silvered spikes opened up at the end of the slope, a wedge of the ceiling clicked downward to reveal three large spouts pointing directly at her. With the quick flick of her wrist, she flung Skeleton Key into the middle one—a spark of magic bursting out before she covered her face with her arms. Jets of fire blasted out from the other two spouts as the slick gel-vomit beneath her shoes caused her to slip into the pit.

With the unholy energy of *[Grave Strike]*, Humphrey cleaved the gel monster in two, and the magic holding it into a cube shape dissipated, leaving the remains across the floor. He leaped over the mess and slid to the edge of the slope, trying to peer down.

"Sally? Are you okay?"

"Bleeding out a little, but I avoided landing on any important organs." She squirmed against the long blades piercing her. Both legs and one arm. Shoulder and perhaps a kidney. The sharp spikes were too long to raise any of her skewered parts over the points without being able to stand. Thankfully, she had grabbed a potion on the way down, and it had kept her from passing out. Or worse.

Humphrey turned to the Party. "Any of you have a rope?"

They shook their heads, but Lucius stepped forward. "I have something that might help. Hold my hand."

The Death Knight narrowed his eyes but did so, as the Shade skirted down the slope slightly to see where the zombie was in the darkness. He held out a hand, and his crimson eyes flickered monochrome for a moment.

[Fade Away]

The base of the trap, along with all the silver spikes, became dark like shadows, and Sally slumped against the floor.

"Ow," she groaned. "Whoever built this place doesn't mess around." Sally stood up on shaking legs and took a deep breath. With her hands now free, she went through her Inventory to grab a rope and threw an end up to the waiting Party.

Once back up the slope, she collapsed on the ground and scowled at the dead slime.

Archie walked over and stood in front of her face, giving her a brief sniff. "This is far more deadly than the System would have created."

"So, you're saying that this is the work of an enemy Unique?" She scrunched her face up in the ginger fur enveloping her vision.

"Certainly one that doesn't want us snooping around," Edward said, leaning against the wall.

Humphrey shrugged and lowered a hand down to help the zombie up. "Or it could just be a bugged dungeon."

If anything, having the basement being trapped with more difficult things gave Sally some hope that they were on the right path. You wouldn't protect something unimportant, after all. She took the Death Knight's plated hand and stood on her feet, relenting to using a med kit to patch up what injuries she had left. She glanced up at Lucius while the progress bar filled.

"That's a neat trick. What are the limitations?"

Ellipses appeared next to his head. "Well, it's one of the new skills since I accepted being undead. One target at a time, several minute durations, and can only be objects. That sort of thing."

"Well, we know what to do next time there's a puzzle or locked door then." She beamed. Lucius was possibly her new favorite for this alone. Being able to bypass troubles would save them a lot of headaches and mouthfuls of acid. "Someone work out how to get across the pit without immolating themselves." She waved a hand at the group. "I'm going to loot the goop."

She kneeled and brought up the handy System menu. Most of it was junk—possibly whatever remnants of the last person to get stuck within it without having a walking tank to shove them out. Still, loot was loot—and hey, there was even a dagger in decent enough condition! A sword and spear had deteriorated enough to be designated unusable, so found no place in her stash.

45 Gold
Dagger
Skull (2)
Acid Gel (5)

Although she wasn't too sure what she planned to do with acidic gel, there was bound to be a use further down the line. Strangely enough, her mind was blank. Perhaps it was just the sudden trauma catching up to her. She tilted her head to look back at the Party to see what they were squabbling over now.

"If you reset it, then it could activate again." Edward had his arms crossed and was glaring at the Death Knight.

Humphrey was grinning, seemingly happier to frustrate the demon more than find a solution. "Just don't activate it again, then."

"I'm *not* throwing you across." Lucius stood holding the cat but was apprehensive about the next steps, a sweat drop emoji beside his head.

"Do it." The cat squirmed in his grip. "Cats always land across gaps."

"That's 'on their feet.'"

"Exactly."

Sally considered just standing and watching them crumble apart. It was more amusing than it should be, considering she entrusted her unlife to these goofballs. If it were Theo and Jackie, it'd be no different. So far, it seemed like she was just a magnet for this type of personality. Now they were her burden to keep from standing in the red circles.

The gap over the pit wasn't even that wide, and the doorway opposite stood there judging them, not a dozen feet farther than the spiked hole. It was difficult to jump due to the slope right before the drop, and there were probably traps on the other side—otherwise, she would have already made the attempt.

"Alright!" She rubbed her eyes as she got the attention of the *Outsiders*. "You had your chance. Lucius, see how the wall on the other side is made of a large block? Shadow it."

The Shade put the cat down on the floor and used *[Fade Away]* on the structural stone.

Sally moved to the edge, ran and jumped over, landing in the shadowy space where she wouldn't have been able to reach the lip of the stone above. She then hopped up onto the floor side and glared at the wall. With a click, she flicked the small switch downward, and the trap reset.

"Quickly now, you don't want to be halfway before it activates again." She smiled and folded her arms, keeping an eye on the switch so that she could give it an emergency flip if necessary. To save them, not to drop them in. Teach them a pointed lesson . . . intrusive thoughts had her hand muscles twitching but kept them at bay.

"Thank you, Sally." Archie beamed up at her as they made it across to where she stood, unharmed.

"Hey, we all help each other, Arch." She kneeled to pet him on the head. "Some of us just have more brains than others."

Edward rolled his eyes. "Most of us don't need to eat other brains to get by."

"Yours tasted bitter, by the way." She stuck her tongue out at the demon. "Now, Humphrey, you lead."

"That would be for the best," he said, as he nodded in return and glared at the rest of the hallway. The flame from the back of his helmet illuminated the ceiling in a ruddy hue as he slowly stepped forward toward the door.

Sally gave Lucius a light jab on the arm, briefly amused that a shocked emoji popped up when she did so. "That ability is insane. I bet there're all sorts of troubles you'll get us into and out of with it."

"Feels like there is a limit though." The Shade rubbed the back of his hood. "I don't quite understand the workings, but it might be like . . . shadow charges?"

"I gotcha." She nodded and turned to watch the Death Knight creep down the corridor. "You just need to work out how to replenish the charges, right?"

Lucius nodded, accompanied by a similar emoji.

Humphrey made it to the end of the hall with no further untoward traps springing. He put an outstretched hand against the door, which did nothing violent toward him. Still . . . he paused.

Sally walked up, followed by the rest, still overly cautious about potential surprises. Humphrey may be big and heavy, but there might be traps that were triggered by other methods that they'd need to be mindful of.

"Everything okay?" she whispered to him, trying to peer past his plated armor to see what the holdup was.

"Yes. Though, I feel odd."

He didn't look any different, at least from the back. Sally exhaled from her nose. "Odd how?"

The Death Knight shrugged and pushed on the door to open it. There was the brief wave of air that blew through the crack as it widened, as though they had popped the seal on a room that had not been opened for a very long time. Although the bottom of the pit trap had no skeletons, Sally doubted that many random Adventurers would have gotten through without issue.

"You forgot this, Sally." Edward nudged her as she tried to glimpse into the next room.

She turned as he held out the Skeleton Key, and she slowly reached toward it.

Bright blue blazed in his eyes as a wide grin spread across his face.

"Thanks, Edward. Would forget my own head if the System let me." She took the dagger and flipped it in her hand.

"My pleasure." The demon gave a brief bow. "We all help each other, after all."

"Sally . . ." Humphrey said from the front. Archie's hair was standing on end.

"There's a really large dog in here."

CHAPTER FIFTY-SEVEN

Silent Generation

Really large was perhaps an understatement. Despite only briefly moving underground, the room here was practically cavernous and had been decorated with pictures of various scenes—figures talking or doing activities. Sally could not see enough detail from this range to make a more precise determination, plus she was also really distracted by said *really large* dog.

Enormous, in fact. With two heads.

Easily house-sized, one half of the animal was off-white, whereas the other was dusty black. Golden collars, decorated with various gemstones, sat about each of their necks, and atop their heads were equally opulent crowns.

"Wow," Sally began, taking a deep breath in.

"Do not ask them to join us," Humphrey interrupted, causing her to deflate.

"I wasn't gonna!" *She was*, and she would hold that against the Death Knight. Look at all the people she had invited—her track record showed things worked out. Eventually.

"Greetings, mortals," the gray-headed one began.

"Or . . . whatever you are," the white one continued.

"They can talk!" Sally hissed. "What are your names?"

"Boros," the white head said.

"Jokos," said the darker dog, with a slight bow.

"I'm Sally, and this is Humphrey, Edward, Lucius, and Archie . . . Arch, come say hello."

The ginger cat had hidden away behind the boot of the Death Knight. The hair on his back was standing on end and his ears were flattened back.

Sally scowled at him. Far be it for her to turn her nose up at something so clearly cliché, but for an all-powerful supposedly the Architect being, the cat could be a bit on the odd side. She turned her gaze briefly between the rest of the Party. Perhaps she shouldn't be the one to judge.

"What do you seek in the pyramid, names I will not remember?" Boros peered down at them.

"Some . . . uh . . . *Humphrey*?" She tilted her head.

"It matters not!" Jokos interrupted. "To pass us, you will need to answer three riddles!"

Sally held her face. This was her worst nightmare. Maybe she could call for a Theo airdrop now. He had a little more brains in him than the rest of them. No—she could do this. She turned to smile at the Party and then grimaced back at the large dog guardian.

"Is there another option?"

"You could turn around." Boros nodded.

"Or perish," Jokos added, helpfully.

"Do we perish if we get the riddles wrong?" She crossed her arms and began to tap her foot.

"You just do not proceed if you are unable to answer."

"But we can eat you if you prefer."

None of the Party looked particularly keen on that outcome—only slightly less so than having to answer the riddles. Seeing no place where she could stick her dagger to avoid this situation, Sally eventually relented. Although she could eat them too, it would be nice for the Party if she didn't drag them into violence for a change. This could be a little gift for them.

"Fiiiine. Give us the first one, then."

"Born of shadows, a void in the light. Invisible to the day, elusive at night. Neither seen nor felt, yet I enhance. What am I in this paradoxical dance?"

Sally scrunched up her face. Why couldn't the answer just be *brains*. Like the word, not actual brains—although she hadn't eaten a good one in so long. Perhaps they should just go back to the starting area and live among the fresh meat again—oh, even better! They could be the new *Zeroes* and gatekeep in the Wastelands. It's not like anyone would survive how harsh it was, or the invincible Toad, anyway.

Or was the Toad invincible? With her new dagger, she might be able to stab it and get revenge. She wondered what it could drop, if anything. There probably wouldn't be anything worth the effort, and its brains probably tasted terrible. But if they stuck about where the previous guild had, she would be able to eat all the Level Ten brains and grow more powerful with little effort.

In effect, it would be a terrific plan B for their conquest idea. They would become bosses in their own right, preventing access to the rest of the world until enough Players got together and found a way to oust her. That definitely sounded more fun that stomping around the desert and rocky land under the constant sun without any brains to eat. Only to almost die to dungeon traps twice, ultimately—

"Sally." Humphrey nudged her. "Are you thinking about the riddle?"

"Huh? Yeah, of course." She tapped the side of her nose. "The answer is—"

"Yes, we know." The Death Knight narrowed his eyes. "Edward already gave the answer while you were glazed over."

Sally shot the demon a thumbs-up and smiled up at the two-headed canine. "Next please."

"Fine, but this one won't be so simple." Boros raised an eyebrow at his sibling—or just his own other head.

Sally wasn't sure how that worked. Were they twins? Same dog, but different brains? It was confusing and very distracting, considering she was supposed to be paying attention. She bit her tongue to mentally stop her brain from running away with the words.

"I speak without a mouth, hear without ears. I have no body, but I shed tears. Wherever I go, darkness is cast. I am not alive, yet I grow fast," Jokos asked with a wide grin.

She immediately looked at the tax collector.

"What?" He shrugged. "Just because I got one, it doesn't mean I have all the answers."

"Not even for a demon coin?" Sally withdrew one from her Inventory and waved it in the air. "Also, Lucius, you owe me two of these you pretended to eat."

"Edward already plied them from me." The Shade slowly recoiled as a sweat drop emoji appeared beside him.

"I think I have an idea," Humphrey announced, standing in between Edward's smirk and Sally's glare. "How about *the night?*"

"No, that is incorrect."

"We can see how you came to that conclusion though."

The Death Knight deflated and rubbed at his chin.

Sally had no intention of getting stuck here when there was a world to save and so many brains to eat. The morsels just had to catch up to where she was and get in the way a little bit. If danger or Theo didn't get to them first. As the Party murmured among themselves, she brought up her chat.

Sally: talking to some dogs
Sally: they have riddles
Theo: that sounds some degree of fun
Theo: bet you're killing it
Theo: i have a coffin now
Theo: won't be long, I promise

She tutted to herself; promises were made to be broken. Like necks. It was good that he had a way to sleep again; hopefully he also had a decent way to transport it. It would be great to see the goof again.

"Very good, weird shadow thing." Boros nodded.

"I'm surprised you got it." The other dog raised his eyebrows.

Sally waved at them. "Third one, please."

"In the skillet's dance, I morph and take form. Layers of joy, a breakfast to warm. A disc of delight on a griddle's embrace. I defy gravity, with culinary grace." Boros raised an eyebrow, while the other head just grinned.

She realized she didn't have anything to distract herself from having to get this last one answered. There was no other option but to blurt out the first thing that came to her mind. "Pancakes!"

They both watched her, stunned. "That is correct, little dead one."

"You may pass."

That was exhausting. She gave them a brief bow before waving on her unimpressed Party. The two-headed dog moved to the side and allowed her to pass, revealing a hidden doorway on the opposite side of the chamber. As she strode across the room, she bit her tongue and managed to prevent herself from asking the hounds to join them. By far, almost the hardest part of this encounter. She wondered how their brains tasted, probably like dog food.

Humphrey closed the door behind them. "Well, that was . . . something."

"I don't think Sally was even paying attention to most of that." Edward tilted his head as his arms were crossed.

She scowled back at him. "I don't need to be in the limelight all the time. You all can get some . . . where's Archie?"

The chamber they were in shook as a dull bass vibrated through the brickwork. Dust fell from the ceiling, and the door opened slightly. Archie walked in, a puff of smoke emanating from his ginger fur as he pushed the door closed again.

"Hello." He beamed up at Sally with large, emerald eyes.

With a sigh, she glanced around the small chamber. Either it was another space to stop and rest, or it was full of unseen traps. Two doorways stood in the wall about thirty feet opposite, around a dozen feet apart. Neither had any sort of markings or way to determine where each of them led.

"Just as tough a problem as the last room." She rubbed at her chin. In the previous dungeon, she had thought going left was the surest way to victory—when in fact, a totally different route was correct. What would she do if she wanted to design a nefarious dungeon? "We may die here."

The rest of the Party looked around the otherwise empty room with a little less suspicion, although none of them made the move to progress without any elaboration.

"We don't have a bag of ball bearings to do the job, or a ten-foot pole . . .

but!" She withdrew a blade and a spear from her Inventory. "We can just throw about the dozens of weapons I still have and prod about at the brickwork with these spears." After passing over the one she held to a skeptical Edward, she brought another three out for the rest of them except the cat.

Slowly, they tapped ahead of them, occasionally making sure there were no pressure plates, false floors, or traps hiding among the walls. Despite their reluctance, they were diligent in doing their part in safe checking the whole way across the room, until finally, they made it to the two doors unharmed.

"Underwhelming, yet that just makes it even more suspicious." Sally narrowed her eyes at the two doors. Caution should dictate that Humphrey go first. Maybe she should just let him pick—that way the blame wouldn't be on her if he died.

She took a couple of steps backward and bowed to the Death Knight. "All yours, sir."

He narrowed his eye sockets at her and then glared at the two doorways. Energy powering over his armor, he took a step forward and kicked the right door open. Despite being made of stone, the door cracked and split from the hinges to clatter into the room beyond.

A wailing noise pierced the air, as some manner of siren blasted back at them from within.

"Thanks . . . THANKS, HUMPS," she shouted back over the constant din.

The Death Knight turned back to her and shrugged. "What? I can't hear you."

"WHAT?"

Edward pinched the bridge of his nose, exhaling continuously, while a mute symbol appeared next to the wincing Shade.

CHAPTER FIFTY-EIGHT

Sliding Forth

The blaring noise ceased, causing silence to wash back over the Party. Sally peered into the room, scowling past the Death Knight to see a chamber lined with boxes—no, these were sarcophagi built into the walls. Just as the realization hit, their stone lids swung open almost simultaneously, the grinding of stone and falling of aged dust combined with a handful of groans.

A dozen mummies stepped forth into the dim light, turning toward the doorway with bright yellow eyes and hunger in their open mouths. Wrappings of dark and dirtied gray covered their bodies.

[Endless Sleep]

They vanished into the ground.

"Neat! Free undead." Sally twirled her finger around. "*Gotta catch* . . . ah, it's wasted on you bunch."

"I'm not sure your skill is meant to be able to pluck random Monsters up." Humphrey scratched at his chin. "However, that is what it did—so perhaps I am in the wrong."

"Just like you were with the door," Edward murmured.

Sally just beamed. The prospect of more undead friends was enough to turn the slow dungeon crawl into a more interesting and lucrative venture for her. They were only here for the silly memory crystal thing the ex-Observers wanted. Otherwise, she would be chewing on brains. Ah, how she missed a proper meal. That's what this second area really needed, some good old-fashioned Player versus Player action.

"I shall try the next one then." The Death Knight narrowed his eyes at the demon. "Unless you would like to go first?"

The confident look on Edward's face slowly slid away, and he gave the wall a glare instead. He may have extra lives to spend, but Sally knew that the demon wouldn't want to waste them on something Humphrey was much better suited to absorb.

Deciding that he had left enough of a silence, the plated figure turned to the next door—this time opening it a little more carefully. It slid to the side to reveal stairs going downward.

"This is the way to B2," he announced, pointing to an engraved sign on the wall.

"The pyramid sure is mysterious, huh?" Sally jostled the Shade, who just looked nervous.

"I hate stairs," Humphrey grumbled, his shoulder pads scraping against the wall of the narrow passageway. As he took the first step, there was a click, and the stairs flattened into a steep slope. Then he was gone.

"Humps!" Sally ran over to the doorway and peered down. Some manner of gloom obscured the end of the slope past fifty or so feet. There had been the scraping sound of metal on stone as the Death Knight had quickly descended, but now there was just silence.

"Looks like we need to find the reverse switch." Archie sauntered between her legs.

She reached down and picked him up. "Are you kidding? Doesn't this look like fun?"

The ginger cat opened his mouth to disagree as the zombie hopped onto the slope.

Things went by rather quickly, the stone not providing as much friction as she would have expected. A handful of wall torches came and went, flickering past her as she descended into the pyramid below. Then, ahead of her, was the Death Knight standing with his arms crossed.

She dug in her heels as much as she could to slow down. The hair on Archie's back stood on end, but nothing could stop her colliding with the metallic barricade. With a hard *clonk*, she bounced back onto the slope. Her head now hurt, but she hadn't squished the cat. Tattered pieces of the Death Knight's cloak lay about the floor.

"Ow. *Why?*" She put the cat down and held her aching skull.

"I knew you could not resist the slope. Just behind me are bladed traps that rise out of the floor as you slide across them." He turned to show his back raked with silver lines.

"That's a pretty mean thing to put at the end of a fun slide," she huffed. "Is there an off switch? Otherwise, the other two might . . ."

"They're coming already." Humphrey grinned.

Sally became pressed against the floor, suddenly covered by something warm and furred. After the moment of confusion, there was a vibrating *thump* that echoed through what she now believed to be a large Archie balloon—followed by a second *thump* and complaining groans.

The cat popped back to his normal size, and she caught him out of the air. Edward and Lucius lay tangled among each other, a panicked face and frustrated emoji alternating from the Shade's head.

"There's danger ahead." She grinned as the pair tried to right themselves on the incline. "It was either that, or slamming straight into Mr. Iron Body here."

"The armor is not made of iron," Humphrey began before she waved him off. With a sigh, he rolled his shoulders out. "I will go disarm the trap now that you're not all going to shred yourself to pieces."

"Thanks, Humphrey!" *[Living Dead]*.

Perhaps an unnecessary spell cast at this stage, but the boost helped everyone aside from Archie and Edward. Unless a powerful enemy was right around the corner, the cooldown would be up before they really needed it. Perhaps slightly necessary, as she watched the Death Knight walk over the blades that rose up from the floor under the command of his weight. It helped with her blossoming headache too.

Only about an inch tall, they would have done some pretty terrible damage to the group going at full speed. As Humphrey rounded a corner, she also saw that the wall at the end of the blades had protruding spikes. She shuddered in remembering the iron maiden trap. The post-gel trap was pretty horrific, too, if she thought about it too much, which she didn't. Some things were just easier for her unfeeling undead side to keep hold of.

With a terrible grinding sound, something snapped, and the floor blades retracted. The stairs also popped back up to their normal form, which again set Edward and Lucius stumbling into one another and tripping into her. She held them back and allowed them to stand and sort themselves. Sometimes she forgot how strong she was.

"Trap is now disabled." Humphrey poked his head around the corner with a grin.

"Any more friends around the corner for me to steal?" She grinned and picked Archie back up, stroking his head as she stepped over the previously dangerous area. The others followed tentatively behind her before they reached the corner.

Humphrey was standing in a small room, arms folded and a grin on his face. On the left wall were the remnants of whatever mechanism worked the trap, the metallics guts of which lay on the floor. A dozen feet away on the wall opposite her was a wide door. Ornately engraved in vibrant colors, with gemstones set in the carved archway. The door itself was a very dark wood but made well—with dark metal bracing across it.

"That says, 'treasure room,' atop it," Archie spoke up from her arms.

"It that where your magic gem is?" She worked her jaw, half excited and half labored with apprehension.

"It's possible." The cat stretched out and jumped down to the floor.

While she hadn't been super keen on the idea, it was important to the two ex-Observers to get some insights on the System and Architect. If that was possible, anyway. They certainly seemed to think so, and they had spent enough time running around after her and her odd questline, so it was only fair that she allow them this. It could even give them some help with the looming dragon fight—at least that was the hope.

"The door is locked," Humphrey continued, grinning from where he stood.

"Good thing we have a—" Sally withdrew her dagger and immediately fumbled it, dropping it to bounce once and then embed itself into the floor. "Rats! That was going to be like a whole line thing. You know, like a capstone that we could quote in future years."

"You anticipate being alive this time next year?" Edward asked, clearly unimpressed with how his time was being spent.

"Sure, unless you plan on killing me first?" She scooped her blade from the floor and pointed it at him, the demon just rolling his eyes in response.

With no further objections, she walked over to the large door and looked for where the keyhole was. Perhaps unsurprisingly, it didn't have one.

"I think it's a key phrase that opens it." Humphrey widened his grin as he stood beside her.

She clucked her tongue. He had gotten her over here all excited to use Skeleton Key for its namesake purpose, and it had all been a ruse because the door didn't open like that. Well, there was more than one way to crack a skull.

With her eyes closed, she put her hand against the door to feel it. Wood. Yep, that about summed it up. But now it looked like she was about to do something cool, so she couldn't just move away yet—but if she stood too long, they'd start getting suspicious when nothing happened. Oh, had that time already passed? Perhaps she could pretend to be asleep.

"This door . . . is cursed," she eventually said, to the slight gasp of at least Lucius—although he had no accompanying bubble. She tilted her head at the side of the wall. The blocks here were around three or so feet wide and deep. "Lucius, can you shadow there?"

"Sure." He pointed his finger at the designated square block, and it turned into a dull gray, slightly translucent version of itself.

Sally crouched down and looked through. Beyond the shadow, the room was dimly lit, and there wasn't much that she could make out. After a moment's consideration, she shrugged and began to crawl through, with the cat joining alongside her.

Clear on the other side, she stood and dusted herself off, thinking that she should probably get a change of clothes in soon. She looked around the room and gasped.

It was large, even more so than the double-dog room. Filled with long treasure chests around the edges, the center of the room was a raised step dais that led up to a container of solid gold—a beam of light from the high roof illuminating it like a spotlight.

With a crunch, a large and shadowed figure stepped among the treasure boxes, looming into view over the pair.

A sharp beak among pitch-black feathers opened and screamed at them, bright white eyes fixated on the intruders.

CHAPTER FIFTY-NINE

Split Treasure

Sally and Archie scattered as sharp claws from the beast descended downward, scoring deep grooves into the stone brickwork.

"What? Is that like an Owlb—"

"It's an Eaglebear!" Archie yelled from wherever he had snuck himself. Being so small, he had the advantage of sliding in the gaps between the mountainous stacks of containers and troves.

Now that she had some distance on it, she could see that the black feathers receded to a gray brown down the creature's body. A large body, much like that of a bear, with four legs ending in sharp talons instead of wings. The plume around the Eaglebear's neck bristled as it peered around for the smaller prey.

It looked neither undead, nor willing to discuss matters. Shame it had to end this way, but maybe it would have nicer brains than everything else here? Dungeons seemed to be the worst place for cuisine—and once she had less danger glaring at her from across the room, she would muse on why that would be.

She stumbled across one of the chests, slipping and bouncing down a couple of them, closer to the Monster. That door needed to be opened. Her eyes scanned it for a lever or switch, as the Eaglebear turned toward her and readied a pounce.

[Mortis Bomb] careened over the space, leaving a trail of green as the skull struck the open switch—not bringing forth any undead, but opening the door for the other three.

The Monster landed on her just after, crushing her through the chests she was standing on and spilling their contents down to the next layer. As it raised a claw up to stomp on her, she thrust her dagger into the gnarled foot, piercing through the center.

Her shadow slashed out at the other foot being used as balance, and the Eaglebear reared up to back away from the surprise pain. Humphrey barreled into it, knocking it down a few layers to collapse through another handful of chests. Sally grinned. That seemed like a quicker way of opening them.

The creature rose and took a step back to avoid the downswing of the greatsword. The Death Knight twisted it to the flat side to block a swipe of the large claws, the metal screaming out from the strike. He blazed red and gray light as his abilities shot into action. From behind the Eaglebear a giant spider burst out from among some storage boxes, bright ginger in color and glaring at the Monster from eight emerald eyes.

Edward mostly stayed near the back, although his weapon was glowing orange.

In seeing that it was now surrounded, the Eaglebear opened its beak wide and screamed—the piercing howl almost bringing a wind with it that buffeted the Party.

The light above the middle of the room became shadowed, and Sally looked up to see a large figure drop through the illuminated opening to land atop the golden chest beneath large brown wings.

"This one has a bear's head and eagle's body," she yelled at the ginger spider with a shrug. "What's this?"

"Still an Eaglebear," the responding hiss came.

Totally ridiculous. They were nothing alike, and would their babies have a chance to make a whole bear or whole eagle? Well, *these two* wouldn't, because she was about to kill them, but . . .

She idly tapped her hand on a withdrawn skull. It was almost time, and as much as she wanted to charge into the melee, she needed to be a bit smarter and use her new advantages. The bird creature turned and leaped toward spider-Archie, who retreated to clamber up the wall. Humphrey had the attention of the bear version.

"Go help Humps," she told her shadow. Lucius popped up beside her with a thumbs-up bubble, hopped down a couple of rows of treasure chests, then vanished into smoke.

She flung her skull attack across the room to strike the winged Monster in the back, the small explosion burning away at some of the feathers. Four zombies rose from the floor and started to grab toward the bipedal legs. It was enough of a distraction to stop the spider-Archie from getting munched by the large maw of the bear's head.

Archie leaped from the wall onto his assailant, skittering around as he drew a length of web from the wall, down over its back and wings. It struggled to move away at the same time as kicking the zombies away—one unlucky corpse getting half stomped by the large talons in the process.

Humphrey buckled under his sword, holding it horizontally as the other Eaglebear tried to stomp down on him. His shadow sliced out at the back legs, gashing just above the feet of both limbs. The creature was confused and tried to dart its white eyes around to see who had attacked it. Five skeletons rose up around Humphrey as he darted forward with a slash of his own, catching the bucking animal across the feathered chest.

Sally watched as Edward slowly sauntered across the battlefield, easily stepping up the layers of wide steps with his long legs. He was still keeping a good distance but was starting to flank both enemies. She held out a hand and cast *[Living Dead]* to regenerate and empower her undead friends.

The winged creature burst into the air as Archie dropped to the floor. One zombie was dead, but three had managed to do a little damage. She commanded them to go assist Humphrey, as their prey was now getting itself stuck in the thick webbing the spider had weaved, preventing it from flying away.

She knew a tasty treat when she saw one. Flipping her dagger around in her hand, she began to hop between containers toward the flank of the battle. Edward jumped from his position opposite, striking the bear creature in the back as he used the Monster as a stepping stone to jump over to where Sally was. Purple energy began to crack and course across the Eaglebear.

"Nice of you to participate." She grinned at him as he followed on behind her.

"Larger Monsters aren't really my thing, and it looked like Humphrey already had a shadow."

"So you came to assist me?" Sally slid to a stop on a long container and looked up at the struggling flying Monster.

"No, I just want first dibs on your loot if you die."

"Ha! If I die, then you will be fu—" They both leaped away as the creature dropped from the sky, crushing the boxes where they had stood into shards.

Sally leaped atop the creature, grabbing at its feathers as it floundered about on the floor. Her dagger rose into the air as she aimed to plunge it into where she assumed a heart might be. Blue illuminated her face as the bear's mouth opened wide, and a large orb of light began to form.

She was blinded and fell from her perching spot, bouncing on the stone floor covered in debris before rolling to her feet. With her right eye, she could see Archie wrapping the taloned feet together, and Edward may have stabbed the creature. *[Living Dead]* bloomed up around her, and vision came back to her left eye. Pain and then a soothing feeling radiated on that side of her face.

With a growl, she stomped on the outstretched wing, stabbing her dagger into the ground to pin it there, then she walked her way across it to the panicked beast. It roared at her, and she grabbed its muzzle to hold it shut. "Bad!"

[Eat Brains]

She rose from the creature, feeling slightly satiated by the meal. Not great, not terrible. It tasted like warm eggs, which was somewhat concerning. Humphrey and Lucius had just finished off the other creature too, in part thanks to the harrying zombies—of which one still remained.

Oh! She would need to get little hats for them. If they persisted through her summoning of them, then she could pick out the best performers and grow attached to them, mourn them when they fell. If only they weren't stuck in a pyramid.

Lucius popped back into being beside the Death Knight. "Wow, that was a lot of fun. Your sword is huge!" A little firework emoji popped beside his head.

"Thanks." Humphrey deflated. "It fulfills a purpose."

Sally stretched out as Archie shrunk down into a normal cat form. Edward walked around the corpse to tilt his head toward her.

"Feeling okay?"

"Sure, a little rough, but what's new?" She yawned and looked around at the carnage. Looting everything would take forever . . . but what if it was some elaborate trap? Like that one movie with the thing. They should take nothing . . . or maybe just the sparkling gold chest? It was the centerpiece, after all.

"It's just that . . ." Edward drew a little closer. "You took a lot of damage from that beam."

She squinted down at the nearest shiny object, trying to get a glint of her reflection. The left side of her face looked pretty raw and discolored, and it had burned away some of her hair, but otherwise she was intact.

"Nah, I'm fine. Let's gather up and argue over what we should do about the loot."

Edward shrugged and then stumbled away as the Eaglebear lurched. Sword drawn, he stepped back as the creature rose to his feet—behind him the bear form one did the same.

[Endless Sleep]

Sally beamed as they vanished from view, alongside the zombie who needed a crown.

"See, that's how we take over the world."

CHAPTER SIXTY

Wrapped Up

The Party gathered around the center stage where the beam of light from above illuminated them.

"So I guess you can just zombie anything now, then?" Humphrey crossed his arms.

Sally shrugged. "You're ex-System, you tell me."

Archie yawned. "Looks like a mix of your abilities, the one that increases your disease chance, but also is guaranteed if you eat brains, but also now your zombies have the same chance, and I forgot where I was going with this."

"Can we not call it a disease, though?" She wagged her finger in the air. "Makes it sound *nasty*."

"You just had half your face blown off, and you're fine with it." Edward narrowed his blue eyes. "Then you ate the brains of an animal."

"Doesn't make it *nasty*."

Lucius remained silent, either listening to something specific or just trying to tune the rest of them out.

"Anyway," Sally continued, "point of order is we need to decide what we are doing with this room. Clearly it's full of stuff, but it could be trapped or cursed. Who would just stick a giant treasure room in the middle of the dungeon, right?"

Humphrey scratched his chin. "*Yes*. I see your point, although the chests that were destroyed didn't seem to be traps."

"We killed the guardians of the treasure, so perhaps that's the challenge here?" Edward sighed and looked around the room.

"Both fair points," Sally relented with a bow. "But we've all seen how insidious this dungeon is in wanting to cause us harm. Something so overtly enticing would surely be just to lure us into danger."

Lucius quietly continued to look around.

"What do you think, Archie?" The zombie kneeled to pick him up, so that he was more at their eye level.

"A nap would be nice."

"What about the potential traps? Or if this place is worthy of looting?"

The cat yawned. "What more could you really want?"

Sally pouted. Whether he meant she had all the treasures life could offer with this found family of goofballs, or that her Inventory was already cluttered with enough garbage—either didn't matter.

"The cat has spoken." She held him up and lowered her head in reverence. "Let's just get the magic stone and be gone from this place."

"I have no love for this place." The Death Knight nodded. "Not that I prefer the endless Wastes, *ha-ha*."

"There's no door out of here," Lucius eventually spoke, causing them all to pause and look around the room.

Indeed, aside from the one they entered from, and the hole in the ceiling, the large room had no other doors or exits. Sally climbed up atop the golden chest to glare around. "That can't be right—surely there is more dungeon down here. Although, I'm basing that on absolutely no prior knowledge."

"The crystal is not here." Humphrey sighed and leaned against the chest. "I had hoped we had gone the correct direction."

Lucius had his gloved hand cupped to his misty chin. Ellipses, followed by question marks, slowly appeared beside him as he thought.

Sally ground her teeth together. They always went the correct direction, even when they didn't. The path would just change to where they were now headed. You were allowed to do that—it was in the guidebook she planned to write once they had taken over the world. Or escaped it. Jury was still out on what she wanted, or what was even possible at this point.

"I don't think that is a treasure chest, Sally."

She looked down at the Shade, who was prodding at the side of it. It looked mostly like some kind of container, and was in the treasure room, surrounded by containers filled with who-knows-what because she didn't want to get cursed. With a sigh, she hopped down from it.

The Death Knight tilted his head. "I suppose it almost looks like a coffin. Perhaps this is some manner of tomb."

"Dibs, then. I'm the expert on tombs." She twirled around and made a show of pushing Humphrey back slightly.

They watched as she turned back and pulled on the lid, straining even with her strength. Eventually, it began to move and slid to the side—as much as it wanted to return to the closed position. It looked like something was inside, but she couldn't quite make out what.

She leaned forward to grab it, and then immediately fell into an abyss as if drawn to something. The tomb closed behind her and plunged her into darkness. "Should have expected that," she murmured to herself as she fell through nothingness.

And then she was sitting on cold flooring in a large room peaked at the top to a point like a pyramid and lit in a strange green hue. Statues adorned the left and right sides of the room, while four decorated pillars rose from beside a walkway up to the slanted ceiling. Engravings illuminated the back wall, past an ornate sarcophagus standing in the middle of the room in a slightly raised area, bright light shining across the golden coffin covered in patterns and gemstones.

Sally stood to better look around. The engravings on the far wall looked to be of kings and queens. Three kings, a queen, a king, and then three queens. Each looked similar, wearing a headdress and an air of regal vision. Around them were carvings of people dancing, harvests, and possibly other things that her brain couldn't process because she became distracted by the elaborate casket.

On account of it shuffling.

Something to add to her undead hotel, perhaps. She grinned to herself and readied her hand to cast the spell.

The casket burst open, and wrappings shot out around the four pillars, encircling them as a figure rose up into the air.

"You dare enter my pyramid and try to steal from me?" The female voice boomed out as two glowing yellow eyes crackled with power from beneath aged bandage.

"No?" Sally smiled, trying to think if she had taken anything or not.

A fifth wrapping shot out from underneath the figure, quickly snaking around Sally's legs. As she went to hop away, the mummy dragged her to the floor and quickly up into the air.

Hanging upside down, she now came face to face with her assailant.

"You're not like the *others* . . ." The mummy narrowed her eyes. "You're . . . undead. And kind of adorable."

"Guilty." Sally grinned back.

The lighting in the room shifted to a more comforting amber, and Sally was lowered to the floor as the mummy sank to the ground herself. The wrappings retracted from the pillars and returned to her body.

"Sorry for the theatrics, hun. I figured it would have been some nasty Adventurers."

"Not quite." Sally held out a hand to be shaken. "I'm Sally."

"Sally, what a lovely name. I'm Norah." She smiled warmly down toward the zombie. "They used to call me the Ever-Living. Now I seem to be the ever undead." With a wrapped arm extended, she gestured toward the engravings on the wall.

"You're the last one?" Sally asked, tilting her head.

"All of them, actually." Norah smiled. "I was granted with the power to be reborn as the Eternal Ruler of the Wastes. Being a king seemed like the most prudent thing at the start . . . patriarchal society and all. After trying out being queen, I just liked it more."

Sally nodded. Being a queen *was* pretty grand. That was some steep backstory for a world that had only existed for a month or two—but that information was from Humphrey, who was an unreliable narrator at best.

"Want to join up with my undead Party and rule the world?" she asked, rocking between her heels and toes with hands clasped behind her back.

"A very generous offer, hun. However, I have all I need here. This is my place to rule, you see, and—"

With a hideous scraping of metal, Humphrey dropped out of the void onto the stone floor, standing from his crouch surrounded by a small cloud of dust and flourishing his greatword to the ready.

Norah blinked. "Actually, *sure*. How do I sign up?"

Sally beamed and waved the Death Knight over, as he looked only partly confused that the zombie was talking to the potential enemy instead of in any real danger.

"Humphrey, this is Norah. Norah, Humphrey." Her smile couldn't get any wider.

"Pleasure." He nodded toward the mummy.

"Humphrey is like my adoptive father figure."

Norah nodded. "He certainly has quite the figure."

The Death Knight stood still, impassively looking between the two women. "Looking for the Memory Crystal," he eventually blurted out.

"We're kind of lost, though," Sally added. "They all follow me, but I have a terrible sense of direction." She punched Humphrey as he nodded along.

"Unfortunately, you are right, hun." Norah smiled. Slight gaps between her bandaging revealed gray-blue undead skin, with dark gray hair flowing out from the off-white wrappings around her head. "What you seek is at the pinnacle of the pyramid."

"Ah, *nuts*." Sally pouted. "Are the others coming down? Oh, you need to meet Theo, Norah. He's a bit of a dweeb, but he's like . . ." She rubbed her chin on how best to describe it.

"He's special to you?" Norah tilted her head, her gaze going between the Death Knight and the zombie as her warm smile continued.

"Yeah, but I'm totes tsundere about it. The whole undead thing, you know?"

Humphrey eventually processed a reply. "The others are too weak to shift the lid."

Norah held up a hand. "Treasure room, right?" She snapped her fingers. A brief wave of energy flowed around them.

The three of them were now in the treasure room, the rest of the Party startled by their sudden appearance.

"Norah. Lucius, Edward, and Archie. Should I be referring to you as Queen Norah?"

"It's so nice to meet you all. But no, no need, hun." Norah gave her a sad smile. "I no longer actually have subjects to rule. It is just my pyramid and what lies within."

Sally wondered if she should tell her about the Monsters they killed and traps they broke—but that seemed like something better left as water under the bridge. Her bridge, her waterway, but it was done now. Maybe her subjects had been erased due to the dragon's meddling with the Wastes. That could be a good thread to drag her along to help them. Although, the Death Knight might be the only motivation the ex-queen needed.

With another snap of bandaged fingers, they were now in a different room. Pointed at the peak, with streams of amber sunlight gleaming through thin slits in the slanted ceiling.

Almost a mirror of Norah's chamber. This one instead had a large crystal hanging in the middle of the room. Almost two feet in height, it shone through all the colors of the rainbow in turn, like shifting oil on water. The glow illuminated the floor and their faces.

"See, Humps?" Sally punched him on the plated arm. "Told you going the wrong way would take us to where we wanted to go anyway."

The Death Knight looked down at the cat, who looked back up at him.

"It is time, little brother."

Archie nodded. "I am ready to be absorbed, big brother."

CHAPTER SIXTY-ONE

Betray Trust

A piercing wail reverberated through the dragon's chamber as Ruben dug his four-foot-long claws through the stone floor.

"I want them *gone* or to yield already." He puffed, blowing the dust across the room.

"Of course, sire." The robed figure before him bowed. "They are proving especially troublesome."

The dragon snorted. "Send two gold Parties along with Claw to kill or capture them. Preferably kill."

"Two, your excellency?"

Ruben tapped his talons on the stone floor. "Are you questioning whether I should send more Parties or fewer Parties?"

The shadowed figure paused. "... *No*, your excellency?"

"Good. If I have to deal with this problem personally, you won't be around to witness it." A wide grin of large teeth picked up the low light of the torches in the room.

"What?" Sally crossed her arms. "What? You can't!"

Humphrey shrugged. "The crystal only works once. We have decided to pool our memories to unlock as much as possible."

She bent down and lifted the cat up, giving him a squeeze. "But, *Archiiiiie . . .*" she whined.

"I grow tired, Sally." He began to purr. "It has been fun, but I am not meant for this world as I am."

The zombie exhaled and closed her eyes. Although it was better than losing a friend due to battlefield death, it still tugged at her undead heartstrings.

"You just need to meet Archie from the next area," the ginger cat continued. "We share meowmeries, so he will recognize you. And he *should* be less unstable."

"*Less* unstable." Edward rolled his eyes.

Sally rubbed her face against his fur, then held him out toward the Death Knight, pouting.

Humphrey took Archie and walked closer to the crystal in the middle of the room. He murmured something that the rest of them couldn't hear, then began the process while they couldn't see.

Bodyguard Removed: Archie, Domestic Cat
Archie has left the Party

Sally rubbed her face and hugged onto Norah, who patted her on the back. A crying emoticon appeared next to Lucius, as he looked down at the floor. Edward seemed indifferent.

Humphrey alone turned his head back to them and gave them a nod, before stepping forth to receive the crystal. The shimmering light coursed from the large stone, circling and wrapping around the Death Knight's form. Slowly, the gem itself became dull and inert as whatever magical power transferred from it to him. After a few seconds, all the waving colors had become absorbed into his plated form, and he stood with arms out.

Silence filled the chamber, as Sally wiped her eyes with the back of her arm. "Everything okay, Humphrey?"

He slowly turned to them. His face looked no different, but there was an almost shocked widening of his eye sockets that quickly faded. "*Yes.*"

"Just 'yes'? Did it work? What do you now know?" She crossed her arms and glared at him.

"Yes. Ah, apologies. This is somewhat overwhelming." He scratched at his chin as he stepped back toward them. "I think we should call Theo back first."

Edward groaned.

Sally: come on over
Sally: arch has gone :(
Sally: humps absorb the adorbs
Sally: and took pyramid crystal
Theo: will be there asap

She felt glum as she closed the chat window. Even with Theo coming whenever he could, she felt bad he wasn't able to say goodbye to the cat. Finding a new Archie seemed weird, but hopefully the next one wasn't a mutated eldritch beast like the one from this area.

After staring at nothing for a few seconds, Edward leaned over beside her ear. "How much do you trust me, Sally?"

"With my unlife." She looked up at him and smiled.

"Excellent." A wide grin spread across his face as his eyes blazed blue before he leaned back away.

Norah has joined the Party

"Hey, Norah." The zombie spun around from the demon to the mummy. "I don't suppose you fancy being my new bodyguard?"

"That's a lot of commitment." The woman rubbed her bandaged chin. "We've only just met and—"

"Humphrey is my other bodyguard." Sally grinned.

New Bodyguard: Norah, the Ever-Living. Mummy Queen.

"I'm also a bodyguard." Edward deflated and put his hands in his pockets.

She nodded but wagged a finger. "You're not undead though, so you're more like the grouchy uncle. Lucius, you're the cousin who spends too much time asking questions and playing video games."

"What's a video game?" A question mark appeared beside his shadowed head.

"See? *Perfect.*" Sally felt pretty pleased with herself. One of the clone Archie's might be taking an extended holiday . . . within the Death Knight . . . but she had managed to condense and enhance the found family.

Now all that was left was to—

Dungeon Complete!

Her STAR began to glow a golden color.

"Think of this as my gift for welcoming me into your little Party." Norah gave a brief curtsy. "You defeated the boss of the pyramid, technically . . . and I may have fudged the numbers a little to give you as much experience as I could."

Sally gasped. "You're the best, Norah! Isn't she, Humphrey?"

The Death Knight was staring off at the wall, as if reading something within his own head. He responded absentmindedly; his eye sockets focused on the horizon. "Hmm. *Yes.*"

She nudged the mummy and wiggled her eyebrows as she opened up her STAR.

> **Level Up**
> **Pick One**
> [Necrotic Aura] Higher averages for undead ability number ranges.
> [Share Burden] For three seconds, any damage is shared around your undead minions.
> [Bone Gate] Create a gateway between two corpses that you can see.

The System didn't make it easy to pick sometimes. She wondered if a leveling process where you only received set skills would be more or less fun. The focus might be more on smart combat than skill acquisition then. She hummed and shook her head from side to side.

Necrotic aura sounded like too much math. Like the Architect had originally intended for there to be tighter ranges over the damage you could do. That ship had long sailed, and the Party already did plenty of damage, with it being marginally better on average. Bone gate also seemed fun, but limited to corpses that she could see—which meant mostly just within the current fight. There were possibly some other edge case uses, but something more functional would be better.

[Share Burden]

It wasn't the flashiest of skills, but she loved being alive. Undead. Something like that could help them punch above their weight. Thankfully, it only worked on minions, so she didn't have to worry about inadvertently killing off Humphrey or Norah.

She snapped her fingers and looked around at the group. The room seemed dull without the active crystal being powered, and some lethargy set on her. Edward was acting on edge about something, and Lucius had been quiet since Archie left.

"Everything okay, hun?" Norah smiled.

"Yeah . . ." She deflated as she sighed. "The Wastes have been very draining on us."

"I've always wanted to see the wider world." The mummy looked up at one of the slits in the ceiling that allowed the constant sunlight to pour through, illuminating dust particles shifting in the slight breeze. "I suppose we'll have to do a lot of fighting?"

"Oh, yeah." Sally grinned sheepishly. "Probably should have mentioned we are constantly bouncing between conflict. Are you much of a fighter, or . . . ?"

Norah nodded slowly. "Not so much when I was a living being, but as the undead monarch of the pyramid I have a number of skills. More of a ranged support role, I suppose."

"Perfect!" Now that was a Party coming together. Summoner, ranged support, flexible support, tank, and melee damage. For a group of undead, plus Edward, that was a reasonable gathering.

"Let me know when everyone is ready, hun. I can take us to the starting chamber." Norah raised her hand up and looked around the group.

They each nodded or grunted their acknowledgments, with Humphrey being a bit slower to respond, as he still seemed distracted.

With a snap, they were back in the room they had slept in previously before taking the stairwell downward. Sally grinned to herself, knowing that she had picked the correct direction, after all. Things always worked out, except when they didn't.

She led them out into the blazing heat of the day once more and immediately stopped.

Ten Players stood in a loose formation thirty feet off. While they each wore different armor that gave a hint of their class, they all had golden tabards on, that gently waved in the slight breeze. Behind the ten, a large figure standing almost a dozen feet tall and almost half that wide, was a bear standing on hind legs. He wore a small helmet atop his head and had loose leather armor in places that resembled something a barbarian might wear.

The rest of the Party spread out around her, growing quiet at seeing the opponents. Once everyone was still, the bear opened his sharp-fanged maw to address them.

"*Outsiders!* My name is Claw, and I have come to take you into service at the behest of Ruben. Or put you back into the ground." He grinned and narrowed his dark eyes at them.

Humphrey began to walk forward. "How about a deal?"

"A deal?" Claw roared with laughter. "What do you possibly think you could offer?"

"You look strong." The Death Knight rolled his shoulders. "Duel for our freedom?"

"I am, and no." The bear shook his head, looking genuinely sad about having to decline. "My objective was straightforward. Either kill you or arrest you."

"What about . . . if I duel all of you at once?"

Sally furrowed her brow. While Humphrey wasn't a stranger to taking on greater odds with overconfidence, this was pushing it a little bit. If all those golds were Level Twenty . . . "I think he is posturing for you," she whispered to Norah.

Claw chuckled. "Seriously? How is that in any way fair? You expect me to believe you could take us all on alone?"

Humphrey rubbed his chin, the metallic scraping sound making some of the gathered Players wince. "Perhaps not. How about I can choose a second? Two versus eleven?"

The bear sighed and pawed at his helmet. "Alright, fine. You'll die either way, I suppose. Choose your second."

Sally stood on her tiptoes, hoping that she would be picked. She held back her excitement and managed to not wave at him.

Edward has left the Party

She looked down at the warm feeling in her chest to see the long silver of a blade punctured straight through her. Blood began to soak through her clothes.

"It was *inevitable*," the demon whispered in her ear, before vanishing in a flash of blue light.

CHAPTER SIXTY-TWO

Dark Night Returns

Sally slumped to the floor. Lucius stood in front of her as Norah kneeled beside her.

"Are you okay, hun?" Worry painted the parts of her face that weren't covered by bandage.

Claw laughed again, a slow, deep chuckle. "I hope it wasn't *that one* you were going to pick. Edward sure is an insidious one playing you for so long, huh?"

Humphrey remained in place, his skeletal face a wide grin, and crossed his arms. "Just like that, our Party has been neutered."

The bear raised up a glowing stone to his mouth. "Claw reporting. Edward double-crossed them. The zombie girl is down. About to crush the small resistance and bring the weaker ones in."

"Norah," Sally whispered, opening one eye. "You need to get that stone."

The mummy narrowed her eyes and then smiled. "Understood, hun."

"Just goes to show who you can really trust, huh?" Claw drawled as he attached the magic stone to his belt. "Now, are you going to pick, or did you want to rethink your choice?"

"A good duel is always worth the wait." The flame at the back of the Death Knight's helmet rose slightly higher. "You will not be disappointed."

The bear blinked slowly. "Well . . . I don't have all day, so—"

Humphrey pointed upward, and all eyes except for his and Norah's looked to the sky.

A circle of dark energy opened in the sky, a light-green grid fading within as a large metal object dropped from the sky. A dark steel rectangle, polished and reflecting the light of the sun, fell and struck the sand with a thunderous *crack*.

Crimson lightning pulsed from the impact, turning a circle of the ground into glass from the heat.

The front of the metal coffin popped open, and a figure dressed in dark leather stepped out, pushing his red glasses up his nose.

"I heard someone was talking shit." Theo grinned, exposing his fangs.

"More little pets for Ruben." Claw shook his head and went to grab the communication stone. His hands patted around the belt as his brow furrowed.

Noah's bandage withdrew from beneath the sand beside the fallen zombie, the magic rock wrapped in the end. "Is that Theo?" she cooed.

"Uh-huh." Sally grinned as she wiped her mouth and got back to her feet.

"Damn, good on you, hun." Norah gave her a wink as she helped her stand.

<hr>

Theo has joined the Party

<hr>

The vampire turned and gave a brief bow to the ladies and Lucius, with the latter just seeming more confused than anything.

"Sorry to hear about Archie." He turned to the Death Knight. "I guess we need to deal with these guys before anything else?"

"*Yes. I told them we would duel them.*"

"Just us two? Hardly seems fair." Theo clucked his tongue and walked over to stand beside Humphrey.

The Death Knight shrugged. "I thought it would be a good chance to impress the . . . rest of the Party."

Theo raised an eyebrow back at Sally and Norah. "Understandable. I'm in."

"Level Ten?"

"Level Ten."

Claw gave up on trying to find the stone. "Alright, no matter. If you two have a death wish, we can just get this over with." He flexed his large paws as long, knife-like claws stretched out. "Kill them!"

[Impenetrable Defense]

As the pulses of skills activating lit up the sands, all readied spells and ranged attacks began to aim toward the Death Knight.

[Perfect Dark] turned the area to night, the sun now replaced by a moon of radiant crimson. Theo's fangs glimmered brightly, and he immediately became a blur. *[River of Blood]* left a crimson wake behind him as he clashed straight into an armored foe wielding a large axe, knocking them to the floor. *[Blood Shift]* into *[Vampire Bite]* onto a spellcaster.

Sparks of magical shields and defensive layers flickered along the sands as his sword appeared in his hands.

"Incredible," Norah whispered, looking between the red moon and the flashing lights of combat.

"Let's have some fun." Sally beamed. "It's not a *proper* duel anyway; they won't mind. Lucius—shadow Theo."

He nodded, a brief thumbs-up beside him as he leaped down the sandbank and vanished into mist.

She brought out a skull, which burst into green flame, and narrowed her eyes. A burst of blue energy sent Theo back away from his target—and her *[Mortis Bomb]* careened in to strike at the unprepared opponent. Four zombies started clambering from the ground as the defensive barrier of the Death Knight faded away.

Norah sent out bandages from each arm, burrowing beneath the ground to wrap around the legs of two opponents. They stumbled in their movements, allowing Humphrey to approach as his skills pulsed over him.

Sally couldn't help but grin at the disarray. While the gold Players certainly had enough damage absorption, and none had died yet, they weren't very prepared for the sudden onslaught. Their ranged users were caught up in the melee, and their melee couldn't land a hit on Theo, who was unnaturally fast. It had all ended up with them tripping over each other, sending spells and attacks in all manner of direction.

"Your boy is really something," Norah purred, her eyes lighting up a brighter yellow. "Watch this!"

[Monarch's Blessing]

Amber light encircled the vampire, and his movements had a sandy blur to them. Even from this distance, Sally could see his grin widen. Wherever Theo had been moving since the start of combat, small globes of blood hung in the air—growing in size the more he drew in the melee against his opponents.

In addition to his sword strikes, his shadow reflected his damage, striking behind and over the side. *[Blood Shift]* into an improved *[Vampire Bite]* and the first of the gold Players fell.

Claw burst forward from the crowd and slashed out at the Death Knight. Humphrey deflected it with a ring as his five skeletons rose around him. "Now you want to duel?" He grinned. The bear didn't reply but sent out a shockwave of force that knocked the plated figure back.

[Living Dead]. Sally rubbed her chin. Standing back and watching was okay. Humphrey was the immovable object, and Theo was the unstoppable force. There was no real need to get physically involved. *No wait!*

Her feet dug into the ground and flung her forward.

Brains!

She used *[Summon Zombies]* three times on her way in, drawing Skeleton Key as she approached. A woman with a bow saw her coming, and a green pulse of energy began to flow around a held arrow. Just as she was about to fire it, a sarcophagus burst from the ground and snapped shut around the archer.

Sally leaped through the air at the container—the magic vanishing just as she arrived to plunge her dagger straight through the defenses of the woman and into her skull.

[Eat Brains]

Delicious! A new lease on life burst forth within her—possibly the best brains she had ever had. System messages could wait. There were more heads to crack open.

[Desecrate Life] [Will of the Dark Lord]

Humphrey used the skill intuitively after hers. Most resisted the stun—but one close to Sally didn't. A flash of a metal dove in front of her as she went for the kill as a knight intercepted the strike, her dagger just sliding down his sword ineffectively.

As he went to follow up, she hopped backward, a bandage wrapping around his leg and keeping him from moving with her. *[Mortis Bomb]* scoured a dark sphere across his polished armor, and three more zombies crawled up around him.

Humphrey stumbled backward, one of the skeletons shattering as Claw swiped through it, his furred arms blazing red. He had grown in size and seemed to be shrugging off any damage inflicted on him. "Let's make this official." Humphrey grinned, his helmet's flame waving brightly in the air. *[Compelled Duel]*.

Whether or not it was successful, the bear continued to slash wildly at the plated figure—silver gashes lining across his dark armor. Every time he blocked, he was pushed back by the overwhelming strength. With Theo's auras back in the group, and his defensive capabilities, the Death Knight was maintaining his footing quite evenly. As *[Decimate]* burst blue light along his sword, he slashed forward, carving a long gash across Claw's chest.

[Eat Brains]. Sally plucked the dagger from the neck of a spellcaster and stuck her tongue out at the entangled knight. A blaze whipped around, the burst of blood from the man's severed arteries spraying across the sand as Theo appeared behind the armored figure, kicking the body over to her after having slashed his neck. *[Eat Brains]*. "Thanks!" She beamed at him as he tipped an invisible hat and blurred away.

Radiant bubbles appeared across the Players remaining, the damage of the Party now almost ineffective as their attacks were deflected or absorbed. There was an element of them wanting to escape or regroup—and they started to gather together to heal and buff each other.

"Unfair," Theo tutted, pushing his glasses up. "But you were already dead as soon as I arrived."

[Death Syphon]

The orbs of blood that had been hanging around the battlefield burst into miniature explosions of crimson that caused the radiant bubbles to flicker—before dark energy pooled like tendrils from all the Players struck, weaving back into Theo.

He held his hand up, a tiny orb of infinite darkness between his fingers.

"Now perish."

CHAPTER SIXTY-THREE

Answers

The crimson moon vanished, plunging the area into stark darkness.

Everyone stood still in shock. All the colors of the various skills and buffs in play dimmed to almost nothing.

Theo walked forward, as if everyone else was in slow motion. Against the pitch-black oblivion, his eyes blazed bright red, and his fangs gleamed white. He approached the Players, his eyes stuck on the female Paladin, who was holding the absorption skill up.

"Goodbye," he whispered, placing his index finger on her forehead.

Like a gunshot there was a sudden blat and the dark sky vanished, flooding the area with intense sunlight once more. The Paladin's entire head now lay as a spray across fifteen feet of ground behind the rest of the body. Any blood or brain matter was just pitch-black goo instead of the expected crimson flesh tones.

The vampire blew the tip of his finger as the woman's body slowly dropped to its knees and slumped over.

"*Holy fuck!*" his shadow said.

Aside from the Death Knight and Claw, everyone else stood in stunned silence.

"Who . . . who are you people?" One of the remaining melee classes shook as he spoke, sweat and tears running down his pale face.

Sally walked up beside Theo and crossed her arms. "Dragon slayers." She grinned as she held up her hand to stop the zombies, a couple of which wore dirtied golden tabards. "You're either with us or against us." She hoped they would be against her. They tasted *so* good.

Most of them either looked at the floor or glanced toward the Champion still fighting.

"Oh, he'll be dead soon too." Theo yawned and stretched his arms out, switching from his armor into his smart suit. "Humphrey doesn't lose duels."

Norah walked over to join them. "Need me to tie them up, hun?"

"They'll be alright." She scrunched her nose up. "Oh! Norah, this is Theo. Theo, Norah."

"Pleasure." Theo gave a slight bow and awkwardly tried to shake hands.

"Great to meet you too." She smiled warmly. "Sally seems to surround herself with good men."

The vampire tilted his head and looked between the zombie and the Death Knight; the latter still locked into a mortal duel they weren't paying much attention to. Eventually, he just shrugged and wiped the blood from his face.

Sally was in a reasonable mood now. "I guess we will catch up when Humps is done. I'm glad you're back though, Theo."

"I'm glad to be back too."

Losing Archie had been sad, and it was a shame that Edward left, but it was good to have Theo back. It seemed as though the System had been content to just give him even more skills as he leveled back up. She didn't even think he had used *[Novice Strike]* in that whole fight.

She shivered, briefly reliving his use of that last skill, before turning her gaze to the Death Knight.

Nothing much had changed. They appeared to be at an impasse where Humphrey could hardly damage the bear, and anything Claw could do to him was eventually regenerated. There must be a time limit or something. They didn't have all day.

"Hurry it up, Humps! We want to press our advantage while they have bad information!"

"Okay," he replied.

Theo licked his lips as he stared down at one of the Players. "What's that about information?"

"Edward pretended to betray us so he could return to the . . . dragon's house? The grizzly relayed the info of it and said I was out of commission, then Norah stole the stone when we attacked."

"Oh, neat." Theo nodded along. "So I can't kill the demon now?"

"He's my bodyguard now, so no. I thought you had buried the hatchet?" She narrowed her eyes at the vampire.

Lucius popped out beside them both. "Hi, Theo!" He waved as a sweat drop emoji appeared. "I'm not a demon either."

"I . . . knew that." Theo nodded slowly. "The shadow thing was really neat, though. I'm impressed you could keep up."

"Thanks, I—"

"Lucius was going to betray us too. He was working for one of the dragon's Champions, but we killed her, and he decided we were cooler, and he isn't going to do anything that silly again." Sally beamed and took a deep breath.

"Oh," Theo said with a nod. "Well, if Sally trusts you, then so do I."

"Seems like you weren't exaggerating about all the conflict." Norah tilted her head as she watched the Death Knight fight. "Certainly seems more fun than guarding the pyramid on my own."

Humphrey slid back across the sand and deflected a downward swipe of the wide claws. "Seems we are at an impasse."

Claw growled and circled around him.

The Death Knight turned slowly to follow the large bear. "Of course, you could always yield. We have ruined your forces. You can escape this with your life."

"I will never surrender," Claw seethed, his eyes reflecting the crimson flame flickering from Humphrey's helmet.

"Then you leave me no choice."

[Kneel]

The word rang out across the area, and the bear hesitated. His posture relaxed, and he dropped to one knee, bowing before the Death Knight.

Humphrey took a step forward. "By power of the Dark Lord, I hereby knight you"—His greatsword cut a wide arc of blazing red—"dead." It didn't quite decapitate the large Champion, but it made it enough of the way through to seal the deal.

"And that makes you the winner!" Sally yelled out from the side.

He deflated at the zombie stealing his line and looked over at the group waiting for him; the mummy fanning herself with some of her bandage. Mission accomplished.

They gathered around in a semicircle in front of the golden Players, who huddled together on the floor.

"What shall we do with you, then?" Sally drummed her fingers on her belt.

"Do you not just kill all the living?" Norah glared down at the figures. "I *hate* Adventurers."

Theo shook his head. "We used to be more . . . loose with our morals. Now we let them go if they don't cause us trouble."

"And some people love trouble, *ha-ha*," the Death Knight added.

"Speaking of which." Sally turned to the vampire and gave him a prod. "How many new Players did you kill and slash or eat?"

"What would seem like an excessive amount?" He pushed his glasses up and tried to avoid her glare.

"*Theo.*"

"Thirty-two. Or thirty-four if you count accidents."

An emoji of numbers and mathematical symbols swirled beside Lucius. "That's just over 10 percent."

"Some of it was self-defense." Theo shrugged awkwardly.

Sally rolled her eyes. "There's no time to teach you about reasonable force. Let's stop yapping and let Humps have the floor for the important stuff."

Norah conjured up a sideward sarcophagus from the ground and sat down on the end, leaving enough room for the rest of them to sit. Humphrey stood in front of them and sighed, glancing back at the panicked Players.

"Is it okay if they hear it?"

Sally rubbed her chin. She didn't want them to go back to the dragon and cry about what really happened here, but killing them in cold blood was rather beyond them. "Any of you remember the world you lived in before this?"

They all shook their heads, confusion mixing with the fear.

The zombie shrugged. Most didn't. Only Theo and Chuck, that she had met so far. For those too deep in the soup, this information shouldn't be too useful. "Go for it, big guy."

"First thing . . ." Humphrey worked his skeletal jaw. "I do not believe there is a way for your souls to return to your previous world."

Sally and Theo exchanged glances.

"That's a rough one to lead with." The vampire rubbed at his eyes behind his glasses.

The zombie clucked her tongue. "*Knew* that would be the case. Things would be too weird otherwise—but does that mean our old selves are dead?"

Humphrey tilted his head from side to side. "Essentially, *yes*."

Sally shuffled uncomfortably on the stone casket. Although she was here, and undead already, she wasn't sure how to feel about her previous life being gone. Part of her wanted to stay here anyway, but knowing that returning wasn't an option . . .

"We'll definitely need to get to max level." Theo rubbed his chin, staring at the floor in thought.

"Yes," the Death Knight continued, trying to gather his thoughts. "The Architect was unwell before the world even started. My understanding was that Players were meant to opt-in and be able to return. Not . . ."

"Plucked unceremoniously." Sally closed her eyes. "That's why near the start one of the System messages said something about a log-in bonus?"

"A proper video game reality . . ." The vampire tapped his leg. "So, originally, death would mean going back to our proper bodies again."

Humphrey nodded. "The release was rushed by a group who I do not have the memories for—they have been scrubbed or hidden from the System intentionally. They both forced the Architect to act and then twisted some of the

Observers into seeing the Architect as a threat to the System. So they got rid of them."

"Presumably they're now working on installing their own Architect?" Theo asked.

"A reasonable assumption. I do not know what they intend to do once that is achieved."

Sally itched to stop that from happening. Just her luck that the Architect was working with good intention but stuffed everything up every step of the way. It sounded like something she would do—not that she would want to become that responsible.

They fell into a brief silence, as there didn't seem to be any further flow of information. The Players and the others in the Party not entirely sure what was going on or what all of it meant.

"What if . . ." Sally hopped down to start pacing. "Instead of breaking the System down—we fix it? Finish what the Architect couldn't, and maybe make it so that souls can return."

Theo shrugged. "Worth a try, if it's possible."

The Death Knight grinned and rolled his empty eye sockets. "So now you want to *save* the System. Make up your mind."

CHAPTER SIXTY-FOUR

Skip the Queue

Theo swung his Demon Killer blade through the air. "We could just cut their tongues out."

"We aren't barbarians, Theo." Sally sighed and rubbed the bridge of her nose. "No mutilating the prisoners."

The vampire pouted and looked off at the horizon, shielding his eyes.

"One of you must have teleports to the other side, right?" She kneeled beside the golden Players and scrunched her face up. "We'll spare you if you hand over all movement and communication items you have."

"And we'll kill you to check your Inventory if we think you're lying," Theo added.

"If we were wrong, then we will apologize, and you can join us." She jerked a thumb back at the zombified Players sauntering around.

[Endless Rest] put them away. Probably a good idea not to let them cook in the constant sunshine. She glanced over to see Humphrey and Norah talking, and she smiled. The Players began unequipping items and drawing things from their Inventories, putting them in a pile on the side under the watchful glare of the vampire.

"Hey, Theo." She grinned and gestured to the rest of the Party with her eyebrows.

Theo tilted his head and smiled. "Huh, who would've thought?"

"I would," Lucius said from the partial shade of the abandoned sarcophagus. "Humphrey has a lot of great qualities."

"What about you, Lucius?" Sally put her hands on her hips. "Any soft spots within you for a little romance?"

An emoji of a thinking face appeared beside him as he tilted his head. "Not particularly. I really enjoy having friends, and that makes me happy enough."

She beamed at him, and her train of thought slid from the track and into a barn. "Oh! Theo, I have crabs!"

"What?" The vampire narrowed his eyes.

"*Zombie* crabs."

"My response is still 'what?', but that makes slightly more sense."

Sally rubbed her eye. "The fight where Lucius went against his boss, she was a demon that could summon giant—"

"—enemy crabs," Theo finished, then whistled. "I missed all the fun, huh? Oh, I have about forty more daggers if you still needed them?"

"Heck yes. Check this out." She handed him Skeleton Key and watched his face, awaiting the change in his expression.

He puckered up his lips and then sucked at his teeth, eventually just exhaling and shaking his head. "*Wow.*"

"I know, right?" She took it back from him. "Plus, I glitched a skill and did so much damage the System had to confiscate it and give me skill reset points."

Theo shook his head again. "Almost wish I hadn't gone back now."

"What about you?" Sally kneeled back down to start to scoop up all the discarded Player items. "Did you get another class?"

"No, unfortunately not. Long story short, it just kept giving skills as if I had never reset. Essentially, I have the skills of a Level Twenty character."

"Ass! So you have your first ultimate? *The most evilest finger gun?*"

He opened his mouth as if to argue, then decided it wasn't worth the effort and nodded.

Sally picked up the last item and put it in her Inventory, giving the group of Players a glare as she stood back up. "I have a kind of ultimate too, so I'm not jealous."

"Oh?" Theo raised his eyebrows and pushed his glasses up.

"You'll have to wait and see!" She turned to the Death Knight and mummy. "You two ready?" She grinned.

Between them all, they marched the Players back up into the pyramid and told them to wait there for two hours. Sally had been sure to remind them if any of them betrayed their trust, then she remembered their faces and would track them down and eat their brains. As scared of the dragon as they may be, the looming presence of the zombie's sharp fangs was more convincing.

"We have three teleport points from here." She grimaced as they stepped back out into the sunshine. "Bronze, silver, and gold. No points for guessing which areas of the Wastes they lead to."

"Going straight for the dragon?" Theo raised an eyebrow.

Humphrey tilted his head. "It would be better if we were Level Twenty."

"I don't think we have the time." Sally sighed. "We've worn out our welcome, and Ruben will get more desperate to finish us off."

"A dragon is a lot for just one Party, hun." Norah rubbed her bandaged chin. "Do you have any other allies?"

Sally wiggled away from the direct question. "My thoughts are—go to the bronze area, rescue Chuck and any other Players that want to revolt. Smash through silver doing the same, then gold—and then by the time we get to Ruben, we either have full stomachs or an army."

After a moment of consideration, they each nodded, a thumbs-up appearing beside Lucius.

"Let's get this party started then." Sally grinned.

"You're back, Edward?" The robed figure looked away from the ledger.

"It was *inevitable*." The demon grinned. "You heard the report from Claw?"

"Indeed . . . you struck at the leader and then ran away?"

Edward deflated and rolled his bright blue eyes. "I used my debilitating attack, yes, then withdrew as I was in the midst of the rest of them. They're all as bright as a box of rocks, but they'll follow the zombie girl into death. Without her, I'm sure Claw can mop up the rest."

"Yes, well . . ." The figure slowly turned a large page. "Ruben will expect you to bend the knee and explain yourself, lest he change your respawn point to above a pit of lava. I wouldn't bother him until the Party has been apprehended, however."

"I didn't intend to." Edward bowed to hide his grin and then continued down the corridor, his bright eyes illuminating the gloom.

"Hey, who the fuck are you?" An angered voice drew the attention of the Party as they completed their teleportation.

Sally spun around. They appeared to be in some kind of room specifically for receiving teleporting Players—circle of magic etched into the ground on the floor below them that was indented in the center of wooden walkways. A high ceiling of white panels and rich wood held a simple candelabra that illuminated the place. On one of the walkways, a man in a silver tabard seemed unhappy with their entrance.

He stepped forward and placed a hand on the hilt of his sword—and then Theo was beside him. The vampire whispered something in the man's ear, and his eyes widened. After a moment of consideration, the guard withdrew his sword sharply and stuck it through his own neck, dropping to the floor in gurgling panic.

"*Theo!*" Sally gasped. "You didn't even let me eat him."

The vampire shrugged, an impassive look on his face. "He's not quite dead yet."

She hopped over. *[Eat Brains]*. "Alright, you're forgiven."

Norah leaned in closer to Humphrey. "Have they always been this cold-blooded?"

The Death Knight grinned. "Theo used to be a normal human, and the first thing he asked Sally to do was murder some Players because they were in his way. If anything, he is a lot worse than she is."

"They're definitely quite the pair." The mummy nodded.

Sally grabbed onto his arm as he pulled her up to the walkway proper. "I feel like this is going to be a near constant bloodbath."

"Don't threaten me with a good time." Theo grinned, exposing his fangs.

"I think I heard something in here."

The Party turned toward the double doors as the sound of footsteps drew closer. With a crash, the doors swung open as three more guards stepped in, all wearing silver tabards.

Bandages shot across the room and wrapped around two of them, encircling their faces and necks. Dark mirrored strands grabbed out at the third as Lucius shadowed Norah.

Theo and Sally ran around the corner of the walkway and finished the debilitated Players off.

"I feel like," she said, as she wiped the gore from her mouth, "we'll have a hard time gathering allies if we kill everyone we meet."

"Valid." Theo shrugged. "I feel like we'd kill a lot fewer people if they didn't attack us first."

"Just let me wow them with my charms first before assuming they're aggressive." She shot him some finger guns and winked.

The vampire looked over at the Death Knight slowly, who just shrugged.

After gathering, the Party began down the hallway. The wooden floorboards creaked beneath them, and the drab paintings along the walls were unimpressive. Although this was the bronze inhabited area, it looked like silver Players ran the place as an authority. At the end of the hall was a smaller room, a desk and a handful of chairs the only furniture. Atop the plain desk was a ledger, most likely for recording who went in and out of the portal.

Theo ran his eyes over it as the zombie strode over to the door outward.

Norah tilted her head. "Uh, hun?"

Sally burst through the door and stepped into the street, hands on hips and intending to charisma the heck out of any Player nearby.

Of which there was quite a lot of them. Two wagons were being pushed down the road, each with a group of bronze and a single silver inside. Another two pairs of silvers looked to be patrolling the opposite direction. A group of bronze Players were sitting at a table across the street and eating. Maybe twenty-five to thirty in total, that she could immediately see.

As one, they all stopped what they were doing and looked over at her.

Still inside the building, Norah pointed at the wall, and Humphrey groaned. Three posters, somewhat familiar, were pinned to a bulletin board they had walked past.

"Wanted," it read, "Dead at All Costs. Promotion to Gold guaranteed."

In the middle of the bold statements was a picture of Sally.

CHAPTER SIXTY-FIVE

Bronze Detailing

It's not like Sally could complain. Their time in the Wastelands had been almost totally devoid of proper Player-on-Player combat. The dragon had perpetuated the myth that the *Outsiders* were a group of merciless Monsters, and in doing so had brought it into being. After offering a way out of the grind he had forced on them, Ruben had energized the Players in bronze and silver—killing Sally and the group was a sure ticket to an easy and prosperous life.

Well, ask all the corpses littering the streets how that was working out for them.

Sally wiped the blood streaked with sweat from her forehead and took a deep breath. Her arm ached. The fight had sprawled out down the street and drew in anyone nearby that thought they had the chance of felling any of them. There were a lot of System-created mixed in, too, who didn't care for the promotion but wanted her dead all the same.

A hand touched her shoulder. "You okay, hun?"

"Yeah." She grinned up at Norah. "Weird mix of giddiness and exhaustion."

"I don't think I've ever had to do so much dirty work myself." The mummy looked back at the carnage left in their wake. "It's exhilarating."

It was clear most of the bronze and silver Players weren't near Level Twenty. Theo looked particularly bored, one hand in his pocket, as he was somehow fighting two people up on the roof of one of the houses. Lucius had shadowed Humphrey, and the pair were a near immovable wall preventing most enemies from getting through the street unhindered.

Sally hadn't even needed to call up *[Endless Dead]*—the bodies from *[Mortis*

Bomb] and eating the brains of anyone that got too close had been enough zombies to pad around the Party.

Now the potential assailants were losing heart. Something about a road running crimson with the blood of others that had tried, and their undead corpses making it an even harder battle, had made the effort seem less worth it. Sally wasn't even sure they were going the right way, but until people stopped trying to kill her, it didn't matter.

She winced as the mummy pulled an arrow out of her back. "Sorry, hun."

"It's fine. I've had a lot worse. Thanks, Norah—I'm glad you're here with us." She grinned.

"How could I say no to a face like that?" Norah smiled back, as her bandages wrapped around a summoned sarcophagus, tossing it into the air ahead of the Death Knight to crash among the wary attackers.

Sally held up a skull, which burst into green flames. With a full undead Party now, things were smooth sailing. All their buffs, auras, and skills that targeted the undead would be fully effective. If she didn't know any better, she was pretty sure Theo would have picked up another aura or two with his extra skills. She wanted to pick Humphrey's skeletal brains about *[Kneel]* as well—that seemed pretty powerful in tandem with his forced duel. Perhaps a single target stun?

The green skull flew out over the Death Knight and struck a System-created townsperson, the flame scouring their flesh from bone as four more zombies rose up.

Theo hopped down from the building to land beside them, now with both hands in his pockets. "How's it going, ladies?"

"Having the time of my unlife, hun." Norah gently patted his shoulder as she passed to go assist the Death Knight at the front.

"I feel great." Sally scratched at the dried blood in her hair. "But . . . something else feels off."

"Mmm, agreed." The vampire narrowed his red eyes back up the road. "The golds will know what has happened by now, so we are mostly killing time until they make a move."

"You think Ruben will come here?"

"No. Not yet. He has too much to lose." Theo turned back to look into her eyes. "But so do we."

"Ass." She snorted. "Don't be such a cliché."

He grinned and gestured to the front of the melee with his head. "Care to dance?"

"They what?" Flame burst forth from the mouth of the dragon.

"Killed Claw and the golds sent, sire. And now they're in the bronze area, causing havoc."

Ruben growled at the robed figure. How did this one Party keep being a thorn in his side? "They must have used teleportation taken from the golds to get to the bronze area." He sighed, blowing smoke from his nostrils. That was the only way to get through the sandstorm without going through the heavily guarded checkpoint.

"What are your orders, sire?"

"Divert all but minimum forces, close off the sandstorm entirely. Send the remaining Champions to me."

Theo threw Sally over the confused guard with a twirl, before slashing up their front with his sword. The zombie landed and stabbed into the Player's back with her dagger, before eating their brains.

Lucius popped out next to Humphrey with a sweat drop emoji and pointed his finger at a rooftop archer, turning part of the house into shadow and sending the figure collapsing inside. "This is exhausting," he panted.

"You're doing fine." Humphrey grinned, planting his sword into the ground. Although he didn't really breathe, or sweat either, his helmet flame was flickering wildly.

"Let the young ones have a bit of fun for a bit, eh?" Norah crossed her arms and smiled warmly at the Death Knight.

"I'm not old," Lucius grumbled. An orb of shadow swirled around in his hand until it reached the tip of his finger. With one crimson eye narrowed, he aimed it at Sally and shot it forth. The projectile swirled through the air until it reached the zombie and then started to orbit her—tiny tendrils of darkness crackling toward the nearest enemy as she moved around.

"The Architect really should have limited it to five to ten skills each." Humphrey shook his head. "Can you imagine us in thirty-six more levels?"

"I hadn't thought that far ahead, to be honest." Lucius cupped his misty chin. "I thought I'd be stuck at my level and still have half my abilities locked, so even now it's quite overwhelming."

"You said Theo has more skills too?" Norah tilted her head as she watched the pair ahead carve through the remaining. "So he's pretty dangerous?"

Humphrey shrugged. "Don't let him know it, but he has the potential to be the most powerful Player in the world. But he could just as easily become corrupted, lose his powers, or be unable to live with what he is."

"Fun," Lucius added, a sweat drop emoji appearing beside his head.

The carnage had warmed the street, even though the area this side of the sandstorm was less parched. Between the smell of death, spent magical energy, and something burning, Sally's smile beamed out past all the terrible things around them.

Theo kicked the body away. "No, I'm pretty sure you've told the pancake one before."

"Impossible." She snorted. "It's my best one!" An arrow struck her in the side.

"Not saying I didn't like it." The vampire shrugged, turning to the archer. "Just that I've heard it before."

"Rats." She pulled the offending projectile from her side as Theo used his glare to stun the enemy. From her Inventory, the trusty crossbow popped out, and she buried a bolt into the immobile figure's neck. "Oh, can you use mounts now?"

He shook his head as he watched the body drop from the roof to crack on the floor. "I'm still technically Level Ten. I just receive skills as if I never dropped back to Level One."

"So when you get to twenty, you'll get the Level Thirty ultimate?"

He nodded and sidestepped the downswing of a halberd. Theo stepped atop the head of the weapon and leaned into the struggling assailant. He whispered in their ear, and after their eyes went wide, they dropped the halberd and ran off down the street, screaming.

"What is that whispering skill? That looks broken." She narrowed her eyes and crossed her arms.

"Want me to try it on you?" He raised an eyebrow.

Sally shrugged. "Sure."

He leaned in, his warm breath brushing against her ear. "I missed you," he whispered.

She pushed him back and shuddered, her eyes wide. "Dickbag! That really does work, huh? *Theo Danger*."

He grinned but furrowed his brow. "Shouldn't we have different surnames, you know . . . ?"

Sally pulled her dagger out and rubbed her chin. "Hmm. We can be married, right? And you took my name? Now you have a new stepmummy."

Theo grimaced and looked around at the rest of the Party, who just gave him a wave in return. "That's a bit presumptuous . . ." He raised an eyebrow back to her. "I'm a hard man to tie down, you know?"

She snorted at him, turning to stab a System-created that got too close. "I'm glad you're still a dweeb. You can be as powerful as you like, just don't . . . change who you are."

He opened and closed his mouth but resigned to just nodding.

"Plus, can you imagine me in a white dress? Ruined immediately." She rolled her eyes. "I can't go three minutes without getting mud, blood, or vomit all over me. Let's catch up to the rest of the family."

Theo looked around—there was plenty of smoke and small fires raging among the houses, but other than the zombies, there was little movement. Then something caught his eye.

"Sally? Sally!"

She turned to follow the vampire's gaze—and there was Chuck.

He waved and ran over, only moderately appalled by the destruction and bodies littering the streets. The Druid looked tired and grubby, but life had sprung anew in his eyes at seeing them.

"Chuck!" She beamed. "We were going door to door to find you."

"I can . . . see." His brow narrowed as he stopped by them. "I wasn't sure if you'd be able to get here—but, holy nine hells, do you both look terrifying. Theo, you look like you exterminate worlds for a hobby."

Theo shrugged and grinned. "Early days."

"And Sally," the Druid continued, "simply horrifying. Like you're a terror beyond imagining."

"You okay, Chuck?"

"It's been . . . tough. I'm overwhelmed." He eventually deflated and allowed them to prompt him toward the rest of the group.

"Chuck, this is Lucius and Norah. They're our new Party members."

"Pleasure." He nodded, looking like it was anything but.

"Chuck is a human, but one of the *good* ones. We Partied together for a while."

A waving hand appeared beside Lucius, making the Druid wince. Norah gave him a brief curtsy. "Always great to meet a friend of Sally's—she has great taste in company."

Chuck glanced between the mummy and the grinning Death Knight, and then between Theo and Sally. He deflated. "I reckon I've just jumped from the frying pan into the fire, haven't I?"

"Frying pan full of blood." Sally snapped her fingers. "We're on the way to kill the dragon."

"That doesn't shock me," the Druid said with a grimace. He went to try to dissuade them, then frowned as he looked into the sky. "What is that?"

They turned around and looked into the darkening sky. Multiple golden streaks began forming through the air, like a meteor storm burning through the atmosphere.

Only the golden objects were coming straight for them.

CHAPTER SIXTY-SIX

Zombie Apocalypse

The ground shook as the first of the meteors crashed into the road ahead of them. Only, they weren't made of stone. Sally narrowed her eyes at the golden object that was twisted like a rosebud.

"I feel this is about to get a lot worse." Chuck grimaced.

The bud split, a hiss of steam rising from the top as a large metallic figure stood up from within.

"Golems," Sally said as she sighed. "Thanks, Chuck."

Another explosion rocked the buildings over to the left as another golem payload cratered somewhere out of view. There were dozens of these Monster-laden projectiles coming down into the bronze district—possibly even a hundred.

A house behind them burst open, stone clattering across the street as an obsidian golem stumbled out. The green glow around its head was only slightly more surprising than the purple-suited figure standing atop it, his eyes a blazing light blue behind the cloud of dust.

"Ed!" Sally beamed. "Nice of you to join us."

The golem moved up to them, and the demon looked down toward the vampire.

"Theo."

"Edward." He nodded in return.

The tax collector turned back to the zombie and smiled. "I've mostly come to share information. I have told them you'll probably intend to fight your way through the zone to get to the gold district. My assumption is they're sending the golems to hold you back while Ruben can gather all forces in the gold area by the mountain palace."

Sally wrinkled up her face and looked back up the street to see one of the golems walking toward them. The ground continued to shake as the area was peppered by more golems—no doubt they'd be breaking through to their current position soon.

She very much didn't want to deal with any of the golems—so fighting their way out wasn't a good plan. Teleporting straight to gold might catch them off guard, but they also might anticipate that and have a trap waiting for them. With a sigh, she looked at the vampire.

"Theo, I need to deleg—"

"I should have known it would be you."

They all turned to see a figure standing atop one of the buildings. The man's cloak waved in the breeze; the hilt of a long sword stuck out from his hip.

"Dent?" Sally grinned.

The swordsman dropped down to the street next to them, his eyes tired and face even more rough beyond his age than when they last saw him.

"You're really doing this, zombie girl? I guess you'll want to call in that favor now."

She nodded and looked around at the group. "I need you to keep Chuck safe. As cool as it is to have all the known faces come back for the final battle against the big bad guy, you'll get squished."

Chuck opened his mouth to complain but looked at Dent and relented.

Theo rubbed his chin. "If they might trap us at gold and want to keep us stuck here in bronze—perhaps the best thing to do would be to teleport to silver and establish a safer place to house those that can't fight."

Sally nodded slowly. "Dent, you know what their plans are?"

He shook his head. "I've been in the bronze area for a while. Things have been tight here since the Champion vanished a few days back."

"Yes." Edward crossed his arms from atop the golem. "They killed Maeve."

"Oh." Dent rubbed his stubbled chin. "That tracks. We'll round up any rebels and bring to silver once you message me, then?"

Sally beamed. "Perfect." She turned as the nearest golem was now almost upon them, a spiked mace rising into its hand.

Bandages shot out from Norah and wrapped between the approaching golem's legs, tripping it to the floor. Theo and Humphrey grabbed one of Sally's arms each and flung her like a slingshot, the zombie landing atop the metallic figure with her dagger plunging easily into the hard shell of the Monster. Her shadow repeated the same action, adding a second gash that she could grab with her hand. As the golem struggled to stand, she pulled the makeshift handle until the metal snapped, and then jammed her arm inside its head.

There was a pulse of energy from the Monster, and then it fell inert with all life leaving its body. Sally hopped down, and Lucius popped up beside her.

Dent whistled. "You guys really are something, huh?"

"You best get going." She wagged a finger. "I'm not standing around showing off in front of you."

"Yes ma'am. Right, Druid, let's go." With a nod to them, he turned and started off down the street, Chuck following along after giving them a worried wave.

"What about you, Edward?" She looked up at him.

"As your bodyguard, it's very annoying when I get the tingle that you're in danger. However, I can't teleport with my golem, and I can't show that I'm double-double-crossing yet." He wrinkled up his face as he looked out to the burning town, the sounds of breaking rock and approaching golems growing ever louder. "I will watch what the golems do and keep you updated. I imagine they are hunting you five only—or at least the better known three of you."

"If you find a way of stopping them . . ."

"I will." Edward bowed and went to move his golem away before glancing at the vampire again. "Theo."

"Edward." He nodded back.

They briefly watched the demon leave before Sally clucked her tongue. "Love to see a future bromance about to bloom."

Theo rolled his eyes. "Let's go then. If we're dragging the golems with us, we'll want to be quick. Establish some control in silver, and then outpace them by going to gold by foot?"

"A better plan than I could come up with." She looked on as the rest of the Party nodded along. "Let's hit it!"

Just as the building beside them exploded outward at the emergence of a large golem, blue light flashed around them, and they vanished.

A wave of vertigo, and then they were in another chamber. Similar to the receiving room of the bronze area, but this one looked better made and more maintained. There were no guards, however.

"You think they've all gone to gold?" Sally rubbed her chin.

Humphrey shrugged. "Seems odd that it would be completely unmanned, however."

"There should be some token force," Norah agreed. "At least to send communication if we came here."

Theo said nothing but looked pensive. Sally understood it—they were in the depths of enemy territory and completely winging a plan to dethrone a potential demigod. If things were going too well, it was suspicious. Failing upward didn't work unless you were actually failing.

She shook the doubts from her mind. "No worries, let's go establish a safe zone somehow, quick as we can—and get the word to the Players." Then they could fail as much as they liked in gold.

They hopped up onto the side platforms and moved through the door. The hallway was even similar, except it had slightly nicer paintings along the walls. Almost made her want to teleport to the next area to see how much better those would be.

No surprise that the main office at the front was slightly better furnished, either. This time she turned to see the bulletin board on the wall—the Wanted posters sitting there proclaiming the great reward for their death. These said, "Dead or Alive", however.

She grabbed the fountain pen from the side table and scrawled an UN next to the "Dead" and crossed the "Alive" part out.

With a smile, she wagged her eyebrows at the unimpressed vampire and then pushed out of the double doors—closely followed by her Party.

And then they stopped atop a dozen or so stairs. The stairs led down to a wide town square—easily two hundred feet wide and deep. Maybe more. Sally was no good with numbers.

This was a shame, on account of what filled the square.

"Regiments" would perhaps be the most apt descriptor. Four of them, standing to attention and looking directly their way. Between the two middle ones, a large figure that was half plant, a cannon-looking object wielded across their shoulder. Between the other regiments were a pair of giant golems decorated with gemstones. They stood at least thirty feet tall and held giant swords of polished obsidian.

"Twenty Players, a Party each leading thirty System-created. One hundred sixty-three including the bosses," Theo murmured to himself.

"Welcome to the end of the road, unpretty ones!" the flowered woman yelled almost melodically from the center.

"Humps," Sally hissed, her eyes wide. "Conditionals are met."

The Death Knight gave a brief nod. "Theo, you need to buy us some time."

With a sigh, the vampire winced at being called up to perform. He took a few steps downward with his arms held high. Eighty-seven of the opponents looked capable of ranged attacks, possibly 112 if you counted projectile skills.

"May we parlay?" he yelled.

"Do we look like pirates?" The Champion laughed, a gaggle of surrounding figures joining in.

"First thing I'm fixing about the System," he muttered to himself. "How about a deal, then? We have plenty of gold if that is what Ruben wants."

The Champion opened her mouth but then narrowed her eyes as if reconsidering. "How much gold are we talking?"

"I can count it out if you're not in any rush."

"Ten more seconds," Sally hissed from the back.

"Bluffs and tricks won't work on us, vampire." The flowered figure brought around her cannon and grinned. "We'll just loot your dead bodies."

"Funny." Theo smiled and pushed his glasses up, his fangs exposed. "That was *my* next line."

"That doesn't even—"

Vibrations pulsed around Sally, disrupting loose gravel. The sky, already a darkening amber color, now started shifting to a dull blue. Lightning flickered across the gathering clouds.

"That's it, kill them!"

Eyes blazing a bright red, crackling with electricity, Sally laughed. A wild cackle, fitting for the most cliché evil villain.

Her hand shot into the air, and the temperature of the area suddenly dropped.

[*Zombie Apocalypse*]

CHAPTER SIXTY-SEVEN

Death Party

The ground cracked and shook. A pale mist surrounded the area, causing all the silver Players a brief amount of confusion and panic.

And then they arrived. *Zombies.*

Hundreds of them, clawing out from the ground and from around all the gathered enemies. Immediate disarray flooded through the regiments, and Player and System-created alike stumbled over each other and into more and more corpses surrounding them.

Theo whistled as Sally hopped down the steps to stand beside him. "That is remarkable. Two hundred and fifty zombies."

"I traded my skills and tricked some weird eldritch god into giving me this. It's like an ultimate, but only boss Monsters get it—and even then, it's super rare."

"Gives me chills." The vampire shook for effect. "Shall we go and join in?" Theo held out his arm with a grin, and she took it as they both started running toward the melee.

Norah knocked the Death Knight on the shoulder pad. "What about you, big guy? Up for having some fun?"

"I have my eye on the Champion." Humphrey grinned. "Lucius, care to join us?"

The Shade nodded, a saluting emoticon by his head. "It would be a pleasure."

Sally swerved through the packs of zombies to slash out with her dagger, taking the guards by surprise. It was great to be among so many like-minded individuals. Her *[Mortis Bomb]* had given them a couple more zombies—and just because they were really driving home the point, she had used *[Endless Dead]* to bring out the ones saved away, including the crabs, mummies, and two Eaglebears.

Theo had become a blur of pink energy, occasionally using *[Blood Shift]* over to her to assist in her eating brains or getting a kill. With a crack of red lighting, he surged up to one of the giant golems, his sword striking over and over as he moved up the figure. The shimmer of a second sword followed him around to flicker in after he slashed out.

Humphrey pulsed out his stun and caught a group of System-created, who were quickly brought down to the ground by the massive horde of zombies. Bandages shot out from behind as Norah stood a little way behind him. Wrapping around arms or legs, she pulled combatants off their footing and toward the Death Knight, allowing him or the shadowed Lucius advantage in striking out at them.

The flowered Champion stomped out at the zombies with one long, vine-wrapped leg, while several clung to her arm and other leg. Anger flared in her eyes. She saw the writing on the wall. "Retreat to the golds!" she yelled out, making to move from the square.

"I don't think so . . ." Humphrey loomed out from the swirling melee; his sword leveled toward her.

She spat on the floor. "I know all about your duels, tin can. I'm immune to such trickery."

Norah leaned forward to whisper in the Death Knight's ear. "You got this, Humphrey. I'm going for the other golem."

He nodded, and the crimson flame behind his helmet rose higher. With a flourish of his sword, *[Grave Strike]* illuminated the weapon with an unholy glow. "What name do you have, Champion, so that I may add it to those that have fallen to my blade?"

"Rose, the Green Lady," the woman hissed, bringing around her cannon. "Now feel my thorns!"

"*Cliché.*" Humphrey exhaled, as a blast of energy washed over him. Vibrant petals, over a foot in size each, burst and scoured the area where the Champion blasted. Zombies were torn to shreds, and deep gashes were scored straight through the stone ground. As the breeze washed away the cloud obscuring the blast zone, the Death Knight remained standing. He wrenched out one of the petals lodged in his shoulder and dropped it to the floor.

Fire sparked in the empty sockets of his skeletal face. "You have picked the wrong side to fight for. Today is the last day you draw breath." Plated boots biting into the floor, he launched forward.

Norah hummed to herself as she moved through the throng of fighting bodies.

Those opposed to her seemed to dizzy and weaken in her presence and were soon overwhelmed by the walking dead. She stopped and crossed her bandaged arms in arriving at the second golem. The giant figure punched down and crushed a pair of zombies, as a dozen more milled around its feet ineffectively.

"My, what a gaudy excuse for opulence," she tutted and closed her eyes. A dark mist encircled her before a large eye of luminous yellow opened above her head. Two dozen bandages zipped out from around her and wrapped the limbs of the golem, the giant turning to her and straining against the attack.

The golem crashed down to its knees as more of its golden form was covered by the snaking wrappings. Its arms struggled against the pull, eventually being almost flattened against the ground.

"That's right, bow before your betters," the mummy purred.

[Become the Sands]

Now fully wrapped up, the golem shuddered and lost its form. The bandages retracted and the large eye faded away as only a large pile of sand remained where the opponent had been.

Sally watched in awe at the display, turning from the pile of sand now blowing about in the breeze, to the blur of pink energy coming from Theo, to the flashes of metal and shadow as Humphrey pushed the Champion on the defensive.

This was it. Surrounded by hundreds of living dead and the wails of the living being snuffed out . . .

This was living!

She beamed and barely registered the last legs of the fight. They had the upper hand from the outset, and every combatant that had fallen had just tipped the scales more in their favor. Hand outstretched, she scooped the crabs, Eaglebears, and whatever other zombies were gathered in that area into *[Endless Rest]*. They weren't really needed now.

Theo slid across the ground to a stop, almost slipping over some spilled entrails. "Everything alri—*whoa*—right, Sally?"

"Better than alright, we're a force of nature! Ever since that first group of zombies back in Hillan . . . and now look where we are."

The vampire looked around and pushed his glasses up. "I imagine there will be an even greater blockade over at the golds. One last ditch effort before he has to get involved himself."

"Psh." Sally crossed her arms. "How tough could the dragon be, anyway, if he has to hide away? We chew through Level Twenties like nothing, and he hasn't done anything throughout this escapade to signal his level of strength."

Theo flared out his nostrils and grimaced. "If he gets stronger the more gold he has, and intended to take over area three, then I imagine he might be between twenty-five to thirty, and boss level, rather than Champion."

"Don't you rain on my parade, pup." She glared out at the zombie horde.

Many of them were now wandering aimlessly as they ran out of nearby targets. "We'll need to start marching, otherwise the golems will catch up."

"Yes, my queen." Theo bowed.

"Don't try to cozy up to me now that you've hyped up the dragon." She shook her head and pushed him away toward the portal building. "Go tell Ed and the boys that silver belongs to the dead." Her nose wrinkled up in contemplation. "But they are welcome guests."

Theo waved her off with a smile and opened up his STAR as he made his way to the building.

What Sally needed to do was to rally the troops. She slunk around some of the groups of zombies, giving them pats on the back and thumbs-up for doing a good job. With unstable footing, she clambered up the pile of sand and narrowed her eyes over the battlefield. Norah wasn't too difficult to spot, and she waved her over. Humphrey was making a show of his duel, and as he glanced in her direction, she gave him the gesture to hurry it along.

The Death Knight was enveloped in another cloud of smoke as the cannon blasted the razor-sharp petals across him. As the smoke cleared, he had his sword lodged in her bark-like chest, the shadow version held by Lucius helping to pry her in half with a quick show of force. There was a *crack*, like splitting bark, and then the Champion collapsed to the floor.

"Good thing I'm really far away and can't see all the gross details." Sally nodded to herself.

"Everything okay, hun?" Norah stepped up the pile of golem sand to stand beside the zombie.

"It was until Theo tempered my expectations," she raised her voice over to the side, but the vampire wasn't there.

"I'll admit I know nothing about the dragon, but if Theo is advising caution, he may be correct." She smiled over at the Death Knight, now working his way back through the crowd. "That boy straight up exploded someone's head with a touch. I wouldn't want to see the things he is scared of."

"To think he used to be scared of me." Sally shook her head and sighed. He probably still was on an interpersonal level. Sheer force of personality was the only step up she had over him these days. Not that she was even complaining. It was nice to have others do the heavy lifting, and she could just point them in the direction her ambition led.

"We're like that anime," she ventured out loud, leaving the mummy confused and without any further context.

Humphrey stomped up the sand, aided by an extended bandage. When he finally got to the top, Lucius popped out beside him. The Death Knight briefly glared at the freeloader before he turned to grin at the two undead women.

"Did you see me kill the Champion?"

"It was very impressive, Humphrey." Norah smiled warmly.

"I was engaged the whole way through." Sally nodded, causing him to deflate slightly at her possible sarcasm. "Lucius, you did great too."

A large smiley face appeared by his head.

Theo hopped up the side of the sand dune deftly, hands in his pockets. At the top, he removed a hand to push his glasses up. "Edward and the others have been notified. They've slowed down the golems somehow, so we should be able to stay ahead."

Sally turned to face what actually lay ahead of them. Across from the mist and gloom of her apocalypse, buildings rose in the distance. Taller and better made than those closest around them. Beyond even those, an enormous mountain stood shadowed before the horizon. The lair of Ruben.

"Undead!" She raised a hand in the air and drew the attention of the horde. "With our dead hands we will grasp and tear the corrupt power from the Wastelands and take it for ourselves." With a deep breath and blazing red eyes, she launched herself from the small hill.

"March to the mountain!"

CHAPTER SIXTY-EIGHT

Shining Buffet

The march went a lot better than Sally had expected. Not that she was looking forward to an extended walk—or any manner of walking if she could help it—but being surrounded by so many undead made it feel like such a big event, she couldn't help but feel giddy.

And it wasn't just the undead. Several groups of silver and bronze Players had joined up alongside them—both in part not wanting to be ground beneath the horde, but there were also some itching to get back at the dragon and break free of the gold farming he had forced upon them.

Edward and Dent had caught up, leaving Chuck behind to deal with the injured or those not capable of fighting. For some, going against Ruben meant certain death—and Sally didn't look down on them because of it. The ones that had the drive to fight always tasted nicer, anyway.

"We are most of the way through the silvers now," Edward called from atop his golem. He stood tall and had his arms clasped behind his back. Lucius sat on the domed obsidian head of the Monster, hand on his chin as he gazed at the horizon.

"Gold is where we'll see the most resistance," Theo added from her side. "They'll not want us reaching the mountain."

She wasn't too worried. After all, they had been able to chew through most things so far, including two groups of golds. Instead, she yawned and waved him off. "Players are soft, most of them don't PvP, so they only have experience fighting System-created—who are rather simple."

Humphrey loomed up behind them. "That has given us the advantage in the past, but we should still be wary. They also have three Champions remaining."

"The tax collectors and council probably won't interfere," Edward added. "I'm the odd one out in that regard. But we still have Sidiv, the Golemancer, and whomever was the fifth."

"Anyone we can recruit to our side?" Sally wrinkled her nose up at the demon. The intended bad guys of the first area turned out to want to live their own lives rather than follow the crazy Cleric. Perhaps there were some faces more friendly in the mountain.

Edward shrugged. "Unlikely, but you do tend to achieve the unthinkable."

She nodded. "That's why I try not to think too hard."

In truth, she was somewhat worried, if only because there was a large element of the unknown baked into this plan. Ruben was some manner of boss, empowered by his ability based on his wealth. Maybe if they just had some way of stealing all his gold, it'd weaken him. Somehow she doubted they'd be able to sneak into the mountain . . . or anywhere, really. Especially not at the head of an undead army.

Sally hummed along to herself as they moved through the streets. If they could oust the dragon, then they'd not only be able to restore some normality in the second area for the newbies that Theo hadn't eaten, but also it would put them one step closer to getting to the third area themselves. It was a risk to come here before Level Twenty, but every day they spent out in the constant sun was an opportunity for Ruben to go after them.

They crested a hill at the end of the silvers and stopped at the sight before them.

Where the streets and houses stopped abruptly, there was a wide plain as if it had been scoured into the land. Maybe a quarter of a mile wide, to where the golds started, and miles long—probably straight across this sectioned off area beyond the sandstorm. The ground looked charred and melted.

"Ruben," Edward offered, as if it wasn't obvious already.

"If he could do this much damage . . ." Norah began, before narrowing her eyes ahead. "Wait, look at that."

As more of their army filtered into this staging area, figures began marching opposite them on the other side. Golden tabards, approaching in formation. And there were . . . a lot of them.

"Six hundred at least." Theo squinted. "It's hard to make out."

"That can't be right." Sally deflated. "How can they have that many Players?"

The demon worked his jaw. "It'll be one Player per regiment, four humanoid golems, and then ten System-created."

One brain in fifteen sounded like terrible odds to Sally. There were three larger figures among the army marching toward them, and there were no points for guessing these were the Champions.

"They intend to head us off before the gold area proper," Humphrey noted. "All their eggs in one basket."

Edward nodded and put his hands in his pockets. "Correct. This is essentially the remaining forces loyal to him. If we can work our way through these . . ."

"He'll have to come out and play personally," Sally finished.

There didn't look to be a way around the army. They could teleport to wherever the receiver was, but the assumption was that they were expected to do that—and they'd be leaving the army behind. They could send everyone into battle and then jump through to attack from the rear . . . but that was probably what they expected. She rubbed at the side of her head.

"Best thing is to kill as many as we can, try not to use too much power." Theo tilted his head and eyed the zombie. "We can try some tricks, but a show of pure strength will be what forces his hand."

"Do dragons even have hands?" She frowned. Theo was right, as always. Churning down Ruben's forces meant less gold being earned and less protection. Doing anything but killing everything in front of them was detracting from their goal of gaining access to the dragon. Simpleminded, maybe, but they *were* undead.

She turned to the gathering, looking down at the sea of hungry mouths she intended to feed. "Theo and Lucius, Humps and Norah, split into two teams to take the Champions out. Edward, take the groups of ranged Players and put them into firing positions. Dent, lead the melee Players into a flank once the first couple of rows of the enemy are engaged." She took a deep breath.

They each nodded along or murmured their agreement.

"What are you going to do?" Theo asked her as she turned to narrow her glare at the approaching army.

"Oh, me, I'm going to *eat well*," she said with a wide grin.

"You think they're just going to come straight for us?" Sidiv raised an eyebrow, a thick yellow snake coiling around his arm.

"They're undead, but they're not stupid." A round figure snorted, shaking out his shoulders. "A protracted battle won't work out well for them."

The snake man exhaled through tiny nostrils. "I suppose even though they look like Monsters, they are just Players at heart. Trying to find some heroic plan to pull the rug out from under us."

The Golemancer, off to the side, tutted. "You two underestimate our opponents. If these were mere Players, do you think our lord and master would have gathered such an army against them? You both saw the panic in his—"

"Blasphemy," Sidiv hissed. "I saw no such thing. You'd do well to watch your tongue, Brakenfold."

"And you'd do well to know your worth," the Golemancer snapped back. "If you fall, you are worth nothing to the dragon. Best hope that you find yourself useful in this coming fight."

They exchanged annoyed glances with each other.

As he wiped his snout, the middle Champion shook his head. "We're standing behind hundreds of cannon fodder. Do you both need to bicker so much?" He narrowed his eyes out over the plains ahead of them. "I'm sure this will be a walk in the park."

It was hard for Sally not to lead the charge. Mostly because the zombies were really slow. She grumbled to herself as she speed-walked her way across the dry plains in front of the horde. The notifications from all the brains she had eaten cluttered the side of her vision, so she waved them away with another grumble.

+40% Melee Damage
+28% Physical Defense
+25% Ranged Damage
+15% Melee Critical Chance
+65% Health Points
+14% Magical Defense
+32% Magical Damage
+18% Mana Points
+22% Magic Critical Chance
+6% Item Find

She hadn't read those in a while, and the numbers hurt her eyes. It was growth, even though the less helpful brains still made her stronger. Zombies weren't meant to eat this many brains . . . but she wanted more.

"I'll try to take out as many ranged opponents as I can on the way," Theo offered to try to lighten her mood.

She nodded. "Thanks. Fighting out in the open isn't the best for our zombie pals. They have us beat on that advantage."

"Defenders always have the advantage," Humphrey added from beside her. "Just because they have better positioning, organization, weaponry, numbers, and . . . uh, I forgot where I was going with that." He grinned as she shot him a tired glare.

Sally clenched her teeth together as they slowly approached. The opposing army had shuffled themselves into the start of the plains, just so there was no benefit of the building and structures for the *Outsiders* to steal. They seemed content enough for the zombie army to slowly march toward them.

"I didn't mention this in the plan before," she said with a sigh, "but it'd be nice if none of you died. At least wait for the fight against Ruben."

"Will do our best, Sally." The vampire smiled, as a sweat drop emoji appeared beside the Shade.

She smiled back at him, despite the weight of the day dragging on her mood. "I suppose this is the point in the adventure where I go through all the potions and boxes I saved up, to use them for the final boss?"

"What if you need them after the final boss?" Theo frowned.

Her hand wavered over the STAR, unsure whether to bring the Inventory up or not.

Lucius nudged the vampire out of the way to stand beside her. "Don't listen to him, Sally. Definitely take every boost you can, and if there's anything you can give me—that'd be great!" A wide smile appeared beside him that only looked slightly desperate.

"Alright." She rolled her eyes with a grin. "Let's go all out."

CHAPTER SIXTY-NINE

Tough to Chew

The first ranged volley blasted through the rushing horde. Some of the arrows or bolts didn't even slow the progress of the zombies, but some spells took a couple out here or there. Sally growled as she avoided a brief ice storm that froze two undead to the ground. *[Living Dead]* pulsed around her to energize those who had been wounded.

Of course, if they were in ranged distance of the enemy, they were also in her range. A skull burned with a green flame in her hand, and she lobbed it into the air in a high arc. Arrows and a couple of spells were sent from her right flank into their opponents.

The golden regiments brought up shields and spears in readiness—the slow zombies soon to be skewered.

"Launch me," Sally ordered.

A tide of corpses washed past her as she paused. Theo and Humphrey grabbed her arms and turned to fling her like a slingshot. She spun into the air, careening over the first row of spears. Some of them rose to try to impale her landing, but bandages shot out and pulled them out of the way.

[Endless Dead]

Past their defensive line, the zombies she had saved pushed up out of the ground, creating a hole the charging horde could push themselves into. Her *[Mortis Bomb]* had struck somewhere among the crowd, but those zombies probably wouldn't last long. Immediately, the melee turned to chaos.

She blocked the slash of a sword and dodged backward, ducking beneath the legs of a zombie crab. Popping up on the other side, she plunged her dagger into the back of one of the golems. Dead, no brains to eat. Disappointing.

Humphrey plowed through the regiment beside her, knocking people over like a freight train. His armor flickered with red and black energy, and his sword burst into blue flame as the minor strikes taken on the way in had activated *[Decimate]*. Blood sprayed through the air as he carved through three figures, slowly cutting his way toward one of the Champions. Every so often, an assailant was grabbed around the neck or leg by a bandage, allowing him to slice into them unhindered.

From her other side, heads burst into the air like fireworks as a blur of pink slid in beside her. Theo gave her a quick bow, his crimson-eyed shadow giving her a wink, before he vanished and appeared behind a Player, sinking his fangs into their neck as Lucius stabbed through their guts.

A fireball, alongside a dozen arrows, peppered the battle in front of her. Edward was standing atop the golem still, ordering the targets for the ranged attackers on their side. A couple of arrows struck the obsidian skin of his ride ineffectively before the vampire bisected the guilty parties.

The undead continued to flood in around her. They had lost a few dozen on the approach but were soon replenishing their ranks. If they could keep up momentum, then they'd eventually overcome them . . .

She moved from a mace being swung at her, then grabbed the offending weapon and pulled the attacker toward her. Headbutt and then a stab to the side of the neck. Even as the body fell, she jumped over it to grab on to the next gold trying to brain one of her zombie pals. Kidney stab, duck beneath the wide side-swipe, stab into the weapon arm, and then kick the knee out. As they buckled, she took their helmet off and ate their brains.

A crossbow bolt landed in her upper arm, and she glared at the man just before a handful of zombies took him to the floor. The Eaglebear zombie with the bear body strode past, a crushed golem in its mouth, and she grabbed hold and climbed up onto their back. They had made it about 20 percent of the way through the regiments, with the Champions languishing around the 60 percent mark.

There were bloody swaths where Humphrey and Theo were carving their way ahead——although the Death Knight was slightly slower. She withdrew another skull and launched a *[Mortis Bomb]* to land on someone just a little ahead, so that the zombies could weaken the formation of the enemy before he got there.

"Let's head straight down the middle, big guy." She gave the large Monster a pat on the back of the neck and it turned to the side, dropping the body from its mouth to screech out. From behind her, the yells of her Player allies charging in under the lead of Dent filled her ears. The regiments were so dense that a melee focused group couldn't flank super well, but if they powered through the weakened side behind Humphrey, then they could eventually help him out.

Arrows passed over her head, the occasional one striking the Eaglebear. *[Living Dead]*. Theo had done a good job of focusing on taking out the spellcasters or ranged Players. As much as she wanted those brains, the System-created and golems didn't seem to have many skills, if any at all.

Sally withdrew her own crossbow and started taking potshots at the enemies ahead of her mount. Humphrey pulsed with dark energy as his skeletons rose up around him, and he used his area stun. Norah used the opportunity to summon a sarcophagus and launch it through the melee, knocking a dozen golds down before snaking bandages around the necks of two.

Theo was a whirlwind of blood and pink energy. Lucius was slashing out at unprotected legs with his shadowed sword, leaving the vampire to carve through necks as they wavered in pain and surprise. He was starting to lag with his progress, taking longer per engagement.

She narrowed her eyes. He was definitely lower level than everyone, so he *should* be struggling—but perhaps the army had been organized by level as well. They had started with the lowest and would be slowly fighting against tougher opponents so they would get tired out and discouraged.

Pretty smart. Sally wished they had some aces up their sleeves. Archie, with some random skills, would have been nice. A powerful ally at the last minute, even. She had scoured her Inventory and not found a lot of things that would be useful without risking more errors. If only she could have used the bugged *[Necroblast]* in the direction of the dragon.

She rocked as the Eaglebear slammed through some bodies. From her Inventory she withdrew the *[Tornado Wand]* and pointed it ahead. The next regiment waiting to engage her was suddenly enveloped by a swirling wind. They panicked and tried to resist—but the weakest of them were flung from the area to land among the melee.

A wide smile crossed her face before she frowned and looked behind. Something was moving along the side of the battle, heading toward Dent's group.

"Look out!" she called back to him.

He caught her warning as he dropped a golem and dived to the side. A massive snake burst out from the crowd and bit down on the Player standing behind him, the venom instantly killing the plated knight. Dent jumped back to his feet and leaped toward it, a flicker of amber beams following his sword as he cut straight through the thick body of the creature.

Sally growled as she turned her eyes back ahead. Thirty percent ahead, halfway to the Champions, but slowing. The Champion on the left where Humphrey was heading was the snake man, and she was sure that wasn't the last attack from afar he would try.

She narrowed her glare to the other side. The one Theo was heading for looked to be the Golemancer—an old man sitting in some manner of mechanical suit made of silver and dark metal. He seemed to be weaving his fingers along something that, from this distance, looked like a keyboard.

Directly ahead of her was a rotund pigman with a large mallet over his shoulder. He had a wide belt across his stomach like a wrestler and fidgeted side to side, as if he was way too impatient for this kind of battle. His beady eyes were focused on her, so she flipped him off in hopes he could see it at this distance. She wondered if those Champion-Outsider matchups were the best. Only time would tell, and they could always help each other out.

If anything, it was a shame the System hadn't given them their due experience for this event. Rebellion had to be worth something, and she would have loved if they could have gotten into this with their ultimates. Well, at least she and Theo had them already.

She frowned and refocused her eyes. The pigman was gone. Surely they couldn't have gone for reinforcements or cut their losses yet? They still had at least three quarters of their forces remaining and hadn't needed to get their own hands dirty. Not that she cared, currently. The less gristle to chew through, the more tasty brain meat that was all hers.

With a quick glance behind, it seemed as though the zombies were mostly stable. They were slow, but in taking advantage of the weakened forces in the wake of the *Outsiders* their numbers were stable enough to gradually make it through the regiments.

"Sally! Watch out!"

She turned to see Edward atop his golem. His bright blue eyes were wide with worry.

Another snake? She bared her fangs and drew her dagger. As she tried to look around, a large shadow flooded over her.

CHAPTER SEVENTY

Pork Chopped

Sally dove from atop the Eaglebear at the last moment, as a large figure landed on the beast with a considerable *crack*. She struck the floor hard and rolled awkwardly into the body of an inert golem. As she rose to her feet, she winced as a sharp pain ran up her left arm. Nothing a bit of regeneration wouldn't fix.

The pigman now stood on the crushed corpse of the Eaglebear, a wide grin across his face as he scratched at his chin. "Aw, I missed."

He was remarkably large, now that Sally could see him closer up—although how he had managed to get across the battlefield so quickly was something else. Perhaps fifteen feet tall and almost the same at the waist, his skin shone in the light of the day as if it was rubber. Oh, that was probably it. She narrowed her eyes.

"What's your name, rubber pig?"

If he had intended to hide his nature, he didn't seem perturbed that she had been able to guess it. "Doinkus Maximus." He grinned, readying his large hammer.

"I don't . . . believe you." She sighed and plucked a skull from her belt. If he was indeed rubber, then it would make biting him difficult, and her zombie pals wouldn't be able to do much other than get in the way. She commanded them to focus on the rest of the regiments, as they slowly passed by her like a tide.

Then, the Champion leaped into the air, far higher than someone his size should be able to. His hammer came down in a blaze of green light as Sally dove out of the way, the ground shattering and cracking behind her. Even as she righted herself, he had begun a follow-up attack—a wide swing that clobbered several zombies and golems on the way to her. She crossed her arms and blocked it; the force sending her sliding backward across the floor by twenty feet. She growled and shook the stinging sensation from her arms.

"Oh? You're tougher than you look." Doinkus tilted his head and licked his lips. "You'll make a fine meal after all."

A volley of arrows bounced off his back from the direction of Edward, giving credibility to the assumption he was rubberized. He ignored the attempted assault and crouched down, ready to pounce toward her. With a bounce, he was into the air again using the same attack as before.

Sally held position and threw out *[Mortis Bomb]* as he came down into her space. The blast slightly obscured his vision even if not doing much damage to him. Shards of rock bounced into the air as he struck nothing once more. He turned his head to the right and struck out with his fist, knocking one of the summoned zombies away. A sharp pain dug into his left knee as Sally zipped past.

"Nice try, little snack, but . . ." he began, before his brow furrowed. He tried to turn around, but his leg was sluggish and unresponsive.

"Oh, were you using that part of your knee?" Sally grinned and flicked her Skeleton Key around. Being able to pierce through nearly any defense had some benefits, like getting into the pesky joints and tendons that made the body move properly.

The pigman growled and went to swing forward, but his weapon was weighed down. He turned his head to see the second Eaglebear clambering atop the end of the hammer. "Get off, you—" He paused and shot his glance back to Sally, but she wasn't there anymore.

With a quick yell, a blast wave shocked through the surrounding area, knocking back all the zombies and golds in the area. As he made to swing for the persistent Eaglebear, a glimmering flash caught his peripheral, and he swung the hammer back around in a blaze of bright green. He connected with the airborne sword and sent it flying off into the fray. Brief confusion painted his face before a second pain radiated in his right leg.

Sally slid away from him and twisted back up into a standing position as the Champion dropped to his knees. "I can't think of any good pig puns, so uh . . . fuck you, piggie." She flipped him off with both hands as she stuck her tongue out.

"You think this will stop me? Goodbye, rat meat."

"Rat meat?" Sally pouted. That wasn't particularly—

Doinkus opened his mouth wide and began to inhale the air continuously. Gradually, it got even more powerful. The air whipped around Sally's hair as she watched some of the inert corpses began to slide across the floor. Everything that got close to him flew up into his ever-widening mouth, sucked straight into his apparently infinite stomach.

She rolled her eyes and tried to step away, but her feet started to slide toward the pigman instead. "Fine. If you're going to play this game, I'll join in."

From her Inventory she started dropping the remaining spare weapons she had collected. As soon as they clattered on to the floor, they rose up into the air and flung themselves into the open mouth of the Champion. She was briefly amused that he seemed to have no issue in consuming these too, but even as she slid closer to him, she could see blood starting to run out from between his thick teeth.

"That should do," she hummed with a small smile. And then she leaped into the air, fighting the powerful draw no more. She quickly flew through the air, straight into his darkened mouth, with her dagger in her hand.

[Eat Brains]

She burst from the top of his head, and the turbulent wind ceased. Dropping down from his deflating corpse, she gagged on the taste of it. "Like eating plasticine." She spat. With a sigh, she stretched out. Imagine fishing for a crocodile and being surprised when it took your hand off. Seems Players weren't the only ones who would underestimate them.

"All okay, Sally?" Edward called from the side.

She gave him a wave, and thumbs-up, despite her arms aching. Nothing broken, but the force of his strikes probably tenderized her muscles. With a crack of her neck, she turned back to the battlefield. Thankfully, the *Outsiders* had stayed on target and hadn't come back to help her. Mutual trust.

Even with slowing, the two sides of the battle were progressing forward. The middle had paused due to her getting distracted, but now all the golds there were stuck between the two growing prongs of the horde. From her side, the Players on their side were clearing up on the left side and making good progress.

"Hey, Dent!" she called and jogged over to him.

"Sally." He nodded toward her. "How goes the front?"

"Slow, but momentum is still on our side." She stomped on the neck of a golem that was trying to crawl after the human. "One Champion is down."

"We grow closer to the final hour, then." He looked around, sighing. "You've done well here. Didn't think much of your group back in the forest, but you've achieved more than I could."

"Don't beat yourself up." She grinned. "Sometimes you need a Monster to fight a Monster, right?"

"Seems so." He nodded, trying not to look at the amount of blood on her face.

She gestured toward the fray. "The middle is falling behind. Want to show me what the greatest swordsman in the System can do?"

Dent rubbed his stubbled chin. "You know what? You're on." He turned his head back. "Carlie, you're in charge of the flank."

Together, they ran back into the main fight.

Another wide snake weaved through the crowds of regiments at great speed, this one heading for Humphrey. A bright ivory color with red eyes, it opened its fanged maw wide as it burst from the crowd toward the Death Knight.

Bandages shot out and wrapped around the snout and lower jaw of the creature. Humphrey slammed his sword into the ground, sharp edge forward, and Norah pulled the large snake through it. The blade carved straight through the back of the snake's mouth and a good third of the way through the thick body before it fell down, slack.

The Death Knight withdrew his sword and flourished it in the air in front of the stunned regiments. "You are quite the delight to fight alongside," he said as he grinned over his shoulder.

"Oh, please." Norah feigned fanning herself. "It's a delight to have a knight in shining armor to keep me safe." With the snap of her fingers, an orange light circled around Humphrey, and he powered forward into the gathered combatants.

"Still keeping up?" Theo slid across the floor and flicked the blood from his blade as two figures slumped to the floor in his wake.

"I'm just glad I can't throw up. Motion sickness is a new experience that I don't enjoy." The crimson eyes in the vampire's shadow shook around.

He grinned, exposing his fangs. "It's rather fun, and I've certainly had my fill. Shame we can't go all out yet."

"This is you holding back?" A shadowed emoji that was indecipherable appeared beside Lucius.

Theo hummed to himself as he moved between zombies, trying to read how the battle was going. "Hmm? Yeah, some of it. Sally said to keep it easy in case we needed everything we had for Ruben."

Lucius grabbed out at the legs of a golem, tripping them so the vampire could spin and lop their head off. "Even seeing you against the demons, it frightens me how powerful you are."

He shrugged at his shadow. "I don't know sports, or what sports you even have here. But Sally holds the ball, and my job is to make sure she can deliver it to the point zone."

"By decapitating everyone?"

Theo narrowed his eyes ahead. The regiments were shuffling and moving around and the Golemancer had his hand in the air.

"Champions are on the move. So, yes." He turned to see if the rest of the gang had noticed, and his blood ran cold as he saw every golem in the area start to glow a bright amber.

Before he had the chance to open his mouth and yell, the pulse of scores of explosions rocked the area.

CHAPTER SEVENTY-ONE

Destroy the Head

There was a ringing in Sally's ears, and the ground beneath her felt cold. No, it was just wet. Strange, as it hadn't rained in . . . oh. Her eyes fluttered open to see the pool of crimson surrounding her.

A burning smell filled the area, which was unpleasant. With a groan, she pushed herself up on her feet. Some of her was missing, but her brain was swimming around in her head. Confused and drowning. By reflex, she brought out a Healing Potion and downed it.

"Sally!"

She turned to see the obsidian golem slide up beside her, and the demon dropped down onto the ground beside her. Panic was in his blazing blue eyes as he helped stabilize her.

"What's up?" she drawled. Her jaw ached, and it clicked loudly as the warm healing magic flooded through her system.

"They detonated the golems like bombs."

With dry eyes, she looked back at the battlefield. The area was scarred by small craters and charred stone. Hundreds of bodies were now just chunks of flesh, broken limbs, and lifeless. Zombies, System-created, and Player alike. A few of the luckier undead had survived, but their massive throng was now little more than a few handfuls.

Over to the left, a damaged sarcophagus stood smoldering. It popped open and Norah stepped out, immediately moving over to the Death Knight. Humphrey was standing motionless, part of his armor bright silver from the damage. The flame at the back of his helmet was radiant rather than diminished, however.

On the right side of the battle, Theo stood panting heavily. Somehow, only his upper body clothing had been destroyed, leaving his muscled torso to gleam in the dim sunlight. Lucius popped out of the shadow to prop the vampire's body up before he collapsed, fiddling around his belt for a Healing Potion.

Sally dropped to her knees and pushed some rubble out of the way. "Dent? Dent?"

"*Dick move*," the figure groaned.

She winced as she unearthed him from the debris. "You're missing an arm," she said glumly. "Bet that's your sword arm too, huh? Half your face is burned off too, like—oh, you wouldn't get the reference."

"Can't feel either of my arms, so . . ."

Sally clucked her tongue. Some of the other Players in the flanks had taken damage, but most of them had been lucky. She took out a Healing Potion and handed it to the demon. "Edward, take care of Dent, please. Also, get your golem to throw me at the rest of the gang."

He nodded. "As you wish." The arm of the golem reached down, cupped around her as she balled up. A brief amount of pressure and then the fresh air rushed past her. *Theo was the one meant to be thrown around*, she internally grumbled, right before hitting the ground.

Broken leg, but she rolled a few times up to her feet. The *Outsiders* were already gathering in the center, and she hit *[Living Dead]* now that they were all in range. Her leg snapped back into place, and she stretched it out.

"Dick move," Theo grumbled as he hobbled over.

"That's what Dent said." She smiled, mostly at his abs.

"He survived?"

"Barely. You might be the best swordsman in the world now. No offense, Humphrey."

The Death Knight shrugged, a grinding noise between some of his plates trying to bend back into shape. "Maybe we can have a duel after all this is over."

Norah sighed. "A holiday would be nice."

Sally stared off at the remaining army. The two Champions appeared to be arguing. The explosion was probably meant to be the final ploy to rid the world of their Party and accomplices. Zombies began gathering behind her. All told, they probably still had between fifty and a hundred. Theo would know—although he was only wearing the broken frames of his glasses so might not be able to count properly.

"Just under two hundred remaining enemies," he responded without being asked. "We have just over a hundred, including the remaining two groups of Players."

Her mouth opened and closed as she felt exhausted. No words seemed to come to mind. "Line?"

"The longer they delay, the more we will recover." Humphrey grinned. "They should have pressed the advantage."

Their defensive and regenerative auras and individual powers made them a tough nut to crack if they were kept together.

"I'm going to need to eat a lot of brains, huh?" She sighed and stretched her back out, resulting in a few more snaps.

Theo tilted his head to the side. "Same plan as before, then. Lucius goes with Sally this time. You two focus on converting as many as you can—and the rest of us will get rid of the Champions?"

"Thanks, pup." She punched him on the arm. "Perfect plan. Ready to eat, Lucy?"

He nodded his shadowed head slowly as an emoji of a shaking head appeared beside him.

The Death Knight and mummy nodded their agreement, and Sally plucked another skull from her belt. "Let's get to killing, then." The green light of the skull bursting illuminated her face from below.

Edward watched the five of them run off into battle from a distance and sighed.

"Wish you were alongside them?" Dent asked. The man was sitting, propped up against the leg of the obsidian golem. His right arm was missing at the elbow, and one leg was broken but healing up slowly from the potion.

"No. I have neither their durability nor stomach for bloodshed. I suppose I just . . . admire them. They always push ahead, no matter the odds."

"What will you do when the dragon crushes them?"

Edward chuckled. "They'll win. Either that, or we all die."

[Eat Brains]

Sally whirled beneath the swing of an axe and jabbed her dagger in her opponent's stomach. Lucius stabbed them in the calf and knee, allowing the zombie to eat the brains of them unhindered.

She wiped her mouth. It was slowly working back into their favor, and their number of zombies had increased. The remaining Players and System-created had lost a lot of heart in seeing both the large-scale collateral damage the detonating golem had wrought, alongside the fact that it hadn't stopped the *Outsiders*.

Theo *[Blood Shifted]* above the Golemancer, landing atop his mechanical suit. "Your time here was wasted," he growled out, as he plunged his sword into the cockpit. A metal covering zipped over the open space and blocked the strike as the piloted golem became fully enclosed.

"Incorrect, bloodsucker." His metal arms swung up and knocked the vampire off onto the ground, sending the man rolling through dusty gravel.

"Hiding away? Is your blood so precious to you?" Theo grinned, exposing his fangs. "That'll make it all the more sweet when I—" He leaped to the side as a circular saw blazed sparks against the floor.

The mechanical suit twisted, bringing up other weapons to bear. "Too many words. I will erase you."

Humphrey spun away from a snake, drawing a line of crimson down its body with his greatsword. Norah slammed a summoned sarcophagus into the open mouth of the approaching creature, breaking teeth and causing it to choke. With the unholy blaze of *[Grave Strike]*, the Death Knight severed straight through the body.

"How many of your pets will you send to die by my blade today?" He grinned, crimson flame flickering behind his helmet as he glared at Sidiv.

"Bastard! You will be a fine meal for my kin." The snake man hissed, his long body stretching up to meet a pointed face of pale green beneath deep emerald eyes.

Four serpent heads rose from around him as a dark green energy pulsed through his scaled body. Smaller than the previous ones but similarly white with red eyes. At once, they burst forward toward them.

The crimson energy of *[Adrenaline]* filled the Death Knight as he struck the first one from the area as it wound through the air. Norah wrapped and diverted the second, as the third slammed into him.

Humphrey stumbled backward and the fourth snake landed on his plated thigh. Both of them latched on, their fangs pierced through his armor and pulsing with venom. He grinned and flourished his blade through them, severing the bodies and leaving the heads still impaled on him.

"I am immune to that," he scoffed and burst forward.

Flame gushed out from the golem at Theo, and he rolled across the worn ground. Bloody scratches on his exposed torso slowly healed up as he tried to get his breath back. This kind of thing was a lot more hassle when he couldn't use any of his abilities. Well, he could use some of them.

"You're a tough nut to crack." He sighed, standing up straight and limbering up his shoulders. The vampire threw his sword on the floor.

"Ready to give up? I could take you as a prisoner."

Theo yawned. "Sure, bud. If you can take me." He held his arms up into the air, grinning widely to himself.

The Golemancer strode forward, metal arms extended to restrain the vampire.

Obsidian punch-blades appeared on his closed fists. *[Novice Strike]*.

Radiant sparks illuminated the ground around the golem as a flicker of pink energy rolled around them, the metal plates slowly denting and buckling against the repeated assault.

"No, stop—what are you—" The arms waved around wildly but weren't able to land a hit.

Eventually Theo stopped, his blades punctured through the cockpit protection, and grunting, he lifted them up to reveal the panicked old man within. The blades went into the Golemancer's chest to lift him up out of the seat as the vampire bit his fangs into his neck.

Sidiv hissed. "Get the fuck off me!" He wiggled and strained against the bandages restricting his movement. "When I get up, you're going to—"

Humphrey strode up and lopped off the Champion's head with little ceremony. "They talk too much. That only works if it is a proper duel."

"You did well," Norah cooed. "We make a great team."

The Death Knight grinned and shouldered his large blade. "That we do, Norah."

Sally stumbled forward, trying to keep her stomach from emptying. A lot of these brains were pretty gross, and even the occasional Player one didn't make up for how much she had consumed. She glanced around to see Theo feasting on the corpse of one Champion, while Humphrey and Norah flirted by the dead body of the other.

The remaining golds could see the painting on the wall, and lost faith—only some of the System-created remaining as the golems fell inert. It wouldn't take long for her to finish these up, and she had gained another large horde of shamblers to join her current one.

All things said, it had gone pretty well. She furrowed her brow. Something was wrong.

Sally looked up, fear sinking into her stomach as a massive shadow rushed across the floor and darkened the sky overhead.

"Why must I do everything myself?" Ruben boomed through the area, his voice vibrating through the ground.

His large wingspan of gold and sandy skin folded inward as he turned in the sky and began to dive straight for her. As he plummeted with burning anger in his eyes, his mouth opened, and a golden beam of light started to form in his mouth.

"Die!"

Radiant light illuminated Sally's face, as she felt unable to move from the attack.

CHAPTER SEVENTY-TWO

Dragon On

Golden light filled Sally's vision. It was calming, in a way. She could just give up and accept the inevitable. Finally, be done with this weird world and constant conflict. Find out where her soul actually went after this. That would be too easy, though. Did she really want easy, when there was so much for her to do? A lot for one small zombie to accomplish, she should just . . .

[Share Burden]

The beam struck, blasting a wide crater around her, the stone cracking and sizzling against the heat of the attack. As it waved away and cleared, the dragon landed before her, wind from the landing buffeting her stunned body.

Immediately, fifty nearby zombies burst into bloody mist.

"Full of tricks, aren't you?" The large dragon growled from in front of her. "Such willpower from a little error-ridden girl."

Another beam formed in his mouth as Sally blinked slowly.

[Impenetrable Defense]

The spike of golden energy twisted in the air and curved toward the Death Knight, melting the ground around him as he shook, holding the attack at bay.

Ruben huffed smoke from his nostril. "How are you all too stubborn to die? It is very annoying." He lowered his head to glare at Humphrey as his defensive ability faded away. "Why must you come ruin my day?"

"You ruined the Wastelands." Sally raised her fist. "Made it hard for Players and System-created alike to live and prosper."

The dragon rolled his eyes. "Oh, please, like you haven't killed and eaten your way through both yourself. There's not enough room for both of us on the high horse."

"Everyone deserves a chance." She glared at him. "Everyone lives and dies, but they have choices and options. You take that away from everyone."

"Is it because I treat the little ones like cattle? That I see you all as beneath me and nothing more than a stepping stone for me to gain power?"

Sally rolled her eyes. "Can't you see how cliché and shortsighted that is? You're falling on my blade because you're tripping on your own ego."

"Falling on you—" Ruben let out a deep laugh. "Speaking of ego . . ." He took a deep breath and another golden spike burst from his long maw.

[Dread Counter]

Theo appeared in front of her and absorbed the attack, his whole body crackling with crimson electricity.

"Put a shirt on, Theo," she whispered. "You're distracting me."

He vanished away, appearing above the dragon and plunging his punch-blades into the golden scales atop Ruben's head. There was a screech of sparks and then he was shaken from the head to drop and roll a little distance away.

"What are you, *Level Ten*?" Ruben sighed. "Well out of your depth, all of you." He loomed his face forward toward Norah. "What about you? Do you have an ability to prevent my attack?"

She just crossed her arms and glared at him.

"No? What about the shadow hiding behind the little dead one?" He raised an eyebrow to glare at Sally.

His head alone was the size of a bus, his full body was massive. Even Theo's critical attack hadn't been enough to puncture through his golden scales. Maybe she should give him her cool dagger. Her eye twitched in thinking that would be a good idea—although they didn't have time to swap all the normal daggers that would make it worth it.

The sound of heavy footsteps came out from the side, and they glanced over to see the obsidian golem approach, Edward standing atop it.

"Edward the Betrayer," Ruben growled, light flickering in his eyes.

"You knew it would be . . . *eventual*." The demon raised an eyebrow and smiled. "I may be a demon, but I'm not stupid. There's evil and then there's evil—"

"Yes, okay," the dragon boomed and rolled his eyes. "This isn't your redemption arc. You don't need to start monologuing me."

Sally rubbed at her chin. She wanted to eat the brains of the dragon, but he probably wouldn't be too keen on that. Ruben seemed powerful enough that it would be hard for them to do damage from the outside—but maybe if she could get him to eat her whole, she could stab him from the inside.

They had already used their strongest defensive skills, and she wasn't too confident they'd do much with the offensive ones they'd saved up. Still, the fact that the dragon had come out from the mountain to stop them meant that he was worried and didn't have many cards left to play. She glanced over past the golds' city to the mountain.

"So, are you really just trying to take over the world?" She tilted her head at him and put her hands on her hips.

"I'm trying to become invincible and all powerful. Isn't that your desire too?"

"Yeah, got me there," she said as she grinned. "Are you going to give us the 'join me' speech part next?"

"No. You will just die now." He opened his mouth wide, and a similar beam grew, but this roiled with red energy mixed with the golden, as if it was empowered with flame.

[Bodyguard Edward has died]

The blue light faded, and the Party stumbled into the gold portal receiving room.

"*Oops.*" She grinned sheepishly. The room seemed to be devoid of any traps, so they quickly rushed to the front office.

"He will assume we came here, so we don't have much time." Humphrey slid across the wooden floor to look through the window. "What is the plan?"

She shrugged. "Try not to die. Edward is now back in the mountain palace, so I'm hoping he has some wits about him."

"Can't believe I couldn't hurt him." Theo leaned in the corner, brooding to himself.

"*Shirt,* Theo." Sally rubbed at her eye sockets. Things were getting real now. They had a hammer and all the nails had been beaten in. Now it was just a giant shark they had to . . . No. Where was that even going?

She turned to the group, somewhat disappointed Theo was now wearing his leather armor. They all looked rather pensive about the whole situation and awaiting her instruction. Her teeth clenched together.

"I'm kind of at a loss, gang." The tension sunk from her shoulders. "We kind of just make it through stuff. I thought this was going to be just as easy."

Humphrey walked up to her and put his hand on her shoulder. "It will be. We just need an opening to do some damage."

"I can feel him approaching from the vibrations through the floor," Lucius said as Sally's shadow shook.

"Alright." She stood up straight. "We're in the gold district—so we have the advantage of cover. We'll need to distract him, split up, and try to avoid him. Hopefully, we can find some way of hurting him."

They nodded, despite it being less of a plan than she had hoped. They flung the door open and stepped out into a beautiful courtyard. Above them, the sky was darkening, clouds of apprehension giving the fight some dramatic flair. Down the short staircase, they emerged into the groups of retreating golds.

In a quick blaze of violence and panic, they were cut down and a few zombies stood up from the carnage. Then, the *Outsiders* scattered among the built up houses and buildings, just as the shadowed form of the dragon slammed down into the courtyard, breaking up stone and crushing plant pots.

"There was supposed to be a group guarding the teleporter," Ruben growled, scouring the area with his large eyes. "Lucky for you, I suppose. But don't think you can just hide from me."

[Perfect Dark]

Night sky shadowed the whole area, as a crimson moon rose into the wide sky.

The dragon looked up and ran his forked tongue across his lips. "Theatrics won't—"

[Mortis Bomb] struck him, marring his chest with a dark green smudge. Four zombies arose from the ground by his feet. With a quick motion, he lifted his clawed foot up and smashed it down on one of the slow undead, pulping it and cracking the flagstones beneath.

With a deep breath, he shot a beam out toward a group of houses, tearing stone and wood into charred cinder, the buildings collapsing into dust clouds. He narrowed his eyes to see if there was any movement. There—he leaped forward and crushed the escaping figure beneath his claws. *A skeleton.*

Something drained his strength. Must be close by, and his tail whipped through another row of buildings.

"I will burn everything to ash to find you," he growled, snaking his head around the rubble. "Do not waste my time."

Sally pressed herself against the back of a building and panted. Too much cardio for one day. She had no idea where the rest of the Party was, apart from Lucius, who was still acting as her shadow. Cooldown on *[Mortis Bomb]* was still ticking away, not that it really did much to the dragon. The sound of cracking stone came from the opposite side of the courtyard, before Theo slid across the stone around fifty feet down the alleyway from her.

"Shit!" he muttered, before running the opposite way of her.

She dropped to the floor as the tail swiped through the building behind her, knocking stone and wooden beams across the alleyway. Unharmed, but that was close. She glared out at where the vampire had been to see a floating orb of crimson down the alley.

Ruben ground his sharp fangs together, searching around for the little man zipping across the way—just as he caught sight in his peripheral, he was prevented from turning by a bandage wrapping around his foot. He yanked on it, and it came loose, to fall limply among the ruined buildings.

Movement again and he leaped forward, snapping his jaws around . . . another skeleton. He gnashed it apart in anger and spun back around. They were toying with him; he was sure of it.

"You are only delaying the inev—" He sighed before finishing the sentence. "I don't play games."

His eyes turned to pure golden light, and a shimmer of energy rolled down across his body.

Like a flash of lightning, he turned and lashed forward with his maw.

There was a crunch, and he rose with the bloodied and limp body of Theo impaled between his teeth.

CHAPTER SEVENTY-THREE

Death of the Party 2

Edward swore constantly and energetically as he slid around the marbled floor of the palace.

"Edward? You dare return—" the Scribe began as the demon sprinted past.

"Fuck you!" he replied.

As much as he held a dim view of the zombie leaving him alone to be roasted in the dragon's Fireblast, it did give him the opportunity to help out in a way that the others couldn't. His dress shoes squeaked across the floor as he stopped in front of the dragon's chambers.

He jammed his glowing sword into the lock, purple energy crackling over the metalwork.

"I can't allow you to do this, Edward." The Scribe shuffled up behind him.

Edward grinned to himself, slowly withdrawing a throwing knife, his face glowing green from the enchantment on it.

Ruben stretched his neck out as the crimson moon vanished and the normally drab sky returned, looking toward the mountain. His brow furrowed, as if he could sense something wasn't right.

Sally slid out into the wreckage of one of the buildings and held an index finger pointed at him. "Let my Theo go!"

"Hmm?" The dragon looked down his snout at the bloodied vampire between his teeth. "No, I don't think so." He glanced back at the mountain, as the talking moved the sharp teeth in and out of Theo's torso.

He spat the limp body onto the floor; the vampire rolling after he landed, causing a spray of his blood to color the dusty rocks of a ruined building. "Undead taste terrible." Ruben shook his head. "I have more important matters to attend to, but I will be back to find you all."

"Too late." Theo sputtered out mouthfuls of blood as he tried to right himself. "You were dead as soon as you met me."

Ruben gnashed his teeth together. "Your ego clearly needs humbling, mosquito." The dragon growled and opened his mouth, the glow of his beam attack forming.

Theo made the motion of pushing up his glasses, even though he wasn't wearing them.

[Blood Shift] took him above the dragon. Before Ruben could abort his attack to look up, pitch-black flooded the area as the blood orbs hovering in the area burst. Any color and light dimmed to a faint gray, leaving only the blazing trail of the vampire's eyes cratering down onto the top of the dragon.

[Death Syphon]. He landed, legs spread atop Ruben's head, and pressed his index finger against the golden scales.

There was an explosion, as the darkness of the sky was sucked out of being and struck the dragon. With all his energy going into the attack, Theo's body fell limply. He crashed down among some rubble, as Sally ran over to hit him with a *[Living Dead]*.

Ruben twitched, then turned his head to look down at the pair with a wide grin. "Really? You think that would . . ." He paused, and his eyes widened.

From all over his body, every golden scale burst into black mist, leaving pale red scaled skin below. Like dominoes starting from his head, they shattered into the air all the way down to the tip of his tail.

"No . . ." He gasped. "Not my *gold*."

Before he had a chance to gather himself, his wide eyes looking toward the mountain again, the Death Knight sprinted out from an alleyway and stabbed his blazing blue sword into the ankle of the dragon's foreleg.

Ruben turned with a growl, opening his mouth toward Humphrey before a sarcophagus slammed into the side of his face. He staggered away, tripping as one of his clawed feet dropped into a shadowed pit. It then turned back into rock, as the Shade ran across the battlefield, sending an orb to orbit the Death Knight just before he vanished to shadow him.

The trapped foot burst from the stone as the dragon righted himself, fury building in his eyes.

"You are all very irritating." His wings opened up, blowing debris around the area.

"Imagine being around us all the time." Theo coughed out blood from where he lay.

Ruben glared down at him. Where was the zombie girl? Oddly, he didn't seem to be able to move his gaze away from the wounded vampire. Something was controlling him, but he could block it—he was a powerful—

Humphrey slammed his sword into the same ankle again, drawing blood as he cut into muscle. It broke the glare, so he turned, just as something landed on his right wing.

The zombie. He turned his glare just as a flaming green skull struck him in the eye. Ruben screeched in pain as the necrotic energy burned away at his vision. Time to leave. He beat his wings in an attempt to shuffle the zombie away from him.

Instead, pain racked the appendage, as a long split ran through the leathery wing.

As he turned toward the dropped woman, he was restrained by four bandages, two of them shadows. "You really are tiresome." He turned toward the mummy with a glow forming in his mouth.

[Kneel]

The dragon paused and turned to the Death Knight, narrowing his eyes. "The *fuck* did you say to me?"

Theo bit into one of his back legs, barely able to drain blood through the thick skin. An Imp from the *[Summon Demon Scroll]* flew into the air. The small, winged humanoid-demon surveyed the scene, rubbing at his ruddy face in disbelief at the sight of the dragon. With a shrug, he grinned and started to build a fireball.

Ruben opened his mouth to bite into the Death Knight, taking up the ex-Observer in his dagger-toothed maw. The jagged teeth scraped and whined against the metal plated figure.

"You'll find me quite unappetizing," Humphrey growled, as he used *[Will of the Dark Lord]*. It didn't stun the large dragon, but with the Death Knight in such proximity to his brain, it made him stagger backward.

The bandages tensed as he moved, now having surrounded the whole wing as several others had sprung out from one of the alleyways. Norah grinned; her brow furrowed as she concentrated with the looming yellow eye above her head. "Thanks for the assist, Lucius." With a loud ripping sound, the wing burst into sand, the bandages falling limply from the space.

Ruben roared, a deep sound that vibrated through the whole of the gold district, vibrating through every structure within miles. The Death Knight fell to the floor from the open maw with a loud *clang*.

There was anger there, but Sally could see the desperation too. His pride was too great to leave any threat unanswered despite his instincts telling him to go and find out who was messing with his gold. Now he just wanted a little self-preservation.

"Why won't you die?" He roared again, starting up another beam attack.

"Tried it once. We're already dead." Theo grinned and wiped his mouth. *[Novice Strike]*.

Now able to puncture the softer scales of the dragon, the vampire began to circle around with his punch-blades, scoring a multitude of small wounds in a manner of seconds. Lucius had joined back up with Humphrey and the pair were slicing at the chest and neck of the large Monster.

Sally stood atop the nearest unbroken building and cycled through her crossbows, firing off the primed bolt and then dropping the weapon to the street below. Most of them did little damage or just bounced from the pale red scales of Ruben, but a few embedded into his side.

Now unable to fly, the realization that he needed to be out of the area overrode whatever pride was bruised. He crouched and tensed up, even with the vampire peppering him with wounds, about to leap and charge away from the group. His back legs then tripped on bandages that had stretched across the area, and he slammed to the ground.

Sally ran up and clambered onto his back, her dagger crackling with energy after using the *[Scroll: Savage Strike]*. With a growl, she ran across his spine and leaped, striking the blade into his head.

"Even if you kill me, do you think that makes you heroes?"

Sally snorted. "*No.* We clearly aren't." She stabbed into his head again, dark dragon blood running from the wounds where her dagger bypassed his remaining defenses. "We are villains. So are you, but we are just *better*."

"Better? That is laughable." Ruben struggled to get back on his feet, his strength draining away.

"It's about sustainability." She plunged the dagger in again. "We will continue to be villains, and you will be a long-forgotten treat for my stomach."

Ruben shook as he righted himself. Angered by their gall to lecture him, but still under the constant assault that drained his energy, he knew he really had Edward to blame. Something was happening to his gold hoard, and it was weakening him to the point of almost his base power.

He closed his eyes and tried to tune out the constant assault. If he couldn't rule this land, then neither could they.

Dark energy began to pulse around him across the floor. Circles of mist pulsed back and forth around his feet. The air grew cold and even the *Outsiders* started to be more wary of their attacks.

Except for Sally, who kept trying to dig through to his tasty parts. Dragons seemed to have really tough skulls—or more likely, he just hadn't taken enough damage yet. As his powered attack chilled her, her next strike came with an additional crack, and the conditional popped up as active.

Ruben hissed, an element of resigned calmness to his booming voice. "You think you have won? This is your end, you filthy fucking bugs."

[Game Over]

[Eat Brains]

Sally dropped from the body of the dragon, rolling across the floor covered in his blood. A pulse of dark energy released from the dragon washed over the area, chilling her briefly. The others ran over and lifted the zombie up.

"We did it." Humphrey grinned. "The dragon is . . ." His brow furrowed.

He tasted pretty rich. That would be the perfect line to cheer the troops up. Sally tried to smile but couldn't. Theo went to put his hand on her back, but it fell away, back to his side. The others seemed tired too. Unable to talk, she felt . . . confused.

Strength was being drained from them, as if their very lives were being pushed from this reality. As her limbs went lax, and her eyes closed, she just felt so exhausted and resigned to leaning into it.

Surely one little sleep would be okay? They'd won, after all. Rest was nice.

The breeze rustled past, blowing charred dust and clouds of powdered stone around the five lifeless figures of the *Outsiders*.

CHAPTER SEVENTY-FOUR

The Incident

Sally blinked her eyes.

They were dry and struggled to focus as her brain tried to wake up. She was breathing, despite not needing to, and her breaths were slow and shallow. Numbness faded away from her hands, and she found she could wiggle her fingers.

Questions cracked like eggs onto her sluggish mind, slipping right past the important parts such as words, and dripping to the floor. Floor. A sandstone color, smooth but not polished. The flickering light of torches drew her eyes upward.

In her peripheral, familiar shapes. She couldn't quite place their names at this stage. But it was . . . family? No, her Party. That was it. The cracks allowed more deserted memories to trickle from the dam. She was a zombie in an undead adventuring Party.

The surrounding chamber was mostly plain, a rectangle of similarly colored stone as the floor. There was perhaps detailing or engravings on the walls, but she couldn't see it from here, and something even more important distracted her.

"Hey, you, you're finally awake." The voice was familiar and spent some time echoing around in her skull before she could place it.

The visual was only helping slightly. Sally furrowed her brow at the ginger cat with an eye patch sitting in front of the group, waving his tail with impatience. His other eye wasn't emerald, but there was something about the confident animal that struck a familiar tone.

The taste of a name clicked across her desert mouth. ". . . Archie?"

"Indeed." He tilted his head. "I am the Archie from the third area."

"Oh!" She smiled but couldn't really connect the dots yet.

"Care to take a brief walk while your companions recover?"

She nodded and with stiff and aching legs, she stepped after the cat, giving one last look at the rest of her friends sleeping while standing up: the Death Knight, mummy, Shade, and vampire.

"I'm sure your memories are a little bit of a jumble," Archie continued as they walked through a corridor away from the room. "Maybe this will jog things a little?"

They stepped out through an open doorway onto a balcony. Before them, a city of sandstone decorated with bronze, silver, and gold shone beneath the moonlit sky. It was calm. She frowned out into the distance. Endless plains of sand dunes and dry stone, the pinprick of a pyramid on the distant horizon.

"The Wastelands? Did we fix it? *The dragon!*" A flood of information burst forth, everything pooling back at once and threatening to overwhelm her. The violence and the struggle. Victory, but also defeat?

Archie hopped up onto the stone wall of the balcony and sat, wrapping his tail around his legs. "Archie Two's last action was to send me a message to come and look after you."

"That's some foresight, huh?" Sally leaned forward on the wall, the cool stone calming the adrenaline trying to get her worked up. Her Archie had been absorbed into Humphrey before they'd even left toward the final battle.

"We are rather clever." He tilted his head. "Although we were worried you couldn't come back."

"Come back?" Things were starting to make her head hurt now.

"Ruben's ultimate, *[Game Over]*, was meant to erase you from the . . . world."

"Okay." She blinked. Just a big killing move then. There was no need to add the mysterious vagueness to it. "But it didn't?"

There was a flash of blue, and a figure appeared beside them. A slim man in a purple suit with bright blue eyes and horns on his head.

"Edward!" She leaped forward and gave him a hug. "I remember you."

"I didn't get a hug." Archie sighed, his wide eye looking out to the city.

"Glad to see you're back among the living . . . unliving . . . after all this time, Sally." He grinned. "I suppose it was—"

"*All this time?*" She raised an eyebrow between the two of them.

Edward crossed his arms. "You hadn't told her yet?"

"I was leading up to it before you interrupted." The cat flicked his tail in annoyance. "While we were able to prevent you from dying, you've essentially been in a coma."

"For how long, Archie?" She loomed over him. "*How long?*"

". . . a little over a year."

"Oh, I thought you were going to say twenty years or something." She yawned and leaned her back against the wall and looked up at the night sky. The most disappointing thing was that she didn't seem to have her undead dragon at her beck and call. Perhaps it stood to reason that he didn't rise while she was potentially dead herself. She would complain a lot more once her brain didn't feel like warm porridge.

Edward grinned. "The sandstorm then cleared away, and normality returned to the Wastes. The System-created returned, and Players flocked here after the forest and have been able to level properly."

"A happy ending," she said as she grinned.

"There's been four other Player waves since you were out of action." Archie stretched out and yawned.

"Really? So you're telling me that the world is a lot more populated now. We aren't in the top percentage of Players?"

Edward nodded. "Most are still between first and here, but the third area is quite populated now—especially after you cleared the blockage of Ruben."

She sucked at her teeth. As much as she didn't like to be behind the curve, more Players meant more conflict—which equaled more brains. That made her stronger, which made it easier to . . . She raised her eyebrow at the demon. "Have you just been hanging around here for the year, since you're my bodyguard?"

"Yes and no." He deflated. "I cannot level higher than you, so I was kind of stuck, anyway. It's been *miserable*, but I am on the democratic council that runs the Wastes now . . . so yay for me?"

"Politics doesn't really seem like your sort of thing." She smiled. "It's not like you to be a backstabber."

He tilted his head in return. "I used the remainder of Ruben's gold to rebuild what I could, including this little fortress to keep my favorite group of rocks-brained undead safe."

"Knew I could trust you." She exhaled from her nose and turned back to look out at the city. It seemed so quiet now compared to when they had fought here. "So, what's the deal with the third area?"

"That's why I'm here." Archie moved closer and rubbed up against her arm. "There are two factions of Players that have organized against each other. One believes the System should be destroyed, and the other wants it to be fixed or saved."

"Huh." She tapped her fingers on the wall. "So I need to decide what side I'm on and then eat my way through the other?"

The cat exchanged a glance with the demon. "It may not be that simple, but sure."

"Neat! I just have to wake the rest of the gang up, have this conversation all over again with them present, and we'll need to level up to twenty to get stuck into that mess."

Archie rubbed the side of his face on her. "Well, your STAR is already glowing."

Her eyes wide, she smiled down at the golden System interface.

"I found a scout trying to sabotage the supply lines, Boss." The gruff figure dragged a man into the wide tent of dark fabric and threw him on the floor.

The detainee looked to have already been roughed up, with a black eye and graze across the side of his shaved head. A green cloth gagged his mouth, while his arms and legs were bound tight with rope. Dark leathers and a muddied black cloak. He certainly looked like a saboteur.

From a wooden writing desk, a figure stood and stepped closer. "And you couldn't deal with him in the field? You know how much I hate to bloody my own hands, Shin."

"Sorry, Boss. This one said he had information."

With a sigh, the figure dressed in long robes of green kneeled and pushed the prone figure onto his side with the tip of his staff. "He could also just as easily want to speak a spell or ability and assassinate me."

The gruff man said nothing now but lingered awkwardly near the tent entrance, unsure whether to remove the prisoner or not.

What patience the caster had left slowly eroded, and he gestured to the hovering man. "I will deal with him. You may leave."

"Yes, Boss." With a couple of half bows, half nods, he left out into the night.

"Now then." The man reached down and removed the gag. "What do you have to say for yourself?"

"There's a new Architect coming. It has been prophesied."

"I put little faith in such things." He stood and rubbed at his pale face. "What purpose do you have in telling me so? To gloat that your faction was correct? Do you wish to switch sides knowing you were wrong?"

"I come to warn—"

"No, no. You do not *warn*." The figure held out his staff over the body. A green energy began to glow around the end and filled the tent with dull light. "If this comes to pass, and it turns out you were correct, well, I have a few friends that could bring you back so I can apologize."

Vines encircled the man, wrapping him tightly and covering his mouth. They continued to constrict the writhing prisoner until bones started to crack and blood ran from his mouth. All the while, the caster watched with an empty look in his eyes.

Eventually, the struggling ceased, and the vines receded. The spellcaster relaxed and exhaled deeply.

A shadowed figure crossed the front of the tent, stopping to step inside. His arm replaced with a slim bar of sharpened metal, glimmering in the lantern light. "Thought I could smell death in the air."

"I don't suppose you could dispose of him, please, Dent?"

The man nodded with a smile. "Of course, Chuck."

About the Author

Kleggt is the author of the Death of the Party series, originally released on Royal Road. Upon clawing his way out of the depths of Scheduling Hell as a Forever DM, he began writing web novels, channeling his love of world-building and oddball characters into his own LitRPG and progression fantasy stories.

www.ingramcontent.com/pod-product-compliance
Lightning Source LLC
Chambersburg PA
CBHW020644120726
47906CB00001B/118